TWO WORLDS

One quarter of all Indian children were removed from their families and placed in non-Indian adoptive and foster homes or orphanages, as part of the Indian Adoption Projects..... One study found that in sixteen states in 1969, 85 percent of the Indian children were placed in non-Indian homes. **Where are these children now?**

"TWO WORLDS: Lost Children of the Indian Adoption Projects" is an important contribution to American Indian history. Trace Hentz located other Native adult survivors of adoption and asked them to write a narrative. The adoptees share their unique experience of living in Two Worlds, surviving assimilation via adoption, opening sealed adoption records, and in most cases, a reunion with their tribal relatives. Indigenous identity and historical trauma takes on a whole new meaning in this adoption anthology.

This anthology covers the history of Indian child removals in North America, the adoption projects, their impact on Indian Country and how it impacts the adoptee and their families.

Since 2004, Hentz (formerly DeMeyer) was writing her historical biography "One Small Sacrifice." She was contacted by many adoptees after stories were published about her work. More adoptees were found after "One Small Sacrifice" had its own Facebook page and the blog on American Indian Adoptees started in 2009.

Two Worlds is the first book to expose in first-person detail the adoption practices that have been going on for years under the guise of caring for destitute Indigenous children. Every reader will be intrigued since very little is known or published on this history.

TWO WORLDS

LOST CHILDREN OF THE INDIAN ADOPTION PROJECTS BOOK SERIES (VOL. 1) SECOND EDITION

TRACE L. HENTZ

Blue Hand Books

Greenfield, MA

SECOND EDITION Adoption Anthology/American Indian History/Narratives

dedicated to Cynthia Lammers Red Soldier (1966-2017)

© 2017 Trace L Hentz

Library of Congress: On File

Hentz, Trace L. [1956-]
ISBN-13: 978-0692372104 (Blue Hand Books)

Book Cover Design: Kim Pitman, FireflyInx
Formatting and Pre-Press: PressBooks
Cover Photo: Lost Children (by permission of participants in book)
Publisher: Blue Hand Books, Greenfield, Massachusetts

bluehandcollective@outlook.com

WEBSITE: www.bluehandcollective.com or www.bluehandbooks.org
Published in the United States

Dedicated to the Lost Children, Lost Birds

I am 72 years old. I was adopted into a white family at age one-and-a-half when my mother died. I realized I was different before I ever went to school. When I asked, my foster parents told me I was Indian, and from that day I identified with Indians, because that was what I was. I didn't know who I was, and that heartache and anguish has been with me for nearly 70 years. I hope your study can help me find out who I am before I die. I don't want to die not knowing my true identity. They (the government) sealed my birth certificate so I could never find my identity and never see my blood relatives. The pain of this is never ending.

*—Participant in **Split Feather Study** by Carol Locust (Cherokee), 1998*

Contents

Part II. First Nations Canada

Reviews of Two Worlds

By **Peter d'Errico**, January 02, 2013 (published in Indian Country Today)

Two Worlds: Lost Children of the Indian Adoption Projects is a new book about the campaign to break indigenous social structures by removing the children: "Governments… paid agencies and churches to remove and Christianize children… and raise them to be non-Indian." Edited by adoptees, the history is told through chronicles by those who lived through it. Ethnic cleansing by Adoption projects take children away permanently, to assimilate them into non-Indian society via non-Indian families. A common element of the stories is painful curiosity, children trying to figure out who they are, and why their biological parents gave them away. What is learned may compound the pain, when the child's displacement turns out to be a subchapter in the parent's (or parents') own survival struggle. The "stolen generations" is only part of the trajectory of Indian genocide. *Two Worlds* shows that the pain of the non-Indian adoptive families often compounds the pain of displacement. For whatever reasons—many are discussed in the multitude of stories—adoptive parents may be trying to escape from their own pain when they take an Indian child into their homes. Those who try a to fill a void or carry out a messianic belief by adopting an Indian child cause pain that multiplies pain; everyone is scarred. As if all this pain were not enough, the stories tell of a whole new world of pain that may open up at the end of the genealogical quest, when the search for the past has led to the present: the pain of re-assimilation; or worse, the pain of not being able to re-assimilate into one's origin community.
***

Judy Leaming reviewed Two Worlds: Lost Children of the Indian Adoption Projects
☆☆☆☆☆ Wonderful resource June 15, 2013
This will be a resource book in a workshop on Native Nations this summer. It's an important contribution to Native history.
***

Jk12 reviewed Two Worlds: Lost Children of the Indian Adoption Projects
3 of 3 people found the following helpful
☆☆☆☆☆ Not Just for Native Adoptees November 17, 2012
This book contains very personal experiences and thoughts of Native adoptees. Their often painful experiences are similar to non-Native adoptees. The authors write in such a compelling manner that it is hard to put down. Its an emotional roller coaster that also includes the history of American Indians

constant struggle with a government determined to exterminate an entire race. Beautifully written, not to sound cliche but it is a must read. The most important book published since DeMeyer's first book.
***

Yassmin Sanders (UK)

5.0 out of 5 stars: **Thought-provoking and moving**

11 October 2012

Two Worlds – Lost children of the Indian Adoption Projects

If you thought that ethnic cleansing was something for the history books, think again. This work tells the stories of Native American Indian adoptees "The Lost Birds" who continue to suffer the effects of successive US and Canadian government policies on adoption; policies that were in force as recently as the 1970's. Many of the contributors still bear the scars of their separation from their ancestral roots. What becomes apparent to the reader is the reality of a racial memory that lives in the DNA of adoptees and calls to them from the past.

The editors have let the contributors tell their own stories of their childhood and search for their blood relatives, allowing the reader to gain a true impression of their personalities. What becomes apparent is that nothing is straightforward; re-assimilation brings its own cultural and emotional problems. Not all of the stories are harrowing or sad; there are a number of heart-warming successes, and not all placements amongst white families had negative consequences. But with whom should the ultimate decision of adoption reside? Government authorities or the Indian people themselves? Read Two Worlds and decide for yourself.
***

Kindle Customer reviewed Two Worlds: Lost Children of the Indian Adoption Projects

★★★★★   We are all related March 30, 2013

This is one of the most poignant, honest and sad books I've read. It tells finally of the unspeakable wrongs done to Native American children those many years ago. The scars remain like scabs that don't heal. The words, the cruelty. We wondered WHY when we were growing up. We looked different. We felt different. We longed for someone that looked like us. I am one of the lost birds and at age 59 the wounds seem fresh at times but better with every revelation, every truth that comes out. It helps to know the stories of others. We may be of different tribes but we are truly "all related." Thanks again Trace, our hearts are woven with our sisters and brothers for all time. This book is a must read for all that want the truth.

PREFACE

Trace L. Hentz

Welcome to the second edition of Two Worlds. This new updated 2017 edition reflects a change in editors from the first volume. Adoptee Patricia Busbee* has learned through a DNA test that her birthfather is a different man, different than what she was first told. With that news, her ancestry changed along with her story. Her earlier contribution is valued to the adoptee narrative – and just when we think we know all our story and all the truth, this can change.

We know that it's a big world. With the invention of a miraculous worldwide web, connecting is fast and free. Humans can interact at the touch of a key. Because of the internet, it connects me to new people every day, new friends who are also adopted.

In this big world, where do adoptees go to find information? How do we reconnect with our tribes after adoption? How do we learn about culture? Do we find other adoptees to get advice? Do we devour and search books, newspapers, or the web for clues? Or do we hear someone, an ancient voice, a soul who lives with us, inside us, who guides us, even inspires us, after adoption?

Reading this book, you'll know the answers.

In their words, adoptees were destined to live in two worlds, and each has a spirit uniquely their own. We adoptees are like birds who migrate by memory and feed our hunger for culture by instinct and blood memory. Our spirit was not killed by adoption, even if we lived far away from our families and our tribal lands. We knew how to be brave. We hoped away loneliness. We felt this was a test. We knew it is not good to be isolated and went to look for other Indian people and relatives when we could. Even as children we were aware we'd need to find answers to find our relatives. More than one adoptee told me they heard the drum pounding inside them, and felt it calling them. I did, too.

Finding adoptees across the globe was possible with this web. Friends emailed or phoned and I heard about their journeys. I trusted the voice inside me that gently pushed, ask your friends to write their narratives and stories; these experiences would be published in a book, an anthology by Native American adoptees. The vision for this book was born in 2008 and it slowly grew into an amazing collection of voices and history.

Because of adoption secrecy, I knew this history should not and could not remain buried. Truth has to be told and shared.

All of our lives the adoptees in this book have lived under an "adoptee stigma" of assimilation. We are often called *transracial adoptees* because we were raised outside our culture and by non-Indian parents. With a book like this, our sense of self-worth would rise, knowing many of us shared this (sometimes difficult) journey. Our success in finding our tribes could make big waves in the adoption world.

Most who read history are aware it is interpretation, told by the same conquerors who declared victory and Manifest Destiny. Indians cannot and do not rely on stories told by non-Indians isolated in their institutions. Some published scholars never visited a reservation or even know an Indian. It is their interpretation of who they think we are and that is very dangerous because we are not dead. **We are still here.**

Even the Smithsonian Museum, an institution called America's national treasure, kill us again with vulgar displays of our bones and skulls, our medicine bundles, our sacred pipes, our regalia, our masks and our drums. This treatment and disregard for what is sacred to our values and **us** can hardly be called understanding of tribal cultures. We are not relics. We are not the past. We are not mascots. **We are still here.**

What about adoptions? Those who interpret its value to society protect their agenda and myths, spouting benefits for the adoptee. But we are called the Stolen Generations for a reason. Children did not ask to be removed. It is undeniable our assimilation was the government's answer to Manifest Destiny, to make us non-Indian prototypes of American citizens, and to take our ancestral land.

Adopting out Indian children would be as destructive as a war but it would last longer: it'd last a lifetime. The adoption program idea was not officially signed like other treaties made in Indian Country. These unique adoption program records were sealed and not made public. (It was acknowledged in an apology I heard in 2001. Read the *Ultimate Indignity* in this book.) The goal was adoptions would be permanent and closed, therefore adoption was used as the ultimate weapon. Native children adopted by non-Indians would be Americans and unable to open their records; and our tribal parents and grandparents were victims since they would never see us again, or be able to find us.

> "The individual pieces are open and honest and give a good insight into the turmoil of dislocation from family and tribe... I think it does have value and a story to tell. I was affected by the stories I read, and amazed by the facts presented.... because it is saying something new, interesting and often astonishing." —early praise for the anthology **Two Worlds**

My close friend Adrian Grey Buffalo, a wise adoptee elder who has returned to his Sisseton Wahpeton Oyate (People) calls us adoptees the lost drums and pipes who were locked away from culture, and stored in Americans homes. We are the people who need to be repatriated back to our nations. Adrian believes **now** is the time. Our People need **us** back.

With the creation of numerous Indian Adoption Projects and Programs, and The Adoption Resource Exchange of North America (ARENA), this grand scheme didn't make headlines. Their plan was not a war, not a signed treaty, but an idea they hoped would catch on and spread. Selling Americans and others on adopting Indian kids would be quite effortless. Essentially all social workers had to imply to parents was, "you'll save these poor Indians kid's lives."

Judgments fell on First Nations and Indian Country in a very big way. This heavy-handed treatment and their adoption idea blanketed North America in every direction. In Canada it's called the 60s Scoop.** It was the same idea for single women who had an illegitimate baby. Women were told to forget they had the baby. Indians were not told anything. Indian children simply disappeared at the playground or from their backyard or babies were taken from hospitals. Some of our mothers were too poor, pressured not to keep us. A big black government sedan was reported in many abduction stories and it was not against the law or illegal. Some Native children were removed to residential boarding schools. Others were placed in orphanages and foster homes, and others would be adopted.

But by the grace of Great Spirit, it failed. Indians who were adopted do find their way home. The writers in this book are living proof. We are still here and with these new stories, we make new history.

Many folks living in America and Canada still see Indian Country as a foreign land, alien like some other planet. In some non-Indian families, racism and ignorance about tribes is/was very strong. Opinions about Indians was never great to begin with and gets even more damaged and complicated with Indian reservations ravaged by poverty and North America's neglect.

For the past century, this truth is not widely acknowledged in history: the government's plan was to ethnically cleanse an entire population of Indian children. Removing culture of Native children would not only destroy future generations of Indians but adopted children would not have treaty rights. Adopted children would disappear.

It's probably a fact that our adoptive parents had no idea as to the motive or why there were so many Indian kids put up for adoption, or why governments ran these programs and projects with public and private adoption agencies who could supply infants and children to non-Indian families. This book series will change their perception.

By the 1970s, Indian leaders took these serious concerns to the U.S. Senate, leading to the passage of the Indian Child Welfare Act of 1978. First Nations in Canada enacted their own law. From the 1960s to 1980s, some of the children were sent out of Canada to the United States, Europe or New Zealand. In this book, we share what one tribal leader said in his congressional testimony.

As Louis La Rose (Winnebago Tribe of Nebraska) testified:

> "I think the cruelest trick that the white man has ever done to Indian children is to take them into adoption court, erase all of their records and send them off to some nebulous family ... residing in a white community and he goes back to the reservation and he has absolutely no idea who his relatives are, and they effectively make him a non-person and I think ... they destroy him."

I know I was stunned to hear it was government policy to run these various adoption programs. Many adoptees claim their adoptive parents never knew about this. Mine surely didn't and would have scoffed at the idea.

When an adoptee becomes an adult, some question whether their family or their tribe will accept them back. Some were unsure which tribe or if it's more than one tribe. Some did not know they had been enrolled in their sovereign tribal nations, filed earlier by relatives. Some learned their parents and tribal relatives were assimilated too, in boarding schools or in relocation programs, severely scarring them. It's a painful cycle of trauma and loss in this past century.

The "adoptee stigma" of assimilation does leave adoptees lodged between **two worlds.** Can we be Indian enough when raised by non-Indians? Can we return to learn tribal culture and customs? Can we take back our identity? Can we be reverse-assimilated? Can we attend ceremony and get our Indian name? I tell them, "Yes."

But neither adoptee or Indian parent will find government help in reconciliation or repatriation in America. It's up to the adoptee and parents. It's up to tribal communities to spread the truth about these Adoption Projects and begin to look for their lost children.

Victims of these adoption programs have not received a formal apology in the United States. Few politician's know or acknowledge it happened. With sealed adoption and closed birth records, this will prevent full disclosure, which is why this book was planned and written. Politicians and lawmakers need to know our birth certificates were amended and falsified. Judges must abide by the Indian Child Welfare Act.

The adoptees I know are some of the strongest-willed humans on the planet.

They got around laws and sealed records, and as you will read in *Two Worlds*, many built their own bridge between these two worlds.

Gathering these stories changed me, enlightened me, haunted me and even astonished me. I only ask that you share these stories with your children so these governments never attempt this idea again. The adoptees in this book are my relatives now. Their courage and spirit shines through their words. We are our own unique band of survivors and warriors.

"A nation that does not know its own history has no future," is a quote I read by activist Russell Means, Oglala Lakota.

So how do we write the story of North American Indian and First Nation adoptees when so few people know anything about this history?

We gather round the adoptees and listen as they share their story, in their own words, in their own voice.

The only way we can change history is to write it ourselves..... and our truth shall finally set us free.

—Trace L. Hentz (Shawnee-Tsalagi-French Canadian-Irish)
Author-Editor of the book series Lost Children of the Indian Adoption Projects: *One Small Sacrifice, Two Worlds, Called Home: The RoadMap, Stolen Generations and contributor to IN THE VEINS (Vol. 4)*

*Patricia Busbee will be updating her story and journey in the next edition of Called Home: The RoadMap (vol. 2) in 2018.

Please read an important update about Canada's 60s Scoop in the FIRST NATIONS CANADA section of this book.

Orphan Honor Song

Orphans be strong,
Listen to our traditions,
They will give you strength,
Hear the Drums' voice,
It will tell you things...

Words sung in the Wablencia Honor Song for First Nation orphans, translated from Lakota to English.

Dakota Spiritual Elder Chris Leith co-founded the First Nations Orphan Association with adoptee Sandy White Hawk (Sicangu Lakota) after the two met at a World Prayer Day ceremony in Costa Rica in 1999. They felt a *Wiping the Tears* ceremony for adoptees (Lost Birds/Lost Children/Split Feathers) was needed.

Leith brought in Jerry Dearly, Oglala Lakota, who wrote the 'Honor Song.'

"It's a healing," Leith said, "to bring back that sense of belonging, of dignity, of identity, and that love and tender care that everyone is searching for."

Generation after Generation, We Are Coming Home
—Trace A. DeMeyer, published in TALKING STICK, New York City (2005)

Another Lost Bird is Home

i went to Wounded Knee

and i seen Lost Bird's grave

i kissed her tombstone

for she knew herself...my journey

i know she lived as i do now with many questions...

some now answered, some still unanswered

But i am okay with it

because i am another lost bird

that found her way home.

Another Lost Bird is Home

© Karen Kaminawaish, M.A.,M.S. (2011) Anishinawbe Adoptee-poet

PART I

American Indian Adoptees

1

I am Lakota

Diane Tells His Name

Diane with her adoptive mother.

For 37 years, I was Teresa Diane Tommaney, a German/Irish female born in Oklahoma City to Mike and Betty. My roots were in the soil of Chickasha and Oklahoma City.

In 1952, when I was six months old, my folks moved to Southern California. I spent my childhood in moderate affluence. My father was a plumbing contractor. He built the Los Angeles Airport, contracted the plumbing for the KMarts in the Los Angeles area (along with many other large corporate buildings), and he was one of the inventors of a device called the Backflow Prevention Valve used in City Water systems. My mother stayed at home until the early 1960's when she went to real estate school and began a successful real estate career.

In the meantime, my folks presented me with a baby sister in 1954 and a baby brother in 1964.

I grew up in blissful suburbia with a nice big house, a swimming pool in the backyard, and at my doorstep the morning of my sixteenth birthday, a new Mustang. I had the promise of an education at any college I wanted. I was devoted and proud to be an Irish Tommaney. Yet, something was missing from my life. (This is a very common feeling that us Native adoptees have, I am finding out.) I felt this 'something missing' even when I was young. My siblings seemed to fit in the family, where I did not. The bond seemed closer between my siblings and my folks. Maybe it was because they all looked and acted alike. Maybe it was because they talked alike. Maybe it was because they thought alike. Maybe it was just my young imagination. I had no idea that I was adopted, let alone Native. I just felt 'different.' Native America and Indian People had always fascinated me. I had a love affair with the West before it was 'acceptable.' I collected Native American items on my family's trips through the Southwest every summer on our way to visit relatives in Oklahoma. I dressed in a Native Way, admired Native Way, and much to the dismay of my folks; I now know I thought in a Native Way. I had dreams about Indian people, old places, and old languages. In 1987 I finally confronted my 'mother' about the possibility of my being adopted. She was shocked that I would ask and admitted, yes, I had been adopted. I heard the chosen child story from my mom and was told I was the product of an affair my birth mother had and that I was probably half (very little) Cherokee. My journey started then to find my Native family. Little did I know my journey would end up with losing my adoptive family, due to their inability to share me. I was told to go 'home' or 'back to the blanket' as they called it; this would be a disgrace. I knew in my heart that I was way more than one-eighth Native, Cherokee or ?

It took me two long years to find my Lakota mother and family. In 1989, my husband and I, our four children, and two foster children, all traveled to Pine Ridge Indian Reservation. My mother introduced me to my Tribe and I participated in some ceremonies.

When we arrived at Pine Ridge, I felt I had been there before and when I heard my many relatives speaking Lakota, I felt as if I should be able to speak it too. My mouth should have been forming Lakota sounds and speaking the Lakota

Mother Tongue. It was a very emotional time for me to be where my ancestors lived, and where my People and Family still live. My naming ceremony was the highlight of our visit in 1989. The tears flowed and the feelings of belonging began to overtake me. Lakota People danced with me when my honor song was sung and they drummed. They cried as they hugged me and welcomed me home. Old aunties wiped their eyes as I, the Lost One, returned home to the People.

Many of these Lost Birds, as we are called, are suffering because of their plight in not finding their Native families. I hear it over and over that they are lost, incomplete, and useless. Some of the people I meet need counseling and cannot seem to get anyone who understands the total disconnection of knowing they are Native but not knowing what tribe they are from, or who their family is. For a Native, that is like being dead. You have no roots, no beginning, no stories and no future. There is a movement of these People to join and form their own 'Tribe.' In Canada they are known as 'Métis.' I am one of the few blessed ones to have found my family and my culture.

I am Diane Tells His Name, Oglala Lakota, of the Bad Faces Band. My family is from Calico, Porcupine and Wounded Knee. My families are the Lone Elks, the White Faces, the Fast Wolves, the Bissionettes, and the Red Clouds. I am learning the Lakota language and the Lakota Way. I know my family stories and my family history. I know my mother and I know my sisters and brothers. I am complete.

Indian Adoption Project(s)

"Government policies shifted in the 1950's towards a more humanitarian view, but not without serious consequences. Humanitarians still viewed assimilation as the best answer to the 'Indian problem' and viewed tribes as incapable of caring for their children. New projects began, such as the Indian Adoption Project, which used public and private agencies to remove and place hundreds of Indian children in non-Indian homes far from their families and communities (Mannes, 1995). Few efforts were made or resources committed to help tribal governments develop services on tribal lands that would strengthen Indian families. As efforts to outplace Indian children continued into the 1960s and 1970s, the Association on Indian Affairs conducted a study in the 1970's that found between 25 percent and 35 percent of all Indian children had been separated from their families (George, 1997). This study also found that in 16 states in 1969, 85 percent of the Indian children were placed in non-Indian homes (Unger, 1977). The long-term effects of these massive out placements of Indian children were only just beginning to be understood in the 1970's, which included effects not only on individuals, but also the well-being of entire tribal communities. Not until 1978, after the passage of the Indian Child Welfare Act (P.L. 95-608), did the federal government acknowledge the critical role that tribal governments play in protecting their children and maintaining their families."

— Act Against Indians, Terry Cross (Seneca Tribal Nation) STATEMENT OF THE NATIONAL INDIAN CHILD WELFARE ASSOCIATION PRESENTED BEFORE THE SENATE COMMITTTEE ON INDIAN AFFAIRS Regarding the REAUTHORIZATION OF THE INDIAN CHILD PROTECTION AND

FAMILY VIOLENCE PREVENTION ACT S. 1601, SEPTEMBER 24, 2003 [online source]

"These are the facts. Between 1958 and 1967, Child Welfare League of America (CWLA) cooperated with the Bureau of Indian Affairs (BIA), under a federal contract, to facilitate an experiment in which non-Indian families removed 395 Indian children from their tribes and cultures for adoption. This experiment began primarily in the New England states. CWLA channeled federal funds to its oldest and most established private agencies first, to arrange the adoptions, though public child welfare agencies were also involved toward the end of this period. Exactly 395 adoptions of Indian children were done and **studied** during this 10-year period, with the numbers peaking in 1967. ARENA, the Adoption Resource Exchange of North America, began in early 1968 as the successor to the BIA/ CWLA Indian Adoption Project. Counting the period before 1958 and some years after it, CWLA was partly responsible for approximately 650 children being taken from their tribes and placed in non-Indian homes. For some of you, this story is a part of your personal history. Through this project, BIA and CWLA actively encouraged states to continue and to expand the practice of 'rescuing' Native children from their own culture, from their very families. Because of this legitimizing effect, the indirect results of this initiative cannot be measured by the numbers I have cited. Paternalism under the guise of child welfare is still alive in many locations today, as you well know...."

—Working Together to Strengthen Supports for Indian Children and Families: A National Perspective, Keynote Speech by Shay Bilchik at the National Indian Children Welfare Association (NICWA) Conference, Anchorage, Alaska on April 24, 2001

"If the Native American population was 2 million and just one quarter of all children were removed before the Indian Child Welfare Act of 1978, then (on-paper) 80,000+ children were removed from their families during the early to mid-1900s. If the population was 3 million, then over 100,000 were removed and relocated via adoption." (You do the math...)

—Trace A. DeMeyer, *One Small Sacrifice: Lost Children of the Indian Adoption Projects*

"In 1984, 80% of American Indian infant adoptions into non-Indian homes were made without notification to the child's tribe or the Secretary of the Interior. Six years since its development, the ICWA still was not understood, was not being implemented correctly or was simply ignored. The problem exists today; and with the time-frame of child adoption procedures being accelerated under President Clinton's new adoption policies, the risk of Indian children being permanently removed from their families, their tribes, and their culture continues to increase."

—American Indian Child Resource Center

An adoptee's 'records' include: the adoption decree; information about birth parents and their families gathered during pre-placement interviews; and the Original Birth Certificate (OBC). Several states offer restricted access, like Michigan. Restrictions include consent vetoes, required parental permission even for adults, mandatory intermediaries, and open records for adoptees born in certain years. Proposals to change the laws are being considered in several states.

(Source: http://www.reunite.com/adoption-records)

3

I will die with all the damage done to me as my legacy

Evelyn Red Lodge (Lakota)

Evelyn Red Lodge

I awake every morning with thoughts that define me. I lie in wait for a better day. As I rise I take a step into the new day, but it is always the same day. It is the day my nightmare began.

Every motivation I have is based on this day.

My ultimate awakening began the day I turned 50. I realized the wasted time I spent trying to make my adoptive family love me. I awake to the fact that I live each day just to get through it. If I came out alive, then I did and nothing more. Survival is my destination, and I will be glad for that for this day.

I was born in 1961. It was the time of the American Indian Adoption Projects and the last vestiges of the horrendous Indian boarding schools. It was one frying pan or the other for me and countless other Indian children as I would find out much later in life.

In 1961 there still were Whites-only drinking fountains and signs on restaurants and bars in my home of South Dakota that read "No Dogs or Indians allowed." (Chapter three *Racism In Indian Country* by Dean Chavers, 2009.)

It was a time that what those Caucasians did to me I will never recover from. I have sometimes severe depression, debilitating anxiety, and fibromyalgia. The damage caused by them can most likely be seen in a study of my brain. I will live out my life never knowing the tools for living and nurture. I will die with all the damage done to me as my legacy.

As adopted by Caucasians, I was dispossessed of my language, culture, traditions and had imposed on me the history and religion that was not mine.

At 51 years old, I still glean for what happened to me. I am at a loss as to why a whole family would make me as a beautiful child feel so much less than them. They are Caucasian and maybe felt the supremacy the United States Government portrayed at the time. Everyone was taught that freedom of religion is a constitutional right. But, I found this to be true, iffen you are White and Christian. The right to practice our traditions was only given to us (the Lakota) in the 1970s. It is a right from God since the beginning of time, but we were heathens and government was based on Christianity as it is today.

So, how does this God of the chosen come up with the Doctrine of Discovery or Manifest Destiny. You see, it was not God who did this, as I realize today. It was man, and I mean man.

I learned in school that Indians massacred and in church my people were heathens. How was I supposed to love myself even in the institutions that were to be most kind? How did God who is love, keep me locked in a nightmare? Did God only love White people?

I tried to believe there was a God. I thought he did miracles and maybe he could do one for me.

So, I remember being so desperate to believe when I was six-years-old that I went inside a corn crib on my adoptive grandmother's farm and prayed hard to God to make me appear on the outside of the crib. Of course that did not happen, and it became clear that God would do nothing for me.

At about the same time, my adoptive mother in one of her rages slammed my head against a piece of wood over and over. My faith was further shaken as my teacher asked me the next day why I had knots all over my head. I told her what happened and thought sure I could go home to my mother Virginia. As with God nothing happened.

God took my adoptive parents when I was fifteen-years-old. Except, he took the most beautiful baby in my life with them in a car accident. She was six-years-old and her mother young. My seven-year-old adoptive sister had to crawl over her and her young mother to escape the car. The baby was on the floor clutching her doll with an eternal heavenward stare.

I remember the baby in her little casket wondering why she had to go with such evilness as her company. Her mother, who I told a long time ago that her husband raped me, failed to report this to anyone.

What was that baby taken for? I would soon find out as my favorite cousin, who had witnessed the alcoholic rape of me said, "I don't think (the baby) could have endured what we went through. I think she would have died." So, there it was that the baby was saved from the rapes that would follow.

She was saved, but my little adoptive sister was put in the same position prior to the baby's death. She was about six-years-old when she told me that the alcoholic uncle did things to her and licked the baby. I told her never to go over there again. I felt it was all I could do as I was about fourteen-years-old at the time. We felt we could never say anything about abuse.

I think the quote from this woman says much about my experience as a result of adoption. She said,

> "I think the cruelest trick that the white man has ever done to Indian children is to take them into adoption court, erase all of their records and send them off to some nebulous family … residing in a white community. And he goes back to the reservation and he has absolutely no idea who his relatives are, and they effectively make him a non-person and I think … they destroy him."
>
> —Louis La Rose, Winnebago Tribe of Nebraska, testifying before Congress on behalf of the proposed Indian Child Welfare Act (enacted 1978)

I used to stand looking in the mirror at myself and wondering why I was so ugly. I wanted to rub the dark pigments from my knees and my face. I used to wonder why people hurt me and why they raped and beat me so bad.

I know now they are most likely sorry in the eyes of their God yet rely on the culture they were raised in order to live with themselves. A culture of men, and a culture of supremacy without a true God.

As the supreme took everything from us, he did lock us in concentration camps known as Indian reservations. His name is wasicu (Taker of the fat which was best part of the meat).

Now the supreme wonder why our culture is so stricken with sadness, and I think Aaron Huey described it best when he said, "The last chapter in any successful genocide is the one in which the oppressor can remove their hands and say, 'My God, what are these people doing to themselves? They're killing each other. They're killing themselves while we watch them die.' This is how we came to own these United States. This is the legacy of manifest destiny." (http://www.ted.com/speakers/aaron_huey.html)

Was there a god? Why would god let this happen to me? Why did he forget me?

God forgot me for 40 years of my life. The son of God I learned to pray to never once saved me from anything.

It took me 40 years to come back home and find the true God for me. His name is Wakan Tanka. I learned I did not have to fear him and was robbed of his love those four decades. Miracles do happen as I have been shown through him that I am not ugly, nor less than any one person.

It is finally my time to just be. To be as one who can look in the mirror and not feel disgust. I am a person who had children and tried to make better their life for them as compared to mine. Yet, I failed so tremendously, and I am so eternally sorry for that. I am a person without the tools for living.

I am a poor person, and I have to live with that. My children paid for what was not mine. They paid in that I had to learn to nurture from others, but I love them and made their lives a hundred times better than mine.

I do not know how to express this to them, and I am still defined as a victim as my brain was damaged. I am damaged, and I will never recover.

I created a family that is damaged by historical trauma, and I beg Wakan Tanka to forgive me and not let me define their actions. I am so damaged. I try as I sit here and think of the damage I caused unintentionally with lack of knowledge. I am a nut-job and my children are paying, because you freaking nut-job racists and you child-savers ruined my life and that of my descendants. Did you child-savers once check on me?

I see no difference from my experience with the experience of American Indian children today. They are taken for cash, and it is true.

I sit here and think of how I fit into life. Of course I am defined as a victim, yet I advocate for those who suffer the consequences of the child-savers. I rise and scream, "Go moms!!! Go grandmas!!! Get the children back!!!!"

Evelyn Red Lodge is a member of the Sicangu Lakota Oyate in South Dakota and currently resides in Rapid City. She is a journalist and author who specializes in Indian Child Welfare Act issues and advocates for ICWA families.

This story contains excerpts from her own book slated for publication.

4

Healing the Wounds of your Ancestors

"… Our 'job' here is to be the light that we already are and reflect that light outward so that others might find their own way in the darkness. The wounds we carry dim the light. As we do the work of transforming our wounds into gifts that help to bring about healing, we literally begin to shine. We become radiant beings who reflect their true nature, which is luminosity. Or, as Carl Sagan said, 'We're made of star stuff.' We are light beings as much as the stars. It takes courage to do the work of healing. It's not comfortable, convenient or easy. It's not 'business as usual,' or maintaining the status quo. It means the end of denial, pretending and avoiding. It means being radically honest with yourself and those around you. This kind of honesty won't necessarily win popularity contests, but it will recalibrate your DNA. If we're healing and transforming the wounds we carry from those who came before, we're also changing the trajectory of those who come after. Those who follow will have a different standard as the foundation for the lineage. If we break the chain of addiction, violence or other inherited, limiting beliefs, our children and their children and those who follow them are given access to possibilities not available to the ancestors. And thus, the entire lineage evolves…."

— Healing the Wounds of Your Ancestors, Dr. Judith Rich

5

"The Only Good Indian is a Dead Indian"

Trace L. Hentz

Every Indian has heard, 'Kill the Indian, and Save the Man,' or 'the Only Good Indian is a Dead Indian.' Both were uttered by Capt. Richard C. Pratt, the head master and founder of Carlisle Boarding School.

Beginning in 1887, the government tried to 'civilize' Native Americans by educating young children. By 1900, thousands were studying at 154 boarding schools in the United States alone. Carlisle, Flandreau, Hampton, Haskell Institute and others were built. The U.S. Training and Industrial School was founded in 1879 at Carlisle Barracks, Pennsylvania. Carlisle provided vocational and manual training but systematically stripped away tribal culture. Students had to drop their Indian names, they could not speak their languages, clothing was burned and long hair was cut off. Cutting off the hair was done in many tribes when a relative died. For some alarmed children, cutting hair meant cutting off contact.

Carlisle's founder Captain Pratt said the following to an 1892 convention, which portrays his frequently brutal methods for 'civilizing' the 'savages.'

> A great general has said that the only good Indian is a dead one, and that high sanction of his destruction has been an enormous factor in promoting Indian massacres. In a sense, I agree with the sentiment, but only in this: that all the Indian there is in the race should be dead. Kill the Indian in him, and save the man.

Pratt decided Native traditions are wrong. Many tribes strongly disagreed with the American/Canadian government's system of residential boarding schools and adoptions. Our culture is our tribal family. Yet in the past 100 years, tribes lost two or three generations to the government's system of removals and adoption.

Pratt said in a speech to the Board of Commissioners in 1889: 'I say that if we take a dozen young Indians and place one in each American family, taking those so young they have not learned to talk, and train them up as children of those families, I defy you to find any Indian in them when they are grown...Color amounts to nothing. The fact that they are born Indians does not amount to anything.' *DeJong, Promises of the Past, 110.

Opposing both the reservation system and the allotment of communally held lands to individual Indians, Pratt wrote, 'I would blow the reservations to pieces. I would not give Indians an acre of land. When he strikes bottom, he will get up.' *D. W. Adams, Education for Extinction, 53.

'Civilization was defined as white, Christian (preferably Protestant), capitalistic, modern and industrializing... Indians were still primitive...,' Margaret D. Jacobs writes in White Mother to a Dark Race: Settler Colonialism, Maternalism and the Removal of Indigenous Children in the American West and Australia, 1880-1940. 'Perhaps the most crucial goal of the nation builders in each settler country was to gain complete control over the land; authorities looked to indigenous child removal, in part, to help them achieve this objective.' *Jacobs, 82-83.

As part of the assimilation policy, Congress passed the 1887 General Allotment Act, also called the Dawes Act, to break up tribal lands and allot each male head of household 160 acres of land. This land was to be held in trust by the BIA for twenty-five years to prevent its sale. All told, Indian people lost about ninety million acres through the implementation of the Dawes Act. *Jacobs, 83.

The act provided eighty acres to single Indian women. * Hoxie, The Final Promise.

Footnotes:

DeJong, David H. (1993) Promises of the past: a history of Indian education in the United States. Golden, Colo: North American Press.

Adams, D. W. (1995) Education for extinction: American Indians and the boarding school experience, 1875-1928. Lawrence: University Press of Kansas.

Jacobs, Margaret D. (2009) *White Mother to a Dark Race: Settler Colonialism, Maternalism, and the Removal of Indigenous Children in the American West and Australia, 1880-1940.* Lincoln: University of Nebraska Press.

Hoxie, Frederick E (1984) A Final Promise: The Campaign to Assimilate the Indians, 1880-1920. Lincoln: University of Nebraska Press.

"In contrast to the biblical book of Genesis, in which God creates man in his own image and gives him dominion over all other creatures, the Native American legends reflect the view that human beings are no more important than any other thing, whether alive or inanimate. In the eye of the Creator, they believe, man and woman, plant and animal, water and stone, are all equal, and they share the earth as partners — even as family. Recurring themes include the idea of Mother Earth as life host, the relationship of reciprocity that exists between human beings and animals, and the Indians' dependence on animals as teachers. The plots are often complex, take numerous twists and turns, and commonly include humor. But any comic elements never detract from the story's sacred purpose."

—The Spirit World, Time-Life Books

6

Red Lake Anishinaabe Split Feather

Joan Kauppi (Red Lake Anishinaabe)

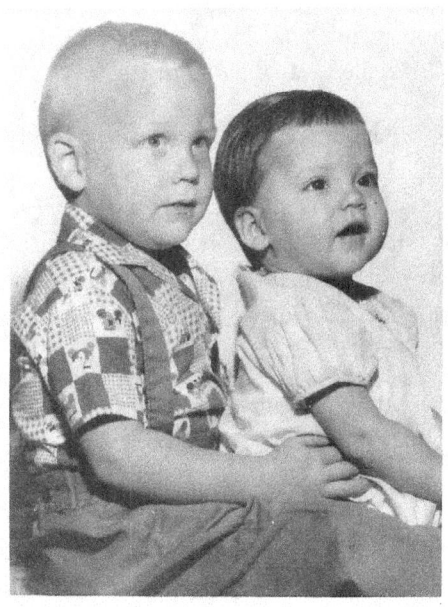

Scott and Joan (10 months)

I was born in 1960 in Minneapolis, Minnesota. Within days of my birth, a middle-class family in Bloomington, Minnesota adopted me. I have an older brother Scott who was also adopted. Several years later a brother and a sister were born to my adoptive parents.

We were a relatively happy family. We went on family outings and went to church every Sunday. I was not abused in any manner and was rarely physically punished. My dad was a very dear and wonderful man. He was quiet and often hard to warm up to, but I knew he loved me. He has passed and I miss him terribly although I know he is around me frequently.

Both my parents were good and kind people, but somehow I knew I was different. I always had a feeling I did not quite fit in. As a child I did not have the ability to intellectualize or verbalize my feelings. I was well into adulthood before I understood why I felt different.

My family regularly attended church but I never felt a connection to Catholicism. I went through all the required motions, First Communion and Catechism. It was expected of me to complete these rituals. I wore the little white dress and promised to live my entire life within the rules of the Catholic Church. The adoption agency was Catholic Charities. Their role in my life felt like a stranglehold. It reached way beyond my adoption.

As a child and a teen I began having spiritual dreams and visions, which were chalked up to my childish imagination. I learned very quickly not to discuss them with anyone for fear of ridicule, yet they were very real to me. My dreams consisted of spiritual messages, occasional precognitive knowledge of future events, and what is known as out-of-body experiences. All of these experiences are in opposition to Christianity. I felt like I was betraying my church.

My parents told me that I was adopted very early on. Since this knowledge was a part of my earliest memories, it was never a shock. However, I did have conflicting feelings. I was picked out, chosen by two loving parents, but my birthparents abandoned me. I struggled to reconcile these two realities.

To add insult to injury I was considered an oddity. I was forced to explain the concept of adoption to my friends. They were curious as to why my real parents didn't want me. Of all my experiences, this was the most painful since I had to keep retelling and explaining my adoption over the course of my childhood.

In the summer I was always darker than the neighborhood children. Many of my friends tried to sunbathe in order to obtain the same beautiful bronze I was able to achieve without the awful sunburn. When they had to stay indoors for several days due to their sunburns I was secretly a little happy. It was one of the few attributes that I owned, one they were envious of.

I began kindergarten at the age of four because I had taught myself to read. I was a very bright child and I breezed through elementary school.

My junior high years were difficult for my parents. I began smoking, drinking, and experimenting with illegal drugs as a means of acceptance. I was pretty tough and became a bully. I wanted the other students to fear me so that they would keep their distance. I believe I wanted an emotional distance so I didn't have to explain my adoption and why my birth parents relegated me to the State of Minnesota.

Things changed when I started high school. Around age fifteen I became acutely aware of my physical attributes and their effect on the opposite sex. Their attention made me feel beautiful and important. The more attention I received, the more I wanted. It wasn't long before this behavior became addictive. It continued into my young adult years and eventually evolved into promiscuity. I was searching for something—anything that would help me reconcile with myself.

By age seventeen I began dating a man who had chemical dependency issues. Several years into the relationship I gave birth to a beautiful daughter. Becoming a mother helped me achieve a sense of responsibility, which I enjoyed and needed. Shortly after my daughter's birth, I left him.

Soon after, I met another man and we were married within a year. I had a second daughter.

During this time I received a letter from the adoption agency. I learned that my birthmother was enrolled in the Red Lake Band of Ojibwa and that she had enrolled me as a tribal member. The letter also stated that I would be receiving a check for approximately $1200 for a land settlement payment.

I decided to initiate a search for my birth family. I spoke to a representative at Catholic Charities. I was advised to request 'non-identifying information.' I immediately began the process. After what seemed to be an endless wait, I received a letter from them. It was exciting to learn where I came from, but more questions than answers started to emerge.

The basic information I received stated that I was the youngest of five; all of us were put up for adoption. My parents were very young and lived in poverty.

During this time my marriage deteriorated and my very controlling husband moved out.

My two daughters and I relocated to a town thirty miles away. I did not know anyone. After we adjusted to our new living arrangements, I once again contacted Catholic Charities. The woman said she knew exactly who I was and said there was an entire file cabinet dedicated to my birth family. The woman took pity on me and provided me with the names of my mother's sisters. I was also given the name of the city where they lived. I immediately found a telephone book and called one of my aunts. She was so happy to hear from me. We both became very emotional. She notified her sister and the three of us met several days later.

I drove to my aunt's house with my two beautifully dressed daughters in tow. Her house was a nice single level home in a northern suburb of Minneapolis. The tears flowed, but this time I was hugged and welcomed into the family. I distinctly remember feeling comfortable and at ease. A sense of peace set in.

We had a lovely lunch. I can still remember what she served and how her home looked and felt. Her sister was also kind and welcoming. After lunch we began talking about my mother. They told me that since the adoption she had remarried and had five more children, two with my birthfather and three during a second marriage. She and her second husband lived five miles south of my childhood home.

She divorced her second husband for unknown reasons and became a recluse. Due to my education and years of research, I now understand her pain along with her historical and generational trauma.

My birthmother, Annetta, frequented a local casino. She maintained her love of bingo. She sat in the back in an attempt to remain invisible, they said.

At the conclusion of our afternoon together, my aunts gave me the names of two of my full-blood brothers. They were unaware of their current home city but would let me know if they ever found out. For the first time in my life, I felt as if I was moving towards wholeness.

Unfortunately, this feeling was short-lived. It was the only meeting I would have with my aunts. I called them several days later, and they were quite rude. I was told that my birthmother was very angry I had contacted them. She told them that they were to not speak to me again. I was dumbfounded.

I decided to try to find my brothers. This was before the internet. I had no idea how to find them. I looked in phone books but could not locate their addresses. During a telephone conversation with my next-door neighbor, I explained my situation and that I was attempting to find my brothers. When I told her their names, she told me to come over immediately. She met me at her door with a photo album open to a page that displayed pictures of my brothers. She had known them for years. She contacted them for me.

At first they did not believe they had a sister. After we met, they said they knew I was part of their family. After meeting, we became close. We keep in contact via Facebook.

Several months later on Christmas Day, I was introduced to two half-sisters who looked upon me as a stranger, like an enemy. They never warmed up and according to other family members they are unhappy women. At that time they both lived within three miles of me. We also have a brother Charlie, my half-brother. He has decided not to meet me. I have learned that he and his wife adopted a child from the Red Lake Nation. They also have biological children. The information I have regarding my four older brothers is sketchy at best. The oldest still lives on the Red Lake reservation and is somewhat of a recluse himself. We met briefly and have not kept in contact. The mother of my cousin, who I met at Bemidji State University, raised him. He expressed interest to my cousin about building a relationship with me, but I have not made the effort. I believe I am hesitant because I fear more rejection from family. Unfortunately I have hurt him in the process. He has little family and tends to be a recluse himself. He lives on the reservation and has expressed interest that I spend time there. From past experiences on the reservation I felt as if I didn't belong there either. I was perceived as an outsider.

I have little information regarding the three boys that were also put up for adoption. One brother, named John, committed suicide, and another brother was in drug rehab. The third brother I know nothing about.

One of my greatest gifts is meeting my two birthbrothers. Both were born within three years of my birth. I experienced them as kind, gentle, and loving. They have their own dysfunction and trauma to deal with; their lives had been filled with abuse, violence, drugs, alcohol and deception. Neither was shown healthy parental or familial affection. One brother has been divorced four times. Sadly, he physically abused his wives. He has married a fifth time and appears to be happy. He has turned to God and has become a minister, although his religion has not helped his anger problem. He is a good, kind and loving man.

My other brother was also tormented by the temptation of drugs and alcohol but has been clean now for many years. He is married with four daughters and a son and is faithful and loving to his wife. He lives in Minnesota and we keep in contact.

My brothers contacted our mother Annetta shortly after our initial meeting and she denied that I existed. At the time it was extremely hurtful but I understand now why she did it. After our adoptions she plummeted into a life of additional childbearing, gambling, alcohol abuse and self-imposed exile.

She and I never became close and only saw each other a few times. I was her fifth born child. She was nineteen at the time of my birth. I wish I could refer to her as my mother, but she never held that role in my life. I questioned her about my birthfather, but she declined to talk about him.

I have a relative who worked in the insurance industry. She was able to obtain a brief glimpse into a file on my birthfather. He was a Sicilian man named Robert. He was incarcerated shortly after one of my brothers was born. He was a member of the mafia in Chicago and reportedly incarcerated for homicide. He was released in the 1990s and passed away in 2000. Additionally, I have a brother on this side of my family tree. He has chosen not to contact me.

When I spoke with my mother, I experienced her as cold and very private. At that time I was struggling with identity issues that I was unaware of. I was unknowingly looking to her to help me understand myself. Our relationship was doomed from the start. I felt further rejection, which was very difficult for me to handle. I now know that someone who was just as broken as I was could not somehow magically make me whole. She did give me one amazing gift and that was the name she was going to give me if she had been allowed to keep me: Caroline Annetta Rossetti.

Unfortunately she began her journey to the next world several years later, alone. She did not want any of us to be with her at her passing. We were instructed not to have a funeral. We honored her wishes. As I reflect on her desire to be alone, I am certain it is due to the loss of children to adoption, death and divorce.

I can verify that she gave birth to twelve children. I was told that there are two more, but I cannot verify this. I still grieve the loss of never really knowing her and not growing up with my siblings. More importantly, I grieve for the pain she suffered in silence. I regret my lack of historical knowledge of our people.

Maybe I would not have held on to the resentment for so many years, which I believe, poisons your body and soul.

I am truly thankful for the gift of my education. Without it I would not have understood all the components of her pain or been able to look at the situation from many different angles. I would not have been able to forgive her. I suffer from prolonged depressed states and have recently emerged from one that lasted over six months. I will always be a broken individual in many respects but I now have the tools to manage some of the negative emotions that have followed me throughout my life.

I have found a path of healing which has ended the intergenerational trauma for my children and me.

Although it's a healing that will take time, patience, thought, and will, the intergenerational trauma in my family will end with me.

Joan Kauppi is an enrolled member in the Red Lake Ojibwe Nation in northern Minnesota. She is blessed with four children and five grandchildren. Currently she is writing an academic paper about identity issues as an adoptee which she plans to turn into a Master's thesis. She plans to write a book on American Indian birthparents that lost children to adoption.

7

Marion Morrison (aka John Wayne)

Trace L. Hentz

> "I don't feel we did wrong in taking this great country away from them. There were great numbers of people who needed new land, and the Indians were selfishly trying to keep it for themselves." —Actor John Wayne (real name: Marion Morrison)

Remember John Wayne? Remember cowboy movies when the American anecdote was to kill and exterminate those savages who stood in the way of progress?

In reality, America's War Chest (dollars and land) was necessary to fight Indians the further west they invaded. In western films, any truth was massacred, slaughtered along with Indians. Yes, it's all we learn about Indians until Thanksgiving, then it's Pilgrims who ate with the now extinct-Indians, the good ones. Portrayed as savages in books and movies, it's not a stretch to see how taking Indian children was part of an overall game plan. Finding white people to raise savage babies would make us white, or so they thought.

If westerns were real, based on true events, you and I wouldn't be able to watch them. Accuracy about Indians wasn't important to the film industry. Few movies captured the beauty, or dignity, or explained reasons why Indians fought back.

Behind the scenes was the Great White Father, the U.S. President in Washington, busy seizing more and more tribal lands, signing bogus treaties or breaking them. Several states forcibly removed tribes west. There were many trails of tears.

More modern American Presidents, Teddy Roosevelt, John F. Kennedy, Bill

Clinton and Barrack Obama have visited Indian reservations. Oprah Winfrey taped an episode on her visit to the Navajo reservation in 2006. No wonder so many Americans seem disconnected from Indian history.

They watched too many John Wayne movies.

> "Good words do not last long unless they amount to something. Words do not pay for my dead people. Words do not pay for my country, now overrun by white men. They do not protect my father's grave. They do not pay for all my horses and cattle. Good words will not give me back my children. Good words will not make good the promise of your War Chief. Good words will not give my people good health and stop them from dying. Good words will not get my people a home where they can live in peace and take care of themselves. I am tired of talk that comes to nothing. It makes my heart sick when I remember all the good words and all the broken promises. There has been too much talking by Men who had no right to talk."

—CHIEF JOSEPH (HIN-MAH-TOO-YAH-LAT-KEKT), NEZ PERCE, 1840-1904

8

45 Minutes

(Nancy) Verrier's work in 'Coming Home to Self,' published in 2003, points to a study by Joseph Chilton Pearce, author of 'Magical Child and Evolutions End,' who states that it takes less than forty-five minutes for an infant separated from his mother to go into shock and this reaction has immediate impact on the brain and functions like sight.

"The secret society of adoption contains two turbulent populations who are by public design held secret from one another—adoptees and birth parents. They are kept apart by a secrecy, which takes the form of sealing of records of the transfer of babies to adoption. The link between the adopted person and his forbears is removed from their grasp."
—*Jean Paton, Orphan Voyage Founder*

"Why is one person's 'crazy' another person's 'genealogical research?' Why are adoptees not supposed to complain when they are treated in a manner that, if occurring to anyone else, would be unjust? Why are mothers expected to forget they ever had a child? If a child dies, the mother is allowed her grief; vice versa if a child loses a parent. But if you're separated by adoption, tough, and if you speak out, you're nuts. Note that the people calling us crazy are, primarily, adopters and adoption 'professionals,' the sole winners (and creators) of The Adoption Game. I say 'professionals' in quotes because any bozo can sell babies, no certifications required. Adoption is a business, a for-profit venture, not a charity...."
—*73Adoptee Blog comment, November 2008*

"Today's Aboriginal youth need their homeland...to understand who they are, where they belong and how they're connected to country, the land, nature, the universe. We need to walk with them and help them feel comfortable living in Two Worlds…"

—*Elder Miriam Rose Ungunmerr-Bauman, Nature Conservancy Magazine (Fish River)*

9

Scraps

Anecia Tretikoff, Sugpiaq

Anecia Tretikoff

An excerpt from her forthcoming book, Loud Blood

Adoption Fallout.

When the US government divided our indigenous American families, crushing languages and traditions, my extended family was in pieces from the cultural genocide maneuvers of the day. It was not ancient times, but 1961; fully affecting we who are alive today in 2011. The shame, physical and mental abuse and

anxiety inflicted at the government boarding school, left young Indians disconnected from their communities, unskilled, alone, and vulnerable.

When my mother and I were separated, it wasn't just my mother and newborn-
me–it was some HUNDRED THOUSAND of us Native American mother-
child pairs being torn apart by the practices of the day. Given these numbers, it
qualifies as cultural genocide.

Yet it seems I'm one of the lucky ones. I know my tribe. I met my mother and
extended family. I got my 'pedigree card'. I know the soul-altering experience
of being held in the arms of my mother – twice. When the social worker broke
the 'Don't Look' rules that were meant for the newborn to be whisked away and
the mother's eyes to never to land upon her newly born, which would somehow make "true" that this birth never happened. But for us, an angel entered
the social worker and brought newborn-me to my mother's arms, so that she
could hold her freshest flesh and say, "I love you. I love you so much. I wish
you a rainbow life. Goodbye." Half an hour later she let go, and love stretched
like a hide over a drum's wooden frame, carrying the pulse of our connection
until our next embrace nearly 24 years later.

The moments that my mother and I met are a brilliant tattoo on my deepest
being. So are the moments of 'goodbye.'

Sometimes the all-encompassing

magnificent joy

of reconnection

is a dwarfed embrace that

goes bouncing

and bounding down,

down,

down

the long, dark mineshaft of loss

for which a bottom

is yet unknown.

One good thing: as the joy of all the cultural explorations and reconnections goes bouncing and bounding down, with it a healing light is drawn into the great shaft, curing and brightening all that hurts, causing new depths of joy.

For this I live, and am grateful.

But to grow, I must take my heart and mind into the wounded places, look around, embrace the sacred joy and sacred sadness, understand, and establish bridges; starting with the scraps.

Scraps

I have been fed, clothed, and sheltered, yet my spirit must live off cultural scraps that I go begging where Native people gather – a story, a song, a weave, a smile… where I feel a resonance and filled and soothed, but sadly, also invisible, broken, culturally orphaned, and lonely.

Will I forever be a guest among my own people? Who will celebrate my joys and triumphs with me? Who will mourn my sorrows? Who will laugh at some shared history? I want to join in my Native community, to participate, to serve, to share what I have, and to receive recognition and feel valued. But even on this side, there are those Indians that I thought were friends who walk past blankly in fuller-blood situations, or those who look at me in public settings with flash-card eyes as they calculate their racist arithmetic with no thought of how they've adopted the blood-quantum mentality constructed by the colonists. I yearn to feel welcome somehow. I need to heal myself enough to come forward to work, for otherwise I remain immobilized, hollow, invisible.

I can hear the critical thoughts of others; I think them myself – Get over it. Geesh, move on. Stop feeling sorry for yourself.

I'd love to. The same as someone uses crutches when they are injured, or someone wears bandages after surgery, or someone wears glasses to compensate for not being able to see on one's own; I am doing the best I can under the circumstances. But I need to be my own auntie and tell myself, 'Chin up. Get over it. Move on with life.' This I can do. It's the smiles, nods, and hugs that are harder. My grandmother's spirit did come with me, but she cannot hold me connected alone. When I am acknowledged with a smile, a hug, a nod – these small acts mean so much to me, reminding me that I am here, less hollow, less invisible.

I must expect nothing. This is not my business, not my community. So what am I doing here? What is the draw? It used to be my honeymoon, my infancy of native identity. What didn't take hold? What connections failed? I am not connected to these people; we are connected as human beings, but not as relatives. I am a guest.

Because my mother was taken into the dominators boarding school and made vulnerable in the world by separating her from her family and tribe, she acquiesced to the stinging, convincing words to let me go to the white man's church-people with the hopes they would find a wonderful family for me. I am indebted my adoptive parents, who did choose to parent me and raise me in the best way they knew how. But I must accept that I am henceforth a guest among my tribe. Anyway, my lack of tribal knowledge and family history must make me seem like some sort of imbecile in a place where the connected members are at home. It is as though when my mother said, "Goodbye," all conscious Native training ceased. When I reconnected with my Native family, and began listening to Native stories, songs, and conversations, my life as a Native resumed. So I gather scraps, like Yvonne, an educator and Chehalis master weaver who collects cedar bark scraps from the weaving tables because she soaks and blends them and makes them into functional, spirited cedar paper. I want to gather the bits and pieces of my life and process them into something functional and spirited. I can't wait to get over this deep-seated wound of detachment and melancholy. I want to heal and live fully the life that isn't about solving disconnection. Once this is healed and resolved, what will I be writing about? What work comes next? Who am I in another context? I long to find out.

It has been so soothing to be present at Native gatherings – witnessing tribal connections, witnessing families, witnessing powerful leaders; seeing Indian faces after growing up among blondes. When attending the 150 Year Anniversary of Treaties Symposium in The Evergreen State College Longhouse, one word stood out: "Quyana", the speaker said. *Thank you* in my mother's original language. Quyana, I heard. Quyana, I comprehended. Quyana, I felt run down my cheek.

Quyana to you, Alaska Native speaker Sally Smith.

A group of young speakers from the Makah Nation stood together at the microphone to share stories about their life and relations. Afterward, I wrote to them:

Thank you for appreciating the beauty of your culture and tribal connections. As a person who was given away from her family and tribe as a newborn baby, who feels so alone in this world, who has no family connections to celebrate big days, like the births of my three babies who are strangers to the people who would be their grandparents, aunts, and uncles. I also mourn my losses alone. This is a heavy burden; a wound I don't know if will ever heal. But perhaps it will, because when I see young people like you that love and appreciate the connections you have to each other and your culture, this beauty gives me healing.

Thank you for appreciating knowing the names of your grandparents and great-grandparents, aunties, uncles, cousins.

Thank you for speaking.

I fully support my birthmother's pseudo-decision to release me to adoption. What choices were there? How is it that she and I are one set among over 100,000 others that experienced this? Whose genocidal plan conceived this "solution?" Instead of creating or supplementing support systems for mothers in great need, they were set up to break contact with their family's next generation; en masse.

Part of my story is finding out that there are so many others. It changes everything. I experienced myself as a Native who stood alone, yet now I know there are hundreds of thousands of other Natives directly affected, and hundreds of thousands more affected in the aftermath. This fact produces in me an empathetic stupor for us hundred thousand humans dispersed and scattered into strangers homes.

On a Dakota-Lakota-Nakota site, a link reads,

For the Children in Exile.

I feel the exile pain. Though I'm not a child anymore, the exile remains. I live free, moving to many places. A tumbleweed. Free. Just the same, the longing for connections to my people, my tribe, my familiar blood, rises in waves like a daily tide. The exile is not punishment from my tribe, but a natural consequence of the benign genocidal practices of the colonists.

In our lives, the security of connection to parents, aunts, uncles, grandparents is absent. I've no older relations to call up and ask important questions or drop-in to witness, observe, share.

According to a quote by the International Indian Treaty Council from the 57th session of the UN Commission on Human Rights in 2001, as Agenda item #13: Rights of the Child, it seems that all or a majority of us have suffered extreme loss:

> Current studies have investigated the damaging effects of transracial placement which include psychological damage, ethnic identity confusion, self-concept formation difficulties, and adolescence repercussions such as alcoholism and high rates of suicide.

Growing up, I thought something was very wrong with me — not looking like others, not thinking like others, and when I could feel, not wishing to live. But fortunately, I didn't feel often.

Ok! Enough of that! Beloved Upper Skagit elder, Vi Hilbert came to the microphone to give an even shorter variation on her signature "Ten line story" about Lady Louse.

> Lady Louse was a sponge. Lady Louse became self-absorbed, and that was the end of Lady Louse.

I am going to be ok. I am willing and able to work, I just also need to heal enough to not fall into that huge gaping wound at my core and walk and talk. I see the hole now and can go around, jump over, build bridges of songs, stories, smiles, hugs, drumbeats, actions, and continue to listen, learn, light up the bridges and work around it. I have encountered many full wings – on my own, with my husband, the spirit of my grandmother, all my spirit helpers – all lifting me up.

I do have my immediate family to celebrate with, to laugh at shared history with, to mourn tragedies with – my brilliant husband, and three beautiful daughters, each bestowed with multiple intelligences.

The day I stepped off the plane and met my mother, brother, and sisters, then, I looked like someone. I met cousins, aunts, uncle, and cousin's children. From that point, I looked like a lot of people and something began to settle. Some new sense of belonging, substance, visibility, and authenticity rose above feeling detached and unseen and mismatched. With this strength growing inside, I must squeeze the self-absorbed sponge, and re-focus and make constant, scraps of beams of Joy.

Sacred scraps. Scraps are no less than a single stroke of paint on the ceiling of the Sistine Chapel, no less than a single spray of water breaking away from a thousand others as it topples and falls over a river's cliff and lands together with itself in a cool mountain pool; no less than the flash of the match that starts the fire for heating the sacred grandfather stones that will share their stories in the ancient sweat lodge ceremony.

Scraps are no less than the words of a beautiful innocent spirited four-year-old Native girl who says to the lost-n-found-soul woman as they lay under the trees cooling off in the shade after the first round of the sweat ceremony, "I never met you. You were a stranger." She sat closer and looked into my face and said, "I'm an Indian. You're an Indian. And we're not strangers anymore."

Anecia Tretikoff, M.A. is Sugpiaq with family roots in Bristol Bay, Alaska. Her life is a pulsing collage of stories, dances, dreams, spirited conversations and lasting connections made together with three daughters whom Anecia feels so privileged to know — Kathleen, Bridget, and Fiona, and friends-turned-cousins in Hawaii, the Caribbean, Alaska, New England, Pacific Northwest, and Ireland. Anecia lives in her blood's home, Alaska.

10

Lost Sparrow solves mystery but leaves wounds exposed

Trace L. Hentz

The Billings adoptees from the Crow reservation

On November 16, 2010, the documentary 'Lost Sparrow' premiered on PBS Independent Lens. Based on a true incident in 1978, two Crow Indian brothers (both adoptees) ran away from home and were found dead on railroad tracks the next day.

Chris Billing's documentary film takes a closer look at what killed these two boys and what truth shattered his entire family.

The filmmaker is one of four biological children. His parents adopted six, with four of them from the Crow tribe. Billing was 16 when the boys died. The family buries them in New York and moves on with their lives. His parents eventually divorce.

The filmmaker narrates how his little brothers Bobby (13) and Tyler (11) were trying to help their sister Lana (who is also Crow). Lana told her brothers she was being sexually molested by their adoptive father. The two boys were going to Montana to get help. They knew who they were and knew their tribe. Authorities believed they fell asleep on the railroad tracks.

As the film unfolds, Billings' story becomes more about the despondent quiet Lana, and how she didn't survive the sexual abuse or find peace after her brother's heroic gesture and unfortunate deaths. Lana runs far away from the adopters to North Carolina. Her pain is so deep the alcohol abuse seems the only antidote she can afford. There are no signs of wealth where Lana lives; unlike the Billings and their homes in New Jersey and the summer mansion in upstate New York.

Journalist-turned-filmmaker Chris Billing said it took three years to make the film. His parents, Mr. and Mrs. Billing, agree to see Lana on film but neither managed an appropriate response to her troubled past. Dysfunctional denial, which Mr. Billing's exhibited while filming, seems inappropriate and not an apology, considering the facts revealed during the course of filming.

The man at the center of the conflict, the adoptive father, an all-controlling philanderer, rich businessman, acts like nothing happened, like he did nothing wrong. What you hope is he was charged as a pedophile and sent to prison. This didn't happen.

What does happen is the filmmaker and his siblings repatriate the two boys to the Crow tribe and have them interned on tribal land. Chris films the boys' father and tribal family who knew the boys were adopted by a rich East coast family but could do nothing to stop the adoption. Their grief leaves the viewer tormented.

After revealing the entire truth, the filmmaker said it did little to bond their family or cure old wounds, 'If it was good for Lana, then making the film was worth it.'

Wounds this egregious and deep are not healed by a 78-minute film.

11

I wanted my Identity

Thomas H. Pierce (Menominee)

Thomas and his adoptive parents

Thomas, now 58, a member of Menominee tribe of Keshena, Wisconsin, is listed on their Descendent roll (because there is a 1/16 blood quantum requirement for their Tribal Rolls) ... his tribal brother told him he has more blood.

I am 3/16 Menominee and also 3/16 Stockbridge-Munsee Mohican. I believe my father was Native American but I can't find him, even though I know his name. I lack the 1/16 each tribe requires for minimum full tribal status.

I was adopted when I was five days old. I found out my adoption was due mostly because my grandfather would not allow my birthmother to bring me home. My mother was a Navy Corpsman. (My birthfather may have been also.) I was born at the Naval Hospital in Camp Pendleton on the Marine Corps military base in California.

I was adopted by a career Marine, Lt. Col. Herbert E. Pierce, a soft spoken "hero" in every respect. My adoptive dad was Cherokee, 1/4 blood, but his family denied it because of racism in Oklahoma. He was a WWII and Korean veteran and highly decorated.

Then there is my adoptive mother, an alcoholic, pill popper, ETOH abuser. (ETOH Abuse means they are abusing alcohol. Most people have not heard of alcoholism being referred to as ETOH abuse and this is because this phrase is predominantly used in the medical and rehabilitation sector. The word ETOH is short for ethanol, which is the primary ingredient in alcohol.)

My mother, I believe, just hated kids. She treated us shabbily but she held a special hate for me. When she was angry, she sailed on about me being a bastard.

My father wasn't around much due to his postings so I was raised by my older sister who was eleven years older than me. When I was about eight-years-old, she went off to school.

Because of my mother's ETOH abuse, she slept in everyday until 10 a.m., so I never had anyone to rely on for getting breakfast, getting dressed or ready for school. As a result, I was a wild child, feral in some ways.

I do remember my adoptive parents were going to adopt a Navajo boy but he was violent—he grew up on the street eating from garbage cans, taking care of his younger brother, so they sent him back. I took that to heart and realized my tenure with my family was tenuous at best.

They always seemed to be sending me off somewhere, every summer vacation. I went to camps or to relatives and finally to a children's home where corporal punishment was practiced liberally.

I even made many trips to psychologists, until they told me my mother was to blame for my problems. I don't blame my Dad though he enabled her and then he was dying, very sick, and passed away at age 54. At that time, I lost my only defender. Then my relationship with my mother turned for the worse, if that was even possible.

She sent me for a summer to an acquaintance where I was sexually abused and where my own alcohol abuse started. She would do things out of spite, like setting me up with a friend for a weekend, telling this friend of hers I was gay, which I am not; but at least by this time I was old enough to fight off my attacker.

Then later, she phoned child authorities telling them I was abusing my own son, all proven untrue.

I was written out of the family will and received no inheritance or money. She gave away land which we had bought but by then I didn't care. Our relationship was irretrievable. I just wanted the few possessions my father bequeathed to me, the only things that would have mattered; and she ignored my sons with their inheritance.

But believe it or not, I mourned at her passing, mostly for the lost opportunity of a decent relationship she threw away.

I had no Indian friends growing up; there are not many Indians in the snooty environs of Wyomissing, Pennsylvania, known for its wealth and society types. In fact, Wyomissing was a great place to learn how to fight. I was teased relentlessly. I learned to fight three or four guys at a time, just to survive as my tormentors waited for me with a beating and racial slurs.

But I was proud to be an Indian and I knew I was adopted from my first recollections. Despite the denials of being Indian from my father's side of the family, they told me to be mum because they were still hanging Native Americans in Oklahoma and Missouri.

I was adopted nine years after the end of World War II and my adoptive parents had been trying to have other children. My father wanted a boy. Since he was part Cherokee, a Native child seemed natural. One of my two sisters (their biological children) looked particularly Native American. After I was adopted, many of my father's friends remarked, in their words, "You certainly can't deny him, Herb." We looked remarkably alike, even when I was in my 40s. I wished I was but alas I am not.

I was told by my mother that due to father's military service (malaria/jungle fevers) my dad was lacking enough sperm. I believe it was her who had medical problems and she had a hysterectomy in 1956-57. With her alcohol and drug abuse, as well as deep-seated psychological problems, perhaps she felt inadequate.

I was psychoanalyzed three times. The psychologists keep saying my problems were a result of her. She had a vicious temper and would assault me many times over the years, like a woman possessed, often when she visibly intoxicated.

My father and I had a good relationship, he was a mellow thoughtful man whom I could confide anything.

After my father died no one could modify her behavior. She kept an article on a blackboard about a theory that some children are "Bad Seeds." This was pointed out to me constantly. She even blamed me for my father's death.

She also had a way of pitting sibling against sibling to achieve her aims.

In early 1977, when she accused me of child abuse, I got so angry I threatened to kill her if she ever stuck her nose in my business again. I was written out of her will and had no contact with any family until the early 90s.

It was established there was no abuse of my children. I have raised six and never raised a hand in anger to any of them. I became my adoptive father.

There was no religious or financial reasons for them adopting me. When they sent that Navajo boy packing, that did affect me. I knew I could also be sent away. I acted out in my older years. I felt my mother just did not want me around.

I have been married three times. It took me three to get it right.

I have been clean and sober for 18 years now. I served in the military, Marines and Navy, as a corpsman. I boxed as an amateur. I love fast cars and motorcycles. I was Pre-Med in college but ran out of money. I'm studying for my Masters in Labor management, converting credits from my B.S. degree in nursing.

I have worked at everything: carpenter, boilermaker, sheet metal journeyman, and have lived all over this country. I've visited 49 of 50 states, lived in 15 states, and visited 25 different countries, as military, or working in the trades, or just for fun. One can never get enough travel, knowledge or evolve and involve oneself politically.

All the lessons I learned from the Colonel, early life with him, was a great civics lesson. He was a born teacher. He taught at Yale and had his PhD in History and also taught ROTC. He taught high school after he retired.

I always knew my first mother's maiden name and was curious in 1995. I felt I wasn't disrespecting my adoptive parents. When I finally found her, my mother and I corresponded, wrote letters. She never told anyone about me so I never met her in person while she was alive, so as not to embarrass her.

About four years ago I reached out to my family in Keshena. Our reunion was grand. I come from such a proud and large family. I am still getting to know them and regret not doing it sooner.

Dr. Verna Fowler is a nun and she started the tribal college. I greatly respect my aunt and admire how she helped Native colleges everywhere. She's truly a beautiful strong woman.

Also, my Aunt Shirley was instrumental in regaining our Nationhood back. (The Menominee were terminated but it was restored.*)

I learned my own birth mother took in and adopted many children, as well as raising my two other half-brothers.

Unfortunately, due to many health issues and funds, I haven't been able to travel back to my rez often. Mostly it's my health. I almost died in 2011 which awakened me to my own mortality, realizing I may have waited too long. It took many attempts to unseal my records and finally be recognized by my tribe.

One of my aunts thought I might be after something. She was right: I wanted my **identity**. My only regret is not starting this process sooner. I am fortunate to have such a wonderful family.

My advice to adoptees is "be persistent." The laws are there but it's just getting the system to work for you and it is slow. Yes, you might not be as fortunate as I was. My Aunt Verna gathered up as many relatives as she could and gave me a wonderful homecoming, catered at the College of the Menominee. I was and still am humbled by her kindness and warmth. I am still awaiting my naming ceremony, mostly due to health reasons, but I have no regrets.

*The Menominee Indian Tribe's rich culture, history, and residency in the area now known as the State of Wisconsin, and parts of the States of Michigan and Illinois, dates back 10,000 years. At the start of the Treaty Era in the early 1800's, the Menominee occupied a land base estimated at 10 million acres; however, through a series of seven treaties entered into with the United States Government during the 1800's, the Tribe witnessed its land base erode to little more than 235,000 acres today. The Tribe experienced further setbacks in the 1950's with the U.S. Congress' passage of the Menominee Termination Act, which removed federal recognition over the Tribe and threatened to deprive Menominee people of their cultural identity. Fortunately, the Tribe won back its federal recognition in 1973 through a long and difficult grassroots movement that culminated with the passage of the Menominee Restoration Act, Public Law 93-197, on December 22, 1973. Read more here: http://www.menominee-nsn.gov/MITW/aboutUs.aspx

12

Reactive Attachment Disorder

Levi Eagle Feather Sr. (Rosebud Dakota)

…We're the evidence of the crime. They can't deal with the reality
of who we are because then they have to deal with the reality of
what they have done. If they deal with the reality of who we are,
they have to deal with the reality of who they aren't." —John
Trudell

2014

Reactive attachment disorder, what is it? Well… mine is a sub-conscious and
conscious reaction to the dark *art* that has been practiced against my people,
the Lakota, for the past two hundred years or more. The adoption experience
is the specific part of that *art* which hit me.

Overall, everything has worked out quite well for it. In harmony with a
multitude of other programs, projects, acts and policies our lives collectively
have been totally altered and we now have to live with the confusion of that
change. Needless to say, the affects of it all have been quite traumatic for a lot
of people.

Many times, emotionally, mentally and spiritually we become lost and tired
within the hubbub of it all. What else can we do but feel lost. As far as
adoption goes the whole basic, being separated from the herd to which you
belong thingy. Something which we all have experienced is pretty much the
icing on the cake of it all. It not only disrupted our natural experience of
familial roots and belonging which is the core of our birthright, but it screwed
with everyone else's experience as well. It removed all of us at the same time

51

from that first belonging which showed us and told us to whom and how it is that we belong. It's been very hard for me to square myself with that even to this day!

While the boarding school process and the relocation process do basically the same thing that the adoption process does as far as removing one from the herd. The adoption process intentionally is a more permanent barrier between you and your roots. When it is all said and done the adoption process literally redirects completely the whole flow of your life and for everyone involved. Redirected it from the original stream that was familiar and which flowed naturally to one that is not only unfamiliar, but to which your original flow must now undergo a lot of shaping and altering. People sense and understand this is happening while it is happening. We sense it and feel it emotionally and we develop memories of it.

The Mayo Clinic has attempted to define Reactive Attachment Disorder. Under diseases and conditions it says that: "Reactive attachment disorder is a rare but serious condition in which an infant or young child doesn't establish healthy attachments with parents or caregivers. Reactive attachment disorder may develop if the child's basic needs for comfort, affection and nurturing aren't met and loving, caring, stable attachments with others are not established. " [1]

I think there are probably a lot of people like myself. That sub-consciously and even consciously realized as it was happening that they weren't experiencing emotional stability. Where ever it was that they got left.

Knowing that belonging isn't there is easy to understand. It also is easy to understand why someone might be skeptical about wanting to have anything to do with who and what they are being redirected to. And it doesn't have anything to do with any wow factor or how cool something might be either.

Naturally, situations like this will affect ones behavior.
The Mayo Clinic says that some of the signs and symptoms of someone experiencing a RAD condition may include:
· Withdrawal, fear, sadness or irritability that is not readily explained
· Sad and listless appearance
· Not seeking comfort or showing no response when comfort is given
· Failure to smile
· Watching others closely but not engaging in social interaction
· Failing to ask for support or assistance
· Failure to reach out when picked up

· No interest in playing peekaboo or other interactive games
[http://www.mayoclinic.org]

I was four when this all began for me. Since that time not much in my life has
been acceptable to me. In a "feeling about it" kind of way. Something is
always missing or just not quite right!

The *Mayo Clinic* says that:

> To feel safe and develop trust, infants and young children need a
> stable, caring environment. Their basic emotional and physical
> needs must be consistently met. For instance, when a baby cries, his
> or her need for a meal or a diaper change must be met with a shared
> emotional exchange that may include eye contact, smiling and
> caressing.
> A child whose needs are ignored or met with a lack of emotional
> response from caregivers does not come to expect care or comfort
> or form a stable attachment to caregivers.

In my situation, whatever was to pass for loving and caring after I was
removed from my family came from something else entirely different. Both,
the attempts at affection and caring, were like gifts that were to be
conditionally given based on performance: **mine.** Their conditions were
based on and guided by the authoritarian principals of their church mostly and
were backed up by what little understanding they had of my history along
with what little they had of their own. This instead of any feeling that I
belonged, or was truly wanted. And I knew this and lived with it every second
of the eleven plus years I was there. People say that actions speak louder than
words. Most of the time this is true, in this situation, my situation, it was.

Naturally, I reacted! From the original crying to whatever I brought with me
that was me. Emotional, mental and or physical from that day forward was
not acceptable and had to be shaped and molded. It goes from the first haircut
to change the wild Indian, and on and on. There was a lot of punitive
discipline along the way and not just corporal punishment but the good old
fashioned psychological stuff.

As I grew older the corporal punishment thing in fact became sort of like part
of a sick game we had to play. It physically hurt sure, at first. But as I grew
older it seemed to hurt less and the fear I had of it morphed into something

Levi EagleFeather

weird for me. It turned into more of "a bring it and fuck you" kind of thing. I remember I was around ten or eleven. Somewhere in there. And I was tied to the telephone pole in our yard with my pants around my ankles. My siblings all lined up in one of the flower beds against the house watching the old man beat me with a bullwhip. I don't remember clearly what it was all about or why I was there. Whether I deserved it or not. What I do remember was looking back over my shoulder and telling him "Fuck you, someday you're going to get yours!" I'm sure that that beating hurt physically. It had to have. But what hurt me more hurt me inside. The embarrassment of being in front of my siblings probably the most.

So in my mind it was the psychological stuff which screwed with my wanting to belong the most. The blaming, shaming and shunning would work in time. Not like it was intended maybe, but it worked. It told me that I was unacceptable and that life for me and everything in it was unacceptable as well.

In fairness, I'm sure that I was a fistful right from the beginning. I was a kid! What did I know about life and living. That doesn't account for what happened to me or how it happened, or make it right! In digging through and unraveling the negative effects all of this has had on me mentally and learning to understand and grow out of the emotional instability it instilled in me is part of that being right. I couldn't dream to wish this kind of right on even the best of my enemies! So throughout my experience I never got to any place in it where I felt comfortable enough inside to trust emotionally. Let alone want to belong! My belonging had ceased for all intents and purposes when I was taken and until my children were born I was alone even in a crowd.

...As long as he's not bleeding he's fine
it's just that
there are so damn many ways to bleed
that at times he's not really sure.....
but what the fuck
he's still standing."
—John Trudell

The Western narrative sucks for a lot of people. Due mostly to the fact that the actual living of it comes nowhere near the glory of its telling. Not even close!

For those of us who are descended from the original caretakers of this land the facts of living this reality get pretty bad at times. The more we become aware and understand why they get even worse and sometimes legendarily so!

By default, those of us who got adopted out, we play a role in all of this. Our role may not be living on a reservation or even living within an American Indian community like a lot of our relatives do. But wherever we live, whatever we have done and whatever we have achieved has been accomplished outside the safety and comfort of our cultural heritage, our birthright. Needless to say, in this we have had no input or choice in the matter.

This we share in common with all other American Indians alive today. No matter the location or condition of our social status or living situation, we are living the consequence of that reality. We lack our cultural heritage, our birthright and choice in the matter. In my opinion we are not better off because of it!

I have never accepted my piece of this consequence as being a good thing for me. I didn't then and I still don't. For me it was not only something shitty which happened to me, but was for a long time beyond my ability to comprehend. In real time people were allowed to fuck me over and get away with it. Without any repercussions for them or reparation to me and it was considered to be something good I was expected to appreciate. It sucked then and when it happens now, it still does!

I spent eleven years of my early years resenting this and fighting back the best I could the best I knew how. When I was old enough and fed up with it enough, I ran. It happened and this is how I dealt with it!

Nothing much changed on the front end of that equation. The only change has been on the back end of it. How I choose to deal with it today. I don't run as much as I used to.

I realize not everyone had my kind of experience. This is a good thing. For those of you who did I would like to think it's gotten better for you by now. Not everyone reacted to their experience the same way that I did either. This also I think is a good thing! I'm glad you didn't. I'm not a person who could wish a bad experience on anyone. For those of you who had less than a stellar experience. I would like to think you're finding your way and are doing better now.

Regardless of what I think or how I felt about it. I was still raised to fit in with the Western narrative. To follow along and feed my energy and effort into the confusion and madness of it's dominance and influence. I've never been successful at it though. At least not willingly and definitely not with any grace or much finesse.

Yes, I went to different schools and got their paper. I even went into it's military, eventually learning some valuable skills, eventually picking up trade experience. I've had several different kinds of jobs and occupations because of this. I've even experienced family and belonging along the way in a variety of places, situations and settings. But overall I never really fit, never liked it or felt like it was me and I suffered because of this.

This is how being westernized, affected me. I think, it affects a majority of us American Indian folk in this way to varying degrees. I think it affects us, mentally, physically, emotionally and spiritually. Not always in the same ways on the same levels or to the same degree necessarily, but I think it affects us all. Not so that we can fit in, but so we can't resist it.

The roots of the suck we experience are not rooted in a race, an ethnicity, a religion, or a creed though. Nor is it rooted in the color of anyone's skin. In my opinion it is rooted in a skewed way of thinking. A skewed way of perceiving reality. We are taught to think this way and we learn it and adapt to it!

John Trudell, a Dakota relative of mine, broke our malfunction down this way:

I've come to the conclusion that there are two perceptions of reality. There's a religious perception of reality and there's a spiritual perception of reality. The religious perception of reality is about guilt sin and blame and that's the trap. That's the chain that holds every citizen.

Spiritual perception of reality…is about the responsibility. We're all responsible. We're not guilty we're responsible.

And it's trying to make our way through these two perceptions of reality: that seems to be the biggest problem we're confronted with as human beings on the planet right now! Cause the religious perception is about dominance, it's not about responsibility, it's about subserviance and male authoritarian figures. And the spiritual perception of reality is about life and respect and responsibility.

I think that the new world order is marching on. To me, in my own mind, it comes closer and closer to that… and is very real… that even though Germany and the Axis lost WWII. I don't think that the Nazi's did. I think that the Nazi's won WWII. And I think that their authoritarian methods of behavioral control, mind manipulation, converting human spirit into energy so that they can feed the need for their technologies. I think all of this stuff is just moving right on down the line again.

And I think that there really is no political solution or an economic solution that exists right now. And I think we need to get a clearer perception of reality and where we are in reality and take responsibility. And by using our intelligence intelligently. Create the solutions that we need to create. Because right now we're just more fuel.

Somewhere under the religious perception of reality a decision was made that the earth was the dominion of man and man therefore could plunder the earth. That man could take whatever they wanted from the earth. But somewhere in the progress of this mindset man has forgotten that we are part of the earth. And just the way that this system of technologic man has devised to take the resources of the earth and turn them into fuel and energy. They've taken our spirit and they're turning it through the process, through their process of civilization. Taking our spirit and turning it into energy to run their system. We need to remember that what happens to the earth happens to us. I'm not advocating anyone's politics or any of it. To me, I just think we've got to continue to do the best that we can do. And that's what I'm trying to do. [2]

Of course this suck didn't happen overnight. It started long ago. Feeding off of and compounding with violence, the fear and chaos which separation from knowing and understanding ones place in nature causes. This skewed way of thinking and perceiving reality was well developed and deeply entrenched in the western mind long before it reached our lands.

It didn't take long for it to take root in our land. It's grown and morphed becoming highly refined and firmly entrenched. It's civilized now! Just as deadly and just as abusive, but civilized. At least in the western mind it is.

Due to it, the destruction of our nature based cultures has become normal operating procedure. Insulating and normalizing our grief and suffering. Each successive generation the grief and suffering has mounted. Until our generation where loss of belonging and tribal identity have become common place.

I look at this part of our history as the incubating process for a collective reattachment disorder. Individually, and as a part of a collective, we suffer this disorder without a clear and coherent way of seeing it. Consequently, we have no way of being able to find our way clear of it.

In addition to this conditioned state of being. Where reactive attachment disorder exists and has morphed becoming the foundation of nearly all our societal interactions. We suffer too from a collective amnesia.

This amnesia of which I speak is rooted in our loss of knowledge and understanding of cultural heritage. A knowledge base and educational body as large and comprehensive as all of that which we have received throughout our westernization process. For folks like myself access to this knowledge is critical.

A friend of mine, Steve Smith, whose profession happens to be in the psychological field offered his thoughts on this subject.

Often when children are placed in abusive situations....situations where they are not cherished, they bond to the anger, to the violence or some other abnormal thing (to bond to). They used to tell us that this is a permanent condition....the RAD or being bonded to abnormal things....but we are learning all the time what the elders have known....the brain is plastic (jargon for flexible), people suffering stroke or brain injury learn to use other parts of the brain to perform basic functions. Those of us exposed to living in places where we were not cherished....or even wanted can and do learn to bond normally to the healthy aspects and of course to those we love. Culture and spirituality are amazing at facilitating this kind of healing as is proper nutrition and exercise." —**Steve Smith** via Facebook

In future writing on the American Indian Adoptees blog [3], I plan to offer more on this subject. It won't be for everyone, necessarily. That is up to the reader to decide. It won't be definitive because our cultures are not that way and never have been. For those who are interested I can say it will be interesting, because it always is. What is more important, however and what I would most like for people to understand. Especially, folk like myself, American Indian folk who mistrust and hurt and don't clearly understand why. Homogenous tribal and cultural lifestyles may be a thing of the past, but culturally based living is not.

You can be educated, undereducated, employed, unemployed, single, married to another Indian, transracially married, divorced, gay or straight, it doesn't matter. At the core of who we are, tribally, non-tribally, fullblood, halfbreed or fingernail is the reality of human beings being human. Our ancestral ways our ancestral cultural ways were the roadmaps the methods and the systems that taught us this. They educated, guided and showed us the why's, what's and wherefore's of how to live. So that we would belong, be connected and know and understand our place and our relationships to all that is. So brothers and sisters stay classy and don't sweat the small stuff!

Hau Mitakuye Oyasin!

Levi Eagle Feather Sr. (Rosebud Dakota) also contributed an essay THE HOLOCAUST SELF in the anthology CALLED HOME (Book 2) Lost Children of the Indian Adoption Projects. Levi is developing the IronEagleFeather Project for adoptees, based in South Dakota.
FOOTNOTES

[1] http://www.mayoclinic.org/diseases-conditions/reactive-attachment-disorder/basics/definition/con-20032126

[2] On YouTube: John Trudell " Religious vs. Spiritual" Perception of Reality, https://www.youtube.com/watch?v=Xbjzujo1Qx8

[3] American Indian Adoptees, www.splitfeathers.blogspot.com

13

The Ultimate Indignity

The Apology: Working Together to Strengthen Supports for Indian Children and Families: A National Perspective, Keynote Speech by Shay Bilchik at the NICWA Conference, Anchorage, Alaska, April 24, 2001

"Indian people knew from the beginning that this (adoption) policy was very wrong. ... they saw this 'as the ultimate indignity that has been inflicted upon them." ... David Fanshel's 1972 Child Welfare League of American (CWLA) study of these adoptions (which only covered five years in the children's lives), concluded that while the children were doing well and the adoptive parents were delighted in almost every case, only Indians themselves could ultimately decide whether this adoption program should continue. "It is my belief," Fanshel wrote, "that only the Indian people have the right to determine whether their children can be placed in white homes." Fanshel came to this realization, as he concluded his research, because of the vigorous Indian activism that was underway in the early 1970s.

"...In the words of the Indian Child Welfare Act (ICWA), Congress endorsed the unassailable fact that 'no resource is more vital to the continued existence and integrity of Indian tribes than their children.' As you have clearly articulated, children are the future. ...While adoption was not as wholesale as the infamous Indian schools, in terms of lost heritage, it was even more absolute. I deeply regret the fact that Child Welfare League of America's (CWLA) active participation gave credibility to such a hurtful, biased, and disgraceful course of action. I also acknowledge that a CWLA representative testified against ICWA at least once, although fortunately, that testimony did not achieve its end. ...As we look at these events with today's perspective, we see them as both catastrophic and unforgivable. Speaking for CWLA, I offer our sincere and deep regret for what preceded us," Bilchik said.

14

Congressional Testimony

STATEMENT OF WILLIAM BYLER, EXECUTIVE DIRECTOR,
ASSOCIATION OF AMERICAN INDIAN AFFAIRS

Senator ABOUREZK. I just have a couple of questions before Mr. Hirsch makes his comments. Can you describe how removal of Indian children in adoption situation is accomplished?

Mr. BYLER. I can cite certain kinds of experiences that we have had. One case, not too long ago in North Dakota, Indian children were living with their grandparents. Their grandmother was off doing the shopping. The grandfather was three miles away with a bucket getting water. While they were away, the social worker happened by at that time and found the children scrapping. When grandfather returned, the children were gone, and I don't know whether, in that case, he was ever successful in finding where the children were. I think they were placed for adoption somewhere.

When that happens, Indian parents or grandparents are told this is confidential information. We cannot disclose to you where your children are. This makes is seem impossible for them to even try to do
anything about it.

Senator ABOUREZK. You mean the children were taken from the home and the grandparents never were allowed to see them again or to try to fight the actions?

Mr. BYLER. That is correct, and as far as they knew, they never received any notice that there were proceedings against them or against the parents. This is very often the case, there is no notice given, or if notice is given, it is in such a form that the people who get the notice don't understand it; It does not constitute a real notice.

—HEARINGS BEFORE THE SUBCOMMITTEE ON INDIAN AFFAIRS

OF THE COMMITTEE ON INTERIOR AND INSULAR AFFAIRS
UNITED STATES SENATE NINETY-NINTH CONGRESS SECOND
SESSION ON PROBLEMS THAT AMERICAN INDIAN FAMILIES FACE
IN RAISING THEIR CHILDREN AND HOW THESE PROBLEMS ARE
AFFECTED BY FEDERAL ACTION OR INACTION, APRIL 8 AND 9,
1974

15

We Carry their Blood

Trace L. Hentz (Shawnee-Tsalgi-French Canadian-Euro)

> You can't live in two places at once."

This quote is from *BUCK*, a movie about Horse Whisperer "Buck" Brannaman, referring to the horrific childhood physical abuse he endured, and how he ultimately healed himself.

For me this quote translates: "Abuse memories will control me **if** I let them. I've lived and learned and truly know what brought me to this moment, right now, where I live, how I live." The past abuse I endured no longer rules me but it certainly defines me... as someone who was adopted by strangers, traumatized numb, colonized, who lived with a fake identity as a DeMeyer, who was sexually molested by my adoptive father and who was raised outside my culture, far away from any biological relatives.

I make no claim to be an expert on any culture or adoption or that in doing this book series, I lead a movement for adoptees. There is no "me" but "we" in this work. I take this work seriously, as a responsibility, a vision, a purpose. I have lived near reservations most of my life and have relatives in more than one tribal community. After I found my father and had proof, I became an Indian Country journalist in 1996.

My father Earl Bland did not live in ancestral territory or on the reservations in Oklahoma or the Carolinas. But he knew his family history. He was well assimilated into American culture, lived in Chicago and Pana, Illinois and died an alcoholic. We had our only reunion in November 1994 and he died in 1996. Yes, I attended his funeral. And I went back when my sister Teresa Kiser passed. Later I lost my brother Danny Bland.

Trace in braids, first grade

In any tribal nation, relatives would need to invite me to ceremonies, to teach and offer friendship. Other tribes offered this kinship to me. My Lakota relative named me Winyan Ohmanisa Waste La Ke.

Today's tribal nations do need to create some form of welcome, but sadly, the only tribe that called out to their adoptees was the White Earth Ojibwe and that was in 2007 and they did it again in 2014. There have been two pow wows to honor returning adoptees on the Rosebud Rez. (There may be more tribes doing this in 2017 but I have not heard about it.)

I was well aware that people claim some Cherokee ancestry then get ridiculed for claiming it. I needed to be absolutely sure what tribe or tribes so I asked my birthfather Earl during our first conversation in 1994. He and my aunts are very proud of our ancestors and explained after the Indian removals, people scattered all over the Midwest and south. Later I found out my paternal great-grand-mother Mary Francis Morris (Conner-Ward) was adopted by relatives (Watson-Ward) and her family had migrated from Tennessee, Kentucky and Ohio to Missouri then to Illinois. Understandably Indians were on the move during Andrew Jackson's Reign of Terror. You either hid out or ran.

Mary and her daughter Lona Dell Harlow (my grandmother) lived our culture, even in Illinois. They did not need an identification card to be Indian. My great aunt Bessie used a common code: Black Dutch ancestry, trying to hide the truth in plain sight. (If you were mixed, you chose to be anything but Indian. If you were Indian, you could not own land.)

Being a breed, a person with a mixed-ancestry, **all** my ancestors (Shawnee-Tsalgi-French Canadian-Euro) are with me so I carry their blood and their dreams.

After reunions with the Bland-Harlow-Morris relatives, I wrote my memoir *One Small Sacrifice*; in those five years it took me to write it, I changed so much I hardly recognized myself. That was a good thing. I needed to change. Understanding adoption required my time, study and research. I was more than willing to learn. And in learning, I changed.

Back in 2010, I wrote on my blog that I desperately wanted my adoption file. In September, I mentioned this to Jackie Willie on my book-tour in the Midwest. Jackie helped Ani (Ben Chosa) get his adoption file so she gave me the email address for the state offices in Madison, Wisconsin. I live in western Massachusetts so this was convenient. I'd write them an email!

Wisconsin, by law, allows adoptees in a closed adoption (like mine) to request and receive their **non-identifying** information. You simply fill out their form and request it (and pay them $75 an hour).

Let me clarify: your non-identifying information is a bit of history with no names. It will not help you locate your natural parent(s). In fact, it's so vague it's really no help at all! It might say you have a Native parent, and if it does, then you call the Bureau of Indian Affairs (BIA) for help as to which tribe or clan and how to contact them for enrollment. But the BIA won't release the name of your natural parents.

I decided to request my **identifying** information (aka the real deal: my sealed adoption file.) They emailed back I would need a court order. I needed to fill out their form, have it notarized and mail it back to them, so I did. Within a month, I spoke to a woman on the phone that proceeded to fill out the legal paperwork for a court order. She would present it to the judge and I didn't need to be there.

What was weird: she asked **why** I wanted my file. Why was this so hard? I have a million reasons but I didn't know what the judge wanted me to say.

What was a good reason? Finally I said I wanted my adoption file to help me understand my early history and where I was the first months of my life: that is what I *think* she wrote down. (I said more than once I was nervous).

Ok, I'm sure the *most used* reason for such a request is the need for family medical history and ancestry. (I could have told her I was nervous dating strangers who might be my real brothers. Had the judge ever considered incest? Well, I'm married now but at one time I had this concern.) There are many good reasons, yes. But what did the judge want to hear? I didn't know.

If the judge read my request form, he'd see I already knew the names of both my natural parents. (I already read my adoption file when I was 22 and found both my families.) Heck I knew their birthdays and when each of my parents had died.

So like all adoptees, I waited and prayed. The un-named judge would review my request. He or she could deny me. But the judge didn't.

Because I wrote my birth parents are deceased—that is why I believe the judge granted my request. It's only a guess. And if they considered my age, I'm no kid. Maybe that is why.

So this white envelope arrived the day after Thanksgiving (in 2010) and I was too emotional to open it. I was a wreck! I knew it would hit me like a ton of bricks. It sat on the table, unread.

My friend Anecia (Scraps is her chapter in this book) met me for breakfast that Sunday and since she is an adoptee too, she said she would read it to me. That was better, we thought. It was best to do this with a friend who was also adopted. So she read and I cried… and cried… and cried (in a crowded restaurant)!

The worst part was not my crying. There was family history on one page and a small post-it note that said the next part (and page) was not on microfilm. Pages missing? Yes. I did not receive the entire testimony my natural mother Helen gave to the social workers. I do not know what else was written down.

In 1956 my mother Helen was 22, and not able to keep me since there was no family support, and no money. It was clear she worried about the money she owed the Catholic maternity home for staying there. (Apparently they charged women rent, so my mother Helen chose St. Paul Minnesota so she could work at the unwed mother's home while she waited to have me.) **She even arranged to pay them in installments!** As if I wasn't enough payment? Obviously she believed the nuns and society who told her she was giving her baby a gift: a set of new parents (two total strangers).

I had a hard time accepting Helen wanted to keep me since she refused to meet me when I finally located her.

This evolving story took place over several years, with as many years to process it all emotionally. I was just 22 when I'd asked a judge in my hometown (Superior, Wisconsin) to read my adoption file. (I could only take notes, no copies.) Now I definitely know this 2010 paperwork is different than the file he let me read since his had more legal paperwork. After 30+ years, the effect on me is greater—and I have my father's version (what he told me) which was very different than Helen's. It's complicated but at least I know.

One of the reasons I didn't mention to the judge: I was in a foster home. Who were they? Now I have their name and address. That was huge for me. Now I know where I was the first days and months of my life.

I feel so fortunate I was able to get my adoption file. What **hurts** me is so many adoptees are still living in the dark about their identity, name, history and tribe. Some do not have the money required to hire search angels or pay court fees. If an adoptee born or adopted in Wisconsin wants to do this—if they need tribal information—it is on the form in Wisconsin and the only way an adoptee can do this is through a court order. And pay $75 per hour.

The Indian Child Welfare Act was signed into law in 1978, after the Indian Adoption Projects which placed children (even with more than one ancestry) with non-Indian parents to end tribal affiliations. If I was born **after** the Indian Child Welfare Act of 1978, then the social workers would have been required by federal law to notify my father and the tribes. I would <u>not</u> have been placed with strangers who knew nothing about me or my ancestry. My dad Earl told me he would have raised me, or one of his sisters would have, which is kinship adoption and tradition in Indian Country. Even if my mother Helen didn't want to raise me, my dad and his family would have.

In a perfect world, a family unit, tribe and extended family raise their own children, in a culturally appropriate, sensitive, familiar atmosphere, all across the planet.

It is in remembering that our power lies, and our future comes...this is the Indian way... —Anna Lee Waters (from The Man to Send Rain Clouds)

16

Know Who You Are

Meschelle Linjean

Meschelle with her adoptive parents

I believe that parental rejection is a shattering, near-mortal heartbreak and soul wound that can result in a deep-seated feeling of emptiness—a lack of grounding and stability, a missing sense of place and purpose. It can cause the "self" to float in a mist, like a dream almost remembered for a split second upon awakening, but too quickly dissolved. What was that ...who am I? The self that becomes tangible for however fleeting a moment is too often lacking a sense of worth and efficacy. It sounds terribly cliché, but if you don't know yourself, love yourself, and respect yourself, how can you relate to others in a healthy, meaningful way? I've learned that the primary heartbreak and soul wound from parental rejection can have longstanding repercussions well into adulthood. You're lost until you're found, or, until you find yourself...

I knew I was adopted for as long as I can remember. When I was a very young child, all that meant to me was that my parents were not my biological parents. The flipside of my parentage—that there was a different mom and dad out there somewhere who *were* my biological parents—did not really sink in until I was about eleven-years-old. My adoptive parents, or at least my adoptive dad, told be proud that I was Indian, but I never knew what that meant, nor was I provided with any resources from which to develop cultural pride. The first heartbreak and soul wound I consciously remember was not from my birth mother, although she was the first one who left me. The primary rejection I remember came from my adoptive mother, when I was about four-years-old.

I was a painfully shy child. I remember clutching on to my adoptive mother's legs and trying to hide behind her when strangers would talk to me. I remember that I kept my head down and wouldn't look at photographers. Someone would always try to lift my chin up before they snapped the photo for a family portrait. I was scared of strangers, particularly men with mustaches.

The first time I was touched inappropriately, I was a toddler. I remember several of these incidents and telling my parents about some of them, but I don't remember anyone getting into trouble for it. When I was a teenager, I learned that my Uncle M had been in prison multiple times for child molestation and rape. He got thrown in prison for fondling a toddler and a very young teenager during my college years as well. When I was grade school age, I can remember him holding me in front of him, his hands on my shoulders, rubbing the back of my head into his crotch, surreptitiously, while others were standing around, oblivious. Perhaps this is when I first learned to ignore situations that made me uncomfortable or when I felt I was being taken advantage of. This mustached Uncle M was a man who was assigned to babysit me on multiple occasions, sometimes overnight, while my adoptive mom was out partying or dating. When I was a teenager, he started asking me about my sex life and fondly recalled how I used to do "cheesecake" for him when I was a toddler. Then he told me that he had known my biological mother intimately and was probably my father. For a while, I called him Uncle "Dad."

Despite some dysfunction, I think I might have been a mostly happy, though shy, child during my earliest years when my adoptive parents were married. I was adopted by White parents as an infant and raised as an only child. When I was adopted, my adoptive dad was 40 and my adoptive mom was 25. My dad was a long-haul truck driver; my mom was a beautician and later took art classes. When I was about three-years-old, my mom began having an affair, running with a younger crowd of hippies or "heads" (this was the early 1970s in a small town in Oklahoma). I can remember waking up in a car, alone, outside of a bar in Chouteau, and crying outside a liquor store because my mom left me there and I couldn't go in. I was taken to parties with beer and pot, and sometimes I was given beer too, starting before kindergarten. This might have contributed to my own drinking problem later in life (learned behavior, alcoholic genes, self-medication, or the ultra combo? It took a lot of humiliation, shame, pain and more heartbreak before I was ready to address that problem). Around this time, I also saw my mom kissing another man. Although she told me not to say anything, I told my dad. He begged her to stay for my sake but they divorced. For a short time before I started kindergarten I lived with my mom in Tulsa, but mostly stayed with her mother, my Grandma H, because my mom was out running around. A few times, my mom left me with Grandma H and then Grandma H left me with another babysitter the same night. I remember them distracting me with toys so they could sneak out when I wasn't looking. I became very insecure and distrustful, scared of being left. I later learned this was referred to as having "abandonment issues" or an insecure attachment style. I would wake up in a strange babysitter's house, scared, and call my dad. If my dad was not on the road, he would always come to get me. He finally told my mom that she couldn't continue doing that to me and that he would take me with him. My dad was my savior. Until I started kindergarten I often went with my dad on the road, riding in his 18-wheeler through Kansas, Texas, and Oklahoma. When I started school, I had to stay with babysitters again and my dad started looking for more permanent care for me.

For about the next six years of my life I remember things but I'm uncertain of their order on a timeline. Basically, elementary school is a jumble, but here are some selections: Not long after I moved back in with my dad, when I was in kindergarten; my mom arrived at my dad's house in a van to pick up a bunch of her things. She was with a "head" named Bobby as I recall, and she was moving to Louisiana with him. I asked her if I'd ever see her again and she said, "I don't know." I was hysterical, inconsolable. Wouldn't she miss me? Why didn't she love me? I don't know how long she was gone—months or a year—but she eventually came back to Oklahoma. Although I was scheduled to visit her every other weekend, she often continued to leave me with Grandma H on her assigned weekends. Uncle M lived with Grandma H so sometimes he was the babysitter. Sometimes he gave me beer. Many times my mom would tell me she'd be back to get me at a certain time and then be gone all night. I would call her apartment and the phone would ring and ring all night long.

One time a man answered and hung up on me when I asked for my mom. Then, the phone was taken off the hook. Into my teenage years I had recurring nightmares about trying to call my mom over and over, but getting no answer or a busy signal. For a while, my mom lived with her boyfriend in the same small town as my dad and me. She lived maybe two miles from me—when I got a bicycle, I could ride it to her house—but I still only saw her every other weekend at best. Sometimes I'd run into her at the local grocery store and she'd buy me a pop or some candy. I was always excited to see her but she might as well have lived 30 miles away in Tulsa. After she moved back to Tulsa, many times she wouldn't pick me up on her assigned weekends. I'd sit on this 1970s velour patchwork ottoman, with my overnight bag at my feet, watching the clock. Hours would go by and I'd sit and wait. Sometimes she'd call hours late and claim she was sick or that her car broke down, or that she'd forgotten about me. Sometimes she didn't call. I didn't have the gumption to get up and do something else, or to hate my mom. I needed her. My dad was often gone on long-hauls and my stepmom, who raised me in his absence, was worse.

When I first moved back in with my dad, he had left me in the care of another of his former wives a few times while he was on the road. She was really mean and told me that my mom didn't love me. So, when my dad hired a Seneca woman who was born in 1917 to be a live-in housekeeper and babysitter for me, I was misguidedly relieved. Because I needed a mother, my dad gave me, at the age of about 5, the choice of which woman he should marry—the former wife noted previously, or the Seneca housekeeper-babysitter thirteen years his senior. To my regret, I told him he should marry the latter. My new stepmother was physically and verbally abusive to me. Without getting into too much detail, my elementary school years were filled with belt strappings, willow switchings, screaming, shaming, humiliation, and false accusations of lying and sexual behavior. My stepmother's grandchildren were close to my age and highly favored. Basically, I was the unwanted, flawed, scorned stepchild, while these other children, with whom I had to spend most weekends, were loved and cherished. Children with more gumption might have acted out but I didn't do that at this point. I was just scared and depressed and tried not to draw my stepmother's attention to me. I think I felt that I didn't have anyone I could count on to help me and I didn't know how to help myself.

The other sad thing is that my stepmother and her family were Indian and had the opportunity to provide me with Native cultural experiences, but that was not to be. Many years prior, my stepmother had been married to a close relative of Fred Lookout, the last traditional Osage chief. Her children had received naming ceremonies and her grandchildren danced in the Osage dances in traditional regalia. My adoptive dad asked her to get me a dance shawl, which she did, but I was never invited to attend any dances. Instead, she told me that because I had been adopted out of my tribe, I was considered White and not Indian. I have no idea why she told me this, because it was certainly not true, as I learned as an adult. So, I grew up with peripheral exposure to Native culture, seeing Osage cultural items and hearing stories about boarding school, but receiving no acceptance as an Indian myself. In elementary school, there were times when they would call all the Indian students into a room and distribute some free pencils and supplies. I always went to those gatherings because I knew I was Indian, but I didn't get the school supplies. There was always this sentiment of, "Oh, you're adopted. You don't have an Indian card." I remained an outsider.

My adoptive dad got ALS (Lou Gehrig's disease) when I was about nine-years-old. He could no longer protect me. His health deteriorated very quickly and he died six days before my thirteenth birthday. The parent who really loved me was gone. About a month later, I moved to Virginia with my adoptive mom and the man she was living with and later married. During the last year of my dad's life, I had moved in with my adoptive mom to escape my stepmother and I still harbor guilt over leaving my dad. I had recurring nightmares about that until just a few years ago. I would dream that my dad was still alive, but dying. He had been waiting on me to visit him all these years. In my dream, I would suddenly realize that he was still alive and I would be watching the house, hoping that my stepmother's car wouldn't be in the driveway so I could sneak in the house and see him without running into her. Also, during the last year my dad was alive, I developed some serious behavior problems. My grades went from A's and B's to D's. I lost my virginity and became promiscuous—looking for love and acceptance from adolescent and teenage boys, I guess. This just compounded my self-esteem issues, experiences of rejection, and fear of abandonment. About a year later, I also started to experiment with drugs and got my first boyfriend. I became crazily possessive, and later, physically abusive towards this boyfriend. I know the possessiveness was related to my fear of abandonment. I think the physical abuse was either me imitating my stepmother's behavior or due to me having so much anger inside that had not been addressed. Although I carried some of these traits throughout high school and into college, I've thankfully been able to overcome them.

During a summer visit to Oklahoma, my Uncle M told me how he had known my birth mother, T. Actually, he said that she was "built like a brick sh*t house," that she used to run with my youngest adoptive aunts, and that these aunts had dared her to get into bed with him. Such was the conversation he thought appropriate for his fifteen-year-old niece. Perhaps this conversation came about because I looked so much like my birth mom did at that age. It turned out that Uncle M had been sleeping with my birth mom when she was only 15 or 16 and he was in his late 20s. She had told him that he was my father. So, Uncle M dropped these pearls of wisdom on me, but refused to tell me anything more or help me meet my birth mom until I turned 21. I suppose I could have done more to find her on my own, but I was living in Virginia and, as a teenager, I just wasn't ready.

I was born at the Claremore Indian Hospital in 1970, but I did not learn this until 1991, when I received my unsealed documents. When my mom gave birth to me, she had just turned 17. She was married to my older half-sister's father, but he had been in VietNam when I was conceived (although he is listed as my father on my original birth certificate). My birth mom had sex with my adoptive uncle, but a DNA test conducted when I was about 30 proved that he is not my father (I still don't know who my birth father is but based on my looks, he must be White). As soon as my birth mom's husband returned from Vietnam, he was paralyzed in a really bad car accident and eventually died in a VA hospital; he was not the main factor in my adoption. The main problem was that my birth mom was extremely poor and did not have a secure home. Her mom, my biological grandma, was a really bad drunk and in no condition to help, even if she had wanted to (she stopped drinking when she was middle-aged). My great-grandma was also unwilling to help at that time. Both these grandmas had been raised in mission boarding schools. My direct ancestors physically survived the Trail of Tears but our traditional ways did not. My birth mom had grown up with a lot of domestic violence and sexual abuse when she wasn't in mission school, and had never had any good parenting role models. When I was born, my older sister was staying with her own paternal grandparents. Grandma H (Uncle M's mom) offered to watch after me for a while until my birth mom figured out what she was going to do. I believe I was four-days-old when my birth mom left me with Grandma H. A couple of days later, Uncle M's sister dropped by and saw me. She decided she wanted me and convinced her husband that they should adopt me. Then they convinced my birth mom that giving me up for adoption to them was the best option for me since she didn't even have a home at the time. The way I see it, it was the best option for *them*. The best option for *me* would have been if they had helped my birth mom find a safe place to live with me.

Although my birth mom gave me a name when I was born, my adoption papers show that the adoption of "Baby Girl" was decreed on March 24, 1971. My original name was legally changed and a falsified birth certificate showing my new name and my adoptive parents' names was issued April 5, 1971. My adoption papers list both my biological parents and me as White. I have some White blood, but I am Cherokee. I became enrolled in the Cherokee Nation when I was 21, after obtaining my original birth certificate showing my original name. When I was 20, I told my adoptive mom that I wanted my Certificate Degree of Indian Blood (CDIB). She agreed to help me by telling me who had handled my adoption. My adoptive had a sister and two brothers that had been adopted out as children but they reunited with their birth family as adults (Grandma H had 11 children), so I think that helped her understand my need for information. I contacted the law firm and told them I wanted all my records. They contacted my adoptive mom to get her permission. Even with my adoptive mom's permission, the law firm still sent my adoption papers and original birth certificate to my adoptive mom, and she sent them on to me.

The first time I contacted my birth mom, also at age 20, I wrote a very stilted letter, identifying myself and letting her know that I wanted her help in getting my CDIB. I had no idea she'd ever tried to keep me or find me—I thought she'd just given me away and didn't look back. I didn't get a response to my letter. About a few months later, I got really angry that I hadn't received a response, so I wrote another letter. This time I let all my personality and quirks fly—including my anger and sense of humor (at some point I asked her if I should address her by her first name, Mom, Mother, or "Mommie Dearest"). I also sent a photo of me and a self-addressed stamped envelope. With that letter, I got a tear-stained response within two weeks, saying, "You sound just like one of us!" and "Call me 'Mom' if you want. Your sisters do." Then I got a letter and photos from my youngest sister, a little rocker that, like me, loved Led Zeppelin, the Rolling Stones and Aerosmith. We didn't have the same father, but we could've been twins, we looked so much alike. I couldn't stop looking at that picture. To finally see someone who looked like me was overwhelming. It was like I had finally been born. I made my plans to meet my birth mom in person that summer, but I didn't tell her I was coming—I was scared she would try to get away and I wasn't about to give her a chance to escape.

I drove from California (where I was in college) to Oklahoma that summer, stopped at the Git N' Split near her small town and told someone who worked there who I was looking for. I feigned that I was traveling across country and that my birth mom was my aunt. The person said, "Yeah, you look like you could be kin to her," and gave me directions. So, I showed up on my birth mom's doorstep and my little niece, who answered the door, thought I was my youngest sister. My birth mom said, "Oh, I know who you are!" and gave me a big hug. She told me that she loved me and that she was so grateful that I found her. All three of my sisters came over to meet me and soon afterwards, I met my grandma, my great-grandma, uncles, and great-aunt. They were all very welcoming of me and my youngest uncle became my pen pal for the rest of my college years. I continued to visit my family every summer and I moved back to Oklahoma after I graduated so I could be near them.

After I met my birth mom, I learned that she had found out where I was staying during my adoptive parents' separation and came to Grandma H's house once, wanting to see me. Instead of letting her see me, they hid me and told her that my adoptive cousin, who was also there, was me. This cousin was a year younger than me and had bright red hair. Since I am part White and my older half-sister has blonde hair, my birth mom thought that it was possible that my hair had turned red although I was born with brown hair. My adoptive mom told my birth mom that she and my adoptive dad were going through a divorce and it would be "too much trouble" for my birth mom to visit me. When my birth mom found out that my adoptive dad had died, she again tried to make contact with me. However, my adoptive mom and new stepdad had moved me to Virginia a month after my adoptive dad died.

My birth mom found my stepmother though, and visited her on multiple occasions to try to learn about me. My stepmother was cruel to my birth mom—told her that I didn't want anything to do with her—and never told me that she was interested in knowing me. I knew nothing of my birth mom's attempts to contact me until I was in my 20s. When my birth mom told me these things, I confronted my adoptive mom and stepmother, and then they admitted they had kept her visits from me.

For years after I met my birth family, I vastly overcompensated for the Native heritage I had been denied. I became very active in Indian political issues and developed an acute disdain for everything I deemed Euro-ethnocentrism. Awareness and activism are good things, but I was out of balance, like a boomerang or a rock that had been released from a poorly aimed slingshot. I had always been different from my adoptive family. For example, I thought differently about animals and the natural world, and my sense of spirituality was out of sync with the southern Baptist and Bible Belt views. My tempo, approach, and views were never quite a fit with my adoptive family. After I met my birth family, I discovered we had many personality similarities (e.g., sense of humor, approach to things). I thought, "Okay, this is what I've been missing! This is who I am!" I endeavored to follow the Indian ways I learned (mostly from California Indians at college) as much as possible, although my birth family members were Christian Cherokees and not so traditional.

When I moved back to Oklahoma after I graduated, I started taking Cherokee language and heritage courses, and spent as much time as possible with my great-grandma—taking her for traditional medicine and listening to her stories. I changed my name, taking my grandma's maiden name as my last name for seven years. I also created the name I use now, "Linjean", from the name my birth mom gave me when I was born. I got a job with the Cherokee Nation food distribution office so I could visit all the rural communities when we delivered commodities. I married a full-blood whose mother had worked with my birth mom and whose grandmother used to run around with my biological grandma. We got married in a traditional Cherokee ceremony and I started spending my weekends fishing on the creeks, looking for wishi, gathering watercress, and hanging out in Indian bars. For a while it was like I finally had the family I was supposed to have had all along. I made a heartfelt (but misguided) effort to forget about everything that had made me who I was up until that point. Traditional Indian people say, "Know who you are." In dismissing 20 some years of my history, I fell out of balance on the other side.

I don't know how I thought I could reinvent myself as "Instant Indian" and "poof," be immediately accepted into a community I'd never grown up in. Well, I was still young. I really wanted to work in the Cherokee Indian Child Welfare department at that point, but my degree was in anthropology and I didn't have the right connections with the Cherokee Nation.

Another problem was that I wasn't a Christian, so I didn't fit in with the Baptist Cherokees. I wanted to be accepted at the stomp dances, but I didn't have any family there except my husband's (his uncle was a groundskeeper but my husband had never grown up with the stomp dance himself; most of his family was Christian). You're supposed to sit with your clan at the stomp dances, and my clan was different from my husband's, as it is supposed to be. I knew what clan I belonged to but I didn't know my people. Furthermore, I didn't know any of the customs at the stomp dances, I couldn't speak Cherokee, and I couldn't play stickball. I felt totally like an outsider. I was an outsider. I became disillusioned and depressed, so my husband and I left Oklahoma to move to Virginia where I had gone to high school. After we got here, we discovered that we didn't really have much in common except being Cherokee and our families' history together. So, we got divorced. I remained disillusioned and depressed, with new and additional identity issues. I couldn't be White and I couldn't be a traditional Native. I felt disconnected and my "self" continued to float in the mist, never quite tangible.

Now in my 40s, I'm still working on the insecurity and self-esteem issues, but I've come a long way. I am gaining a greater sense of strength in myself, an ability to accept myself for who I am—learning that I don't have to choose between one world or the other. It is okay to walk in two worlds and I even have special contributions to make because of how I was raised. Standing with one foot on two different mountains does not have to mean you're about to fall into the gap in between. It is a very significant place with its own purpose.

I still live in Virginia, but I've been working for a Native-owned federal contract company for six years. There isn't always a project to work on that deals with Native issues, but more often than not, I've been able to work in Native education research or curriculum development. I have reconciled with my adoptive mom for the most part (though I am still working through some resentment) and I maintain frequent contact with my birth mom and my sisters. The most difficult life lessons seem to be the ones that have given me a jolt in the right direction. One door closes and another one opens. For me, finding myself has been a journey. I reconnected biologically, racially and culturally. That was good and vital for me. It filled in some holes in my core, but the fillings were sloppy and jagged for a long time—not quite filling some holes and overfilling others.

Years later, I'm finally learning how to smooth out the fillings, find my balance and, with a good heart and a good mind, live as a person of integrity.

My very recent experiences with talking to other Native adoptees who share experiences similar to mine have been such a blessing. For my final Sociology M.A. project, I wanted to conduct research about the experiences and perceptions of Natives who were transracially adopted. I was excited to find Trace (DeMeyer) Hentz's blog and contacted her for resources. She put me in touch with the Native American Indian Adoptees Facebook and American Indian Adoptees Google groups. From those places I found adoptees willing to participate in a survey and interviews about their adoption. In talking with these people about how our adoptions have shaped our lives, I found a type of understanding that had previously eluded me and I am grateful for it.

Thank you, Trace and other fellow Native adoptees.

17

Unanswered Questions

Nolan Littlewolf Walling (Yakama)

I grew up in Vancouver, Washington, the same state as my biological family. I found out at age four I was adopted. They got me from an orphanage when I was three. My adoptive mother told me I was given up at birth to an orphanage in Seattle, Washington. I was born on October 27, 1961.

I didn't understand what 'adopted' meant, not at first. I did when my adoptive parents divorced.

I just knew I didn't belong there. I was rebellious, so I went with my mother to her psychiatrist. She thought I was a problem child. I didn't really act out until I was older, but I would just shut down. I grew up with their birth children, one boy and three girls.

I never did ask questions about my adoption and never really thought about it much after my adoptive mother told me my birthmother was dead. Now I find out that may not have been true at all. I didn't ask about my natural parents much because my adoptive parents were not easy to talk to about anything, let alone my birthparents. My adoptive mother would get upset over some things but my adoptive father, no.

When I was a kid, my adoptive mother was physically abusive; she drank and took a lot of medication until she finally became a born-again Catholic. I was nine when they divorced, and I lived with her. The abuse was physical and emotional. I was beat with anything that was handy by my mother. She would leave marks. She was either married or in five relationships by the time I was fifteen. Then I went to live with my dad and his new family. I was not welcomed with open arms by my adoptive father or my new stepmother or her children. All of my adoptive siblings were grown by this time.

My adoptive parents were about thirty when they adopted me. I was told he was an accountant then he became a motel salesperson. My adoptive mother was from a wealthy Vancouver family. I'm sure she was educated, but she became a stay-at-home mother who dabbled in antiques. Her family disowned her for marrying him.

I wasn't treated differently in my adoptive family because I am Indian. Not because I was Indian and not by the siblings when I was younger. I was just a kid. I think mostly it was just because I was adopted, but I am not really sure. However, now I really don't have any contact with my adoptive siblings.

I had good friends as far as friends go and I was just trying to be a kid. I never really talked about me being adopted. I never really told any of my friends I was Indian until I was older.

I didn't meet other adoptees, none that I am aware of. When I married my wife, she began to question me and ask things about my adoption.

I did try to find my natural parents but just briefly; it happened when I was eighteen and I was working with Job Corps on the Yakima rez but I got freaked out and did not go back. I didn't go back to my rez until after my daughter was born but I didn't do a detailed search.

I had papers to read about my adoption and my actual birth certificate and my adoption picture when I was three.

I didn't use any adoption registries since I had those papers. I don't know if it was a private adoption or a religious organization or the state who handled it. I don't know the exact details.

I have not had a reunion yet but I am enrolled and so is my daughter.

The papers and information I was shown were given to me by my adoptive father when I was eighteen. I do not know exactly when I was enrolled but I am in the process of writing the tribe for my enrollment date. I was told at eighteen that my adoptive father had just enrolled me.

My adoptive parents didn't take me to a reservation, unless you consider the Pendleton Roundup which is on a rez. I did my first powwow when I was in Job Corps at twenty or so.

What I am dealing with now is who am I and are there people who are my family and my children's family? I haven't met other Yakamas. I have not been invited to my rez for a powwow or ceremony. My father's name is Littlewolf and my mother's name is Woods.

I did get advice from Trace DeMeyer on how to proceed and how to approach them. She is the only one who helped me. My wife found her blog and she sent us her book.

A few year ago I had wrote the tribal enrollment office through the mail but it was only for an address change. I did ask them how I could get a hold of a Johnny Littlewolf and they did reply that I could send letters to the Tribal office and they would forward them to him. This man is supposed to be my sibling.

Some years ago I had a lawyer contact the tribe about an issue with my son and the state of Oregon removing him from his mother's custody. I was never contacted or told why he was removed until many years later; he lived with his maternal aunt and uncle in San Jose. My memory is kind of hazy but the tribal council either never responded or were not very helpful in the matter. I am now beginning to reconnect with my son and build a relationship.

I did contact the BIA. That is where I first heard about the government and their program to adopt Indian children for profit.

Years ago on my rez, once I was picked up by someone who thought I was someone else. I was told I looked identical to this person so this is possibly one of my siblings. But I was twenty or so and the whole thing just freaked me out. Last time we were there, my daughter was one and she is thirteen now.

As far as ceremonies I missed growing up, I know about them but I don't know any details about them. I have never really been invited.

As far as a name, the interesting thing is that I do carry my parent's name, my father's name which is Littlewolf. I have not had a naming ceremony. I do receive a per-cap from my tribe but I am not sure I would ever move there.

I did not do well in school. I missed a lot, was behind, and had learning disabilities that labeled me as slow. My wife believes I am dyslexic and recently I was informed that my son is dyslexic, go figure. Art was my favorite subject and reading was my worst. As far as discipline, I was sent to the principal's office.

I was affected by my adoption: emotional hurt, distrust of others, unable to feel at times, anger and sadness, all of them. Of course I did self-medicate with alcohol and drugs. Yes I have committed a crime and been imprisoned.

As far as successful relationships, like marriage and girlfriends, yes and no. Our marriage has not been easy! I do have trouble with trust in relationships.

I have two children and they have helped me emotionally. Yes! I wish for them to know and embrace their ancestry, definitely! They too need to know who they are and where they come from and to embrace it.

As far as my tribal id card, I do not have one now but I did have one.

Nolan and his daughter Hailey are both enrolled with the Yakima tribe and receive per capita. His son however is not and even though paternity was established, Nolan has been unable to get a certified birth record to give to the tribe. Nolan believes the only reason he met any of his family (an aunt) was totally by chance. He was hitch-hiking after an Indian basketball game and someone picked him up said he looked exactly like Johnny Littlewolf. It turned out Johnny is his sibling and the women was his aunt. There was a meeting set up for Johnny and Nolan to meet but Nolan was too nervous and never made it to the meeting. He went back to his rez about 14 years ago on other tribal business and was told he could inquire about Johnny Littlewolf by writing a letter and they would be sure to forward any mail. Nolan's wife said it's because of fear and frustration he has not made contact, after what happened and no help to get his son enrolled. His wife Julaine decided to find his son Jovan and through social networking, they met and are now building a relationship. Jovan is a wonderful young man and totally eager to embrace his heritage and very supportive when it comes to finding his dad's family. Nolan has now met his Yakima family, according to an email from his wife is 2014.

18

My Secret Life

Gail Huggard (Ojibwe)

Betty, Ronald, Donald (the twins) and Gail (100% siblings blood–related and reunited)

I always knew I was different from everyone in my adoptive family. My personality was the complete opposite of my happy-go-lucky, outgoing, and gregarious family members. I was extremely quiet and painfully shy. I stood out from everyone else due to my red hair and freckles. I was considered a loner because I took long walks by myself and I enjoyed the solitude of my bedroom.

I had my first adoption conversation when I was seven. While I was eating my breakfast I asked Mother where babies came from. I wanted to know if I was in her tummy. She told me that I was not in her tummy. I was adopted. 'Why was I was adopted?' She explained my parents were unable to take care of me.

Throughout my childhood and into my teenage years if I got into trouble my mother often said, 'Watch it, or you'll be sent back to the Indians.' I remember being told on a few occasions that nobody wanted to adopt me because I was a 'half-breed.'

When I reached my teenage years I needed to know more. I asked questions about my birth parents and my heritage. Again, I was told that my parents could not take care of me. Simple answers no longer satisfied.

Eventually Mother provided me with bits and pieces of information about my biological parents. 'Your father was tall with red hair. He was an artist.' I decided this was where my artistic abilities came from. My birth mother was described as short. She said my father was part Indian, maybe Cherokee. She wasn't sure. She went on to say that once when she and Daddy were at the Seafair races in Seattle, they spotted my birth parents. I was shocked. I questioned her further, but it was clear that this was the end of the story.

After Mother's brief description, I began drawing mental images of what my birth parents looked like. My father wore a suit and tie. He was tall and handsome with red hair. My beautiful mother was at his side. I imagined that she also wore a suit. My parents were movie stars. I came to the conclusion that they were so busy making movies they couldn't take care of me.

When I was fifteen, Mother took me to The Seattle Children's Home Society. I wasn't given any warning or explanation. When we arrived she announced, 'This is where you lived as a baby and this is where you'll be sent back to if you act up again.'

I was not the only one adopted in our family. My younger sister was, too. Our childhood included many advantages. We lived in a lovely home one block from Puget Sound. We took yearly vacations and went camping on the weekends in the spring and summer. We often dined at fancy restaurants. I had private art, flute, and piano lessons. Mother shopped for our clothes at the best department stores. What she didn't purchase, she and Grandma made. Grandma was a professional seamstress.

Our public and private worlds were very different. From the outside it looked like I was living an idyllic life. This was not the case. My mother constantly complained about how I looked and acted. I was always being compared to my sister. 'Why can't you have curly hair like your sister? Why can't you be smart like your sister? Why do you have red hair?' I didn't have the answers she was looking for. If I tried to explain myself, the threat to send me back to the Indians surfaced. This threat always silenced me.

One of my memories as a child is driving by Indian reservations. My mother would point at people, 'Look at those dirty, rotten Indians.' My sister and I never saw a 'dirty, rotten Indian.' We just saw ordinary people with darker skin.

My eighteenth year was very eventful. I graduated high school, became pregnant, and married my boyfriend. My mother was against the marriage and wanted me to abort the baby. I was horrified! I was secretly excited to bring a baby into the world—a person that would look like me—someone that would love me just the way I was. My baby was born with curly red hair and 'grew' freckles at the age of one. He was so beautiful and unique and he had my blood flowing through his veins. We were connected.

Two years later, I birthed another son. He was also a darling red-haired, freckled-faced boy.

Two years passed, and we found ourselves welcoming another son. Our third son was a dark-skinned, black-haired baby boy. When we went to visit him in the hospital nursery I noticed that people were gathered together and they were cooing over the 'little Indian baby.' 'What Indian baby?' I asked. 'That one over there.' They were all looking at my baby!

Three years passed and my husband and I adopted a baby girl from Korea. That was one of the most exciting and happiest days of my life. I remember her being carried off the airplane and placed in my arms. My daughter's birth completed our family.

Even though I was a busy mother, the need to gather more information about my biological family never went away. The longing started shortly after our third son Steven was born. Steven was shorter than his brothers and he didn't resemble any of us.

I decided it was time to write a letter to the *Longview Daily News*, the local newspaper of Longview, Washington. (I was born in Longview) I requested a list of women that birthed a baby on my birth date. They sent the names of several couples and their addresses. I wrote to each of them. All the letters were returned with an apology. No one had any memory of my mother in the maternity ward. Only one letter came back unopened, the letter to Mr. and Mrs. Woodrow Tully.

I decided it was time to ask Mother to tell me my real name. This time there was no hesitation. 'Delma Pearl Tully.' I thought, what an odd name. Yet, this was my name. She repeated the story about the Seafair Races, the Cherokee heritage, and the red-haired father. She also told me that a female attorney helped with the adoption and that this was a rarity in 1949. I was placed in the Seattle Children's Home Society, and was classified as hard-to-adopt because I was a 'half-breed.'

I made an immediate trip to Longview. As I walked down the street I stared at people's faces. When I went into stores I studied people for clues. I looked at people as they drove by. I was attempting to find someone, anyone that looked like me. I made several trips to Longview, searching for my parents. This sort of gut-response searching did not produce any results. Eventually, I phoned The Children's Home Society in Seattle and made an appointment to ask my questions in person. My best friend, Sue, and I drove to the Society together. I was able to ask my questions.

I also knew that they would not be able to give me any identifying information. A few weeks later I received a phone call from the Children's Home. I was told they had some information. Sue and I drove back to Seattle.

The following is the information that I was given. My parents were married. My father was dark-skinned and Irish. He was 5'6,' and had curly black hair. My mother was short, just like me, 5'2', but dark skinned, with long black hair. She was part Chippewa (Ojibwe).

The social worker also told me that my mother had physical disabilities. I was informed that twins ran on her side of the family. My parents birthed several other children but relinquished them due to psychosocial and economic reasons. I was thrilled! I was part Indian and I had brothers and sisters somewhere! Now I knew whom my son Stephen resembled, my biological mother Lenore.

Since I knew my last name I decided to change my searching strategy. I wrote to everybody in southwest Washington and even parts of Oregon with the last name of Tully. I received no responses. A few months passed. Then one afternoon while I was fixing lunch, the phone rang. A man asked me why I was looking for Woodrow Tully. He told me he was my uncle—my father's youngest brother. And, he said he was sitting next to my sisters! I had sisters! I eventually spoke with both of them. We made plans to meet that evening at my sister Sharon's house in Kelso. My whole family came with me. When I arrived I saw a boy on the porch. He looked like my son Steven. His name was Bob.

I met my beautiful sisters! We are all one year apart. I am the youngest. My sister Betty was very pregnant and had silky, long black hair. Sharon had shorter hair and dark skin. I met my Uncle Paul, and my sister's husbands and children. I will never forget that day as long as I live.

That night I discovered my biological parents gave up twins. 'What twins?' I asked. 'Oh, we have twin brothers.' I learned that the boys were one year older than Sharon. My sisters had visited with them on and off throughout their childhood. I wanted to know where the twins were. 'They live here in town, but we don't see them anymore.' This was told to me matter-of-fact. I was beside myself.

During our next visit, a reporter and photographer from the newspaper was there to take our picture and to write an article! We were front-page news. When the paper hit the stand, one of the twin's wives called my sister Sharon to tell her that looking at me was like looking at Don, my brother, and that we had to get together as soon as possible. That night Sharon, Betty, and I arrived at Donald's house. He was waiting for us with his twin, Ronald. It was like a dream to be reunited with my beautiful and handsome siblings. We could not stop staring and touching each other to see if this was really happening. Donald had red hair, too!

Regarding the 'Indian' part of my life, my biological mother was born and raised on a reservation in Montana. She did not speak English, only Chippewa/Ojibwe. She lived in a teepee. One day (and this is where it gets a blurry), my father was on his way to Washington State when he happened upon my mother on the reservation. Somehow, he put her on a train with him and took her home to my biological grandma. Grandma apparently had to 'pick things out of mama's hair and give her a bath.' Also added to this story was the fact that she was wrapped in an Indian blanket. Lenore, (my mother) was not registered in the tribe, as her mother would not let her due to her congenital hip deformity and blindness in one eye. Apparently, my maternal grandmother was ashamed of her. Lenore was sent to a white Catholic school but this only lasted through the second grade. According to my sisters, she was illiterate and had a strange accent that they thought sounded Cajun.

Our story is complicated. My twin brothers were adopted out, my sister Sharon was given to our father's mother, and my sister Betty was in foster care as a teenager. All of us were raised by someone other than our biological parents.

Sadly, Donald passed away last summer. But somehow, his death deepened our relationship with our brother Ronald. The four of us are in constant contact.

There is also another brother somewhere 'out there,' a half-brother, whom we have been trying to find for many years. He was given to a Catholic orphanage in Montana.

Regrettably, the girls were subjected to things they should not have seen and heard or experienced at home. The boys, like me, were raised in a fairly affluent household and had a wonderful childhood. All five of us wish that we could have been raised together in one household. We still talk about what it would have been like to grow up together. My sisters wish that my mom and dad had adopted them, too.

Sadly, Mother disowned me after I found my biological family. Up until seven years ago, she refused to speak to me. Right when we finally became close, she suddenly passed away. So many years wasted...

When Donald was alive, the five of us would fantasize about what it would have been like if we had all been raised together under the same roof. We never actually discussed who our parents would have been in our fantasy — our birth parents, my adoptive parents or the twins' adoptive parents. We all just decided that we would have one big bedroom with lots of bunk beds and the boys would teach us girls how to climb out the window at night, teach us how to smoke a cigarette and introduce us to our first drink.

Now in our 60s, Ron, Betty and I are actually considering the idea of buying a home together where we could live out our fantasy as a real family, making our dreams come true.

2011: After working as a medical office manager/medical transcriptionist for over 30 years, I retired earlier than planned on the southwest coast of Washington state. I have four grown children and seven grandchildren, three of whom live next door. When I am not traveling, I enjoy collecting Depression glass sherbet dishes and reading nonfiction.

19

Loranda Costello: Yakama Adoptee

Loranda Kay Costello (Facebook
Photo)

[From the CONNECTICUT LAW TRIBUNE, August 20, 2007]
Loranda Kay Costello is $180,000 richer and met her birth father for the first
time, all thanks to her attorney's successful efforts to open Costello's adoption
records.

Born a member of the Yakama Indian Nation in Washington state, Costello
was whisked away to Connecticut at the age of 6. Her birthfather was imprisoned and her birthmother had a drinking problem. Here she was adopted by a
Stratford couple, and her name changed from Laronda Peter to Loranda Neu-
pert. (Later when she married, she took her husband's last name.)

Growing up, she and her brother, Joseph, had vague knowledge that they were Native American, but didn't know the name of the tribe to which they belonged and had no contact with their birth parents, according to Costello's attorney, Allison M. Near, of Hurwitz, Sagarin, Slossberg & Knuff in Milford.

In college, Costello grew more interested in her heritage and learned that members of certain tribes may be eligible for scholarships, Near said. As it turns out, members of the Yakama Indian Nation receive financial payments from the tribe generated partly from the tribe's timber lease. "That's something that would have been paid out [to Costello] in various installments throughout her life, had [the tribe] known her whereabouts," Near said.

Over the years, the installments added up. Online, Costello eventually learned the U.S. Office of the Special Trustee for American Indians was holding benefits under her birth name that had amassed to roughly $180,000, according to Near. The problem was she needed proof that she was, indeed, that little girl who was separated from her biological parents some four decades earlier.

The agency that handled Costello's adoption attested, in a letter, that her parents were, indeed, Yakama tribe members, and gave her some other non-identifying information about them. To satisfy the requirement for proving her name change, however, she needed to obtain a copy of her adoption decree. In April, the Stratford Probate Court directed the adoption agency to release a copy of the decree with non-identifying information about her birth parents pursuant to C.G.S. § 45a-748. That still wasn't good enough to satisfy the Yakama tribe. It required a copy of the decree certified by the probate court itself.

Costello's husband is a longtime Hurwitz Sagarin client. Represented by Near, she petitioned Probate Judge F. Paul Kurmay to allow her access to her court adoption record under the Indian Child Welfare Act (ICWA).

"Under Connecticut law, you really can't get anything without parental consent," said Near. But in the interests of promoting the stability and culture of Indian tribes and families, the ICWA provides Native Americans who were adopted access to information about their biological parents 'as may be necessary to protect any rights flowing from the individual's tribal relationship.'

Kurmay found Costello had a 'powerful due process and equal protection of the law argument' and held that the federal law took precedence in the matter before him.

Last month (July 2007), with a certified copy of her adoption decree in hand, Costello traveled to Washington and collected what is owed to her. Though her birth mother has since passed away, she and her brother reunited with their biological father who had long been in search of their location.

"She's got siblings she didn't even know about," said Near. "It's really been an incredible experience for her."

[Source: Scott Brede, CONNECTICUT LAW TRIBUNE, August 20, 2007]

Laronda now lives in Florida and sings on a drum. She is friends with Trace on Facebook.

20

PAPAL BULL

Papal Bull declares the legitimacy of Christian domination over (Indian) pagans, sanctifying enslavement and expropriation of property:

> Romanus Pontifex, January 8, 1455 — ...We bestow suitable favors and special graces on those Catholic kings and princes, ...athletes and intrepid champions of the Christian faith... to invade, search out, capture, vanquish, and subdue all Saracens and pagans whatsoever, and other enemies of Christ wheresoever placed, and... to reduce their persons to perpetual slavery, and to apply and appropriate... possessions, and goods, and to convert them to... their use and profit.*

> (*European Treaties bearing on the history of the United States and its Dependencies to 1648*, Editor Francis Gardiner Davenport, pages 20-26)

Note: Papal Bulls are the fabric of United States and International law. Papal authority is the basis for United States power over Indigenous peoples, not generally understood in America. The Doctrine of Discovery is still being used as an active legal principle. Empirical attitudes are not dead. —Editor Trace Hentz

> "I would like to quote a very prejudicial doctrine that was handed down by the Supreme Court in 1823. It said that the Indian Nations do not have title to their lands because they weren't Christians. That the first Christian Nations to discover an area of heathen lands has the absolute title. This doctrine should be withdrawn and renounced to establish a new basis for relationship between indigenous peoples and other peoples of the world."

> —Floyd Westerman (Sisseton Wahpeton Oyate, Lakota)

21

Job, age 9

From a sales document of a child:

Know all men by these presents that I Zachariah Thomlinson, of Stratford in the County of Fairfield and Colony of Connecticut in New England, for the Consideration of eight barrels of good merchantable pork already in hand Recd of Joseph Woodruff of Milford which is to my full satisfaction and contentment, Do relinquish, release and pass over to him the said Joseph Woodruff and to his heirs and assigns forever, all my right, title and interest in, and unto the Servitude of one Certain malatto boy named Job, aged nine years, born of an Indian woman named Nab, to have and to hold said Malatto by free and clear from all claims and Demands made by me or my heirs and further I the said Zachariah Thomlinson Do for my Self and my heirs Covenant with the said Joseph Woodruff and his heirs that he and they Shall Quietly and peaceably possess and enjoy Said Malatto boy Job without the Least Interruption or molestation from or by me or under me or my heirs forever. In witness whereof I have hereunto set my hand and seal, this 21st Day of May 1765.

The collection of the Fairfield Historical Society, Connecticut Colonial Records, Public Records of the Colony of Connecticut, Volume 1 [Source: http://www.cslib.org/ earlygr.htm]

22

The Adoption Era, defined: Native Americans expose a forgotten period in their history

Stephanie Woodard (Story and Photo)

"I'm an angry Indian," Roger St. John, Sisseton Wahpeton Oyate, told the First Nations Repatriation Institute's second annual adult-adoptees summit. The elite panel included child-welfare specialists, judges, lawyers, community activists and scholars. The most important experts, according to the organization's founder/director, Sandra White Hawk, Rosebud Sioux Tribe, were adult adoptees—such as St. John—who related their experiences at the three-day meeting at the University of Minnesota, Twin Cities in St. Paul.

"I'm more than glad to tell you I'm pissed off," continued St. John, a 49-year-old truck driver with dark hair pulled back in a ponytail. "I was the youngest of 16 children, grabbed at age 4, along with three older brothers—no paperwork, nothing. The other kids in the family escaped because they took off."

Soon, St. John and his siblings ended up in New York City at Thanksgiving time. The year was 1966. "We were on the front page of the newspaper, along with lots of good talk about the holiday and adoption. We were brought up without our culture, which took a terrible toll on our lives. I grew up angry and miserable."

St. John's experience was replicated all over Indian country in the mid-to-late 20th century. The boarding-school era that had begun in the late 1800s was winding down, and the abusive residential schools set up to isolate and assimilate Native children were being closed down or turned over to the tribes, a process that was largely completed by the 1970s. Meanwhile, another means of separating Native children from their communities was gathering steam.

The Indian Adoption Project was a federal program that acquired Indian children from 1958 to 1967 with the help of the prestigious Child Welfare League of America; a successor organization, the Adoption Resource Exchange of North America, functioned from 1966 until the early 1970s. Churches were also involved. In the Southwest, the Church of Jesus Christ of Latter Day Saints took thousands of Navajo children to live in Mormon homes and work on Mormon farms, and the Catholic Church and other Christian denominations swept many more Indian youngsters into residential institutions they ran nationwide, from which some children were then fostered or adopted out. As many as one third of Indian children were separated from their families between 1941 and 1967, according to a 1976 report by the Association on American Indian Affairs.

"People have heard of the boarding-school era and know it was bad, but they don't know our adoption era even exists," said White Hawk, who was taken from her family on the Rosebud reservation as a toddler in the mid-1950s. "A few small studies of adult adoptees have been done, and we're just learning how to talk about what happened. We need think tanks and conferences and scientific research to explore what occurred and how it affected us."

Then, White Hawk said, that information will inform current Indian child-welfare cases. "When experts take the stand to testify in a child-welfare hearing [about placement of a child or termination of parental rights, for example], they need academic backup to explain the relationship between, for example, suicide and being disconnected from your culture," she explained. "The courts want Ph.D.-level research to back up what we tell them."

A paper by Carol Locust, Cherokee, describes Native adoptees suffering from what she calls Split Feather Syndrome—the damage caused by loss of tribal identity and growing up 'different' in an inhospitable world. "Lost bird" is another phrase researchers have used to refer to the group, recalling one of the earliest Indian adoptees. A Lakota infant who survived the 1890 massacre at Wounded Knee sheltered by the frozen corpse of her mother was claimed as a war trophy by a general who named her Lost Bird, according to her biographer, Renée Sansome Flood in *Lost Bird of Wounded Knee*.

Thanks to newspaper coverage of the massacre and its aftermath, Lost Bird became her generation's celebrity adoptee, but fame did not save her from a fate that was a harbinger for too many Native children. She endured intolerance and isolation, and when she rebelled as a teenager, was shipped back to her birth family, where she no longer fit in. After a stint in Buffalo Bill's Wild West Show and the loss of three children—two died and she gave away the third, according to Flood—Lost Bird was felled by influenza in 1920, at the age of 30. "Throughout her life of prejudice, exploitation, poverty, misunderstanding and disease, she never gave up hope that one day she would find out where she really belonged," Flood wrote.

At the summits and other events White Hawk has organized or spoken at since 2003, modern-day adoptees have recounted their dramatic life journeys, sometimes for the first time. "The stories vary from the most abusive to the most beautiful, but that's not the point," she said. "Even in loving families, Native adoptees live without a sense of who they are. Love doesn't provide identity."

"I never felt sorry for myself," said St. John, "but if I ever got hurt, it wounded me to my soul, because I felt no one was there for me." In recent years, he has found his birth mother and connected emotionally with his adoptive parents. "They were so young, in their 20s, when a priest convinced them to adopt four Sioux boys from South Dakota. It was too much—for all of us."

During the adoption era almost any family problem—from minor to serious—could precipitate the loss of an Indian child. Two Native people interviewed prior to the summit said they were separated from their families after hospital stays as young children, one for a rash, the other for tuberculosis. A third was seized at his baby-sitter's home; when his mother tried to rescue him, she was jailed, he said. A fourth recalled that he was taken after his father died, though his mother did not want to give him up. A fifth described being snatched, along with siblings, because his grandfather was a medicine man who wouldn't give up his traditional ways. As in St. John's case, no home studies or comparable investigations appear to have been done to support the removals. "Indians had no way to stop white people from taking their kids," said yet another interviewee. "We had no rights."

Eighty-five percent of the Native children removed from their families from 1941 to 1967 were placed in non-Indian homes or institutions, said the Association on American Indian Affairs report. The aim, said White Hawk, was assimilation and extinction of the tribes as entities, as their younger generations were removed, year after year—just as it had been with the boarding schools.

"We can't be afraid to use words like genocide," said summit participant Anita Fineday, White Earth Band of Ojibwe, managing director of Casey Family Programs' Indian child-welfare programs and a former chief judge at White

Earth Tribal Nation. "The endgame, the official federal policy, was that the tribes wouldn't exist."

As Native adoptees struggle to recover their identities, some have trouble accessing their original birth certificates. Many states seal adoption records to protect the confidentiality of the process. "In a state that does this, you have to be a detective to find out where you're from," said White Hawk.

Or lucky. According to Sharon Whiterabbit, Ho-Chunk Nation, a business consultant and internationally known rights advocate, the son she'd given up as a teen mother found her because he lost his social security number. To get a new one, he had to petition the courts for his original birth certificate and, using the information he found there, tracked her down.

Could something be done on a tribal level to keep adoption records open and available for those who want them? Whiterabbit asked the group. This summit was about solutions, as well as problems, and Fineday had an answer: "Tribes have a right to know their members, so we can demand the records. We're not requesting, though. We're demanding. At White Earth, we were successful with this tack in a couple of cases. When the [adoption] documents arrived, I got goose bumps."

Carrie Imus, director of social services and former chairwoman of the Hualapai Tribal Nation, suggested that tribes do pre-enrollment of children who are being adopted out, to ease their return.

According to Terry Cross, Seneca Nation of Indians and director of the National Indian Child Welfare Association, nontribal child-welfare workers usually did not recognize the large support network that Native children enjoy: "In the 1950s, '60s and '70s, children were removed from Indian families because auntie was taking care of them, and the system called that neglect. But it was simply a different cultural way of meeting the child's needs. To this day, social workers who remove Native children don't know what an Indian family is and what supports are available in the extended family and tribe."

Decades of stolen children caused unresolved personal and community-wide grief and high rates of alcoholism, suicide and other social ills that stalk individuals and tribes to this day. "It took me years to realize nothing was wrong with me and the response I had to the trauma I'd experienced as an adoptee," said Sandra Davidson, White Earth Band of Ojibwe and a program manager for Praxis International, a nonprofit dedicated to eliminating violence toward women and children.

Often referred to as 'historical trauma,' the pain can't be cured with quick-fix programs, said Cross. "In Canada, we looked at places where suicide is the highest, and it's where the culture is most broken down," he said. "In such cases, do you start suicide-prevention programs, or do you restore balance in the community through more self-governance? I have found that unless you change a community systemically, you can't affect the symptoms of imbalance, such as suicide."

Linear thinking—see a problem, apply a solution—is ineffective, he added. "Mainstream society's services are so fractured. Medical doctors get the body, psychologists get the mind, judges get the social context, and clergy get the spirit. But, in fact, we are all whole people, and real solutions have to address that."

Cross pointed to the sweat lodge as a way of caring for the whole person. "It's done in groups and includes teachers, stories and protocols for how to conduct oneself, which relate to the social context," he said. "You sweat, and you experience aromatic herbs, which heal the body; you participate in prayers and songs, which are in the realm of spirit; and when you come out, you feel better and have moments of clarity that are aspects of mind."

That type of healing is required for entire communities, as well as for individuals, and is a part of what Cross called the 'remembering' of indigenous cultures. Colonization has pulled indigenous cultures apart worldwide, as colonizers have taken land and resources. "They also usurp sovereignty and attack spirituality," he said. "The last item is removal of children to educate them in the language and worldview of the colonizer. Now, though, we Native people are remembering our traditions and remembering our communities. We're healing from within."

The adoptees' stories must be articulated so they can heal, so their communities can be restored, and so the experiences can help remedy Indian country's ongoing child-welfare crisis, said White Hawk. The percentage of Native children cared for outside the home remains disproportionately high across the nation, despite the Indian Child Welfare Act (ICWA), a 1978 law that sought to ameliorate the situation—but has yet to do so. In Alaska, Native children make up 18 percent of the child population but 55 percent of the children in foster care;

in South Dakota, Indian kids are 15 percent of the state's youngsters, but 53 percent of those in foster care. Other states topping the list for skewed numbers include Minnesota—where the overrepresentation of Native kids in foster care increased substantially from 2004 to 2009—Montana, Nebraska and North Dakota.

Another summit attendee, Gina Jackson, Te-Moak Tribe of Western Shoshone Indians, is helping educate judges through a model-court program of the National Council of Juvenile and Family Court Judges, in Nevada. The program helps jurists understand ICWA and relevant best practices. "We've signed up 66 jurisdictions and will help them work for compliance," she said.

Education of the judiciary is crucial, said Arizona state judge Kathleen Quigley: "ICWA cases are not the bulk of a judge's work, so many are not familiar with the law." And the concept of the 'active efforts' needed under ICWA to find and notify a child's tribe of a possible removal from the family is not dealt with sufficiently in case law, she said.

"At this meeting, it has been critical for me to hear from folks who've been in the system and to understand how being taken from their families and communities affected their lives," Jackson said. "I want everyone who works with kids and families to hear these voices." Michael Petoskey, Grand Traverse Band of Ottawa and Chippewa Indians and chief judge of the Pokagon Band of Potawatomi Indians, agreed. "Thank you for sharing your stories," he told adoption era survivors. "We judges may underestimate the impact on people's lives when we terminate parental rights."

"You're saying that is medicine for those of us who've been through this," White Hawk responded. Going forward, the repatriation institute will work to affect policy and will organize a day of prayer and healing for Friday, November 2, 2012. "We're hoping to have events at state capitols nationwide," said George McCauley, Omaha, head of the Institute's board of directors.

Jerry Dearly, the renowned Oglala Lakota storyteller and educator who serves as White Hawk's advisor, told the group that healing is about identity, understood on a profound level. "You have to find out who you really are, who you really were," he said. "Go to a quiet place where it's just you and the Creator. All of us are beautiful, but you have to believe in yourself."

"Now I have cancer and am waiting for an operation," St. John told the summit. "But I believe in myself, and I can survive anything."

A version of this story was first published in *Indian Country Today*. More of Stephanie Woodard's writing on Native issues can be seen there and on her blog, *stephaniewoodard.blogspot.com*.

Cross says child-welfare workers too often ignore the large support network for Native children.

23

Lost: Incarceration and Reincarnation

Jessup Floyd Neubert (Cheyenne River Sioux Tribe, Lakota Nation)

Jessup and Tashea (on his 11th birthday) (Family Photo)

On October 24, 1984, my nineteen-year old mother Cheryl Fasthorse brought me into this world on the Rosebud reservation in South Dakota. She gave me the name Desmond Jacques Fasthorse and planned to raise me by herself. My father is of the Cheyenne River Sioux Tribe and a few vague, shadowy memories are all that I have of him. On my fourth birthday Cheryl had moved us to Utah and that is where much of my story would eventually culminate in loss.

I've lost many things during my twenty-six years of life. One might even say that my life has been characterized by incessant loss. I lost my mother to addiction. Then I lost her again when I was adopted. I don't know where she is. I've also lost something that many people take for granted, freedom. These losses began twenty years ago.

I was six-years-old when the police carried me and my two-year-old sister Tashea to the cruiser. Our mother had been fighting with Tashea's dad again. As the red and blue lights flashed I watched them restrain our Mom with hand-cuffs and lead her to another police car. I held my baby sister in my lap as she cried on my shoulder. Though I didn't comprehend the full gravity of our Mother's alcoholism, I knew something had gone drastically wrong. I tried to comfort Tashea while the police drove us to an unknown destination. It was a shelter for children, a house in Provo on a lake. Although our first stay would only be a couple days, it was the first of many.

The first separation from our mother, Cheryl, was the catalyst that forged an unbreakable bond between Tashea and me, one which lasts to this day. We only had each other. It was my duty to protect and comfort her as we went through the gauntlet of an alien system.

After the state of Utah allowed us to return to our mother, it was only a matter of time before her addictions manifested again and we found ourselves back at the children's shelter. This cycle of being taken and then restored was not only endless it was progressive. The separations grew longer in duration. Eventually we were kept from our mom for months at a time.

Sometimes we were treated like welcome guests in the white foster homes and other times we were treated as temporary visitors. It was in a foster home of the latter kind when I first exhibited my anger toward the white people who had control over us. It was also one of the first times I heard the word 'orphan' used, referring to Tashea and me.

They were a Mormon family with children of their own. Their eldest child never failed to remind me that his parents were his, not ours. We didn't want his parents. We just wanted to be returned to ours. Tashea would often cry when I left her sight and the white foster parents could not understand why. One time after they locked her in a room alone, Tashea began crying for me. They told me, 'This is for her own good.' I would have none of it. When the foster dad knelt down and tried to patronizingly explain his reasoning, I snapped. With my small six-year-old fist, I swung at him. His nose immediately filled with blood. His wife ran to his aid. While they attended to his bloody nose, I went in the room and calmed Tashea. I don't recall what they said, but I knew they wanted us 'orphans' gone. Soon after, our caseworker arrived and took us to another foster home.

This process of being taken to and from strange foster homes went on until I was eight. By the time we were about to be returned to the custody of our recovering mother, we had entered the household of the family that would eventually adopt us five years later. This was the fourth or fifth foster home that Tashea and I were subjected to. Thankfully this family was unlike any of the previous ones. They actually treated us like we were their own children. They were a large Mormon family that had nine children of their own. Four of their children were still living at home. I will always recall our initial stay with the Neubert's as a loving experience. This was also one of the first times I remember that Tashea didn't cry when I left her.

Our first visit was temporary. We were returned to our mother. This time we had a new baby sister to help with. Her name was Tonika. Both Tashea and I were thrilled to finally get our mother back. Unfortunately it didn't last. Within a year, our mother would lose herself again to her addictions.

When we were first reunited, we lived in a small pink and white trailer. I told myself that things would be different. In the beginning everything seemed to be right in our world. I'll never forget how good it felt to be home and around some of my own kin. During those first few weeks it appeared our mom had changed. I almost forgot the adversities Tashea and I endured over the last two years.

When our mom began to disappear, Tashea and I already knew how to take care of our new baby sister and ourselves. Peanut butter sandwiches, macaroni and cheese, and cereal were the main staples of our diet. We quickly learned how to make formula for Tonika and how to change her diapers. When mom began to disappear for days, I had no choice but to skip school. I simply could not leave my two sisters alone. It was now the three of us against the world. We adapted to our circumstances. Together we found solace. We had each other.

Sometimes our mom would come home drunk or with some strange guy. I learned to keep Tashea and Tonika away during those times. When there wasn't any food in the house I learned how to steal from the grocery stores. Sometimes I would borrow food stamps from our neighbors. Because our mother wasn't around, we had to pretend we weren't home when a caseworker showed up unannounced. We didn't want to be taken away again. This happened several times.

Once Sandra, our last foster mother, came by for a visit. It wasn't until she was about to leave that I realized who it was. I had to run and catch her before she left. Sandra was checking on us. Tashea and I would often call her when we could. Sandra became a beacon of light during our time of darkness.

As we approached the last time we would ever live with our mother again as a family, I was aware that things were changing. My mother was losing her battle with alcohol. Before we were taken the final time, our newest baby brother Miguel was born. Now there were four of us. Reliving this time in my life evokes deep pain. We lost more than just our mother. We lost each other.

The state of Utah decided we were to be separated. Tashea and I would go to one foster home; Tonika and Miguel would be sent to another. Thinking about this still brings tears to my eyes. I wonder what might have been if I had told the white caseworkers no, that we didn't want to leave. But I didn't. The ramifications of our mother's alcoholism would produce even more suffering, as we grew older. We would lose things that can never be completely recovered.

Tashea and I did return to the wonderful and loving parents of our last foster home. We were allowed to visit our mother Cheryl. We could see Tonika and Miguel once a month and on special occasions. Shortly after we left, our mother became pregnant again. She named our new brother Emilio. After he was born, the state of Utah gained custody and he went to the foster family that had Tonika and Miguel. When I was twelve we were all adopted by these two families. All the boys had their names changed. I went from Desmond to Jessup. Miguel became Michael and Emilio became Steven. Tashea and Tonika retained their birth names. When I lost the name Fasthorse I was born with, I lost a vital connection to my Lakota identity. I didn't understand the full magnitude of this until many years later. My understanding came after many years of inner suffering, disconnection, and imprisonment.

We lost our mother to her addictions. We lost our names. I lost my connection to our blood because we were adopted into white Mormon families. I lost three of my siblings when their adoptive family moved to another state soon after our adoptions. All the memories we might have shared were taken from us. Lost.

Even though we lost so much in the devastating wake of our mother's addiction, I discovered many positive things about living from our new white family. I discovered that the meaning of family isn't limited to genetics and skin color. The meaning of family can and does go beyond such superficial characteristics. The meaning of family is love. I have only good things to say about the Neubert's and the five or six years I lived with them after our adoption. I too carry the last name, Neubert. They will always be a part of who I am.

When my last sibling was born, our adoptive parents Sandra and Danny made sure that my new sister wasn't lost to the system. Anna was adopted into our white Mormon family, too. Thanks to them, I have Anna in my life. She is truly a blessing.

Though our past may drag us down with the weight of sadness and regret, I am convinced of our very real potential to transcend the limits society places on us, and the imagined limitations we place upon ourselves. In spite of writing this in a maximum-security prison in Arizona, I understand that loss isn't the only aspect of life. There are many good things, too.

My 'loss' today is a loss of freedom. This loss was my choice. It belonged to me and me alone — no one else did it to me, or for me. Because I lost myself to the bottle and drunken violence in 2007, I am now losing eleven years of freedom due to my involvement in an armed robbery.

Separated from my people, culture, and history, at an age when I already knew I belonged to my Lakota nation, wasn't without inner conflict. I now know that my past, including the time I lived with my mother, made me stronger. But I have to ask, where was my tribe when my family needed them? Do my people even know I exist?

Even though my mother failed in many respects, I have unconditional love for her. I understand how she could lose herself to drugs and alcohol. My empathy comes from my own experiences with alcoholism. I started drinking at age seventeen. Now I understand the terrible role that drugs and alcohol often play in the circumstances surrounding the neglect and abuse of our Native children and the subsequent removal of those children from such dangerous situations. Instances like this are but symptoms of the underlying epidemic of alcoholism and drug addiction that has been tearing at our people's spiritual and cultural fabrics since those poisons were first introduced to us. If we are to address the many issues that affect our people effectively, we need to remain aware of those issue's underlying causes. Otherwise we are only dealing with the symptoms while neglecting the actual disease. Our approach to the problems of losing our children to interracial adoption — must be holistic in scope and nature.

Currently, I am trying to correct my wrongs and shortcomings. I am working on reconnecting to the things I lost while remaining grateful for the many things I gained.

Reincarnation

Today is the day I die. As I languish in this concrete cage, I often wonder what might have been. Initially I believed I was absent the day they taught, 'Life and How to Live it.' After numerous failures I became convinced that the curriculum of life was beyond my intellect and ability. With my life in shambles and shackles, what other plausible explanation could there be? Was there something lacking in me? Why did tragedy always occur?

My reality at that time was that people, places, and things could not be trusted or relied upon. Before my eleven-year sentence, I was blinded by addiction and denial. I was positive that I had no intentions of ever harming another person. Yet it became apparent that in most, if not all of my interactions with other people, I imposed suffering. I have come to understand we are all interconnected. We will always affect one another, whether we intend to or not.

Shortly after I began to realize this, the remorse actually made my heart colder. I came to the conclusion that an individual with my disposition couldn't possibly belong with the rest of society. This twisted desire to be alone was birthed from the idea that if I am alone, cut off from society then I couldn't inflict any more suffering. The judge and state prosecutor agreed. Their ineffective justice system discarded me. I was labeled a 'Menace to Society.' It was argued I should be removed from society for no less than fifteen years. I actually wanted to be alone with my suffering. My heart became the coldest it has ever been. I became an outsider looking in—or to put it more succinctly, I became an insider looking out.

A solitary warrior became my identity. I was selfishly attempting to protect myself from the realization that my choices had hurt other people. Prison with all its deprivation humbled me. I had time to objectively and consciously examine the notions I had previously held on to. I was able to determine that a certain amount of narcissism was involved. I internally romanticized my struggle. How I self-identified was no longer consistent with reality.

Seneca's Epistle XLVIII helped me to recognize the need to destroy my identity of solitude. 'No one can live happily who has regard to himself alone and transforms everything into a question of his own utility... you must live for your neighbor, if you would live for yourself.'

If I was going to remain intact during my incarceration, a spiritual rebirth and psychological awakening were required. I realized that in order to begin the healing process; I had to risk experiencing even more suffering. This process demanded that I sift through the wreckage of my life. Cultivating optimism, selflessness, and insight through honest introspection and spiritual reflection, became paramount to my recovery.

So with these realizations in mind today, I begin to dismantle the isolating defense mechanisms.

Today, I begin to trust and make myself open to the peace that reality offers.

Today, I commit the quiet suicide of my misguided self.

Today is the day I die. I die so that I may achieve my freedom, so that I may live.

This is my reincarnation.

I have sincere aspirations to attend and graduate from a four-year college after my release from prison. Education is the primary avenue of positive change for me and my main objective is to apply all of the knowledge I gain towards helping my Native people. I'm presently single but plan to marry and start a family of my own as soon as I find the right woman. My hopes, thoughts, prayers to Wakan Tanka remain with all who suffer—especially my fellow Split Feathers. May Wakan Tanka continue to guide us all in our struggles toward peace.

Mitakuye Oyasin!

Jessup is currently incarcerated in Arizona. Diligent and resolved to further his studies, he is earning college credits through Rio Salado College and plans to earn degrees in Chemical Dependency and Business.

24

Good Medicine, Bad Medicine

Trace L Hentz

The lesson (is) to realize the value of an alternative perspective. And that is why we are here. That is why the Creator allowed some of us to remain, in spite of all the attempts to destroy us. — Tall Oak (Everett Weeden), Absentee Pequot/Narragansett, *500 Nations documentary*

For 150 years and counting, Indian Country has been dealing with weakened immune systems, sugar diabetes, amputations and heart disease. Loss of traditional foods has reeked havoc on our bodies. Genes do remain a factor as an adult. Without medical records, every lost child/adoptee is a time bomb. When we don't know our own medical history, we are at a greater risk.

Tribal leaders do struggle to make things right or better, but it's not easy in this 'conquered' Third World, fighting for **scraps** we call food, sovereignty and dignity. It's as important to understand what these removals and adoptions accomplished in America and Canada as it is to see where Indians stand today. Some American Indians say if we keep our languages strong and return to our ceremonies, our tribal nations and people will grow strong again. That is good medicine, they say.

For those living on their rez, they too have experienced upset and turmoil in ever-changing traditions, living in their two worlds.

As the United Colonies became the United States, spreading and erecting more and more fences and boundaries, Indian people were the first to be removed, the last to be consulted, and not on the majority's conscience. Over 400 peace treaties were signed with promises made to care for the Indian people sent to reservations. No one really expected Indian people to survive, let alone thrive.

"We are at a place in this world where we need to recognize that we need to go backwards in order to move forward, reclaim those parts of tradition that embraced respect and dignity. Teach our children the things that our great-grandparents were taught as children. Until this is done there cannot be unity among us, any of us..."

—James Magaska Swan, United Urban Warrior Society, Black Hills Chapter

25

A Work in Progress (Adoption or Adaption?)

Andrea (Andy) Miller Hill

I have made six attempts at documenting the search to find my birth family. If I had written with pen and paper the past five tries would have ended up in the waste bin. Luckily the earlier drafts were not lost and I was able to go back and decide what I wanted to include. This is my final attempt.

This is not the story of how I came into 'being.' This is the story after that. My story is about my search for my biological family.

Where to begin? I thought long and hard about this. My earliest questions came from pure human curiosity. Who am I, where do I come from, what makes up the whole of me, my eye and hair color, height, and health, etc.

For most people, these basic questions are easy to answer, but not if you are an adoptee. I am fifty-one years of age, and until 1999 I lived with guesses, dreams, and bits of pieces of a history that may or may not be true.

I wanted to write this with as much accuracy as possible so I pulled out my adoption paperwork along with the few photographs that I have from childhood and onward. I sat on the floor with everything spread out around me. When I began looking at it all I realized that instead of answers I had questions.

After reviewing the documents, I now know that I was placed in foster care with my prospective adoptive parents at the age of two months in October 1959, not at three months, as I previously believed. My adoption wasn't finalized until November 1960, not November 1959. I discovered that they were already a family, complete with their biological daughter, who at the time would have been three years old.

I always knew I was adopted and that my older sister was not adopted. There

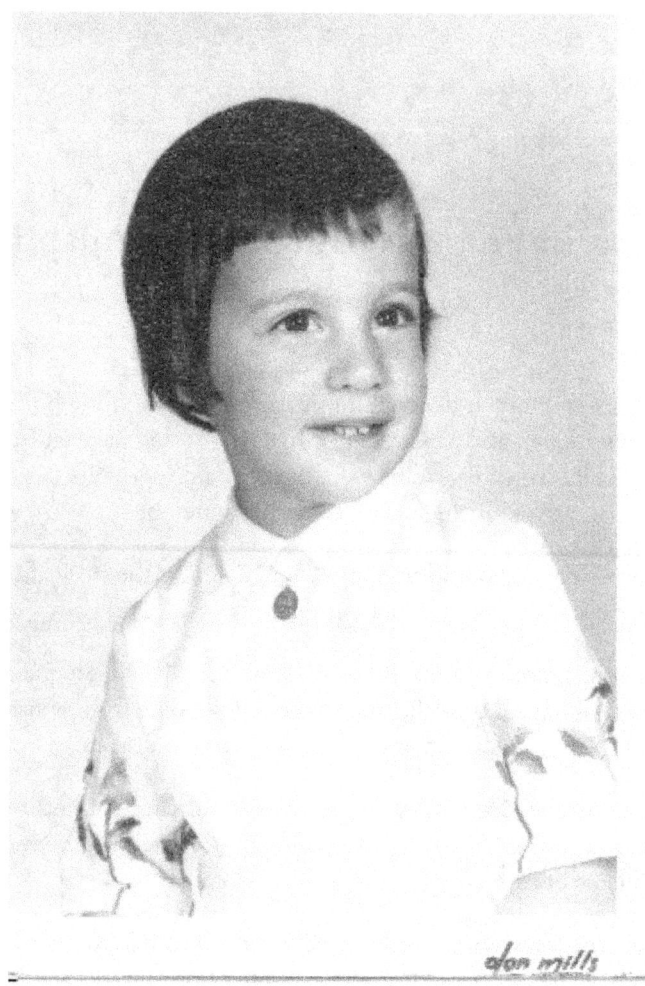

Andrea (Andy) Miller Hill

was never a sit down explanation at the age of five, six, or seventeen, etc. There was always the understanding that I was not theirs. One of the books read to me as a child that I enjoyed, but also felt conflicted about, was *Are You My Mother?* Like the bird in the story I realized I was different, but the bird eventually found her mother. I wondered if I ever would find my mother.

As I reviewed my life through photos, I felt that the word adoption could be replaced with the word adaptation. From early on I learned how to adapt within the family as the adopted daughter. I tried to be somewhat hidden while the day-to-day in the household carried on. It was not a horrible life, by any means, but it was also not what my friends experienced. There was no comradely between my sister and myself. At a young age I began blaming myself for this. At times I fall back on this way of thinking. If only I had been five inches shorter, worn a size one at the age of fifteen, had curly hair rather than stick straight dark brown hair, was smarter and more aggressive, then maybe, I would have fit into my family, but then I would have been their biological daughter and not me.

Along with the photos and the court documents, I made chronological lists from my childhood to present. In doing so I realized that my closest friends became my family. With them, I was me, not the masked child trying to be what her adoptive family expected her to be. With my childhood family, I always stood before them with an invisible hand across my mouth out of fear of being rejected and judged not good enough and returned to the grocery store where my adoptive sister told me I came from. Unfortunately to a certain extent, I still bring that mindset to other relationships. It puts one's life in a whole new perspective when you allow yourself to touch what has been causing you pain. I choose to let go of the pain and to live positively. I view myself as a work in progress. I am an artist.

In 1992, my adoptive father gave me an envelope that contained the court papers and a brief history of my biological parents. The reason he gave them to me was he hoped that they would help me uncover which Native American Nation I was from. He was interested in the monetary aspect. He wanted to defer some of my college costs. I was in the middle of a divorce and raising my two young daughters when this happened.

At the time of my adoption, possession of court papers was totally unheard of. My adoption was handled through the law firm where my adoptive dad was a partner. The lawyer that was in charge of the adoption felt it was unfair to leave me, the adoptee, to be in the dark about my past.

For the first time in my life, I told my father no. I wanted the information, but I refused to use it for college expenses. I explained to him that I would not take monies away from someone who was more needing than me. I have Grandpa Jack, Dad's father, to thank for my views. He was raised in foster care and made it on his own in life. He did so well that he was able to provide his children with all the luxuries that anyone could ask for.

It was during one of Jack's LONG afternoon drives through the north country of Arizona, Navajo Land (as the adoptive family called it back in the 1960s) that I learned this lesson. As we pulled up in front of a tar paper shack with a torn faded black cloth for a door, a skinny tan and white dog tied to the side of the structure, and the air conditioning blasting through his new Cadillac's vents, he turned to look at me and said, 'You may have come from this, but this is not who you are.' This, of course, was his notion of what it meant to be Native in America in the 1960s, in Arizona. It was the only trip that I ever took with him that my sister Victoria was not invited. It made a huge impact on how I viewed my life and the lives of those less fortunate.

In 1997, five years later, my friend Tim Thundering Hawk Warner (Lakota) and I were having a conversation about what Nation I might be from. He recommended that I start looking. Knowing that it could have a large impact on our lives, I went to my daughters with it. The consensus was unanimous: we or I would start the search into which Nations had the Miller family (my birth name) in their communities. I discovered the Miller name was in the Mohawk, Mohegan, Mahican and/or Cherokee Nations. My searching came to a standstill as I only had two generations of biological names.

With the Mohawks, I was able to send a letter of query to Six Nations in Canada. Three weeks later I received a very lovely letter telling me to keep in contact and that any further questions I may have would be answered if possible. However, with the scant information I had given they were unable to find any direct link.

My daughter and I decided to do a direct search for the family to see what came up. It became a central part of her social/history class. We began by looking in the social security (SS) archives online. Thank goodness for the internet! I found my mother's name with the correct birth date, but the archives stated that she had died in the 1970s. We moved on from her name with the hope that she was somebody else's mother. We tried her mother's name next. It was a hit, not only her name and dates but we also located the state of residence. According to SS, she had passed in 1985 in Susquehanna County. The county she resided in was less than forty minutes away. Katie and I followed up at the county courthouse. I hoped to confirm or deny the fact that my mother had already passed on.

To shorten the telling of the story, in Montrose, Pennsylvania—Susquehanna's county seat, their local paper no longer archived their newspapers. All of the county court paperwork was warehoused in Scranton, PA. A stop to the Montrose library was now in order. It was 10:30 a.m. and of course they didn't open until noon. After brunch we went back to the library. It was a success! They did have the newspaper's obituaries on microfilm. I found the one I was looking for. Half of the surviving children that were mentioned had her name, the other half had a different last name. I assumed she had married.

We decided to call one of mom's local half siblings to see if I was accurate in my presumptions. He lived in Appalachin, New York. After many tries, I was finally able to speak to a human instead of an answering machine. I was told all the information I'd need was in the phone number given to me. So I dialed it and called the United Way of Tioga County. I, of course, apologized for having the wrong number. The voice on the other end asked what I was calling for, so I told her. She confirmed that my mother was married and that her maiden name was Miller. Then she asked who I was, so I said I was a distant relative hoping to make contact with her. At this point, the conversation came to an abrupt end. 'I can't talk to you, but if you give me your number, I'll give it to my Uncle Milt who will know what to do.'

Of course, I said thank you and that was that. I left it all on hold for over a year while waiting for the return call. Frustrated, I finally did a search using the white pages and looked up my mother's name on the computer. There were three possibilities. Only one was from Tucson, Arizona where she resided when my grandmother's obit was written in 1984.

On June 6, 1999, I am volunteering at the Otsiningo powwow, when my friend Tim came over to talk to me. It was the end of the day and all the artists were packing up and getting ready to head home after the weekend art and music festival. What I was told would be the pivotal piece in the finding of my mother.

I had decided the year before that I wouldn't look any further, feeling that it wasn't my right to come barging into my biological family's lives. Tim told me that he felt that now was the time to connect with my mom and if I waited, it may be too late. I took his advice. He seems to be always right about what he sees and feels!

Monday morning, June 7, 1999, I mailed a letter to my biological mom at the address in Tucson. The body of the letter started off with an apology for intruding in her life. I asked if she was the correct 'mother' and I stated that I wanted contact. 'Please send back the stamped postcard that I included.' I recall I asked her to write 'yes or no.'

If she was my mother and she didn't want contact, the postcard with 'no contact' should be sent back. If she was not the correct mother there was a stamped postcard for that as well. With my letter I included photocopies of the adoption papers.

On June 11, 1999, Katie and I were working on her math homework when my phone rang. I answered it and the voice asked if I was Andrea. The person on the line gave me her full name. I said she didn't need to call me Andrea, and she said, 'That's what moms do.'

I started crying. Kat came in and asked me, 'Who's on the phone?' I told her, 'It's your grandmother.' She started crying. Mom asked me, 'Who is that?' and I told her, 'It's your granddaughter Katharine.' Mom started crying. It was a long-distance lifelong-awaited happy crying fest.

I had found my mom and my sister Beth. We kept in touch by phone for weeks. Towards the end of June I was asked what I would be doing on a certain weekend in July. We planned to be in Victor (New York) at Ganondagan for their Native American art and music festival. Beth finally let the surprise out of the box. They would be flying into Syracuse, New York on that weekend, staying overnight, and then driving into Binghamton the next day to meet us. April, my oldest daughter, and I drove up to Syracuse to meet their flight. My first impression was, 'well now I know what Kat will look like when she's my mother's age, except Kat is seven inches taller.' It was a wonderful weekend. There would be two more trips east for mom and my sister Beth over the next two years and the last one included my niece and my brother-in-law.

In the fall of 2002, my daughter April and I packed our truck for a cross-country drive for a three-week trip to Arizona so that we could spend time with our family. It was wonderful!!! I made two more trips in 2006, and again in 2007. (I hope for another trip to Arizona in the fall of 2011.)

We are always in contact, laughing, loving, and missing one another. I have an extended local family as well. There have been deaths in my biological family and those gone are greatly missed. Most deaths were cancer-related. Mom was diagnosed with cancer and was still recouping from the surgeries when I visited in 2007. She is still cancer-free and I believe in my heart that that was the overlying shadow Tim had seen that prompted him to push me in 1999 to complete my search for her.

Through the help of one of my great aunt in-laws, on my mother's side, my biological father was contacted in the fall of 1999. It did not go well, but then my aunt's view of my mother's story was not the true picture. Knowing the pain that was caused by my father, up until recently I left that side of the family alone. This past summer (2010) on Facebook my father's son came forward asking questions. We have connected and will stay connected, regardless of the fact that my father refuses to acknowledge that I even exist. It's his loss, not my brother's or mine.

My adoptive father died on August 27, 2010 in California. Their biological daughter Victoria had relocated both he and my adoptive mother in March.

My two daughters and I were able to connect with my adoptive mother through Skype. We wanted to speak with her Easter evening 'face to face.' She told my adoptive sister, 'Those people are not anybody that I recognize.' It was very sad for my girls and me.

Choices that we make affect many people—sometimes generations.

I hope to stop in California to see my adoptive mother on my trip to Arizona, knowing that it will very likely be the last chance I'll have to talk with her about our lives together. At the very least I can hold her hand and say thank you and goodbye.

My name is Laura Lee Miller by birth and Andrea Ragine Hill by adoption. And thank you to the U.S. Department of Social Security for allowing me to become Andrea Miller Hill in 2004, honoring my past and my present.

To family and friends, I am Andy, mother, daughter, sister, aunty, artist, of mixed ancestry and memories, with Mohawk, Pawnee, Shawnee, British Isles ancestors and who knows what else on the side of the family that I recently made contact with—all of which makes not the sum of me but rather enriches the whole of me.

I recognize that I am in the small percentile of adoptees that found their birth families and had a positive outcome with regards to that finding. So to those of you who are still searching, may you find what you seek with love and blessings.

Andy works as an artist and is a student of healing arts.

26

Ani's Story

Ben Chosa, Jr. (Lac du Flambeau Ojibwe-Menominee) with Jackie W.

Ani and his father

I found out fairly young that I was adopted. It wasn't really hard to figure out that, 'one of these things is not like the others.' I was the short dark one amongst the tall willowy blonds. For the most part, it never meant much to me. I had no clue what was missing so I had no frame of reference. It was only when I got around other Natives that I began to understand the scope of what had been taken away from me.

Growing up I heard the usual comments about being Native. Since I didn't have a frame of reference, most of what was said was pretty meaningless. For the most part I identified more with whites than I did with Indians.

As a child I was told on numerous occasions how my adopters had 'chosen' me. Attached was the unsaid implication: I had better be grateful, I had better behave, and I had better be a better son.

I was an uneven student. I had a lot of natural gifts, but I didn't do well in school. I didn't graduate from high school and got my GED at Ethan Allen School for Boys where I spent four years of my life from age fourteen to eighteen. This trend extended even into college where, without much effort, I pulled a 3.0 GPA. This feat was accomplished despite the fact that I was in prison, or possibly, because I was in prison.

I seemed to do really well at certain things that led people to expect things of me that I couldn't sustain. Knowing this pattern, I'd find myself pulling out when the bar got set too high. Better to move on to something else than come crashing down, disappointing everyone around me. I was average in sports. The only team sports I participated in as a child were wrestling and track. In juvie, I played football, but I was too much of a security risk (I tended to impulsively walk away from places) and was kicked off the team.

Academically, I did better at things that required reading, and multiple-choice tests. I remember always being able to read. I used to pour over the encyclopedia at home, and when I'd skip school in junior high, you could often find me in the town library, looking through art books.

I never wanted the name of my adopters. Even before finding out about my history, I wanted to change my name. Like a lot of other things, I wanted to change the world. I never managed to break the inertia of the helpless. After coming home in 2002, one of the first things that I asked for was an Indian name. I had been taught that the reason that Indians have names is so the ancestors and the spirits know who to look after. White names are too common. How can the spirits tell the difference between me and another 'Scott'? I received my name and now the ancestors and spirits know me.

The name on my birth certificate is Ben Chosa Jr. I like its brevity. No middle name or even an initial. The 'Jr.' is misleading as I am actually the third in my family with that name. I kept that name for the first few years of my life. Like so many Native Americans from northern Wisconsin, destiny would soon drag me far from my family, reservation, and culture. Destiny took the form of social policy and Christianity. I then became Scott Carl Kieson, the stolen child (adoptee) of Gary and Barbara Kieson, and the unwilling brother to Cindy and Tammy Kieson. I never fit in with them. I was a dark, short boy, in the land of tall, willowy, blond Germans. I was chosen to be the standard-bearer for the Kiesons, who were unable to produce a natural male heir. And while that plan didn't work out for them, I find myself stuck with this name. I call this name my 'government' name that was thrust upon me when I was adopted.

I'm fond of the saying, 'all things by the will of the Creator.' Not that I'm always in agreement with the Creator. But then again, he saw fit to bring me home to my people even if it was 30 years later: addicted, convicted, filled with confusion and anger, but at least metaphorically home, if not physically.

Since one of the first things I wanted was a name, I asked my natural father to help me. I wanted a name I could use when I was at ceremonies. I'm not sure the ancestors knew who the hell Scott Kieson was. So my newly re-found father made arrangements with a medicine man to hold a naming ceremony. The medicine man prayed for many days for the Spirits to send a name, but nothing came to him. As he left Minnesota for the long drive to my rez in Lac du Flambeau, Wisconsin, a storm began to form behind him that followed him as he drove East. The storm was filled with black clouds, thunder, and lightening and chased the medicine man to the borders of my reservation where it broke up and dissipated. I guess a medicine man's main quality is being observant. As he experienced the storm chasing him, he received my spirit name. Animiki-igiizhig (Thunderbird Sky). A thunderbird sky occurs during a thunderstorm where lightning arcs from cloud to cloud as opposed to striking the ground. The lightning is said to take the form of a thunderbird. It's a good name, a name of power, a name I have my doubts that I can live up to. But if it's all the same to you, I think I'll try.

So this brings me to the last name I have, the diminutive of Animikiigiizhig. Admittedly, Animikiigiizhig is a big old Ojibwe mouthful, not only for thick white tongues, but for most Natives too. Thus, all my friends and loved ones call me Ani. Just like my enemies, and the white people who run these iron houses, they know me as Scott Kieson; just like my family knows me as Ben Chosa Jr.; just like my ancestors know me as Animikiigiizhig. Whatever you choose to call me is your choice, but I hope you would call me Ani.

I've had one long-term relationship that has withstood the test of my buffoonery. When I was younger, I was not particularly available emotionally, but I wasn't dead either. My problem was that I trusted no one, which meant that I wasn't all that truthful with my girlfriends. To a certain extent this is true today. My philosophy is that it's easier to ask for forgiveness than to ask for permission. I've never had problems attracting companionship.

My best friend is Jackie W. I met her when I was fourteen or fifteen. Oh, one of the things you will come to realize is that one of my many disabilities is not being able to accurately place chronological events. If time is like a train, and events are box cars, then my box cars don't connect to each other. They just sort of bang up against each other and will move and shift their place in line. If my brain is the locomotive, let's just say that this train moves kind of s-l-o-w-l-y. I'm just saying.

I met Jackie when I was locked up. Having pretty much nothing in common, we nevertheless (sort of) clicked. She has her version of what attracted her to me. What I remember the most about her was a pair of white shorts that she wore. In my defense, I was a fifteen-year old boy and none too sophisticated. One of the things that stands out to me is that the woman always told me the truth. I was always acutely aware of the lies adults told children. Call it an adoptee's sixth sense. One of the more insidious lies I was told by my adoptive parents is that 'we chose you.' The implication is that my birth parents simply did not want me. I could get into how my adoptive parents were no prizes, but that would be a bit off topic. I knew that I wasn't some sort of item left in the bargain bin at the adoption agency.

Jackie always tried to give me some control over my life. Not that my being in control is always a good thing, but her heart has always been in the right place. Even from the start, we had a complex relationship. By the time she met me, the Kiesons had all but given up on me. She would smoothly transfer from role to role as needed. She was a confidant, a friend, and even a mother figure, even though she has three children of her own. Even now, from time to time, she still acts in those roles. While it's a bit confusing to me, it seems to work for the most part. I can say with some sense of certainty (and a little embarrassment) that I seem to have gotten more out of this relationship than she has. Not only has she been with me in my darkest hours, she has withstood my most outrageous and chaotic behavior. I am not the easiest child/man to know. I have lied to her, stole $7,000 and shot it up my arm, been unfaithful to her, and generally been an insensitive bastard. I can't blame my misdeeds simply on being an untrusting, unreachable, deeply flawed human. I am all of that, but sometimes I just can't stand the closeness and intimacy of another person. I am working every day to change those things and right what I can. I am repaying the money I stole, and while the truth and I have a nodding acquaintance, I try to avoid the big fat bald-faced lie. The problem with that is not only does she know me so well, I have discovered that I don't have a poker face. My deceptions tend to be fairly transparent to her. Jackie will also ask the most pointed questions that leave me no room to wiggle. She has taught me that with her, truth really is the best policy.

For example, recently I had to take a piss test that I knew I was going to fail, since I was high when I took the god-damned thing. In the past, I would not have told her—not only was I going to go to segregation, I would most likely have denied my guilt, even in the face of overwhelming evidence. It's a convict thing: You never admit anything, even if they bust you with a bag of weed and the pipe in your mouth. But the truth always does have a way of coming out—so I've learned. This time, I told her ahead of time that not only was I smoking the ganja, but I was too stupid to get away with it. (It's ridiculously easy to avoid detection in prison, unless you're careless, or in my case, too stupid.) With her being far from thrilled with this news, we dealt with it pretty quickly and moved on. So admittedly, they can train bears to ride tiny bicycles faster than teaching me not everybody is my enemy. I have proven that I can learn and change. Some things just take longer than others.

Now let me tell you about Sally. I met Sally through Jackie, who met her through an online Parents of Adoptees' organization. I tend to cast a jaundiced eye upon some of the people Jackie finds online. Most fall into the category of quacks and cranks. However, like I said, I'm evolving. I now give the benefit of the doubt to people. I am so glad that I did because then I met Sally. Even though she lives in Australia, half-way around the world, she has had a large influence upon me. So often people will instantly write off people like me as beneath contempt. Being me, someone who would dismiss another human being without thought, I understood the dynamic. I like to believe that Sally looked beyond my obvious flaws as a human being, and saw the spark of good within me. I'm a far more humble man when I think that another human finds enough value in me to include me in her life. Holy Crap. I just made her sound like a saint. I know Sally is human, imperfect like everyone else, but she works hard to make the world a better place for her family. If she can do that, then I can face my own short-comings and be a better man.

That's a fairly small circle of humanity, eh? I believe that a person is pretty lucky if they can find one or two good friends in a lifetime. At least that's what I used to believe. It was fairly naive. I'd surrounded myself with junkies and criminals and was somehow shocked my life was empty. I closed myself off from the world. I never connected with people; a legacy of being born to a woman who was ill-equipped to deal with her own losses. Her inability to attach to me as an infant resulted in me never fully attaching to others in my life. My understanding of that process shakes me to the core of my being. Since I was never able to emotionally connect with people, I never learned how to empathize. I could cause pain in others, but not feel that pain. Never once during any of my crimes did I feel the damage I was inflicting. Even today, I struggle with my past by not being as emotionally available as I want to be, as I can be. I am also overwhelmed by the trail of devastation I left behind me. I can't undo that, ignore it, or wish it away. All I can do is accept my responsibility in causing that pain, face it every day, and work to never be the same man I was then. It's a small restitution, but it's all I can do right now. Maybe tomorrow will allow me to do more.

I didn't think of doing much about my adoption until I got around other Natives. It was then I realized knowing where I came from was important. The adopters gave me some information, but it wasn't all that accurate. I had no knowledge of the circumstances of my birth or how I ended up being adopted. I didn't actually set about finding my family until the adopters were dead. I'm not sure how they would have reacted.

I think that someone told me that there was a law in Wisconsin that allows adoptees to get their adoption records. All I needed to do was fill out some paperwork. I think I learned that in 1993, but it didn't actually get done until 2002.

I'm not too sure I want to talk about my family other than acknowledging that most of what has been said about them is true—as far as I know it to be. I tend to live my relationships rather than analyze or understand them. My brain doesn't work like that—nope, I don't do abstractions.

My birthfather (my only father—I never refer to the adopters as parents, mother or father) enrolled me some time in the 1980s. I was very young when I was taken. Both of my parents at that time were drinking and that had a lot to do with why I was taken. I've read the records of why and how but I have a lot of anger about how things were handled by tribal officials and employees of the state and the adoption agency.

That being said, here's what my relationship with my birthparents was like: I only knew my father Ben Sr. when I met him at my sentencing in 2002. He died a few years after that. This left me feeling very angry and cheated.

Maybe I do understand that once he sobered up, he really tried to do his best by me. But so what? Understanding doesn't do shit for me. It seems to do more for other people. So he's gone and I'm not. Knowing him was nice, maybe even great. I have a dad. He existed. And he was a billion times better than the other one that thought he could buy himself an heir. Since I don't think I have much to say about 'fathers,' let's move on to the next crappy exhibit: Mothers.

To me, my birthmother was a drunk who chose to go boozing with my 'Aunt' rather than take care of her child. Maybe she was more than that in her later years but that means little to me. Maybe there is a reason, a damn good reason, for being such a failure of a human being, but that doesn't change things for me. Do we see a pattern forming? Let me break it down for you—family is a weapon the universe uses against people least equipped to defend themselves from its deprivations. I have a family, but for the life of me, I don't know what good it is or what to do with them. There isn't much to say about this subject.

I miss my dad, Ben. I miss what I was denied. I will never be complete and I will never stop being full of rage the way it all turned out. Best never to talk about this again. I think I'll just steep and stew in my bile for the next few decades.

My tribe has a casino, as well as other financial means of support. In a normal year I usually receive a per-cap. The recession and a bit of mismanagement affected our tribe and for two years I didn't receive a payment. I got one this year. I have a strange sense that the tribe owes me for not being able to stand up for me when I really needed them back in the 1960s. I was born in Chicago and at the age of six months, my mom and dad brought me to my dad's rez in northern Wisconsin. A month later, I was taken from my parents and I never saw them again until I found my dad in 2002. I've never been back to the rez since I learned that is where I am from. I haven't been able to. This time I've been locked up since 2001. But I also have mixed feelings about it. I'm somewhat conflicted about being enrolled. I feel the tribe, and to some extent my family, let me down, so I have no problem saying that a per-cap is the least that my tribe owes me.

Life history from Jackie: Ani's story

The story that I tell now I learned mostly from Ani's birthfather when I met him for the first time in 2002, and from Ani's birth aunts and uncles, and from history books that tell the story of the Indian Relocation Movement in the 1950s and 1960s. During that time, people came to the reservations and told wonderful stories and showed pamphlets about life in 'The Cities' for Indians. The pamphlets said that people would be taken care of and they would get wonderful jobs and make lots of money, and that life would be better in 'the city' than on the reservation. For many reasons, Ani's family was a prime target for these ads. They were intelligent and ambitious people, and the eldest family male had for generations left the family at an early age to explore the world. And they were not afraid to try new things. Ani's father, Ben, said that his family was the first one to have a radio and how they always had a car when he was growing up— in the 1930s and 1940s, when most others did not.

So Ani's father went to Chicago, with Ani's Aunt May, Aunt Betty, Aunt Yolanda, and Uncle Mike. In Chicago they looked for jobs, and socialized with other Indians, and became politically active in AIM for a time. A lot of this socializing went on in bars on Chicago's near north side—on Clark Street. It was in a bar that Ani's father met Ani's mother, who was from a different reservation and a different tribe. But in Chicago, this didn't matter so much, as being Indian is what drew people together.

Ani's mother, Betty Pierce, came to Chicago from the Menominee reservation in Wisconsin in 1966. At first Betty stayed with her sister Shirley and her husband who had come to Chicago to find jobs in 1959. Betty soon started hanging out on Clark Street, which her sister Shirley referred to as 'ghetto,' and Ben's sister referred to as 'Skid Row.' But that was where the action was, even if some of it was on the rough side. That was where you could meet people and that is where Betty Pierce from the Menominee reservation met Ben Chosa from the Lac du Flambeau reservation. Before long, they were living together and about nine months later Ani —or 'Baby Ben' as he was called then, was born.

Ani didn't know any of this story or who his parents were until he met his father Ben for the first time. He was thirty-five years old. The last time he'd seen his father was when he was seven months old. Ani never saw his mother again, after his adoption. By the time we found his father in 2002, his mother Betty had died.

Ani loves his birthday. It is a great pleasure for me to share with him his delight and glee over the day of his birth. To be with Ani is to be given the gift of unabashed pleasure and fun as a child feels these things.

I can only wonder if Ani's mother and father felt some of this excitement and anticipation over his impending birth. I have the feeling they did. I knew Ani's father from 2002 to 2006 and spent quite a bit of time with him. He had a great respect for relationships but also some fear of them. As I learned more family history, I understood more about the complexities of the Chosa family. I do not believe that Ben would have given a son his own name if he didn't intend to raise him. There is love and pride, promise and anticipation, in the act of giving his name to his son. And Ben Sr. was capable of huge amounts of these things. He was a man of very deep feelings.

From everything I heard about Betty, Ani's mother, she was a fun-loving and caring person. She also had a very complicated family history from what I know about it. It will be important to get more information about Ani's mother before her relatives who store this information are no longer with us. Betty was her mother's oldest child. At some point, Betty lived with her grandmother and was adopted by her at age fourteen. At this time, Betty changed her last name to be the same as her grandmother.

When Ben and Betty met in Chicago, they were not teens. Betty was twenty-nine and Ben was thirty-six. Betty had already had seven (possibly nine) other children before Ani. This was at least her eighth pregnancy. Modern science tells us that a mother's emotions create a chemical bath that passes through the placenta. In this way, her baby feels at a physiological level what his mother feels. If the mother is calm and peaceful, the baby's nervous system grows in an environment of different hormones and chemicals than a mother who is under stress. Ani's experience of family starts here, with a combination of genes, family history, culture, health, and intimate body states as he grew inside of his mother for nine months, listening to his father's voice. Ani has a basic knowledge of what it means to be loved, and so I believe that joy was in Ani's mother's heart as she waited for her eighth child to be born. Perhaps she also experienced an uncertainty.

Ani was born at 7:17 p.m. on Christmas Eve in 1966 at Cook County Hospital in Chicago, Illinois, and was named by his parents Ben Chosa, Jr. On his birth certificate, it states that parents lived at 4131 N. Sheridan Road, that his father was a mover from 'Laflambeau, Wisconsin,' age forty one, and that his mother, Betty Marie Pierce Chosa, age twenty-nine was born in Neopit, Wisconsin.

This information is not available to many children and adults who were adopted. Ani was able to obtain it with the help of an attorney in 2002. This original birth certificate is an incredibly precious document. I would like to thank Attorney Michael Edmonds for helping us to obtain it and Jacy Boldebuck of the Adoption Search Program in Madison, Wisconsin who sent Michael Edmonds the adoption file. We were told that the county who took custody of him in 1967 might have more records. We did contact Vilas County and got a court order — which was not difficult. After the court order, they looked in their basement and found Ani's record on microfilm. They printed it out and sent it to us and their file had the original birth certificate in it. We would like to thank Beth Moore at Vilas County for helping us to get these Vilas County records.

As I have learned firsthand about Ani's experiences with family, I realize how I take my own family for granted. I take the fact that I know my mother and father for granted. Family members have repeated the story of my birth to me many times on my birthday. I take for granted the feelings that I store in my body that create my assumptions about permanency and security and who I am. It is difficult to realize that my beliefs and assumptions come from these experiences that shaped my world view from infancy through adulthood... and that my experience is just not true for Ani. I often state things about 'the way life is' with such certainty that I must sound incredibly naive or superior-sounding to Ani. What must he think when he hears these unintended assumptions about parenting and family as if they are the only way life happens...and yet they exclude his experience entirely?

I was taught to 'feel sorry for' children who didn't grow up like me. As a child, I sensed that there was something disrespectful, arrogant, ignorant, and downright dangerous about that teaching, yet I think that I was an unusual child. Aren't we wired to learn our culture's way of doing things so that we can succeed in it? And so wouldn't adoptive parents naturally try to teach their children how to succeed and give them the best they know? Yet, this wiring must get confused and criss-crossed when a child is taken out of his own culture and raised by strangers who don't share his DNA, his instincts, his language, his history, or his culture! There was little or no education for adoptive parents in 1968 about raising children from another culture.

In 2002, Ani learned who his parents were and was told the story of his birth. During a visit in the prison visiting room, Ani's father told him the story of his three children. 'I always said that you (Ben Jr.) were my Christmas present, Linda was my birthday present (born near his birthday), and Barbara was my turkey (born on Thanksgiving).' We all laughed at the family joke. I can still hear him saying this and it is a glorious memory.

Ani has said he can never make up for what he lost. The loss sits there, huge, and yet there are good things, too. Families are never perfect. But Ani has one. In fact, for better or worse, he has four — his father's family in Lac du Flambeau, his mother's family in the Menominee tribal nation, his adoptive family, and now my family.

This is Ani's story.

Ben maintains a blog http://www.scottckieson.blogspot.com/ and is working on several art projects.

27

Becoming Cricket

Susan Smith (Grand Portage/White Earth Ojibwe)

Suzie and family

I found out I was adopted when I was maybe 7 years old; I do not know the exact age, but I know I was in grade school. I overheard my adoptive mother Virginia telling my sister Connie. Connie was also adopted, four years older, and of Irish ancestry. I attended a private Catholic grade school, and was the only little girl that was **dark**. I remember how my mom immediately tried to express I was "special," that I was picked out of the crowd of other children. I don't really recall feeling any particular sort of way but I just knew that I was different. Eventually I would learn that *other* people had compassion for me because I was adopted. At times I learned they would actually feel sorry for me!

I would not know this until later, when I reached 6th grade. Friends felt sorry for me that my adoptive parents were much older, often confusing them for my

139

grandparents. I didn't look like my siblings so they felt sorry for me about that, too.

At the young age of 7, I was not aware of what being adopted meant. I gradually became more aware, especially at doctor's visits when my amother Virginia would tell the doctors, "Suzie is adopted so there are no details of her health records." This always left me with a hole in my heart, reminding me that I had no records. As I grew older, I scheduled my own doctor's appointments. I recall doctors asked, "Any history of *this/that* in the family?" I'd say, "I am adopted, so I am unsure if it runs in my family or not."

I did not pursue any search until I moved out of the house. I moved out before I graduated from high school. This was against their wishes but I had already made up my mind. I moved into a beautiful English Tudor home with three friends from high school. We shared the second and third floor of a house near Lake Calhoun in South Minneapolis in the same area they filmed the *Mary Tyler Moore* sitcom.

Once I had my freedom, I figured I could begin my search. It would not involve or hurt them in any way. I was no longer hiding the desire to find my biological information. I could write and receive letters in the mail without consequences!

I knew that it hurt my adoptive mother that I wanted to search. To this day, I do not know how it made her feel. She discouraged it from the very beginning. My adopted sister Connie has no interest in a reunion with her biological family. We have very different paths now.

I did try to find answers. I received some detailed genetic background information from Catholic Charities. This non-identifying information was three pages long. It contained information about my mother, her height, her education level, and her siblings. The document stated, 'At the time of your birth she had a sister who was seventeen years of age. At the time of your birth she had a sister who was nineteen years of age.' It covered all of her siblings including a younger brother who was blinded at an early age due to rheumatic fever. It indicated that my mom moved out east to live with her uncle who was an artist at the time. (This artist turned out to be the famous Ojibwe artist George Morrison). With this three-page letter, I was able to post my information on the Internet on an adoption search-board. I posted the duplicate information on three or four different search-boards hoping I would someday get a hit.

I had a house fire in 1987 and that letter was lost in the fire. When I tried to go back to the state to get the letter again, they told me they could send it but it was going to cost me. After I calmed down I wrote them a letter verifying that I had lost everything I owned in a fire. They sent a replacement copy at no charge.

As far as my search, I had given up hope, totally. I figured that if someone/anyone had wanted to know where I was or what had become of me, it should have been years ago. I thought, 'I'm forty, my life is half over. Nobody cares.'

Then I got the phone call that changed my life. In November 2002, my half-sister Sarah called me. On one of those adoption search-boards, I had left my full name as Susan Fedorko, and she had performed an Internet search and was able to pull a work number for me. Sarah got my voicemail and left a message. When I came back to work from a long weekend, I retrieved this voice mail from Sarah. She did not tell me who she was, so I was not sure if it was my mom or an aunt? I never expected it to be my half-sister trying to find me. Sarah had narrowed the search down by State/Date of Birth/Female and the information I had posted.

Catholic Charities handled my adoption in Minneapolis. I have over twenty-four letters that I wrote to them in which they did absolutely nothing but let me down. I will never contribute to them, not in this lifetime. In fact I have thought about suing them for the injustice they did to me. But how does that look if you sue a charity?

They could have helped me get enrolled in my appropriate tribe. They had all the right information. However they did NOTHING to help me. They did however send me copies of each and every letter I'd sent to them.

I have been in reunion for just over nine years. I am Cathee Dahmen's first-born daughter. Her second daughter Sarah found me. Both of my parents were deceased by the time I was located. My father Tom Conklin died in 2001 of stomach cancer. My mother Cathee died in 1997 of emphysema. No DNA test was performed. Each side was one hundred percent certain, beyond a shadow of a doubt, that I was their relative lost through adoption in 1962.

I have met all my biological family members with the exception of some distant cousins. The reunion has been positive with only a few instances of turbulent waters.

My mother Cathee never hid the fact that I existed. Everyone was well aware she had a daughter. There were times (I was told) I was like a storybook character come to life. I did not replace her at the family table, however I am a different version of her that now occupies her chair.

Ironically I was enrolled in my tribe before I knew. Somehow I was enrolled in 1992. My half-sister Sarah did not locate me until November 2002. I was enrolled under the name Susan Smith Fedorko back in 1992. When I went to the enrollment office in 2002, the enrollment clerk took one look at my name and immediately told me, 'You are already enrolled. You are on the long lost members rolls.'

I was eleven months old when my grandmother took me and adopted me out. This was done without my mother's permission. Cathee went to high school one morning and came home to find me gone. Her mother had taken me away. I can only imagine what that did to my mother Cathee. I will never know the pain that caused.

As I understand what happened, Cathee did not want to be just like her older sisters. She didn't want to be strapped with kids and unmarried. She saw how this pulled her sisters down. They were unable to even think about their goals or dreams. Cathee really wanted to do something with her life. But when she gave birth to me, this all changed. Cathee kept me for the first eleven months, and shortly before my first birthday, her mother (my grandmother) Mary Morrison, adopted me out without Cathee knowing. I heard this story that Mary Morrison was a visionary, and she saw GREAT things happening to Cathee in her life. So Mary gathered up my things and dropped me off at some adoption agency.

People talk about forgiveness, but I will never be able to forgive Mary for what was done to me. I run the questions through my mind, 'Why me? Why was I the only one in the family deemed unfit to live as a family member?'

I have no intentions of ever forgiving that woman. She is not my grandmother. When I hear other cousins talking about how GREAT a grandmother she was, it makes me sick. When I go to visit my mother's grave, I walk right past Mary's. And if I ever make it to the pearly gates, I am walking right past her then, too!

Grandmothers are not supposed to act or behave like that. She has hurt me in a way that is unforgiveable.

I truly believe that Cathee had something to do with my enrollment. I have learned that usually the parent has something to do with getting their offspring enrolled and my mother Cathee died in 1997.

The first pow wow I attended was in August 2003. I attended The Grand Portage band's Rendezvous Days, their annual powwow. I have attended every August since I was found! I love attending and feel like it's a part of my religion. The drums call and I am calmed, and with family. I am protected and am at peace. I have a sense that overtakes me, and have no worries or cares. There is only peace and drums, smoke fires, sweet grass burning, jingle dresses, great tales being told, and kindness.

My adoptive parents never took me to my reservation. We never embraced my culture. I remember camping in Canada and there was a powwow going on, but we did not visit the powwow grounds.

I reconnected with friends after years of being separated and relayed my good news about being found, and come to find out, they were adopted too. Now I've bonded with Sandy White Hawk's adoptee-fostered group for Native Americans. I have been with the group since 2003. I try to get to her monthly meeting as often as I can. I have had friends at certain stages in my life that have helped me through good times and bad times. I think it is helpful to have an adoptee friend within your circle.

Is being adopted a life-long test of emotional suffering, sacrifice and endurance? Yes, I believe it is! If asked this when I was younger, I would have given a different answer. Reflecting on my past and figuring out how it fits into my present is something I needed to do for myself.

Having the support of other adoptees that have experienced all the emotions and situations can be so helpful. When I wrote and posted on the search and reunion website, it was like trying to find a needle in a haystack. I guess it is possible to find one after all! After a three-year span, I had actually given up on my search. I'd waited twenty years. It was very frustrating to write the adoption agency and get no results, no answers and no help. I would write and each time I would get a response such as, 'Thank you for your current address information, so that when contact is made on your biological family side, we can get a hold of you quickly.'

I felt as if I was given a shallow hope, if my biological family had decided to look, the adoption agency could have quickly reached me. There was a great deal of confusion about who to contact. I always thought I was dealing with Catholic Charities—but would get responses from both Catholic Charities as well as State of Minnesota Department of Human Services. This was very confusing.

I started my search at the age of eighteen and was FINALLY found when I was forty. That to me seems like a lifetime, many years of missing out. I missed out on embracing my culture, too. The Internet was instrumental in my reunion. I was listed for several years, and never thought in a million years I would get a phone call out of the blue! All it took was for one family member to break the ice and get through the system.

I never paid for a search; it was always too much money. In the 1980s it was a couple hundred dollars and I never had the money. In the 1990s, it went up to a thousand dollars. I still did not have the money and they always told me there were no guarantees.

Thinking back, the state had my file, and they could see that my mother was Cathee Dahmen, a descendent of George Morrison. Why wouldn't they say that? They probably could have located her by the end of the business day. It's miles of red tape designed to help nobody. Minnesota needs to open up the records. We are entitled to our birthrights.

My childhood was happy and stable. It's not that I wanted to replace my parents. I just wanted to know where I came from and who I looked like. I would have been happy with stalking them from a distance, as long as I knew it was truly my family! I needed to know for myself WHO they were, and where they were in their life to complete my own. I may be the only one who thinks this way. But I just needed to know for myself. I was not planning on replacing my adoptive parents in any way, which is what I think they feared.

As far as any advantages to being adopted, none come to mind. What is the advantage of being left at the doorstep? I get the feeling that neither one of my parents would have refused to meet me.

My mom Cathee came from a huge family. She was one of nine children. She gave birth to me and kept me for the first eleven months. Everyone in her family knew I existed. She eventually got married (twice) and both times she told her husband I existed.

My father, Tom Conklin Sr. knew that I existed, however he told only one person. I heard from my half-brother, Tom Conklin Jr. that his father tried to tell him about me. Tom Jr. was certain that Tom Sr. was trying to tell him something when he was near the hour of his death.

I was a dirty little secret until about a year after he had died. My sister Sarah was able to tell me who my birthfather was, and I tracked him down. I had some lucky breaks locating him. I tried calling his house hoping to locate my siblings, but received information from his grieving wife. I was a total surprise to her. She had been married to Tom Sr. for years and he never once told her about me.

I spoke with her, and reluctant as she was, she gave me the phone numbers of each of his children from his first marriage. She was shocked, too.

I was surprised to learn that both my parents were married twice. This was something I would have not guessed or even thought about while 'reunion dreaming.'

After finding out my siblings phone numbers, I made several attempts to reach them by phone. Nobody was available. I thought, 'I just can't leave this kind of message on a voice mail.'

My father's wife Linda must have had her doubts because she called her sister-in-law, Evie Shew and asked her if she knew that I existed. Evie was the only person that Tom Sr. had told. Evie and Tom were friends of my mom Cathee when they were young teens. Linda gave Evie my contact information.

I eventually got a call from my Aunt Evie and she was ecstatic over being able to talk to me. I think she was also really nervous, but she handled it very well.

Both of my birthparents are from a Minnesota Chippewa tribe. I could be enrolled in White Earth Minnesota or Grand Portage. I chose Grand Portage because my mother was registered with them. I actually have blood relatives on the tribal council.

My Minnesota Chippewa Grand Portage tribe did not help me. It would have been nice to be given a 'Welcome to the Tribe' packet, but they are just not available. You learn quickly that it's about who you know. Now I have bits and pieces of knowledge. We have a national monument on our reservation. There is also a well-known 'Little Spirit Tree' or 'Witch Tree' on reservations grounds. It is a 400-year-old cedar tree that reaches out over the shores of Lake

Superior. I learned this from other family members. In eighth grade I learned all about the Iroquois Indians. It was so interesting for me to learn about them. Now I learn about my own nations from my family.

Cathee's mother was Mary Dahmen Morrison. Mary and George Morrison were brother and sister.

George Morrison is considered one of the greatest Native artists of the 20th Century. He was one of two featured artists when they opened the National Museum of the American Indian, part of the Smithsonian in Washington D.C. in 2004.

I went into the Grand Portage Enrollment Office with my auntie Barb (my mom's younger sister). She helped me, but we both were shocked to learn that I had somehow been enrolled in 1992 and were very surprised to learn that I had accumulated several thousands of dollars under that enrollment number. That would amount to a nice tidy sum of over $20,000. I thought, 'Great, enrolled and a bonus!' That was quickly destroyed when the tribe ruled that my enrollment in 1992 was an error. And they tried to tell me the 'good news, 'We are giving you a new enrollment number and a new date of rolls.' The substantial amount vanished.

Basically they ripped my previous enrollment from my hands and replaced it with a different number so they would not have to pay me back per-capita payments. This was the rude awakening I received about tribal politics, and the 'who knows who' game. There was no fighting it due to the tribal sovereignty. I learned very quickly not to trust tribal council members. I received my first taste of how unfair tribal council members can be, if it is not their own immediate family benefiting from such a ruling. I really do not see how my blood changed from 1992 to 2002. They know what they did to me. I wonder how they sleep at night?

I did contact the BIA after the injustice I received with Grand Portage's enrollment and re-enrollment, but they told me I had to work that out with the Grand Portage tribe.

I traveled to the White Earth Reservation first. My aunt Evie and my dad's children (my half brothers and sister) were going to meet me there in 2003. We had thoughts of trying to enroll me on the White Earths reservation, however my Auntie Elaine really wanted me to enroll with Grand Portage.

When I went to White Earth in Minnesota, I only dealt with the enrollment clerk. When I went to Grand Portage I was with my Aunt Barb, and she knew everyone. I even got to meet my cousin Briand Morrison for the first time. He was standing out in front of the headquarters.

I am learning as I go. Each August when I go home to the reservation, I learn more and more. I always worried about NOT being Native enough, like they would stop the entire powwow and single me out. It must just be fears of rejection and not belonging. Or it could be that I watched *Invasion of the Body Snatchers* too much.

I think the struggle to feel accepted is very real for many adoptees. Feelings of rejection (much like my enrollment process) are very apparent with most of the adoptee's I have become friends with.

I do struggle with NAMES. My birth name was VERONICA ROSE DAHMEN. However the Dahmen family called me by my nickname, which was: CRICKET DAHMEN. When I was adopted, it was changed to Susan Smith. When I got married it changed to Susan Fedorko.

My mom's family still refers to me as CRICKET. When I go home to Grand Portage, during the five-hour drive, I morph into Cricket.

I have always wanted an Indian Name, but do not know how to obtain it. I have not attended a naming ceremony. I would like to attend one someday.

My adoptive parents were in their forties when they adopted me. They are now in their nineties and both are alive. I do not go into details about my reunion or new family, because I have never wanted to hurt them. I have sheltered them from all of my discoveries. Anyone reading this book will know more about me than they have been told. They are elderly and I do not want their last few years clouded any more than it is.

My father (Lloyd) retired from the federal government service in the 1970s. He had a successful career in administration. I am proud of his career and have followed in his footsteps. I have over fifteen years of service myself. I remember him telling me to go apply when I was looking for work and direction.

As far as having white families 'save' children from their tribe, it worked for me. However, I am the rare exception. I can think of maybe two other people who had this work for them. Out of hundreds of Native American adoptees, there are only a few where this worked. It worked in a sense that I was provided a positive upbringing, good health, guidance and education. However I never opened up to my culture until I was found by my birth family. I was not nurtured to be Native. I question myself (again and again) will I fit in? Am I Indian enough?

I did all right in school. I transferred to several schools. I often wonder why that was? I truly believe that I had an attention disorder, being referred to as 'a dreamer.' I applied myself when I wanted to, when I was interested in a subject. I did not care for school and disliked the subjects except for art. I hated science. The hallways always smelled and the idea of dissecting a frog grossed me out. My favorite subject was (and still is) art! I always wondered why I enjoyed it so much, and why I was so good at it. Art runs in my blood. Being the great-niece of George Morrison makes me very proud. I attended the opening of the National American Indian Museum when it opened in 2004. I was blown away by all his work and his accomplishments as an artist. Now I know why I love art so much. Art runs deep in the family gene pool. My mother Cathee was an artist, too, besides her other career accomplishments. Art shadowed in comparison to her career as the first Native American Supermodel.

Yet I do feel like an outsider on my reservation. Especially after the enrollment process, and how they treated me. I will never trust council members and have realized they make their own rules. I truly believe they wished that I had never shown up. I have family that lives on the rez, and will always feel welcome by them. We are all individual feathers and deserve respect. I do not see them giving us the same consideration, except when it comes to voting time.

It's as much my rez as it is any other tribal member. I am respectful and take solace in all that it has to offer. I love the environment there. Grand Portage is such a beautiful part of Minnesota. I have always had a fondness for moose. On my very first visit I was hoping to see one. I was thinking on the drive home, several miles away from the Casino/Lodge, 'I had a great weekend —but NEVER saw one moose.' Shortly before the rez border, I looked up and saw one standing along some rocks. This was such a poignant moment for me, because this moose stood there looking down at my lonely truck. It was almost like it was telling me, 'Good bye Cricket—please come back again soon.' I teared up, convincing myself what it was telling me. I love my reservation. It will forever be in my heart.

I am sure that I am entitled to land on the rez but I might get a different answer if I asked the Tribe. I do receive a per-cap payment one time a year. From what I understand it has been the same amount for the last 10 years, even though the casino continues to make profits. With the I.H.S and health care, I do not understand the I.H.S. subsidy. I have my own health care plan. I am very concerned about my physical health. I found out that my mother died of C.O.P.D. in 1997. Poor lungs run in the family. My father died of cancer in 2001. I sure hope my health holds out. As I was discovering my family's health history, I have been very pro-health with my own. I already struggle with chronic bronchitis, and have the 'Dahmen Cough.' HAD my sister Sarah not contacted me, I would still be wondering about my asthma condition. Why was it NOT going away?? Why do I have chronic bronchitis?? I have very bad asthma and am probably slowly following the same route as my mother.

Now that I know the lungs are a health issue in the Dahmen/Morrison family, I have better prepared myself and conditioned myself to take every precaution available to sustain good health. I also know that my father died of cancer and I will be tested for various types. If you do not have this information, it cripples you. EVERYONE has the right to know what runs in their family gene pool.

I investigated rez housing but you have to live there full time and I am not willing to make Grand Portage my full-time living arrangement. That may change in the future. I am not opposed to living there; it's just that I am already established in the Minneapolis area, and have a lake home in northern Minnesota. Gaming has changed their financial outlook somewhat. It is not a very big casino, and outdated compared to others. They do all right, I am sure.

I met the whole Conklin family back in 2003 on the White Earth reservation. My father Tom Conklin Sr. was enrolled there. White Earth hails a lot of notable Indians. Well, I saw my siblings and thought, 'How is this possible?' The Conklin's are really tall. They all look really REALLY Native. Even in their photos they are dressed in full regalia. I kept thinking, 'This is not possible! Maybe Cathee wasn't truthful with her family telling them that the father of her child was Tom Conklin?' I was raised in such a white world. I did not know how to react to them being SO NATIVE. I questioned myself repeatedly about what I had gotten myself into and would question myself at times, 'Am I Indian enough? Will I be stopped at the front door and questioned?' There are no 'Welcome Home Adoptee' booklets/guides.

I did need my original birth certificate. I do not remember if I received my original birth certificate before or after I attempted enrollment. My Conklin siblings did draw up an affidavit and had it notarized that all three Conklin siblings signed that I am their biological sister. It was not something I needed for enrollment but a very heartfelt gesture. I was blown away at how accepting the Conklin side was.

I have two grown daughters. They have helped a great deal, and are good support for me. They are not too comfortable with me being called 'Cricket' as that is very weird for them. It has been nine years since I am in reunion, and things have gotten much easier. At first it was a little strange to have all these new relatives to talk to, but my daughters are now adjusted and have met several family members. Their comfort zone is a little bigger than what it was the first year. Time heals most things, and it has for this situation. I would like for both of them to embrace their culture. They were raised thinking they were white too, so this is the only way they know. It would help if they could get enrolled, but I tried and was denied. More bull and rules set for only the chosen people.

Looking back, I never enjoyed my birthdays. People just did not understand why. It was never a happy day for me; it reminded me that I was given away because somebody did not want me in their life.

I do trust, but it takes a while to build that trust. And if it is violated, especially when it comes to my own family, that trust is lost forever. That also rings true with other acts, such as overstepping your bounds, or hurting my family. I do not forgive easily and rarely ever let anyone back in my sacred circle.

I do not feel that I have a lot of self-confidence. I struggle with this, and know it is a problem for me. I doubt myself. Perhaps that comes from knowing you were not wanted in some way. I know adoption has taken its toll on me. I think I am stronger than I appear. I am proud of my work ethics and accomplishments. I have worked hard and am dedicated. I have a great deal of self-worth. I sometimes consider myself a perfectionist on the job. As for my self-esteem, that is very low. I often have to pump myself up to get through a speech or presentation. I wish that part of me were different.

I often think of myself as unworthy, and it sometimes gets in my way. I try to work through it, and immediately recognize it is stemming from my adoption. I am rather harsh on myself at times. Adoption is NOT for the weak. If you're weak, it could eat you alive. These are just my own observations, after dealing with a lifetime of rejection. Rejection is very hard to swallow. Adoptee scars are on our hearts.

I have been married for almost twenty-nine years. My children are my world. I am very protective of them. I recall looking at both my daughters when they were eleven months, the same age when I was let go. I could have never let them go in the way I was. Their precious tiny little faces, they had the world ahead of them with so many possibilities. I would have been devastated to have my mother rip apart my life like my grandmother did. So it takes a while for trust to build up.

As far as reunions, I am not close to my half-brother, Cathee's son. I am not sure why. I really wish I was closer to him, but that is just not the case. I was close to my half-brother Tom Conklin Jr. When he divorced years ago, he was upset that I was still talking to his ex-wife. When I met his family, I met them as a whole family. Just because he was divorcing his wife, I did not feel as if I should not talk to her. He made it very clear in a phone call that he did not like me talking to his ex. Tom eventually cut me out of his life as well as his children's lives. I still sent his girls Christmas cards and gift cards since our falling out. We did not speak for at least four years. Then in July 2009, Tom was killed in a tragic car accident. He was gone forever in one afternoon. I never got the opportunity to tell him I was sorry, and he couldn't tell me he was sorry. My brother was Chief of Police in Horton, Kansas for the Kickapoo tribe. He was a very well-known man and respected in their tribal community and in the city of Horton. He was buried with full honors and I attended.

As for my adoptive parents—our relationship has crumbled, and I think that my adoption reunion has a minor part in that, but the other percentage has a great deal to do with something other than my reunion. They are elderly and in their nineties. Both parents are forgetful, and do not recall many things. It's a sad situation for me to be in. They are not the same people I knew three or four years ago.

The only difference for me with having two sets of parents is trying to differentiate them in conversation. I do consider my adoptive parents my parents. And when it comes to my biological parents, I refer to them as birth parents. My birth parents are both deceased, so it's not a problem accepting them. It would have been much harder if they were both alive.

I believe that I live in two worlds. There is the 'Cricket' world. And there is the

'Susan' world. Just like there is home life and work life. I do not like these two worlds to clash, but often they do.

Susie, a member of the Grand Portage Band of Ojibwe, was born June 23, 1962 in St. Paul, Minnesota, and has lived in Minnesota her entire life. She married Tim Fedorko in 1982 and they have two daughters, Samantha, 28 and Sasha, 26. Suzie is the birth-daughter of Cathee Dahmen, the first Native American Supermodel in the 1960-70s. Suzie's birthfather is the late Thomas Leroy Conklin of Horton, Kansas. Her birth-mother died in 1997, less than 36 miles from Suzie's current home. Suzie works in administration for the U.S. Federal Government. Her memoir CRICKET: The Secret Child of a Sixties Supermodel, was published in 2012.

28

Tosh's daughter

Rhonda Serges-Teeple (Bay Mills Ojibwe)

Rhonda's favorite past-time is riding

I guess you have to start somewhere, even though being adopted starts right then and there at your birth.

I really can't blame my natural parents. They were only human. I can't blame the wonderful people that adopted me. I got lucky and had pretty good parents.

But my earliest memories are me wanting to go home, to family, to where I felt safe.

Because of unknown delays, I wasn't given to my adopted parents until I was almost six months old. I obviously was in a foster home. When I was finally adopted, I really didn't want to be there because I'd bonded with them, my foster family.

It wasn't that I didn't have a loving Serges family of parents, uncles, aunts, grandparents, but I didn't feel as if I belonged to them.

It is kind of funny but I never missed my natural mother or thought about her; I missed my father. At that time, there was no reason for it; it was just how I felt. I felt guilty for feeling that way. I also thought I would never disrespect the people who raised me by looking for answers to my existence as an adoptee.

So I never really knew who I was; I just stumbled along trying to make myself fit. I made it work. At age thirty-nine, raising my son alone, I got very ill, and while I was recuperating, I began to wonder about all these unknown medical problems I had, including diabetes. I didn't know where they came from. I knew my adopted parents medical issues and saw how they related to their family history. But their medical history was not mine. So I began my journey, not knowing how it would end.

My first step, since I lived in Michigan, was to contact the Child and Family Service of Michigan. Through them I was able to obtain my non-identifying adoption papers. I got my first surprise when I read them and found out that my father was a Native American; along with the fact that my natural mother had five sons who are my half-brothers.

My next step was to contact the Bureau of Indian Affairs. They told me since my father had passed away, there was no way to prove genetics, so 'sorry.' I did get the information as to what tribe before we hung up. But not his name! My father was a member of the Bay Mills Indian Community in Brimley, Michigan. They are Ojibwe and have always lived on the banks of the St. Mary River.

So how do you prove anything without a name? Well, I wanted to look around on the reservation so I went to Brimley with my adopted mom. I'm glad she went since it was one of our last trips together.

We stopped at this little railroad car museum and I found the book 'The Place of the Pike (Gnoozhekaaning): A History of the Bay Mills Indian Community' by Charles E. Cleland. Well, of course this made me more curious, like who am I related to in my tribe. So I had to pay Child and Family Services of Michigan to get more information.

Since my birthmother had already passed away, they were able to release her name: Gordene Cook. They were also able to get me in touch with my oldest half-brother John. (I'd like to add Child and Family Services will not guarantee results from their search. You pay them regardless.)

I really got quite lucky. On the 4th of July weekend in 2005 I met four of my five brothers: John and his wife Linda, Joe, Tom, and Tim. I also met my nephew John Jr. and his wonderful family. At that time John was able to give me a nickname my father used: Tosh. My brothers were very young when they knew him and were unable to remember much, except my dad was really good to them. They did give me names of relatives who knew my mother and knew about her pregnancy and my birth.

I truly love my brothers and am so glad I am part of their world, too. They knew about me and said they planned to try to find me some day. I just beat them to the punch.

So back to the phone book I went. I found my birthmother Gordene's cousin who had dated my birthfather's brother. She told me what I had been searching for—my dad's name—Clifford Teeple.

Wow, what a feeling that came over me. I felt almost complete.

Being me, I went back up to Bay Mills reservation to search for family. I booked a room at the Bay Mills Resort and Casino. After wandering around for a bit and finding my dad's name on the wall of past officials and leaders, I went into the Back Bay Grille where I started talking to the bartender Laura LeBlanc. It turns out she was my father's neighbor for seventeen years and knew him well. We talked.

Through Laura I was able to contact Corrine Cameron, the head Tribal Judge on the reservation, who is my one aunt's daughter-in-law. She was kind of stand-offish at first but told me to come back to talk to Carrie Kuzmik later in the day. So I did. As I faced Carrie for the first time, I felt her look into me, my soul and my dad Tosh must have been waving at her; she must have felt I was related to her.

I told her my story as I have written here, then she embraced me.

Carrie is my first cousin and her mother is my aunt. Her mother had ten children and five of them were still living on the reservation.

By August 2005 I started meeting my extended Native family and made new friends. For the rest of that year, I made trips to my reservation. I also found out why the family questioned me so intensely. Well, about four years before I found them, a lady went up there claiming to be me! They did a blood test and found out she wasn't related. It was a strange thing to happen. Then I showed up.

Later, during one of my visits, Carrie and I went to the community picnic. They were playing bingo and the winners were allowed to send a prize to any-one of their choice. My Aunt Marie, who I wasn't able to meet prior, sent a barrel of monkeys to me. I knew then I was accepted.

Aunt Marie is the oldest and her acceptance was very important to me.

In April 2006, my uncle Jerry (my dad's brother) and I took a DNA test that proved I was truly a member of their family. I moved up to the reservation in August and worked there for three months until my adopted dad's health forced me to return south to help him.

Now I am enrolled officially in my tribe. Living there I really felt like a part of the community and miss my family on the bank of the St. Mary's river. I can hardly wait to move back. I consider it totally heaven and my true home.

My father had three sisters and three brothers: Marie, Beatrice, Norma, Frank, Lawrence and Gerald. There was also a baby that didn't survive, and Beatrice died at 12 from appendicitis. Lawrence died in 1974 from drowning. Frank passed from a heart attack. My dad Tosh died of complications from diabetes. My Aunt Marie married Harold Cameron and had 10 children. My Aunt Norma (Carrie's mom) married 'Mutt' Jesse and had 10 children. Uncle Jerry married Gloria and they have 5 children. Uncle Frank had 2 children and married Ethel.

What have I found out about me? I found out adoptees have four sides to them. And we can have family and more family. But it is important to really know who you are and where you came from. Genetics are more than how you look; they have a lot to do with how you think and feel, too. My tribal family gets me. We truly understand each other and laugh at the same jokes.

Yes, I am now a complete person who doesn't have to feel guilty about wanting the truth that was hidden from me. I can truly love all of my families. Having found out who I am doesn't interfere with who I have been or how I was raised. It just opens the windows and allows more light in.

EDITOR NOTE from Trace: In my adoptee journey, meeting relatives took several years. I met Rhonda in 2006. For her, in her early 40s, it took her under a year to find her tribe and relatives in Michigan, and she was officially enrolled on March 19, 2007. After a few more legal formalities, on May 20, 2007, she received her official Tribal identification card and paperwork from the Bureau of Indian Affairs. Rhonda said she was born too early (in the 60s) for the new open records law in Michigan to help her. She had only her non-identifying information, a common occurrence for Native adoptees in too many states. It appears adoption advocates believe secrecy protects our birthparents identity. Both of Rhonda's birthparents were deceased. Who would secrecy protect in her case? Receiving her tribal ID card and meeting relatives makes her story so uplifting and inspirational. Rhonda met her relatives and told them she wanted to know about her father. They gave her that and so much more.

29

Congressional Testimony

STATEMENT OF WILLIAM BYLER, EXECUTIVE DIRECTOR, ASSOCIATION OF AMERICAN INDIAN AFFAIRS

Surveys of States with large Indian populations, as you point out, show that about 25 percent of all American Indian children are taken away from their families. In some States this is getting worse. For example, in Minnesota, presently, approximately 1 out of every 8 Indian children is in an adoptive home, but as recently as 1971 and 1972, 1 out of every 4 Indian children born that year was placed into adoption.

The disparity in rates for Indian adoption and non-Indian adoption is truly shocking. I'd like to read some of the statistics. In Minnesota, Indian children are placed in foster care or in adoptive homes at the rate of five times, or 500 percent greater than non-Indian children.

In South Dakota, 40 percent of all adoptions made by the State's department of public welfare since 1968 are of Indian children, yet Indian children make up only 7 percent of the total population.

The number of South Dakota Indian children living in foster homes is per capita nearly 1,600 percent greater than the rate of non-Indians. In the State of Washington, the Indian adoption rate is 19 times, or 1,900 percent greater and the foster care rate is 1,000 percent greater than it is for non-Indian children.

In Wisconsin, the risk of Indian children being separated from their parents is nearly 1,600 percent greater than it is for non-Indian children. Just as Indian children are exposed to these great hazards, their parents are too.

—HEARINGS BEFORE THE SUBCOMMITTEE ON INDIAN AFFAIRS OF THE COMMITTEE ON INTERIOR AND INSULAR AFFAIRS UNITED STATES SENATE NINETY-NINTH CONGRESS SECOND SESSION ON PROBLEMS THAT AMERICAN INDIAN FAMILIES FACE IN RAISING THEIR CHILDREN AND HOW THESE PROBLEMS ARE AFFECTED BY FEDERAL ACTION OR INACTION, APRIL 8 AND 9, 1974

30

Finding the Truth

Martina Marie Bodonie (Navajo)

Martina (Facebook Photo)

I was born January 30, 1969, in Lukachukai on the Navajo reservation in Arizona and was named Martina Marie Bodonie. I was the baby of ten children and stayed with my Navajo family until 15-18 months of age.

My oldest sister Kandee was taking care of another woman's children and asked our family if I could come out and visit with them in California. This is the story told to me after being re-united with Cheryl Brown (now deceased) who brought me from the Navajo reservation to Ridgecrest, California.

The story goes my sister Kandee wanted Cheryl to adopt me, telling her she needed to go to the reservation to get me. Cheryl said adoption had always been a part of the plan, and that it was understood that she would be bringing me out to California for purposes of adoption. That year, 1969, Cheryl's husband was killed in a parachuting accident. My sister Kandee still insisted on her getting me. Cheryl had two boys of her own.

Cheryl told me how my sister Kandee was having break-downs and was very promiscuous; how she didn't want to be an "Indian" anymore, she wanted to be white and that she wanted to save me from it. That she'd become a drug user and prostitute and a porn actress, and that she was causing trouble and was put in psychiatric hospital and was told that she could leave but ONLY back to the reservation.

Cheryl said she will never forget the day she picked me up; she remembers the hogan, the dirt floor, the sheep running around and me sitting on a mattress in a corner. She said there was a man there crying over me (she assumes that was my father). Cheryl said that when we left the reservation, she did not want to look back and knew from that moment on, she did not have the heart to return me. She said she stopped at a rest area to clean me up, that I was dirty and had fleas. She took me to Dr. Pinto, a doctor in Ridgecrest, California, where the reports said I was malnourished and sickly. I do question that.

With no husband to support her and my sister sent back to our reservation, Cheryl felt she had no choice but to put me up for adoption. The word went around that there was this Navajo baby that needed a family. It was even asked of known Navajo families in the Ridgecrest area to adopt me but apparently no one wanted the responsibility (*shrug*) and they questioned why I wasn't returned to my own family on the reservation but no answers were given. The one man that did want to adopt me was Anglo and married to a Navajo woman but she did not feel that she could care for me (she had cancer and was very ill).

This man Mosbie, was previously married to a woman and they had three children, so he asked his ex if she would be interested in adopting me but she had her hands full with five children and one on the way but she knew a couple that might be interested. That couple, Howard and Peggy Mavis, just married and out of high school, met with Cheryl. Cheryl said that Howard was very affectionate towards me and Peggy was very stand-offish. Cheryl said that it seemed that Howard wanted me more than Peggy did.

Cheryl admitted to me she had a strong feeling of hesitation about them but decided this would be "my" family.

My adoptive mom Peggy also thought long and hard about it; she had graduated with a male Navajo and had heard of the conditions on the reservation and had always wanted to help but she couldn't do anything for all those other babies. Now there was something she could do for "this" baby, me.

Growing up I was told that they had been trying for a baby and could not conceive on their own. My adoptive mom Peggy told me that day they brought me home I was her proof of God's Love; I was an answer to a prayer. The adoption proceeded, papers were sent to my biological family. (They received many papers but didn't understand them, so they threw them away).

Cheryl Brown was no longer allowed contact with me. So on top of losing my family, I lost three more important people in my life: Chery, and her sons Rick and Rodney. Because they had not heard anything back from my biological family, I was adopted under the legal terminology of "abandonment."

That is what I was told, that I was abandoned, and that is what I grew up with, burned in my mind. They took lots of pictures but couldn't figure out why I wouldn't smile. I hated my first bath. I screamed the first five months they had me at every bath time. I have many photos of myself as a child not smiling. To this day, I'm very hesitant around water.

I started school but was having dreams of this dark, cold, grey woman chasing me (Peggy?) and she was always trying to get me. I had dreams of these parents deciding that one day they were done with me, leaving me all alone. I tried very hard to convince myself that that woman and that man were NOT those people in my dreams. THESE people wanted me or they wouldn't have "chosen" me. I did grow up being told that I was "Indian," not what tribe though, not yet.

I had many cousins then the day came when Peggy's belly got big. I was about seven years old when ta-da, I had a baby sister. "I" was a big sister and it was my job to teach and protect and be an example for this new little person who would look up to me. Heather and I were VERY close. We shared EVERY thing and when another sibling, Brian, showed up the following year, we even ganged up on him. I don't doubt that we made life miserable for the little guy but we took delight in it but we were mad protective of him. (Later we were always getting into fights to save him).

Things were good on the home front. Peggy and Howard were doing everything they could so that I wouldn't feel "different." Then school started for my siblings. They were excited for everyone to meet their big sis, then questions started for them as to WHY I was different from them. They'd known me all of their lives and NEVER once questioned it.

Come to think about it, neither had I. We were the same; we were family. So the years came and went, yeah I was Indian, but now I had found out that I am "Navajo" Indian but that didn't mean much either. I mean we'd always been given pages of Native Americans to color but not once was I told, "this is a Navajo, this is what YOU are." Later, in elementary school, there was a woman that started a Native club. We got together and made beads and sand paintings and learned songs; we were taken places to be viewed. I even had a well known artist take a picture of me and the teacher to be painted. I saw that picture in my adult years and even told people, "that was me!"

When I was 16, I guess that's when things started to change but more noticeably, the story came that there was another baby in need of a family. We had another baby sister, Alyson, my little dream; another baby like myself who was adopted. For me this would be our connection and bond forever!!

This is when I grew angry at the word "abandonment" on my adoption papers, and had a lot of questions about my own adoption, about me and where I came from.

My adoptive mom Peggy had told me that it was her wish that we both together find my biological family.........when she felt I was ready. I had tried a search on my own but with no support from her. I came close enough to correspond with the nurse that was present at my birth in St. Isabelle's Mission Clinic but she was dealing with cancer and had witnessed a lot of births and couldn't offer me much.

I wrote an angry letter to Father Carron about these "evil" people that abandoned me and he wrote back he understood but I was too young to be coming to such conclusions. I gave up that search.

At this time I was beginning to understand that I was no longer a part of this "family." I married early to get away. I had already lost contact with them, finding myself pregnant and having been raised in the Mormon religion, things were NOT good. Somehow, somewhere, "I" became the "enemy" and was treated as such. I received no "motherly"support with my pregnancy but when my son Joshua arrived, Peggy was like my best friend.

I thought things were different but they weren't. Now I was hearing the begging from my baby sister, who was suffering the same torment I had suffered at the hands of our parents and there was nothing I could do but hug and reassure her that everything would be OK. Peggy couldn't stand to be around me, not for any length of time.

It was around this time that I found Cheryl Brown again and she told me how she regretted allowing the Mavis' to have me. She informed me then that she had always kept an eye on me by sitting on the playground, and she watched me play. She adored me and my babies.

Anyway, my youngest child was around 4-6 months when I got a call from Peggy that she wanted to talk to me and it was this BIG thing. She had information that my Navajo family had contacted a family friend, the same Navajo friend who told Peggy in the beginning that she was stealing me from the Navajo Nation. I don't know how long she had this information but Peggy was very controlling with it.

I finally talked to my sisters Kandee, Rose, Esther and Lisa, and we wrote back and forth. Things were very wobbly for me then. I didn't know WHO to trust. AND to this day I have not learned my Native language. There is a story that my biological mother wants to tell me but she doesn't speak fluent English. So far all I can get is a "I love you, baby."

I learned then that I did not have the same father as my siblings, that I was a "love child." I was even introduced to my father's wife. (LOL)

It was then that I was accepted back into my Navajo family and learned of the anger and disappointment that my family felt towards Kandee, all those years, for "losing" me. The only solace my Navajo mother received was that I was in a better place and to trust that I would come home.

Kandee said there was never a plan for adoption, that she was told to leave and that she could not come back to get me. She tried many times to come to California to find me.

Peggy says that was lie, that they had always known where I was.

Kandee denies what Cheryl Brown told me.

I only know that after all this time, my Navajo family have been there for me and loved me, even after I had left my current husband and started living with my life partner Debbie.

I have known NO pain with this family but still was and am drawn back to the only family "I" knew and remembered.

I have not seen my adopted mother in 12 years.

I have not spoken to her or the rest of the Mormon family for three years now. Only a few knew of my depressions, my suicide attempts, my drinking, my "love" searches, my self-mutilations, and my hatred for myself.

If the "adopted" family could just let go of me like they did, WHAT is there about me that THIS Navajo family sees???? Only that I AM the baby and they did NOT want give me up.

I was torn for a long time, what family? Which family do I belong?? WHERE do I belong.............to date I've been diagnosed with severe depression, post traumatic stress disorder, general anxiety disorder and still fight with panic disorder, taking Paxil and Xanax for the depression and panic.

There is so much more to this.....and I'm left to piece it all together, so it fits for ME, not anyone else because I'm the only one responsible for my ultimate healing and recovery. No one can do it for me.

Martina lives in New Mexico and is friends with Trace on Facebook.

31

Finding His Family

After more than 50 years, man finds his family through a letter to the editor

The Begay family poses with their long lost brother James, second from left, including Tom Begay, left, Susie Begay, second from right, and Frank Begay, right, at their reunion on Aug. 17 in Prescott, Ariz. (Navajo Times photo)

Navajo Times, GALLUP, NEW MEXICO, Aug. 26, 2010

For 56 years James Weems knew he had family on the Navajo Reservation. So he submitted a letter to the editor to the *Navajo Times*, which was published in the Aug. 12 (2010) edition. What came next was unexpected.

"My uncle, Jerry Homer, he lives in Cedar Ridge, was home," said Bernice Curley. "My uncle said he bought the newspaper but he hadn't read it yet. But something was telling him to read the newspaper.

"So he said, 'OK! I'm going to read the entire paper,'" Curley recalled from the discussion with her uncle. "Then he read the part where he saw 'Looking for Family.'"

Immediately telephone calls were exchanged between family members and there wasn't a doubt in their minds that Tom Begay, 74, Frank Begay, 66, and Susie Begay, 60, found their baby brother who was originally named James Begay, now 56.

"He called us and shocked us with the news," Curley said.

They looked at the letter in the newspaper and the information didn't leave any doubt.

"My mom broke down crying," Curley said. "She finally found him."

The parents of James and his siblings were the late Blanche Tallman Begay and the late Hasteen Nez Begay.

James was less than a year old when he was taken from his family and placed into foster care by an Anglo nurse and a lady named Helen Tallman (no relation).

Hiding from the feds

"Back then if you saw a government vehicle children would run and hide from them because they were known to take children from the family," Curley said. "My grandma, James' mom, was sick with tuberculosis and was in a hospital in Tucson and was hospitalized for four years."

James was only an infant and Susie remembers that she and her brothers Frank and Tom once saw a government vehicle approach while they were helping their father in the cornfields in Cedar Ridge, Ariz. They ran to hide.

"They hid in a ditch," Curley said, recalling stories that were told to her. "James was an infant then and was with their father when he was taken."

James was placed with the Weems family in Flagstaff for foster care. In 1962, the Weems family legally adopted him.

While in the hospital, Blanche was given a picture of James taken in Flagstaff showing him wearing a cowboy hat with two toys guns in a belt and holster around his waist.

Around that time, Blanche returned home and she and her husband began searching for their son. One of their drawbacks besides not knowing where to go or start was their inability to speak English.

They did their best to find him. Blanche found out that Helen Tallman, no relation, was married to the owner and operator of Wauneka's Trading Post near Flagstaff.

She tried to see Helen Tallman, a social worker, but was unable to see her.

Blanche and her husband then tried to look for the location where the picture was taken. They asked people if they knew the child in the picture.

Adoption papers

They had no luck and returned home. Blanche got sick again and this time was taken to Colorado for a hospital stay. That was where nurses, who were Navajo, presented her with adoption papers that needed her signature.

"She didn't sign the papers because she wanted her son back," Curley said. "There was a nurse that was Navajo that translated what the paperwork was for. She refused to sign them.

"I guess what happened was that the adoption papers were also sent to my grandpa and maybe because he didn't know how to read or understand, or maybe he was lied to, he signed it," Curley said.

Blanche returned home thinking that because she didn't sign the papers her son would be home as well. That's when she learned the horrible truth that James was given up for adoption.

Blanche took the news hard and blamed her husband for losing her baby.

"(Hasteen Nez) never talked about it," Curley said. "He never said anything about it."

Blanche, with her health problems, resorted to drinking alcohol to ease the pain.

The reunion

On Aug. 17, Frank, Tom and Susie along with their families traveled to Prescott, Ariz., to finally meet James at the VA Medical Center. It was an emotional reunion as brothers and sister closed one chapter in their lives.

"I always knew. I'm home now. I have a family," James said in an interview Aug. 20 with Susie, Bernice and other family in Gallup. James had come home, first to meet relatives in Cedar Ridge and then on to Gallup.

As they spent time together it was a shock when they realized that they all lived so close.

"The residence areas shown in the photo of James has Mount Eldon in the background," Curley said.

When James showed them where he had lived, Susie said that sometime after James was taken the remaining family members moved to Flagstaff.

"My mom said they had lived just down the street from them," Curley said. "They lived in a trailer not too far from where James is standing in the picture."

The news was too much for Susie to think about during the interview and she was overwhelmed with emotion and tears welled in her eyes.

James also recalled spending time at Naanizhoozhi Center in Gallup last year and hitchhiking back to Flagstaff on U.S. Highway 66. He unknowingly passed by the Begay's home in the Western Skies trailer park in west Gallup.

Finding his heritage

But James had known he was different and wanted to know more about his heritage.

"I always felt something missing," he said. "I knew I was different."

"I'm happy and I'm already attached to him," Susie said. "I'm glad that I found him."

"I'm not alone," James said. "I have two brothers and a sister. I'm home."

Without a word more, James and Susie embraced for an emotional hug.

The hugging has not ended and James believes he has more coming with extended family members still to be visited.

In the meantime, the VA hospital is caring for him and providing assistance with employment. He plans to return to the reservation to be with his family and also plans to legally change his name back to James Begay.

He is now learning about his family, his heritage and, above all, his clans.

He is Tahneezahnii (Tangle Clan), born for Tabaaha (Edge Water Clan). His maternal grandparents are Tlizi Lani (Many Goats Clan) and his paternal grandparents are Biih Bitohnii (Deer Springs Clan).

James is a veteran of the U.S. Army and served a year before being honorably discharged.

(Reprinted with permission from the Navajo Times)

32

Weaving a new life

Leland Morrill Kirk (Navajo/Dine)

An amazing resemblance: Leland and his relative
Benaynee. Leland's photo by Mary McNurlen (2011)

My name is Leland Morrill and I am one of ten Native children adopted by a Mormon family under one of the ARENA adoption programs. [ARENA, the Adoption Resource Exchange of North America, began in early 1968 as the successor to the BIA/CWLA Indian Adoption Project.*]

I was adopted on July 15, 1971. I was four years old.

I found out it was my Navajo mother Linda Carolyn Kirk's responsibility to enroll me in the tribe and she should have obtained a census number for me at my birth or within a reasonable time. She didn't... I will never know why because she was killed in a car accident in Albuquerque in September 1968. She was living off the reservation. After she died, I was taken to St. Anthony's orphanage, not affiliated with any tribal nation. My natural father, whoever he is, never claimed me. From the orphanage I was returned to the Navajo Nation, to my mother's relatives. I have been able to piece together that I was abused

173

and neglected by them. When I suffered severe first, second, and third degree burns, and broken bones, I was admitted to Keams Canyon Indian Health Services clinic then transferred to the Gallup Indian Hospital. The BIA intervened and assigned Ms. McCray of Arizona Social Services as my caseworker. She found my Mormon foster parents, Stan and Gwena Morrill, so I was placed with them upon my release from the Gallup Indian Hospital. I was in foster care for twenty-two months then adopted by the Morrill's.

As far as the tribe or lawyers at my adoption proceedings, someone named Andy G. Smith, a DNA Legal Aid advocate, acted as guardian to the estate of Linda Kirk, my mother. She had life insurance since she was working at the Albuquerque Federal Building. DNA People's Legal Services is a nonprofit who provides free legal aid for seven tribes in three states, helping low income people get access to tribal, state and federal justice systems.

I have not read my adoption file. I do not have access to it because I am not yet a member of the Navajo Nation. I applied for membership to the Navajo Nation on March 22, 2011. After that, I'm assuming access will be granted by the Navajo Nation but I am not feeling that is a guarantee.

Being adopted did affect me. I have been weaving together my pre-adoption life up to my adoption, though the tribe has not supplied me or my adoptive parents any credible documentation or explanation concerning my lack of enrollment. I have a theory. By not enrolling me into the tribe in 1968 when my mother died, the Navajo Nation avoided the 'prior approval of the Advisory Committee'... they'd set up these rules in 1960 concerning Navajo children being adopted out. Since the BIA had a role here, they would have advised against enrolling me, possibly, which made me adoptable. Navajo Judge Joe Bennally should have had me enrolled; it was his duty, but he didn't. The Navajo Tribal Council would have never investigated because I was never enrolled in the tribe by my mother or by the judge.

About my childhood: Me and my nine adopted siblings did convert and become Mormons but none of us became missionaries or went on missions. Only one of us, Virginia (Ginny), is a practicing Mormon now. As far as money compensation as foster parents, my parents would have been paid at least $65 per month, per child, before our adoptions and $65 each monthly after the adoption, for a temporary period of time. My sister Virginia, also Navajo, and I were handled under ARENA, funded by the BIA. Our (mixed blood) brother Shaun was adopted as a baby out of a court in Phoenix, not tribal court. The Morrill's moved to Canada the day after Ginny and I were adopted.... effectively removing me, my sister and my brother from any biological family or tribal connection. I have asked myself, 'Why so far...why Canada?' My father says they were transferred. With the LDS Church Education System, doesn't one request a transfer? In Canada, my adoptive parents adopted seven more kids, all Ojibwe siblings. I'm assuming there was ARENA money for them, too.

We did meet other families who adopted Native children. My mother's friends, the Johnson's, adopted Native children, but I am not sure which tribe. They lived in Chinle, Arizona when we did. John Christensen was my mom's boss at LDS Social Services in Rapid City and they also adopted a Native child. My adopted mother eventually worked as a secretary for LDS Social Services, a division which handles Mormon adoptions.

Growing up in a house full of twelve kids, what we did on a typical day as a (Mormon) family would depend on the day and the year. We had specific rituals as a family. We woke up by 6:30 am, read scriptures from the Old/New testament, Book of Mormon, Doctrine and Covenance, rarely from The Pearl of Great Price. We did the children's versions then graduated to The Standard Works.

After scriptures, we had family prayer, went on a fifteen minute walk/run, got ready for breakfast then off to school. As the years progressed, we would rise earlier and go to early morning seminary. My dad was the local ecclesiastical leader and the area coordinator for the LDS Seminary & Institute program for the Mormon Church. I think his title trumps the Bishop and Stake President.

We were encouraged to do extra-curricular activities, like I was in the band, and ran track and field. We'd come home after school and had assigned chores that would rotate; sometimes it was cleaning the bathrooms, sometimes the living room, shovel snow, chop wood, wash the cars...we all rotated without regard to our sex. Of course kids had favorite jobs and sometimes we'd trade each other. Then we'd eat dinner and do homework. By 9-10 p.m., we'd go to sleep.

Later, when I was nine, dad set up the Morrill Family Services, a janitorial company. We kids cleaned buildings like a cytology/histology lab, then a local blood clinic. I did it for seven years until I was sixteen, in addition to having a paper route. Some of my brothers were hired out to do yard work and shovel snow.

On weekends my adopted mom liked to go to garage sales so sometimes we'd all end up at them. Of course we'd clean houses since the Morrill Family Services had jobs on Saturdays. We had a huge garden and all of us were assigned weeding, taking certain areas. I always traded for the strawberry patch because I like them. Every Saturday we'd prepare for Sabbath, cooking, cleaning, setting the table, washing clothes, ironing, things you'd do on a normal day; we always set up for Sunday Sabbath.

Sundays were for church. We'd be up 7 a.m. then get ready for three hours of church. We'd come home, eat, mom and dad would have their alone time and us kids would go outside and play quietly, or take a nap. My sister Sheila liked to tan so sometimes all ten of us would be outside tanning our brown bodies on the deck or the side lawn. We rarely included the other two, Kaelyn and Shelly, who were our parents 'natural' kids.

Today I live in Los Angeles, California. Oddly I felt I was called here. I found out 50 years ago (in 1961) my mother Linda lived here in LA.

My siblings live all across the country: Shaun and Adam live in Salt Lake City; Keith is in Pueblo, Colorado; Sharon is in Springfield, Missouri; Robert is in Tennessee, he just moved; Ginny lives in Magna, Utah; Cindy lives in Madison, Wisconsin; Debbie is in Raleigh, North Carolina; Shelly is in Denver, Colorado; Sheila is in Mount Hope, West Virginia; and Kaelyn is in Draper, Utah.

I was number 8. We counted off 1,2,3,4,5,6,7,8,9,10,11,12, eldest to youngest, when we went anywhere...like the Von Trapp whistles.

I first went to school in Burford in Ontario (Canada), then elementary, junior high and high school in Rapid City, South Dakota, then Salt Lake Community College in Salt Lake City and Brigham Young University in Provo, Utah.

At school, I was fascinated with almost any subject. My problem is the structured class; I can read a whole textbook and take a final exam in three days. Our classes lasted for three months. I can be impatient. I really liked my computer classes in the 1980s when 'Windows' came out, and especially real estate law... in fact I went to a seminar at UCLA School of Law in April 2011. I actually didn't finish college but I studied real estate, statistics, family law and computer science.

My first job out of college was working for AIS, working my way up from data entry to Assistant VP of operations for our Seattle/SLC/Denver offices,

16 to 18 hour days with a great salary, of course. I was a lead researcher for Fidelity Information Systems, only to be replaced by cheaper Phillipines and India work-mills. Previous to that I worked for the Federal Reserve Bank writing training manuals, and I worked as their information security liaison-reconciler. I'm self-employed now, but it's very tough in this economy. I have two businesses, Desert Power LLC, and My New Blinds.

Identity

As far as getting counseling for being adopted, I have not gone for being adopted. Therapy, group sessions, AA, even seminars are all good ways to understand and improve yourself. Actually no one tells you you've been robbed of your identity. But I would recommend therapy, especially for older adoptees who remember their past. I would recommend therapy to deal with dynamics of the parent/child non-biological relationship, how to verbalize, how to ask, tell, state your wants, needs, desires, how to operate as a human being. Non-biological parents don't understand you and you don't understand them; each person should understand this and have tools to communicate.

I did not feel isolated or injured as an adoptee. No. I was taken away from abuse, neglect and malnutrition, from those who injured and traumatized me, a child one to three-years old, long before the age of reason. I think as an adoptee, isolation comes with the new territory. It becomes the new normal for me because there is no biological connection. Sure, I tried to read, do sports, swim, run, bike, hike, etc. Yes, I am still alone. But now I enjoy being alone. I also have chosen my own friends and support group who I can and do call on when we need and want to be around each other.

Some adoptees say they have issues with bonding, low self-esteem, trust and love. Here are my thoughts.

Bonding: I choose who I can bond with and made many platonic friendships easily. My best friend and I have been friends for twenty-six years and talk at least twice a day in addition to texting, emailing and Facebook.

Low self-esteem: I really don't understand that. Perhaps this doesn't apply to me. Yes, I have low moments and recognize them. If I need help getting out of my funk, I have mentors, friends, AA, to bounce things off. By the way, on the AA thing, my older sister Sheila had to go to AA so when I was younger, I went with her for something to do...I still go on occasion... just last weekend I went to an AA meeting.

Trust: I trust my true friends, support group people I choose to love above any-one else.

Love: Intimacy I never learned. We Morrill's never hugged, kissed or any of that until I was in 12th grade. We got therapy to teach us—this coming from a father with a bachelor's degree in psychology.

I found my tribal relatives when I was studying at Brigham Young University (BYU) in 1984; I met Leanne Begay from Ganado, Arizona and she knew several people in my Kirk family. The following summer a friend and I went to Ganado to visit my mother's uncle, John Kirk. He took the place of father when my grandfather abandoned them. I also met John's wife Ruth Shirley Kirk. Both spoke only Navajo so my cousin Calvin Kirk interpreted....it was awkward for me since I only spoke English and French.

I'm still reacquainting with them all. Most relatives went to boarding schools off the rez; some lived in Wisconsin, Oklahoma, New York, Los Angeles, all over. I think culture remains on the rez. Overall they haven't shared that with me. From another perspective, the government's assimilation and boarding schools were successful in hurting culture.

Back in 1985, I went back for a day, and they did kill a sheep; the women cooked and we men ate first. I assumed it was customary. I treated it like a for-mality. I have not attended ceremonies, just the pow wows put on by Brigham Young University's Lamanite Generation. According to the Book of Mormon, a Lamanite is a member of a dark-skinned nation of Indigenous Americans that battled with the light-skinned Nephite nation. I really do not know which tribes were representative of the Lamanite Generation at BYU.

I once had a photo of my birthmother. There was only one photo and I lost it in a move. A box went missing with my memories and that was in the box. I looked stunningly like her. I have my father's crooked smile, if it was him in the picture. I had that picture less than a year, back in 1985. I know statis-tical things about her, where she went to boarding school, her social security number, birthdate and date of death. I know where she died, and approximately where she is buried.

My dad could be Navajo/Dine. Anything is possible. I've heard he's San Felipe Pueblo and San Domingo Pueblo, too.

I was told by relatives I had a brother and his name was Christopher Kirk. He was younger and he died. That's all I know. I never saw a picture so I don't know what he looked like. But strangely I have feelings for him. It's like something is missing. I've grieved for him. WHY? I haven't a clue.

As far as my future, I haven't thought about living on my rez, not really. I might if I could design programs that would help my nation, such as writing and research, something useful. Oddly I could do everything I'm doing now on my rez.

Thinking about taking back my name, actually I've kidded over the years, Kirk is easier than Morrill. After all those 'Moral jokes,' I'd rather be Captain Kirk.

My relationship with my adoptive parents who live in Draper, Utah, comes and goes. It's not the same as a biological connection. It takes work and maintenance over and above what Kaelyn and Shelly take for granted being their biological kids. I talk, facebook, text every sibling except my one sister Debbie.

As far as being adopted, we didn't discuss it at all. We were kept busy at all times. We just never brought it up; it was never talked about.

I understood some Indians at church were foster children and went home to their parents. I stayed with Stan and Gwena. At ten and eleven-years-old, I truly understood.

I didn't hear derogatory terms about Indians from my parents. From others, yes. We grew up in all white neighborhoods, went to all white schools. I just dealt with it. I had good friends who took care of me. I found this out at my ten year high school class reunion.

As far as learning about language, my relatives haven't taught me much. Many of the Kirks speak English. I've been learning some words on YouTube… some white friends are now greeting me with Ya at ahee, which makes us all laugh.

I was closer to some siblings more than the others. We have two sides to our family, the American side and the Canadian side. The seven Canadians are all from one family. They all have their own way of communicating. The Americans: Kaelyn, Shelly (the Morrill natural kids), Ginny, me and Shaun all hang out together more. Shaun and I run My New Blinds business together. We are the tricksters, the jokers and tend to keep the family lively. He just broke into mom's Facebook account and sent out some hilarious commentary. Ginny and

I are like twins. We read each other and know what the other thinks. We were adopted together on July 15, 1971.

I'd say I am the 'peacemaker' in our family. I can speak to anyone, and I do. I can be the most candid and talk about what most would prefer not to, with ease. I bring out why certain people in our family don't talk to others.

There wasn't abuse in our family. With the Morrill's, it was just old fashioned punishment with a belt or a switch; with them there was no sparing the rod. But we're all alive and we've all dealt with what we considered abusive. There was no sexual abuse, but we did run away… constantly.

With the Kirks, I was malnourished and weighed (at most) 30 pounds when I became a foster child. Those severe burns, I have the skin grafts to prove it; I had two broken arms. My right eye still gets tired easily… something that was wrong before my adoption.

All of my siblings have found their tribes and relatives now. I was the last one. My search was the hardest because I was an orphan and undocumented.

Lately I have been dealing with documentation issues. I had my wallet and identification stolen riding a bus here in LA. The California Department of Motor Vehicles (DMV) said I needed a state-issued birth certificate because of the new Real ID Act of 2005; it's a post-9-11 act. I still had my old Utah driver's license so in May 2010, I went to the Utah DMV and received a temporary driver's license using my adoption papers, social security card, and my Mormon baptismal record. For any new driver's license, you'll need an original birth certificate. I didn't have that. Not many adoptees do. I found out states will only issue a temporary driver's license or temporary identification card. The temporary was good for a period of one year.

Hopefully my Facebook page, *Adopted Native American Citizenship Affected by The REAL ID Act of 2005,* will help. In early 2010, I e-mailed Representative F. James Sensenbrenner (R-WI) to explain how 'H.R. 419 The Real ID ACT of 2005' is affecting me and how it could affect other Native adoptees. When we apply for an identification card or driver's license, we will no longer qualify. Rep. Sensenbrenner's office did not reply. Once a temporary license expires, Native American adoptees, me included, become undocumented, thus illegal with no papers.

After 22 years, I now have a copy of the State of Arizona 'Certificate of No

Birth,' issued on December 21, 2010. I did continuous research beginning September 7, 1989. With the help of close friends, family, people willing to help, using my own financing and tens of thousands of dollars later, I had my State of Arizona 'Certificate of No Birth' and a second six-month temporary driver's license expiring July 13, 2011. Then my United States of America citizenship would expire.

In 2011, I met Chai Feldblum, the U.S. Equal Employment Opportunity Commissioner, to discuss the Real ID Act of 2005. We discussed how it affects Native Americans who are adopted out of their respective tribes without a birth certificate, Census number, or Certificate of Indian Blood. When the Final Decree of Adoption does not state our biological parent name(s), birth date, birth place, or census number, it's separating the adoptee from their birthright and now it affects our employment, creating a sub-class of unemployable *former* US Citizens who now are forced to find their way back to their respective tribal heritage.

With over twenty years of advocating for adoptees, I am now in process of writing an Amendment to The Real ID Act of 2005 with Ms. Feldblum. She will present it to the author of The Real ID Act, Jim Sensenbrenner (R-Wisconsin).

On May 14, 2011, my California state-issued Identification (plastic) card came in the mail.

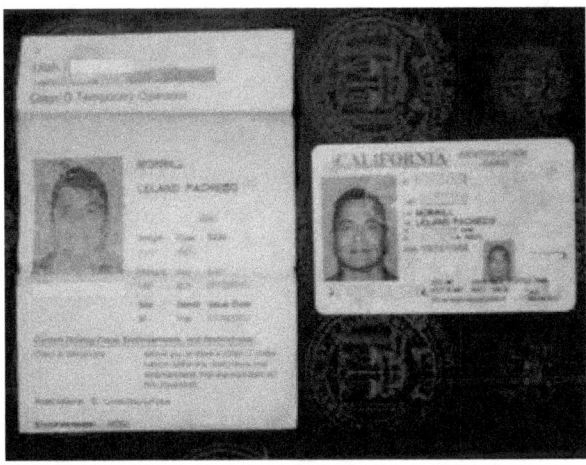

Left: my **paper** State-issued Identification. Glad I don't have to carry that anymore because no one accepts that for ID then I have to continually explain it is State-issued Identification. Right: my **plastic** State-issued Identification card. Finally! A sense of completion and accomplishment. The ability to be part of reality returned. Every time I look at that card I understand freedom in a different way.

*see Indian Placement Program for more about ARENA

Leland is currently working in Los Angles as an actor. Leland continues his journey and writes about his reunion with his father in this book series.

33

Congressional Testimony

STATEMENT OF WILLIAM BYLER, EXECUTIVE DIRECTOR, ASSOCIATION OF AMERICAN INDIAN AFFAIRS

Mr. BYLER: Few Indian parents, few Indian children are represented by counsel in custody cases. Removal of these children is so often the most casual kind of operation, with the Indian parents often not having any idea of what kind of legal recourse or administrative recourse is available to them.

The employment of voluntary waivers by many social workers means that many child welfare cases do not go through any kind of a judicatory process at all. The Indian person has to come to a welfare agency for help; that welfare agency is in the position to coerce that family into surrendering the children through a voluntary waiver.

The Indian family is also placed in jeopardy by the fact of going to a welfare department for help, just to get enough money to live on and money that they're entitled to under law. This exposes that family to the investigations of the welfare worker to see how that family conducts itself; and, welfare departments originate most of the complaints against Indian families and exercise a kind of police power. We think this is an inappropriate way of administering the laws.

There are certain economic incentives for removing Indian children. Agencies that are established to place Indian children have a vested interest in finding Indian children to place. It's interesting to note that in many cases, the rate of non-Indian people applying for Indian children for foster care, or especially adoptive care, raises dramatically when there is an Indian claims settlement.

It has been alleged by some tribal leaders that, especially in rural

183

communities where non-Indian farm families may have a difficult time in making ends meet, some foster parents have an economic incentive, make a net gain by bringing Indian children into the family and using the foster care payments for general family support, and also have extra hands to help around the farm.

On Training in Indian Values

Senator ABOUREZK: Are there any States in which the State welfare workers are given training in Indian values or Indian culture?

Mr. BYLER: I don't know that they are given training in Indian values, Indian culture. I don't know of any that are. We can't believe that it is generally effective if it is given, because of the figures we see. There are Indian communities, or tribes or individual BIA social workers who do a fantastic job. There's one community, an Apache community, in New Mexico that had a large number of Indian children out of the reservation. A BIA welfare worker was appointed and those children were brought back in, those that had not been placed for adoption, and few children there are placed off the reservation today. But then, there was a strong tribal input, a compassionate and concerned BIA welfare worker, and when you have that kind of combination, it works.

Senator ABOUREZK: Would you recommend that as one alternative, that the BIA, or some other agency, supervise a program that would, at least, make social workers aware that perhaps Indian people do have different standards and different values of their own?

Mr. BYLER: Yes. I would say, to train the welfare worker, to train the judges and to provide education for attorneys working in the community. More importantly, if, for example, under title I of S. 1017, Indian tribes contract for and operate the whole child welfare apparatus themselves, if they have tribal welfare committees that function to determine whether or not a child should even be recommended for removal and then tribal court passes on this or some tribal agency passes on this question, that's the answer.

A part of the answer is not to orient non-Indian social workers, although that can be helpful and necessary, but to have far more Indian social workers.

Senator ABOUREZK: Did I understand you to say during your testimony that as far as reasons for removal of Indian children from the families are concerned, that alcohol problems in a family was given in only 1 percent of the removal?

Mr. BYLER: Physical abuse, the beating of a child, child battering, was cited in one percent of the cases. All the others were based upon somebody judging Indian behavior or the environment in the home. For example, there is often the case that a welfare worker will see a father, let's say, or a mother every weekend going to the local bar, and maybe spending the night in jail for public intoxication. That is assumed to be grounds for removal, but there is never any need for proof, professionally demonstrated, that that mother or father's behavior is actually damaging the child. In fact, it could be argued in some cases that because the parent has enough problems in life and has found no better outlet for them, or for resolving the problems, getting drunk Friday night may be the best thing that can happen to him or his kids.

Another kind of thing that can be advanced for taking children away from their families is immoral conduct, and yet there's never any evidence to demonstrate in this case or that case that the behavior of the parent is damaging that child. Immoral conduct is often judged by the wildest stretches of the imagination. For example, on one reservation more than 50 percent of the people live in common-law situations. These unions have lasted 5, 10, 15 years. The people don't have enough money to afford divorces and they want a family life, so they live with a person for 5, 10, 15 years. Police will sometimes, then, make a sweep of a whole reservation and arrest the people that are living in illicit cohabitation. People living in illicit cohabitation are subject to having their kids taken away from them.

Senator ABOUREZK: I wonder if this may not be a question better reserved for some of the professional psychologists that we have coming up, but I will ask you. You don't have to answer it if you cannot. If you know, what is the effect on the Indian family of this kind of removal?

Mr. BYLER: I think they will, in fact, give documentation on that, but what we have observed is that by taking the child away from the parents, you remove the main incentive for those parents to fight to try to overcome the difficult circumstances they have. Taking children away does not cure alcoholism. It may aggravate alcoholism. Taking children away does not encourage somebody to take a job, but discourages him. He may see no point in having a job.

—HEARINGS BEFORE THE SUBCOMMITTEE ON INDIAN AFFAIRS OF THE COMMITTEE ON INTERIOR AND INSU-LAR AFFAIRS UNITED STATES SENATE NINETY-NINTH CONGRESS SECOND SESSION ON PROBLEMS THAT AMERICAN INDIAN FAMILIES FACE IN RAISING THEIR CHILDREN AND HOW THESE PROBLEMS ARE AFFECTED BY FEDERAL ACTION OR INACTION, APRIL 8 AND 9, 1974

34

Two Worlds – Johnathan Brooks' Story

Johnathan Brooks

"The aim of life is self-development. To realise one's nature perfectly – that is what each of us is here for." ~ Oscar Wilde

It has become popular in counselling for clients to be encouraged to write their story and to come to recognize how detrimental experiences can be used as opportunities for living life to the full. In a sense this could be called allowing oneself to move into new situations, places or environments where this can happen. This is my story, an artwork.

How I found out

I was six years old when I found out that I was adopted. I was watching an old black/white western film at our family home in Victoria, London. I was kneeling on the carpeted floor only a few feet away from the TV screen. The film scene was a typical stage coach fight, with the Indians as always depicted as the baddies, attacking the coach on horseback with rifles and yelps of war cries.

Caught in the high energy of the battle scene, with two fingers pointed at the TV and with my make believe handgun, I began shooting, "Bang...Bang." At that point my mother walked into the downstairs TV living room. I had always noticed that she never liked me pointing guns and shooting things, but today I was in the mood to test those boundaries and continued to shoot away.

But this time was different. There was no telling off, she simply knelt down to my eye level and asked, "Who are you shooting at?"

"The baddies of course," I replied, and continued shooting.

"And who are the baddies?" my mother continued to question.

"The Indians are, of course," I said, looking at her rather oddly as to why she couldn't tell the difference between goodies and baddies.

Her reply was, "You shouldn't shoot Indians, because you're one of them. You were adopted."

That somehow confused me. Not in the way adults might think in terms of identity crises...yet, but in a six year olds mind: If I couldn't shoot the cowboys because they're the goodies and I couldn't shoot the baddies because I was an Indian, who could I shoot?

Nobody... so I never shot at anybody ever again, as far as I can remember.

Adoption Background

Adoption and fostering offers a unique opportunity for adopter and adoptee for personal growth and the healing of the wounds we all carry, and may have to re-experience several times in order to except the wisdom of their lesson and move on. Before we are born our spirit/soul chooses the particular set of circumstances and the environment that will give us the greatest opportunity for growth into self responsible adult instead of remaining a victim.

My adopted mother was born Countess Barbara von Bismarck-Schönhausen, the great granddaughter of the "Iron" Chancellor Otto von Bismarck of Germany. After she had studied art under the tutor of Marc Chagall at a Paris university, she took off to Hollywood, California, not wanting to conform to family expectations by marrying a Diplomat, and she became friends with actor Yul Brynner. There she met her future husband, Steve Brooks who worked for Yul Brynner as his Publicist and ran Yul's production company as General Manager.

While in California, Barbara had noticed the awful poverty levels of the Native Americans and would buy jewelry and traditional costumes (regalia) from their small stalls that were at the sides of the roads, as a way of giving them money. That was her way of helping them. Soon Barbara and Steve married and had a son called Niall in 1960. After the birth, Barbara had been told that she would not be able to have another child.

By now, Barbara wanted to give in a bigger way to the Native Americans and found Father Emmett Hoffmann who ran St. Labre Mission in Montana for the Northern Cheyenne and Crow tribes, and became a donator. She often would sell her paintings at an art gallery then would double the money and send the cheque to Father Emmett. Business was not her strength!

One day in the early part of 1964, Barbara received a letter from Father Emmett asking her if she could do the biggest favour for the Northern Cheyenne's and adopt a baby due in a few months time. Her reply was yes without even consulting her husband Steve. That was just the way she was, generous.

I was born 10th April, 1964 in Oakland, California and adopted ten days afterwards. The actual adoption took place between the two mothers in a hotel lobby in San Francisco, probably over a coffee as one does!

As the years went past, my adopted parents moved to Europe partly because Yul Brynner now lived mainly in France but also for other reasons, like their kid's education. By 1969 we found ourselves based in London, England. My adopted mother wanted to be near her family but not too near! I guess some sea was needed for distance.

Bonding

<u>When</u> we are born we are totally dependent on others, but if we are unable to bond

with a parent or nurturing figure with any degree of closeness, we may find it difficult to become self-reliant and free to create a life of our own.

We may allow the values of others and the culture to dictate the patterns of our lives and try to fit in, or equally restricting, being constantly at war with that culture instead of freeing ourselves to fulfill the reason for incarnation.

I loved my adopted father very much; we never had any real problems together, but somehow my adopted mother became rather distant emotionally and we never really bonded. She used to say that she felt it was because she had not given birth to me and never really knew if I would still be around. My natural mother apparently in the early years, in Barbara's words, was blackmailing her that she would come and take her baby back unless money was given to her. Barbara hadn't told Steve of the blackmailing as she was too scared to tell him, but it stopped when Steve one day answered a call and it was my biological mother asking for more money and he told her "If you want him, come and get him." She was never heard from again.

I learned over the years that you couldn't always trust what my adopted mother would say, either because she would make what she thought into a better story or she wanted to get her own way or her mind had become so *distorted*.

Barbara's sister had died in 1969 and she never really ever got over it. She was extremely close to her sister Vendaline especially since their parents had both died in a car crash when Barbara was just ten years old. Somehow, Vendaline's death had triggered something deep within Barbara and she became depressed and couldn't sleep. Refusing to go to seek help from psychiatrists out of principle, the doctors prescribed her heavy dosages of barbiturates and valium, which was typical at the time, especially with American doctors.

Unfortunately, Barbara became addicted. By age six or seven, I didn't know what was going on, other than being woken up at night with sounds of crashes. Barbara would wake up, not that late at night, feeling hungry, sluggish, and unable to think clearly and no coordination and she would fall down the stairs and not make it to the toilet. She would be out for the count! I would peer down the banister and watch as my father, who was a large man, struggle and try and pull her up the stairs to bed. One day I came down to help him, he looked rather embarrassed about the situation but we cracked into action. This became a nightly routine, and I began to resent her, how could she do this to him.

Her moods during the day were rather downbeat and could snap at really small things and would hit me. This did not help our relationship but she eventually stopped slapping me when she realised that I became of age, where I was bigger and stronger than her.

By age eight, I was sent to Michael Hall, a Steiner school in Sussex, England. My mother had hated boarding school as a child and didn't want me to go through what she went through so I boarded with a family called the Pichlers. They were Austrian/Australian, his English wife together with their son, who was in the same class at school, and four days older than me. This son's name was John to my Johnathan; in a sense we were like dissimilar twins finding each other after a long separation.

However, by this time I had become so inhibited and unable to express or be myself in any way to my adopted mother. I was considered a bit slow and unresponsive. In fact, I still felt lonely, imprisoned and separate from the love of anyone who understood me, and I believe I was re-living a prison-like isolation experience when the Cheyenne's were split into two and vanished from their tribal grounds.

As I was under the age of sixteen and living with another family other than my own, legally I had to be registered with the local council as a foster child in order that a social welfare officer could check up on me periodically on how I was doing. My foster parents took their role seriously and never regarded me as anything but a welcome second son, and frequently said, "How lucky we are to have two such good boys," and they missed me when I was away during the school holidays.

My foster mother regarded the extraordinary world-wide travelling experiences on both our parts that had brought us all together as a sign of a beneficent and supportive universe, pointing to the fulfilment of the cosmic plan for Humanity. To unify everything and return to Source through the magnetism of Love.

It was my foster mother who discovered I was Dyslexic. Dealing with this problem and wound led to me studying acting and later to become a NLP Master Practitioner, giving talks and workshops. Who would have thought that a dyslexic who couldn't express himself clearly would later in life be involved in 'communication'? So a wound became an asset.

At the Pichlers, I was encouraged to keep at my education and learn about my background. Over the years I bought and read many books about the Native

Americans, both about my tribe in particular, Northern Cheyenne, but also other tribes. This was something I kept quiet about when going home for holidays as my adopted mother disliked me talking about my heritage.

Welcome Back

Years passed and in the summer of 1985 when I was twenty-one and had finished with university, Barbara bought me a return ticket to Montana. I was to fly to the St. Labre Mission and stay with Father Emmett on the Northern Cheyenne reservation. I was gob smacked! She never wanted to talk about it and then bought me an open return ticket!

There was one condition, though. I was not to tell anyone that I was Northern Cheyenne and adopted because, as her story goes, that after my birth, my biological mother had to go back to the family and say it was a 'stillborn' child. So it was all very hush hush!

When I arrived, Father Emmett gave me a volunteering job as a Relief House Parent at St. Labre Home for underprivileged children. These were children that the courts had ordered that they stay at St. Labre Home on the Catholic Mission. These children came from really disturbed families. So poor that the children lived in old rusty cars or had witnessed their father shoot their mother, some horrific stories.

I kept my word and secret for awhile but as time went by, it became clear to me that I was looking just like them. I thought to myself, if I hadn't of been adopted, then this would have been a place where I could have ended up.

I made friends with one of the older boys in my care called Rudy, and told him my little secret. He simply replied, "Of course you are, you can see it." I realised it was no real big deal. But I did make sure that I didn't say anything to Father Emmett in case word got back to Barbara. Otherwise, all hell would have broken loose when I got back.

I certainly felt more at ease with myself that I wasn't living a lie while working there. Now that it was kind of in the open, I decided I wanted to know who my biological parents were. I managed to get a date set to go to the Northern Cheyenne Tribal Court. I represented myself and told the Judge Judith Spang why I wanted to know who my biological parents were. She listened and then with her hammer banged it on the bench and ordered that the Bureau of Vital

Statistics in Helena, Montana, open their file on me. Little did I know at the time, but a few years later Judge Spang turned out to be my aunt.

Boy was I pleased that I had won a court case single handed with no preparation. However, this was a bit like clutching straws as I knew I was actually born in California. The Northern Cheyenne court only had power within the state of Montana. I had nothing to lose, and it gave me hope that by some miracle something might be there and it was a start of my quest. That made me feel good. It wasn't too long before I heard that the Bureau had found no records of me. Avenue closed.

I had made some good friends during this trip. One was called Joe Fox Sr. who used to cut the grass on the Mission but was also the Keeper of the Elk Horn Scrapper Society of the Northern Cheyenne, a very spiritual society. He was a man of few words but when he did speak you listened to everything he had to say, with respect. He had been awarded two Bronze stars with the United States army. I knew it was something to do with a knife and killing people in trenches. I asked him about the Korean War and he simply thought for awhile and replied that he wasn't proud of his past and that if he could relive his life again, he would be a priest.

Every Sunday morning he would go to church on the Mission and late afternoon on the same day would invite me to a Sweat at his home. There I learned about how to use Sweats to pray. And I loved it. I also became his Sundance 'Helper', twice.

The second family that I became good friends with was Jimmy and Juanita Little Coyote and their beautiful daughter Dewanda who I would hang around with a lot of the time. Jimmy was a Chief and made feathered head bonnets; they worked in the Mission museum selling their silver and turquoise jewelry and beadwork like moccasins. I bought many things from them. Dewanda, being eighteen or less, had just graduated from high school and had a white sports car as her graduation present. Lucky girl, but I got to go for rides in it, and we had fun.

September arrived and I knew it was shortly time for me to leave. I had no snow gear if I was to stay longer and more importantly, it was the start of the field hockey season back in England, and so I went back.

That Christmas was the worst family Christmas. By now, both Barbara and Steve were physically very ill. Barbara had cancer of the colon and not much left after numerous operations. And Steve had leukemia about thirteen years and was now seventy-one years of age and had two chemotherapy treatments. It was normal in our family that we celebrated on Christmas Eve around 5pm. We would dress smart, Christmas music was played and Steve would read the same passage from the same bible every year.

But this was very different. Every time Steve tried to read aloud, the words came out jumbled up. On hearing his own voice he would stop and start again, and still the words came out mumbo jumbo. This was a man who made a living from reading scripts and who had an intelligent sharp mind.

My brother and I looked at our mother who looked at us and shook her head not to say anything and she tried to act all jovial as if nothing had happened and handed a present for Steve to open. Niall took off downstairs to his room and I knew, we all did, that Steve didn't have long to live; clearly his body and mind were completely stressed out.

After Christmas I went back to Sussex to the Pichlers and looked for work. I had tried a few universities to do social work after the impact of working at St. Labre Home. I didn't get in to any and even had one head of social studies tell me that he thought that I would change my mind again. So I began looking for work while I figured out my next step in life.

March arrived and one evening had a phone call from my brother. He never rang me, and I could tell by his low voice that he had bad news and it had to be about Steve. It was. He had died at the Royal Free Hospital at Hampstead during a routine check up. They wanted him to stay for a few days and while there had picked up an infection, had no white cells to fight the infection, had a heart attack and died.

I visited Barbara every weekend afterwards and we spoke a lot about things. There were only us. Niall was living on an old sinking wooden ship moored on the Thames. We became closer and closer and I would take her to Steve's grave where she had covered it in colourful flowers, typical of her style. She told me that she had bought the plot next to him for herself. There was a wooden bench opposite Steve's grave and she would arrange the flowers and sit on the bench for an hour and just stare at them.

Our relationship was getting stronger that I even thought of moving up to London and living at home for awhile, just making sure that she was OK. As a kid I used to think that if Steve ever died first, that she would die shortly afterwards, since he was the backbone of the family. She had her religion and that seemed to be giving her strength she needed.

By July I had found a job as a van driver for a retail chain, thinking that it might lead to their trainee management scheme; after all I had passed my Business and Finance Diploma. It meant occasionally working on Saturdays if there were lots of deliveries to be made. By the time I had finished work one Friday, my foster mother, Gill Pichler, told me that Barbara had rang and said that I wasn't to come tomorrow as she didn't feel well and then hung up abruptly as though in pain. That was just as well I thought and I would call tomorrow to see if it was worth me visiting at all. The abdominal pain was nothing unusual for Barbara; it happened with regular occurrence.

I went to work the next day, loaded all the deliveries to be made and set about my business, occasionally popping into the shop to drop off and pick up more 'white' goods when my manager said that a man had called for me, and would I call home immediately, which I did.

A strange man's voice answered my home phone, "Who are you?" I said a bit shocked. "The coroner," was the reply.

I sat down on the office desk and listened to the questions the coroner had to ask me. On finishing his set of questions, he made the suggestion that I come home as soon as possible as there were strangers walking around the house. On hanging up the phone, my manager asked if everything was ok, and I broke down in tears as I told him that my mother had just died. One of the other members of staff drove me back to the Pichlers where I changed and tried to concentrate as I drove carefully back to London. My mind was a bit spacey by then.

It took about a year, sorting out my parents things. Niall continued to live on a houseboat struggling to be a recognised writer and I decided, as it was the summer again (in 1987) and August, I knew it was the best month to go to Montana as it was Pow-Wow season. I loved to watch the traditional dances and admire those beautiful Native American girls in their gear. Occasionally, I would dress and dance as well.

This time when I stayed at the friary with Father Emmett, I felt that whatever agreement that I had with Barbara was now void. It was my life and I wanted to meet my biological parents.

The US laws had changed regarding House Parents; now you had to be a married couple, which meant that I was out of the question. I decided to help Jimmy and Juanita Little Coyote in the museum. As I knew a bit of history and spoke the Queen's English, I became a bit of a novelty around the offices and with the tourists.

Determined to find my natural parents, I spoke to Father Emmett, and asked him straight, "Did he know who my natural mother was?" Unfortunately, he told me that he couldn't remember her name but did remember her as the most beautiful Native American woman that he had ever met. I didn't push him further. Another avenue closed.

The friary had a new full time cleaner called Ruby Braine and as I saw and spoke to her every day, I opened up and told her about my adoption. On hearing me, she looked at me. I could see by her eyes and the way she slightly tilted her head up, the gaze of someone accessing their memories, and then said that she knew of a young mother back then who had had a baby boy adopted out, and that she would contact the mother. This seemed like a real long shot but a day later, Ruby said that I was to have my birth certificate at hand and wait by the phone at 9pm, and that I would get a call from Rosalia, a potential mother.

By now I had learned that adopted children receive new birth certificates with the new parent's names and a new baby name on them. But the rest of the information was the same.

On the stroke of 9pm the phone rang and I answered it. A kind woman's voice on the other end started to ask questions about my birth certificate. I answered all the questions including a description of myself. At the end, Rosalia apologized that she wasn't my mother but wished she was. The doctor's signature was wrong, the hospital where I was born was wrong, the time of birth was wrong and the description of me was wrong. It was yet again another avenue closed. However, she then added that she knew who my real mother was, and went on to explain how she knew.

There had been two other pregnant women who all had babies around the same time as each other and she knew which hospitals, which day and time each gave birth to their baby and therefore knew who my biological mother was. She clearly had never forgotten. This sounded really promising for the first time which led to me asking a question. What was her name?

She decided not to tell me the name but would contact the biological father's sisters as she had not seen my biological mother since my birth. It would appear that my mother had made a new life for herself outside the reservation as far away as she could.

I was happy for myself on this new lead but I could hear in Rosalia's voice sadness as she said goodbye. She added that she hoped one day her adopted out son would search and find her as well.

A couple of days later, Ruby clearly still wanting to help me, allowed her house to be used as a meeting point, as she lived across the road from the friary. I was to meet two aunts, Nathel and Rosalia Fisher on my biological father's side; Rosalia was the same woman that I had spoken to on the phone just a few days ago, who had given birth to a baby boy the same week that I was born. She happened to also be one of my aunt's as well. Both Nathel and Rosalia knew me as a baby and had helped take care of me as a newborn for the first three months of my life until my adoption. It became clear that Barbara's version of me being adopted after ten days couldn't possibly be true.

I was to go there after lunch which I did. I walked across the road and knocked on the front door. I open it and walked in. Sitting on the couch were my two potential aunts, who simply stared at me for awhile then seemed to simultaneously look at each other and nod that I was that baby all those years ago. I wondered briefly how they could possible know. I had changed surely. This thought was interrupted as one aunt muttered, "That's Troy," to the other.

Troy I thought, I knew that name, a name that I had not told anyone on the reservation or in England. I had simply forgotten it.

When I was younger, during the school holidays, I'd go swimming at the Holiday Inn swimming pool in Swiss Cottage, London. It wasn't far from where my adopted parents lived in Hampstead. My adopted father would swim most days as a way of keeping his flexibility. On one occasion while we were in the pool, I asked my adopted father if he knew what my Indian name was. He said with a vague look that he thought it was Troy Fisher but couldn't be certain. I had never told anyone as my adopted father wasn't certain himself.

It was a short visit and the aunts got up to go and still perhaps still not completely certain then turned as they were leaving and Nathel asked me, "Do you know your name that you were given?"

"Troy," I replied.

"You're my nephew," Nathel said with certainty.

I knew then that I had found my roots and my family.

I asked who my mother and father were, and they too said that neither of them had seen my mother since my adoption. But her name was Betty Bahr and she had a brother, Lester Bahr, who worked here as the maintenance man at the Mission, and that my father was called Eugene Fisher but he didn't live on the Northern Cheyenne reservation.

They explained that another sister of Eugene's called Juanita (Nita) Fisher had also helped Betty with me and that she was the third mother, and had a baby girl called Vickie Lynn. I was later to find out that my middle name was also Lynn after her. The sisters had flocked around Betty as I was the first born of their only brother. Betty had kept it quiet of her intention to have me adopted, I was there one day and then gone the next which caused an upset amongst the sisters as Nita would have adopted me. Somehow, with my presence, that old wound could now be healed. Troy had been found.

The aunts said that they had to leave and drive back to Billings, a good two hour drive, so after my goodbyes to them, I set off back to the Mission to find my uncle Lester. I was told he was digging a trench repairing a large pipe in the grounds somewhere. I found him in a trench and said, "Lester?

He was wearing an old scruffy baseball cap, and looked up at me and said, "Yeah."

"I've got something to tell you." I said it as if I had a big surprise.

Lester's eyes opened wide as they could and he tipped up the tip of his cap to have an unobstructed detailed look at me, and said again, "Yeah?"

"Well, you're my uncle!" I replied.

At which point he leapt out of the trench, now with a look of disbelief, and stared at my big earlobes, relaxed and then flicked them with his finger and said, "You got the Bahr earlobes alright......I knew this day would come."

After a quick conversation about the physical traits of the Bahr earlobes, we agreed to meet after work at one of three Ashland bars on the edge of the Northern Cheyenne reservation for beers. There was much to talk about.

After dinner, I made my way to the Ashland bar as we agreed, walking distance from the friary. This was Lester's usual watering hole most nights. He was there dressed with blue jeans, white t-shirt and the same baseball cap; he was tall, and thin. He was sitting there with a couple of his half-sisters, more aunts of mine.

We stayed there most of the night chatting away and they too had not seen my mother Betty. Lester did say that he had a phone number for her and in time would call her. My only concern was, how old was that phone number and would she contactable at that number? Lester was never one for ringing, writing or any form of communication. He spoke about their earlier life on the Northern Cheyenne reservation and clearly there was emotional pain and resentment of his and Betty's childhood. A picture of their background was beginning to form in my mind, a harsh life living on a reservation. Who could blame Betty for not wanting to get off the reservation?

Lester and I and those aunts became good friends for the rest of the trip and in subsequent visits I made to the US.

September arrived, and again it was time for me to make my way back to England and it wasn't long, while at the Pichler's, I got a phone call one evening. True to his word Lester had called his sister and told her all about me and had given her my England phone number.

I had done it; I had found my natural mother against the odds. But not only had I found her but we got on really well. She continued to keep in contact with me calling sometimes once every two weeks, and I loved getting the calls.

I wasn't to meet her until 1989, even though I had been to Ashland the previous summer as well. I couldn't get enough of it.

From my adopted father Steve's first marriage, I had a half-brother and half-sister who both lived in California, near LA. By this stage of my life I was interested in getting into the film business and had contacted my half-brother Steve Jr. who worked in the business driving the trucks and running the generator to power the film sets. His advice to me was to arrive around March, when the film industry season would pick up and there would be much more work around.

So I did. I flew to LA and stayed with my half-sister Tammy who was married to Mark Cutler, and they had a wonderful house in San Fernando Valley. First thing, I took the California driver's license exam and passed first time. I also brought my modeling portfolio and photos; I had been asked in England to do some modelling. I brought it in case I might have a lucky break and looked into modeling in LA. Models were a dime a dozen there and I soon lost interest pursuing it.

Steve Jr. told me about a company called Cinelease in Burbank. They specialised in lighting and grip rental equipment and needed a driver to supply the various film sets. I went for it.

I arrived at the interview on time. The warehouse manager, who would be my boss, on noticing my English accent, asked me in the interview if I had a driving license. I did and showed him and then he asked how I would find myself around the big city and surrounding deserts. Having never been to LA before could have been a problem. I simply quickly replied, "Well, I got here for the interview on time, didn't I? And I know how to read your city map." He looked at me, smiled and agreed that I had done just that, and he gave me the job.

It was hard work lifting heavy cables, boxes and lights, and delivering them in the very hot California temperatures but I had every weekend off, a rarity in the film business and I got to drive around to various-sized film sets. I nearly reversed my large van into Telly Salavas wearing a white robe as he made his way to his caravan on the film set of *The Hollywood Detective* (it was a kind of Kojak but without the lollipop.)

Around mid-July, I knew that I would want to head to Montana by August. I had Betty's home phone number and called her and explained that this was the nearest I'd probably ever get to Albuquerque, New Mexico where she lived, and I proposed the opportunity of meeting. She agreed. I handed in my notice to Cinelease. They were sad to see me go and told me to look them up if I ever wanted work again.

On the plane to Albuquerque, I suddenly realised that despite knowing the sound of Betty's voice very well, I had no idea what she looked like. I had not said what I'd be wearing to identify myself. Albuquerque would be full of Hispanic and Native Americans.

After collecting my bag from the collection point, I walked and stood in the middle of the airport and systematically scanned left to right looking for a mid-forties looking Native woman. As I scanned to my right, in the distance I saw a woman looking at me. I walked over to her and said, "Betty?"

She nodded, "Yes," and we hugged each other politely and walked towards her blue small pickup truck that was parked just outside the airport entrance. I threw my bag in the back of the pickup and sat in the passenger seat. We looked at each other and she said, "I've got a two week holiday, where shall we go?"

With nothing really planned, I replied, "Well, I was planning to go to Montana and I'm sure there would be room for you at the Friary in Ashland." She said OK and we started to drive north towards Montana. We took turns driving each day and paying for gasoline and we stayed at cheap motels or with relatives that Betty had not seen for years. One night we stayed with some older relatives that told me that I had five uncles, brothers who were bank robbers in Northern California. In total they robbed five banks until they were caught. This was something that I wasn't use to. From my adopted family background, I was used to uncles who were Diplomats, Politicians or Bankers, in a very different way though. Bank robbers, however, was much more exciting!

On our first day of driving it was all very polite questions that we had for each other but as the days went by, we started to ask more personal and deeper questions. We had a high level of rapport and we clearly really liked each other's company. She was a very quiet sort of person and told me things like she had rattlesnakes in her garden but they never rattled at her when she walked through her garden. But if anyone else did, the snakes would rattle away. I knew then this was evidence of her calming nature that the rattlers never felt her threat and nor did I. This was a nice change. With Barbara I was always anxious if she was in the same room with me and I would often leave if she entered it.

By the third day of travelling, we had run out of the superficial questions and now it was time for the real emotionally charged questions. I wanted to know why I had been adopted.

As a child, sometimes when I went to bed I would cry and wished that I had never been adopted or even born and even wished that I was dead. I would watch one of my favorite TV programs like *Happy Days* and be so jealous that a family could be so happy. It was like a revelation, and why couldn't ours be like that? I had even read in one of my historical Native American books that if one sister had no children and the other sister had say ten children then if she had an eleventh baby she would give it to her sister with none. And the baby was brought up with two mothers. So why didn't that happen to me? Was I not loved or wanted? This basic core wounding of *rejection* was to become my life script. It affected my relationship with my adopted mother and future girl-friends. But who was rejecting who?

Betty's Story

Betty started to explain her side of the story. She had been twenty-one and Eugene Fisher twenty-four and they were in a relationship and fell pregnant with me. Eugene didn't want to know and left her. As Betty had no money, she didn't feel confident that she could take care of the baby as a single mother and thought that I would do better off if I was adopted out to one of Father Emmett's rich donators. She clearly had done this with a positive intent, with the love of wanting the best for me. She had felt awful doing it and thought about me every day until the day she started a family herself and became too busy, thinking about her immediate family's needs.

I completely understood her, now that I knew it wasn't that I wasn't wanted or loved. I told her it was OK. I then asked her the next question, "did she really blackmail my adopted parents?"

Betty's reacted a bit shocked by the question and initially said no and was con-cerned that I must have grown up hating her if I believed what Barbara had accused her of. No, I actually hadn't. It was more about me. Later, Betty said that some money had been handed over but not by blackmailing. I could see that I wasn't ever going to know the full truth and never asked again and dropped the subject.

Betty, having heard various stories about what my adoptive mother Barbara had done to me, said the way Barbara told me I was adopted made her angry. Betty thought her good intentional adoption plan, despite being based on the fear of coping as a single mother, hadn't in her eyes worked out, not how she had imagined it would. But that's life; that's families for you.

Despite some highly charged emotional questions, we still liked each other very much and loved each other. We were now about twenty-four hours from Montana when Betty asked me, "How would you like to meet Eugene one day?"

I thought about it and said, "Sure, one day."

"We'll be in Montana by tomorrow afternoon; I can call Nita Fisher, his sister and tell her we're coming and we can see him," Betty said adventurously.

"You mean see him as well….when was the last time you saw him?" I said this as I went into overwhelm. Meeting my natural mother for the first time was one thing but to meet the natural father as well, on the same trip, now I was getting a bit nervous but mostly excited!

"Oh, I haven't seen him since I gave birth to you, and I'd like to see what he's up to these days," Betty said curiously. She called Nita at the next service station pit stop.

Nita informed us that Eugene was busy fire fighting somewhere miles away and that she would call him to come on over.

We arrived in Browning, Montana where they lived in the late afternoon. Browning is a town which is the largest community on the Blackfeet Reservation. The reservation is about 1.5 million acres large, situated northwest of Montana; Browning was known as one of the roughest reservation towns around. Eugene had since got married to Anna and they had six children, one of which he had adopted. He had married a Blackfeet woman.

We had pulled into a typical reservation gasoline station, one with only two pumps and it was my turn to pay. I went in to pay, bought cigarettes and the attendant noticed my funny accent. He wanted to hear me speak some more and so I told a bit about my background. It seemed like every Native American I met wanted to know my background. I paid then left. Little did I know actually how small Browning was and how fast gossip flies!

We drove on to Nita's house and on arrival Nita, on greeting us, says to Betty at the top of her loud voice, "Jesus Christ girl….how the hell are ya?" in a regional Montana accent.

Nita was always very fond of me as I was, after all in a way, her lost baby as well. We sat around in Nita's house waiting for Eugene to turn up. Eugene on hearing from Nita that we were coming had got into a fire truck and driven non-stop back to Browning straight to Nita's home, without swinging by his own home first. But he had picked up a male friend of his called Two Bulls.

We sat and drank Budweiser all night. I was used to stronger beer in England; I found that Budweiser didn't really touch the sides but was perfect as a session beer as this was going to be one long session.

At some point during the night Betty and Eugene talked privately; they had much to talk about and no doubt I was part of their discussion. Soon afterwards, Eugene came to talk to me and said, "Never blame Betty, it was my entire fault. You have to understand that I was only twenty-four and I had more women than you could shake a stick at." I had never heard that expression before and chuckled. He continued, "Two years later I regretted leaving her but it was all too late, she had gone." Clearly Betty must have said something to him along the lines that I blamed Betty for adopting me out. I was glad to hear him take his part of the responsibility and understood him as I was about the same age as he was back then.

We continued drinking and taking photos of us all together when about 2am Nita's home phone rang. Everyone stopped chatting and looked at Nita wondering who would call at this time of the night. Nita said that it could only be one person; it had to be Eugene's wife Anna wondering where he was. The room went quiet as Nita answered the phone and we heard her as she denied that Eugene was there. When Nita hung up, she said that Anna had heard rumours that a mother and her son were in town and that Eugene was the father. The question was then, how did she know? Oh no, I thought and told them about the short conversation that I had had at the gas station. It became clear that Eugene had never told Anna about that aspect of his past. A woman thinks she knows her man but actually she doesn't. In reality everyone has secrets.

I knew we were on borrowed time and the overall thought was that Anna wouldn't come around at this time of night so we carried on until around 4am just before sunrise.

As Eugene got up, he knew it was time to get home and face the music. Two Bulls turned to me and asked if I owned a pair of cowboy boots. I didn't, so he took his black boots off and handed them to me to keep. I at first refused them worrying what he would wear instead, but was also aware that it was customary in Native tradition if given a gift you accepted it. Eugene and Two Bulls left the through the front door. I stood in the doorway and watched as they walked through the plains towards distance houses and wondered how far Two Bulls would have to walk in his socks before getting home.

We woke around 9am and had breakfast and Betty and I felt an uneasiness hanging around in Browning. We didn't want to cause any trouble, our visit meant well and we decided that it was best that we left sooner than later. We thanked Nita who understood why we were leaving so soon and got back into our pickup truck to start our last leg of our travels to Ashland.

After a few days at the friary, Betty and I drove to Billings to pick up Lisa, Betty's youngest daughter; I was going to now meet my half-sister. Lisa looked completely different to me; she was blonde, blue eyed and very pretty who clearly took after her father Mac Farley, a non-Native. Betty was a bit worried what Lisa would do as a profession; Lisa then in her late teens was unsure what to do with her life.

What I could see was how different the relationship was between Betty and Lisa and Betty and me. Betty had a typical parental relationship with Lisa and my relationship was different. I was happy with our relationship; we had more of an adult friendship with mutual respect and love.

Betty had now been travelling over her two week break and it was now time for them to make the long drive back to Albuquerque. They packed their bags and it was one of hardest goodbyes to ever say in my life, even though I knew we would stay in contact.

Betty and I embraced each other and she turned and handed the truck keys to Lisa telling her that she could drive, as she put on her sunglasses. It was after all a sunny morning but I could see by Betty's body language that the sunglasses were not for the sun but to hide her tears and she stared at me through the windscreen with a blank facial expression. Betty was feeling the anguish again of a mother letting go, as if it reminded her of the emotional turmoil she went through the day she handed me over for adoption. I knew I had to be strong and keep smiling as a signal to her that it was still OK, otherwise I would have broken down and made the whole thing worse. I swallowed hard my tears internally.

As they drove off, I waved and shut the friary main door and made my way to my bedroom. There I cried as I lay on the bed, and released. It had been a roller coaster of emotions those past few weeks but was able to relax by telling myself that over all, I had more things to be happy about than sad.

If life was a jigsaw puzzle, with each piece representing a part of my life, the missing piece labeled 'history' was now complete.

Johnathan Brooks MAC, PG Dip is an enrolled member of the Northern Cheyenne tribe and resides in Tunbridge Wells, England with his wife and child. He has his own private practice and blog www.spiritbearcoaching.com as a Cognitive Behavioural Coach who has trained in Cognitive Behavioural Therapy (postgrad), Emotional Freedom Technique, Master NLP Neuro Linguistic Programming and has a Post Graduate Diploma in 'Coaching and NLP'. He is writing a book.

35

Drew's Lyrics

Drew RedBear Rutledge

(2012) How did I survive, able to be alive, 'cause I was born to fail, just ridin' the rail of brutality and abuse, there was no excuse for the bullying or anger, just give me the hanger to end the pain, the tears of rain, goin' insane, it is not in vain, for my head is low, the blood don't flow to my heart, can't you see, it isn't meant to be, that I live a good life, cause 'dad' and his wife don't give a shit about me.

Well I did survive, despite your strife, a better man, you are now banned from my uplifted spirit, so hear my lyrics, you failed to cease my living lease, and I will not die 'til I'm ready to say goodbye!

Compounded Feelings...(2017)

She took in vain, my pain, no constrain, a thirty year reign that put a strain -n- sprain on my brain, detained to maintain your profane domain to attain and sustain an insane -n- inane disdain, for your gain was my tears of rain, down tha drain, wasted champagne, I dare not complain or explain my pain, stained bloody chain, your ruthless deign..

And I'm supposed to care? To dare to glare in those eyes of primeval, medieval evil for the retrieval of her heart? Well she can pluck the duck in which she can fuck cause she's outta luck..

Drew, a Lost Bird adoptee, is a poet living in Missouri. He contributed his story in CALLED HOME: The ROADMAP *(Vol. 2)*

Editor Note: We love the word Drew used: DEIGN: to think fit or in accordance with one's dignity; condescend.

36

Indian Placement Program

Trace L. Hentz

There was a reason Indian leaders went to the Senate and demanded an inquiry into the staggering number of children disappearing in Indian Country. It was not just boarding schools creating this mass exodus of children.

Programs like the Adoption Resource Exchange of North America (ARENA), established by the Child Welfare League of America in 1967, funded in part by the Bureau of Indian Affairs, paid states to remove children and place them with non-Indian adoptive families and religious groups like the Mormon and Catholic Churches, happening after the Indian Adoption Project run by the CWLA and BIA. ARENA expanded to include all Canadian and United States adoption agencies and offered them financial assistance. One state New York called theirs "Our Indian Program." Maryland and Connecticut ran a similar program.

As William Byler, executive director of the Association of American Indian Affairs, testified back in 1974, for many tribes, survival was at stake; Congress agreed tribal stability was as important as that of the best interests of the child, which eventually lead to the passage of the Indian Child Welfare Act of 1978. (Read excerpts in this book)

One striking example is The Church of Jesus Christ of Latter-day Saints *Indian Placement Program*. By the 1970s, an estimated 5,000 Indian children were living in Mormon homes in the US and Canada.

Francis R. McKenna wrote in the *Journal of American Indian Education*, "... Christian churches have developed massive programs for adoption of Indian children. Adoption of Indian youth is some 20 times the national average. For Navajos alone, some 2,000 children are spirited away for adoption annually by a single agency, the Mormon Church."

37

Buffy, Mary, Chris, Mark, Star

Native American Adoptees Make their Mark on History

Trace L. Hentz

Buffy

First Nations adoptee Buffy Sainte-Marie, Cree, is asked all the time: Where has she been for, oh, the past 20 years? Her answer: "Canada, mostly. Europe. Japan. My most creative times are when you're not hearing from me. If I'm out on the road, I don't have time to make paintings or write songs," she told James Reed of the *Boston Globe*.

For years she's been educating schoolchildren on Native rights and history through the Cradleboard Teaching Project, a non-profit she founded in the 1990s. In addition to recording and painting canvases on her farm in Hawaii, her digital art has been exhibited worldwide and she's taught university courses on the subject.

Sainte-Marie has not been on the music charts in a long time but in August 2009, she released Running for the Drum, an album with all new material, a rare occurrence since 1992's Coincidence and Likely Stories. Back in the 1960s, her music was made famous by other musicians. Bobby Darin, Cher and Elvis Presley all had hits with love song *Until It's Time for You to Go*, and Donovan is still more associated with *Universal Soldier* than she is.

She turned 70 in 2011. "I haven't changed much," she told the Boston newspaper in 2009. "I was not about folk songs. I was about songwriting, self-expression, and communication with an audience who I thought might be interested in the same thing that was showing up in my head."

211

Since the 1970s, she kept a low profile in the US, after the Johnson and Nixon administration's blacklisted her because of her outspoken politics. Even the CIA kept a watchful eye on her.

Born on a Cree reservation in Qu'Appelle Valley, Saskatchewan and later adopted, she grew up with a family in Massachusetts and spent most summers in Maine. Her adoptive mother was Mi'kmaq. But she obviously has mixed feelings about those years, quietly alluding to 'predators in the neighborhood." After studying education and oriental philosophy at the University of Massachusetts at Amherst, Sainte-Marie followed her aspirations to New York's Greenwich Village where a scruffy young Bob Dylan suggested places for her to play. Sainte-Marie was more visionary and pioneering than anyone realized at the time of her first recordings for Vanguard Records. She dabbled in folk, rock, country, electronic music, film composing (she won an Academy Award for co-writing *Up Where We Belong*), and originated what she calls 'powwow rock' in the mid-'70s, according to the Boston newspaper.

Her very first album she was voted Billboard's Best New Artist. She made seventeen albums of her music, three of her own television specials, spent five years on *Sesame Street,* scored movies, helped to found Canada's 'Music of Aboriginal Canada' JUNO category, raised a son, and earned a Ph.D. in Fine Arts. Whew! She's had more than nine lives—from troubadour and rocker to activist and artist and academic. Buffy invented the role of Native American international activist pop star.

"The new album *Running for the Drum* has dance-floor-ready tribal beats with steely songs about corporate greed (an incendiary No No Keshagesh) and lost love (the spook-jazz rendering of When I Had You)," one newspaper writer said.

She told the *Boston Globe,* "If I'd had [major] success, if I had had a Madonna kind of lifestyle where you have to hide from the public and you can't have a real life, I bet I would have gotten locked into something... but I didn't, and I think I have an interesting life now. I look back on the past and say, 'Wow, yeah, that was rockin',' but it's all about right now—tomorrow and the potential of what we can do."

Buffy operates the Nihewan Foundation for Native American Education whose Cradleboard Teaching Project serves children and teachers in eighteen states and lives in Hawaii.

Source: James Reed, Globe Staff, August 16, 2009, New York Times Co, www.boston.com

*****

Mary

Grammy winning flutist Mary Youngblood was adopted and raised in California. In 2009 she gave an interview to Mary Noden Lochner of the *Northern Light* student newspaper in Alaska and said, "I grew up noticeably different from other children in school. I had the only brown skin in a sea of white faces... sometimes my peers were cruel about it."

Youngblood credits her adoptive parents who paid for the classical training in music, particularly the flute. It was a means to cope, she said. "In the mid-1970s, when kids were experimenting with drugs, I delved into the arts....boys wouldn't date a brown girl. The way I handled that pain was through the arts."

At the time, Youngblood didn't know about her birthparents, or their ethnicity. After she married and had her first child, she started thinking about her natural mother. With very little information, she joined groups who help adoptees search and learned how to improve her query letters to agencies and organizations. When she received an envelope from the Chugach Corporation in Alaska, Youngblood was 26 and at a critical time in her life. Her husband was caught up with drugs and alcohol and left her with two children. Her music took a backseat to survival and providing for her young ones. A number of times she hawked her flute at a pawn shop. What Youngblood found in that envelope was a whole family tree with her birthmother's family, and the name of her ancestral home: the village of Port Grahm, Alaska.

In 1986 Youngblood made contact with her mother and siblings she never knew she had. Youngblood's website lists Aleut on her mother's side and Seminole (Florida) on her father's side. "I got involved in my community after I found my mother in 1986," Youngblood told the newspaper. "I got involved in an Indian community in Sacramento, I was on the board of directors for a local Indian clinic, and a member of a women's Native group."

All the while, Youngblood kept the dream of being a musician alive, especially during those hard years, and she wrote a story about a woman like herself where the main character, a single mother in dire financial straits, overcomes the challenges to become a successful musician and eventually win a Grammy. She succeeded. "I was writing my way out of my situation," Youngblood said. "I think that's a powerful tool for us as human beings, and especially as young people, to write out our dreams."

It wasn't until Youngblood was in her early 30s that she first picked up the Native American flute. She felt drawn to it, and eventually made a demo that caught the interest of record labels. Her first album, The Offering, which contains the track Aleut Wind, received acclaim. Her second album, Heart of the World, picked up a number of awards, and by her third album, Beneath the Raven Moon, Youngblood landed her first Grammy in 2003.

Shortly after, Youngblood visited and performed in her mother's village of Port Grahm for the first time. She arrived in a twin-engine Cessna in the middle of a storm that whipped the plane around as it landed on the gravel runway of the village airport. A group of people ran after the plane down the runway: a half-sister, a niece, an uncle, a cousin, and other relatives.

"I was sobbing," Youngblood told the newspaper. "I thought, 'This is where my mother grew up. And this is where she played as a child. This is where our ancestors are from." Youngblood's family held a potluck of traditional food for her and she played a concert for them. She told them Aleut Wind is in their honor.

Today Youngblood works to be a role model for young people, especially those who are struggling and aren't sure how to make their dreams a reality. "If you visualize your dream and what you want in your life, you can make it happen," she said. "It's important for young people to never let go of that dream and that vision."

Source: published in Northern Light University of Alaska-Anchorage Student Newspaper: http://kasenna.uaa.alaska.edu/~tnl/?page_id=8696

******

Chris

Cheyenne-Arapaho filmmaker Chris Eyre, born December 4, 1968 on the Warm Springs Reservation, was adopted by a non-Indian couple in Portland, Oregon. By high school, Eyre had learned 35mm still-photography and immersed himself in shooting black and white film, developing and printing. His high school photography class—and historical Native American images of

Edward Curtis—inspired Eyre into a career behind the camera. 'It came from wanting to touch those people. I kept wondering who they were,' he told *Cowboys and Indians* magazine in May 2009.

At age 18, he traveled to Oklahoma and received tribal enrollment in the Cheyenne-Arapaho tribe; and later tracked down his mother. Chris describes his first days of life, "I'm always inspired by the rebirth of the seasons. After I was born to Rose, of the Southern Cheyenne and Arapaho tribes, I was reborn within days to my adopted parents, Barb and Earl, in a white middle-class home in Klamath Falls, Oregon. As a dark-skinned five-year-old, I would ask my mom what I was going to be when I grew up. 'Anything you want!' she would say." (He told *Smithsonian* magazine in the July/August 2010 issue.)

Growing up Indian in a white environment, he said, "I have never seen things in black and white but always in many colors and shades of gray." He found his birth mother when he was 25. On finding her, he told *Cowboys and Indians* magazine, "I had ten years with my biological mother before she died, and afterwards I was still angry that she left me twice."

Through his love of photography, Eyre attended Mt. Hood Community College and enrolled in the Television Production Program to learn basic three-camera television studio directing and the techniques of color processing and printing photographs. In 1989, Eyre received his Associate's Degree in Television Production and transferred to the University of Arizona to study filmmaking and received a bachelor's degree in Media Arts. By then he'd made three experimental films and wrote his first feature-length script. Chris returned to Oregon in 1991 and set out to make this first feature based on a script he wrote in college, 'Things Learned Young,' inspired by his childhood as a Native adoptee and his search for his mother Rose. (On his website, Chris plans to make a documentary about Native American adoptions and his own experience someday.)

Chris applied to New York University's prestigious Graduate Film Program and was accepted in 1992. Independent cinema allowed Chris to concentrate on his vision and work with filmmakers who'd been his idols. At NYU, Chris made three sync-narrative shorts on 16mm film. His second year film, Tenacity, about two young boys that encounter 'rednecks' on a reservation road, garnered much attention and won 1st Place in the Graduate Film department. The 10-minute short went on to screen in numerous film festivals worldwide and was Chris' first distributable production. It was screened at the 1995 Sundance Film Festival.

1995 was an outstanding year. With the unexpected success of Tenacity, Chris started to attend film festivals and received numerous awards: a Rockefeller Film Fellowship, The Haig Manoogian Award, the Martin Scorsese Post Production Award, a Warner Brother's Post Production Award (1995) and Best Film of 1995 in NYU's Graduate Film Program.

Later that year, Chris participated in Robert Redford's Sundance's Directing Workshop. Chris' project, a short story-turned feature-length script, would become *Smoke Signals*. (Chris' work with Redford continued with Skinwalkers (2002) and A Thief of Time (2004), where Redford was executive producer.)

Miramax Films Co-Chair Harvey Weinstein bought *Smoke Signals* after a private screening and helped launch the film at the 1998 Sundance Film Festival, where it won the Audience Award and Filmmaker's Trophy. Smoke Signals won awards worldwide. Nearly everyone living in Indian Country has seen *Smoke Signals*. Many can accurately quote any given line; a favorite is 'Hey Victeeerr.' The film also received critical acclaim and is known as the first feature length film directed by a Native American to receive national theatrical release. *People Magazine* called Chris Eyre '...the preeminent Native American filmmaker of his time.' Geoff Gilmore, Director of the Sundance Film Festival, simply called him 'a great American Filmmaker.'

Chris went on to direct Skins (2002) produced by Jon Kilik. Graham Greene was nominated for Best Actor by the Independent Spirit Awards for his role as Mogie Yellow Lodge.

Chris' follow-up Edge of America (2003) took the highly coveted spot as opening night film at the 2004 Sundance Film Festival. It won several awards: a Peabody Award, a Writer's Guild Award, a Humanitus Prize, and the highly prestigious DGA (Director's Guild of America) Award for outstanding directorial achievement.

His film A Thousand Roads (2005) was executive produced by Rick West, Jr. and Peter Gruber, a Hollywood veteran, and with the feature Imprint (2007) he was co-producer. Then Chris signed on for the five-part miniseries We Shall Remain for PBS, and directed People of the First Light, Tecumseh and The Trail of Tears.

Eyre has said, "I love making movies and telling people's stories. However, cultural aspects of a film mean nothing if you're not personally and emotionally engaged in the characters you are watching. I am interested in the people I'm portraying. For that reason, the films that have interested me the most are the ones I'm making." Eyre was named a 2007 USA Rockefeller Foundation Fellow and given a $50,000 grant by United States Artists. Eyre directed *A Year in Mooring* in 2010.

In a recent editorial, Chris wrote, "Today, it is inspiring to see the number of strong Native American youth eager to learn more of our ancient traditions and cultures from the elders, who are more than happy to share with those who respect them. The youth renaissance is rooted, I think, in the elders' tenacity, 1970s activism and a backlash against the mass media's depiction of Native Americans…. The dismal portrayal of Native reservations is inaccurate and harmful. The media focus solely on poverty and the cycle of oppression. What most outsiders don't see is the laughter, love, smiles, constant joking and humor and the unbreakable strength of the tribal spirit that is there. Some reservations are strongholds of community, serving the needs of their people without economic gain but with traditions leading the way. My hope is that Native evolution will be driven by a reinforced traditionalism passed down from one to another…. Negative stereotypes are causing a youth renaissance; it's the only good thing about them. I like the thought of Native youngsters fighting back against the prevailing view of Indians. It means they're mad as hell and not going to take it anymore. They're not going to invent excuses for racism like (some of) their elders have."

Another project, 'Native Century' will be a four-hour documentary he directs that recounts Native American history in the century after Wounded Knee and chronicles how Native Americans sustained ancient traditions and preserved sovereign nations while adapting to the 20th and 21st centuries, according to information at www.katahdin.org.

Eyre currently resides and teaches in New Mexico. His website is http://www.chriseyre.org/

Sources: his website, http://www.cowboysindians.com/art-entertainment/tv-film/2009-09/reel-west.jsp and http://www.ouradopt.com/adoption-blog/jul-2010/lisas/transracial-adoptee-movie-director-talks-about-adoption.

*****

Mark

Mark Yaffee, who performs at Laugh Out Loud Comedy Club in California, is a late bloomer when it comes to stand-up comedy (he was in his late 30s when he began in 1998). And he only discovered his Navajo roots at 25. He was born in East Los Angeles, adopted at birth by a Mexican-American mother and Jewish-American father. Only when he was contacted by his birthmother decades later (a Fed-Ex package with photos and a letter) did he learn that his biological father was Mexican and Navajo. "It was pretty awesome,'" said Yaffee, 49. He connected with his birthmother two months later. It was tough on his adoptive parents.

"That biological pull is awful strong," said Yaffee. He never met his real father, however. But he delved headfirst into American Indian issues.

Yaffee's comedy, which moved away from adoption humor and to exploring his Navajo heritage, pokes fun at stereotypes—bingo, casinos, and drunkenness and smoke signals. At the same time, he imparts humanity into the act.

"Non-Natives are really supportive," he said. "The Native perspective is so original. We don't do it with maliciousness. We show we can laugh at each other and realize that whatever happened in the past, we remember, but from that pain there is humor about it. Not every Indian owns a casino and no one's around crying over people littering."

Source: http://www.mysanantonio.com/entertainment/stage/marc_yaffee_leading_native_american_comedy_wave_95029144.html

*****

Star

Musician and adoptee Star Nayea challenged herself over a decade ago to not only change lives but to **save** lives. To do this, she would create workshops that combine motivational messages with educational facts and her music. After twelve years, Star did accomplish her mission to become a successful motivational speaker, musician, actress, recording artist. It is not a surprise she won Native American Music Awards 2008 Songwriter of the Year and she has her own record label Raven's Last Laugh. Star says she is proud to represent a wellness movement growing in Indian Country.

Her many accomplishments include 2001 (NAMA) 'Best Independent Recording' for *Somewhere In A Dream;* guest vocalist on Robbie Robertson's Contact from the Underworld of Redboy; featured singer in the Broadway-style production, TRIBE; she's performed with Testament, a west coast heavy metal band and guest vocals on their album Live At The Fillmore; she's performed with Rita Coolidge and Walela, Buffy Sainte-Marie, Ulali, Joanne Shenandoah, Indigenous and others; she accompanied Robbie Robertson on stage for the first annual Native American Music Awards at Foxwoods in Connecticut; and she performed with Robert Mirabal at the New Orleans Jazz Festival.

Star, described as 'the little lady with a big voice,' launched her career in Austin, Texas, then New York City. She developed a unique contemporary bluesy rock with folk and traditional Native American vocals. Three songs on *Somewhere In A Dream* topped southwest radio charts at number one for three consecutive weeks; she co-produced and wrote this album with longtime friend David Shelley. Then she made a holiday album *Christmas Dream.*

Most proud of the birth of her son and being a mom, she is taking wellness to a whole new level with the Healing Power of Music, a program she started in 2000. Star says she survived her childhood to grow into an adult who exists to make a difference. She has not been able to open her adoption or find her tribe but that didn't stop her heart.

On her My Space page, Star admits, "I'm not a perfect person, or a perfect mother. Like every human being, I am full of flaws. I PRAY every morning to be guided in a better way! I made mistakes along the way, better to grow from these mistakes than to claim perfection. However one mistake I pray to never make is be like my adopted family from Michigan who raised me and put a roof over my head, clothes on my back, food to eat and clean water to bathe in. But what was missing, you ask? Love. Nothing but fear and dysfunction existed there. Any laughter that arose was false, always bearing conditions, and usually meant someone was drinking. My adopted mother and father attempted to be parents but failed miserably. Instead they were subconsciously molding me into a highly dysfunctional young woman, one who would grow up to have children of her own. I was not ready for my son nor did I feel I deserved him."

She added, "Abuse, neglect, emotional spiritual cultural disrespect, I pray to never abuse or neglect my own son. I will do everything humanly possible to make a difference and continue to lead my sober lifestyle, be a good mother, sister, friend, mentor, teacher, and maybe one day a wife. Most of all, I want to be a GOOD HUMAN BEING. Sacrifice is a given. However, retaining integrity, compassion with that daily sacrifice, is the key."

About being a mentor, she said, "There are no words to describe, or capture the feeling I get sharing the gift of music. It is an honor to make a difference in someone's life! Today's teen promiscuity is at a dangerous level. The number of teen pregnancies and sexually-transmitted diseases (STDs) increase each year. With all the latest technology, Internet dating, cell phones for SEX-texting, youth are being exposed to a way of life that will most certainly get worse if we do not speak up and stop them from desecrating their bodies, their spirits and their hearts. In the 19th century, a 15-year-old was married with children. In this century, a different set of social rules apply, with good reason" Star intimately addresses this in her workshops. In her diabetes and 'O factor' workshop, Star teaches, "Genetics and ancestry is a road map—why our bodies react to certain foods, commodities, beverages, lack of exercise, moods, based on the blood type 'O.' Managing the 'O factor' is better for the mental and physical health of all Native people."

By offering songwriting, poetry and recording workshops, Star believes, "Regardless if the youth want to do it for a living or not, it is a healthy form of release, a way to communicate. I should know. Youth today in so many ways are the mirror image of me back then. Sadly some kids were extremely abused as I was, or they are neglected. Or they're being shipped from home to home because of alcohol problems in the adults who are supposed to be taking care of them. Some are feeling so lost, searching desperately for answers and attracting the wrong kind of attention. Some incredibly do not want attention anymore. I pray for them and for ALL MY RELATIONS!!! AHO! CHI-MIIGWETCH, BAAMAAPI!"

Star, possibly Ojibwe or Potawatomi with ancestors in Michigan and Canada, is still seeking her own birth family. She lives with her son in Seattle, Washington. Her website: www.nativestars.com/bands/star/

38

More adoptees

Brulé, aka Paul LaRoche, has a unique story to tell. Along with amazing music, theatrics, and traditional dance troupe, Paul tells the story of how he came to realize his Native American heritage after nearly 38 years of separation from his biological family, who resides on the Lower Brule Sioux Indian Reservation in central South Dakota. Paul, adopted at birth off the reservation, discovered his Lakota heritage in 1993 after the death of both adoptive parents. He was reunited on Thanksgiving Day 1993 with a brother, sister, aunts, uncles, nieces and nephews. The discovery of his true heritage has greatly affected Paul's life and those around him. Paul writes, "Ironically at the beginning of the Brulé journey, the term reconciliation was seldom heard or understood. As time went by and we shared my story of homecoming and reunion during each performance. It became clear that the story was as important as the music itself. Not more or less but the combination of the two seemed to have a profound effect on the audience causing what some might term a transformation or paradigm shift. The result was a unique examination of the reconciliation process that is on-going between Native America and mainstream America." His website: https://www.brulerecords.com/news

Paul DeMain is a member of the Oneida (Wisconsin) and Ojibwe tribes, and was raised by a non-Native family in Wausau, Wisconsin. 'I grew up with some compassionate liberals who never tried to hide my identity and encouraged me to inquire about it,' DeMain says. In the early 1970s, he made contact with the Oneida tribe, where he is enrolled. He has met his biological family. In 1986 he launched *News from Indian Country*, an independent newspaper that covers tribal politics, legal issues in Native and US courts, reservation crime, education and Indian art, with a circulation of 9,000 readers worldwide.

Eric Schweig was born to an Inuit mother and a Chippewa-Dene father in Inuvik, the Northwest Territories. At six months, he was adopted by a German-Canadian family. During his childhood in Inuvik, Bermuda and

Toronto, he was systematically and physically abused by his adoptive parents then he ran away from home when he was 16, and became a laborer on construction sites. In 1987 he was 'discovered' while walking down a Toronto street and cast in the movie *The Shaman's Source*. At least 16 films followed, most notably as Uncas in *The Last of the Mohicans*. During this time period he endured a 'roller coaster of alcohol, drugs, violence, failed relationships, despair and confusion' [Schweig said] due to the abuse and racism and ethnic identity deprivation of his childhood. In 1996 he began to regain his cultural identity and is now primarily a carver, especially Inuit spirit masks, living on Vancouver Island, and he continues to act in films. He is a passionate opponent of the adoption of Aboriginal Native People by Europeans. Read Eric's adoption speech in this book. www.mohicanpress.com/mo05005.html

MORE:

- Quanah Parker, Comanche Chief
- William Apes, Pequot(d) minister-author
- Charles Alexander Eastman, Lakota doctor-author
- Senator Ben Nighthorse Campbell, Cheyenne/Apache/Pueblo (foster child)
- Peter Catches, Lakota author
- William Big Day, Crow
- Horn Chips, Lakota
- Clarissa Pinkola Estes, Mestizo author
- Jumping Bull, Assiniboine
- Lone Wolf II, Kiowa
- Billy Mills, Lakota Olympic winner
- Minik, Inuit (living exhibit in NY museum)
- James Pipe Mustache, Anishinabe Medicine Man
- Sacagawea, Shoshone/Hidatsa heroine
- Mary Tall Mountain, Koyukon-Athabaskan
- John Stands in Timber, Cheyenne
- Kateri Tekakwitha, Mohawk saint
- Bear Woman, Inuit
- Baby Veronica

39

To Dry the Eyes of Indian Adoptees

Mary Annette Pember (Photos and Story)

Before 1978, most Native American adopted children were taken into non-Indian families. Some of those 'Lost Birds' have found a way to make peace with the past and reclaim their Native culture.

A girl in a traditional jingle dress dances with a stuffed animal at a powwow of Native American adoptees, in Minneapolis.

The arrest of white missionaries trying to adopt allegedly orphaned Haitian children struck a chord with me. Similar media stories about well-meaning white celebrities adopting pretty babies of color from poor third world countries have also rubbed me the wrong way. You see, American Indians have a long history of white folks trying to help us by taking away our children. It is estimated that between 1941 and 1978, white parents adopted 35 percent of American Indians in the U.S., often forcibly. Indians have learned that no amount of good intention can wipe away the painful loss of our culture.

Not long ago, I traveled to Minneapolis to report on the Lost Birds—those Indian people who were adopted by non-Indian families prior to 1978. This story caught me by surprise; it touched the center of who I am as an Ojibwe woman and as a mother.

We adopted our son Danny from my tribe in 2005 when he was seven months old. Danny came into our lives as though directed by an outside force. Both my husband and I felt that he was meant to be raised by us and that he was meant to know he is an Ojibwe man. That 'knowing' has been a deep wordless tie between us and one to which I feel all people, non-Indian and otherwise, are entitled.

So, it was with some trepidation that I began a story about Rachel Kupcho, an Ojibwe woman and her adoptive white parents. Would I be able to keep my feelings about interracial adoption in perspective?

I worried about this and other things during my flight to Minneapolis. Unexpectedly, I noticed the Mississippi River or Great River in the Ojibwe language as the plane descended into the Twin Cities. The power of that great water pinched my heart in a nameless, primordial way and I felt a homecoming not without pain. With relief, I recalled that in Ojibwe tradition, we women are the ones who care for the water and I was comforted. I thought of our traditional Ojibwe stories describing this connection with place and the land. Again, I was awed by the wisdom and nuance of my culture that at once understands yet celebrates the ineffable. A wave of calm washed over me; I knew that the story would emerge in the way that it should.

In the end, I came to see that many mothers, Indian and non-Indian but all women who care for the water, built Rachel's life and strength, like the Great River.

At first glance Rachel didn't look like much of a Lost Bird to me. In fact she appeared to be just the opposite. Confident and beautiful, she strode around the Minneapolis Indian Center with calm authority. She seemed to carry easily the pride that is so typical of an Anishinabikwe or young Ojibwe woman, as she worked to organize the annual Gathering of Our Children and Returning Adoptees Powwow.

Sandy Whitehawk originally organized this powwow several years ago. She is the executive director of the First Nations Orphan's Association, an organization that helps Lost Birds find their way back to their culture. Since Sandy suddenly took ill, Rachel stepped in at the last minute to coordinate the event. Organizing a powwow is no small task. There is quite a bit of protocol involved and the potential for drama is high. Rachel, however, seemed born to the task; to look at her I would have never suspected that this was the first time she had overseen a powwow or that until a few years ago she had had very little exposure to her culture. Like many who attended this powwow, Rachel was adopted at birth and raised by white parents.

Rachel Kupcho, herself adopted by non-Indian parents, welcomed participants at the Gathering of Our Children and Returning Adoptees Powwow in Minneapolis.

When the doors of the Indian Center opened up, people began to trickle in. It was easy to identify the Lost Birds. Their fear and guarded emotions seemed almost palpable as they stepped uncertainly into the gym. They were drawn by the sound of the drum that they may have been hearing for the first time on that day. Looking more deeply into their faces, I sensed hope, a hope that they might begin to return home.

I noticed Rachel ushering people into the gym with a calm smile and I wondered how she has come by such self-assurance. The simple yet enormous answer begins with her parents, Keith and Lisa Kupcho. Typically, they are in the background, quietly helping set up tables for the event. They discreetly excuse themselves once the heavy lifting is finished. They will return when their daughter needs them later in the evening for the Wanblcheya, the Wiping of the Tears Ceremony.

Like so many Indian children prior to 1978, Rachel was given up for adoption by her birth mother from the White Earth Ojibwe Reservation in Minnesota and placed with a non-Indian family. Rachel, however, does not share the typical Indian adoptee history that is so often filled with physical, sexual and emotional abuse. Painful and more insidious than the physical abuse that adoptees report has been a rejection of their natural spirit. The shame of being Indian and therefore inferior is a lasting wound that remains open for countless adoptees. Too many try to medicate these wounds with alcohol and drugs, vainly trying to ease their pain.

This generation of 'Lost Birds' as they are often called, resulted from the well-intentioned U. S federal policy of assimilation that sought to integrate Indians into mainstream culture. The policy was intended to help lift Indians out of the poverty and address social ills that plagued the reservations. Instead, it supported the near wholesale removal of children from their homes, families and cultures.

Before the 1978 Indian Child Welfare Act, that gave tribes jurisdiction over their own families, thousands of Indian children who entered the social services system were adopted into non-Indian families. Churches and social service agencies mistook Indian culture as the culprit in the community's problems; therefore, all things 'Indian' were to be stamped out. Language, culture and the Indian tradition of child rearing that includes extended family, were viewed as backward and wrong. Understandably, many Indian adoptees internalized these messages and have had difficulty returning to their cultures. Rachel Kupcho, however, seems to have made her way back to her people with relative ease, achieving a comfort level that is enviable. To fully know her story, I needed to meet all the mothers, the water caregivers who contributed to her life and journey home.

Rachel is one of four ethnically diverse children adopted and raised by Lisa and Keith Kupcho in Chanhassen, Minnesota, about 20 miles outside of Minneapolis. Small and brown at the front, the Kupcho home sits a bit further back from the street than do the other houses. I imagine a certain sweet shyness about the house. Inside, the walls are richly covered with paintings, photos and prints of women of color and their children, lots of children. Photos of the Kupcho children and a seemingly endless convoluted photo storyline of their friends' children and grandchildren are everywhere.

We visited over coffee in Lisa's kitchen. There was an aura of love in that room that seemed to speak of bottomless acceptance. I found myself moved to tears several times during the interview.

"Fortunately, I learned early on that I couldn't fix everything in my children's lives," said Lisa.

Potentially, there was a lot to 'fix' in being a white mother to her racially diverse clan. Now grown, the children are Aaron (Filipino and Norwegian), Sarah (Scotch and Irish), Rachel (Ojibwe and Italian), and Eve (African-American and German).

Lisa recalled being confronted by an African-American instructor years ago during a parenting class about adopting and raising mixed race children. She recovered from her sense of feeling unjustly accused and resisted storming out of the class. "I realized that I needed to hear what this woman had to tell us. She prepared us for not thinking we could fix everything with parental love alone," Lisa recalled.

Not only did she learn that she wouldn't be able to isolate her children from the hurt of racism, she learned to be open to those who could mentor her through the parenting process.

Enter Sandy Whitehawk, a challenging mentor if there ever was one. Sandy recalls her birth mother handing her, at 18 months, through the window of a pickup truck into the hands of white missionaries who had come to the Rosebud reservation in South Dakota to 'help the Indians.' Sandy internalized her adoptive parents' message: that she was and ever would be a pagan, a member of an inferior race. She was also physically and sexually abused. Seeking to soothe her wounded soul, she turned to drugs and alcohol. Nothing seemed to take away the hurt until she found recovery and 'came home' over 20 years ago to her people and culture. She recalls the sense of relief and healing upon hearing the American Indian drum for the first time.

"The drum goes to that place where there are no words," Sandy has said. "As adoptees when we first hear it, we realize it has been what we were longing for."

Since, she has been compelled, almost obsessed in an effort to share this experience with other adoptees, knowing in her belly that a healing path lies therein. Working with a number of elders and spiritual leaders including Jerry Dearly, Lakota, she helped bring the Wanblecheya, the Lakota Wiping of the Tears Ceremony, to Indian adoptees. It was during a Wanblecheya that she came into the Kupchos' lives.

The first Wanblechaya offered by Sandy's group was presented at an annual National Indian Child Welfare Association conference in Duluth. Rachel had recently been hired at NICWA and was helping to organize the conference. Typically, her parents were there as well, pitching in where they could, happy to be of service to their daughter. The theme of the conference was, 'Reclaiming the Stolen Ones.'

Lisa recalls Keith's look of surprise over the theme's name. "Stolen? Ooooh, a bit harsh," he said. Rather than feeling threatened, Lisa saw the conference as a learning opportunity. Soothing Keith, she reminded him of their motto: "Whatever is good for our kids is good for our family."

Lisa has come to believe that there is a core piece of something missing for adopted kids, a piece of abandonment for which they must seek healing in their own way. She has spoken often to her children about this need and assured them of her support if they choose to explore their biological background and culture more fully.

"Whatever I can do or bring into their lives that makes them more healthy and whole advances our relationship. When you're a mother first, you do whatever you can to make your child feel well and whole and supported." She was excited and honored to participate in the Wanblecheya. In the end, "Rachel's growth has been our growth," she affirms.

Lisa and Keith stood firmly behind Rachel during the ceremony, their hands resting on her shoulders. Tears streamed uncontrollably down her face during the Wanblecheya.

"I felt so unbelievably loved. It was the most profound moment of my life," Rachel recalls.

For Lisa, the ceremony represented a healthy sense of completion. "It was an embrace and acknowledgment of loss," she said.

Although she has never felt lost or misplaced, Rachel felt the relief of being welcomed into the circle of her culture at last. Not only was the event a homecoming, according to Rachel, it was an acknowledgment from her parents that her quest for her heritage is important. "Up until that point, it was the only thing they weren't able to give me, but they were present when I received this gift," she remembers.

Rachel is now convinced that without the unconditional love and support of her parents, she would not be strong enough to do the work that has now become her passion and her calling. Working to support the Indian Child Welfare Act is now her life. She is a court advocate for ICWA and helps Sandy in her efforts to gain funding for a project to create a social work curriculum that includes knowledge about Indian families and culture. Rachel believes, "Everything that has happened in my life has prepared me to do this work."

Lisa sees Sandy as a wonderful mentor and role model for Rachel. "It has almost been a relief to have others in our lives who could give Rachel what she needs," Lisa laughs, recalling some mother-daughter challenges. In the end, Lisa has gained a friend in Sandy.

The passion of these three women, from such different backgrounds, has intertwined to form a tapestry of family love and support. I am reminded of my earlier vision of the Great River, how it unites its many channels into one big river, much as these women or water-caregivers have united to grow Rachel into an Anishinabikwe.

As the Adoptees Powwow comes to an end, the Sisseton Wahpeton Vietnam Veterans Color guards insist on having their photo taken with Rachel. Wearing full eagle feather headdresses and military fatigues, they surround her, creating a vision of embrace, acceptance and support—of home. She has, indeed, arrived.

Note: The reporting and writing for this project were supported by a grant from the USC Annenberg's Institute for Justice and Journalism. This story was published in the Daily Yonder (March 16, 2010). This story was also published by Indian Country Today Media.

40

A Mother's Day story: Mother, Daughter both given up for adoption

Mary Annette Pember (Photos and Story)

Rachel (right) and her 19 month old daughter, Mika, and Rachel's birth mother, Jeanne Winslow (left).

This year, for the first time in a long time, Mother's Day didn't bring with it the painful unknowns for Jeanne Winslow and Rachel Banks Kupcho of the Leech Lake Band of Ojibwe. Jeanne and her daughter Kupcho met for the second time last October (2010), more than 35 years after Winslow gave her newborn up for adoption.

"The day I got the call was the day I knew my life had changed forever," says

Winslow. That call on a cool October day carried the news that her daughter had found her and wanted to meet.

Their reunion was not a made-for-TV event filled with balloons and flowers. Winslow recalls that seeing her daughter for the first time in such a long time was quietly powerful, a bit like the first time she heard the drum and knew deep in her body that she was American Indian.

Like Kupcho, Winslow was put up for adoption as a newborn and raised by non-Indians.

Their story puts a quintessential Indian twist on the standard Mother's Day tale of maternal perfection, and shows the inexorable pull of blood and spirit that so many Native people describe when they speak of wanting to know their culture.

I first met Kupcho in Minneapolis back in 2008 while doing a story about the challenges faced by American Indian adoptees who want learn more about their cultures and their birth parents. At the time, she knew only that her birth mother was Ojibwe from Minnesota. Her adoptive family was supportive and understanding of her efforts.

A bright, confident young woman, Kupcho is convinced that without the unconditional love of her adoptive parents she would not have been strong enough to pursue her passion and calling of working to support the Indian Child Welfare Act (ICWA). While working with the National Indian Child Welfare Association, she met Sandy White Hawk, executive director of the First Nations Repatriation Institute in Minneapolis. White Hawk, an adoptee herself, founded the organization to advocate for Native adoptees in accordance with ICWA and to help unite adoptees with their birth families, cultures and tribes.

In October, they informed me that they had found Kupcho's birth mother, Winslow, a children's counselor living in Iowa.

Winslow and Kupcho, along with Kupcho's 18-month-old daughter Mika, quickly arranged a meeting. Kupcho recalls that Winslow seemed to be in quite a hurry to meet her. She soon found out why.

Winslow's birth mother (and Kupcho's grandmother), Audrey Banks, who

Winslow had met 20 years earlier, was dying. Winslow immediately rushed everyone to her mother's bedside.

"There were four generations in that room meeting for the first time," Winslow recalls. "That was the first thing Rachel and I did together. It was the greatest privilege and honor to be there with her. It was a very healing experience. This has all been about circles connecting. At first, it was just my circle but now I see that so many others are interconnected."

Kupcho didn't know it at the time, but she had previously connected with her grandmother—Audrey was well known and respected in the Minneapolis Native community for her work helping social service agencies maintain compliance with ICWA.

Like Kupcho, she earned a master's degree in social work in order to better serve Native children. "There has definitely been something bigger at work in my life; there has been a path I am meant to walk," Kupcho says of this coincidence.

In many ways, Audrey's experience as a young Ojibwe woman may have helped set the direction of that path.

Born on the Leech Lake reservation, Audrey was sent to the Pipestone Indian boarding school at age nine and remained there for the remainder of her childhood. After moving to Minneapolis she gave birth to three boys and three girls.

According to her daughters, social workers from Catholic Charities showed up at her bedside after each birth, pressuring the single mother to give the girls up for adoption.

"She said that she felt coerced by the social workers that said that the girls would have better lives if they were raised by white people," recalls Bernadine Harroun, Audrey's second daughter. "I think that influenced her decision to go into social work and help keep Indian kids with Indian families."

Bernadine and her younger sister, Winslow were adopted by the same family and raised together. Bernadine initiated the search for Audrey and Winslow and was responsible for their first meeting in 1989. They learned that Audrey, all of her children and Kupcho, all lived and grew up within 20 miles of each other.

"Most of the stories of Native adoptees finding their families are like miracles,"

White Hawk says. The distinguishing factor for Native adoptees, according to White Hawk is that the children were prayed for by generations of parents who knew hard times were coming. "Native people have that spiritual pull, like a spiritual umbilical cord that compels us to seek out our families," she says.

Many Native adoptees report that hearing the traditional drum often activates that spiritual pull. Indeed Winslow recalls the first time she heard the drum. "I heard it and I knew I was Indian. The drum goes to some place so deep," she recalls. (She didn't know it at the time, but her uncle, well-known activist Dennis Banks was one of the people at that drum. He was giving a presentation at Winslow's suburban high school about the happenings at Wounded Knee.)

Except for the strange longing awakened in her by the drum, Winslow says life in her adoptive suburban home was good. Ironically, because of this positive experience, she was able to make the difficult decision to relinquish her own daughter for adoption. Newly independent and sexually inexperienced, she found herself pregnant at age 19. "I knew that I couldn't give my daughter the chance she deserved unless I did something drastic," she recalls.

With the support of her adoptive family, Winslow put Rachel Kupcho up for adoption. "Leaving the hospital without her was the hardest thing I've ever done in my life," she says. Over time, however, she was at peace with her decision although birthdays, Christmas and Mother's Day were hard. "I never stopped wondering about her," says Winslow.

There was always a lingering, fear, too, that Rachel would be angry with her if and when they reconnected. She says, however, that her meetings with Kupcho and Mika have been smooth and joyous. She compares it to dancing in the circle for the first time with Audrey. "Somehow my feet knew what to do," Winslow recalls.

"I can't imagine the pain Winslow went through in making the brave choice to give me up for adoption. I give her tons of credit," says Kupcho, adding that Winslow needn't have feared she would be angry. "If anything her love gave me the wonderful life I have now. The home I was adopted into has afforded me the ability to do the work that I do."

Kupcho is starting a new job with a non-profit organization that licenses foster homes for Native children. Her main focus is creating permanent, supportive homes. Although her adoptive placement was loving and good, advocating for a child to be in a loving home is not specific enough.

"Being with family is ideal," Kupcho says. "Love is not always enough. Going to the occasional pow wow is not enough. We need to know about our traditions and culture. Even knowing you're Indian is not enough. With the experience of meeting my birth family, I understand this more fully. As a mother and as an adoptee I have a better sense of myself. I have a stronger, more confident gait. This is the only thing my adoptive parents haven't been able to give me."

Finding her birth mother, however, was not the whole key to Kupcho's search. "I needed to know where I came from and make that tribal connection. When visiting the reservation I am suddenly among family and I feel good," she says.

Both Kupcho and Winslow report that they are going forward with their new relationship without expectations and going with that process as it unfolds. Their first Mother's Day was one of quiet joy. "I'm a mother, now I have somebody," explains Winslow. "Plus it's great to be a grandma."

"Mother's Day is definitely more complicated now, but only in my mind. I'm taking it as it comes," says Kupcho, laughing.

Sandy White Hawk's message for Mother's Day and every day thereafter: "We need to encourage our birth mothers to forgive themselves and remember we wouldn't be here without them. We need to tell them that regardless of the kinds of lives we have had, we can have good lives from this day forward and for that we are grateful."

NOTE: This is an update to a 2010 story that was published on DailyYonder.com on May 14, 2012. This story was also published by Indian Country Today Media Network.

41

"We are the answer to their prayers"

"Seven generations ago someone was praying for us. We are the answer to their prayers. We take this responsibility seriously. When you are working with children, it is sacred work. Our children are sacred."

—Tribal Court Judge (The Judges Journal, Vol. 50, #2, Spring 2011)

"One by one, as the years pass me by, I still find it so amazing that the grief and trauma that I still carry from being separated at birth from my mother continues to follow me around and exposes itself at the most inconvenient times. I feel like my heart and spirit is that of a gypsy where although I physically stay in one place, my soul keeps wandering around searching and gets so lost….. I often stuff it back into its compartment but at times it just creeps out with no warning and slaps me upside the head and I am forced to confront the emotions time and time again. I don't know that I will ever actually organize this all within myself and find a place of comfort and peace with it all."

—Janey Martin Hart, Red Lake Ojibwe Split Feather Adoptee, 2011 (sent to Trace)

"…Lorraine 'Punkin' Shananaquet, a healer and a member of the Tribal Council of the Match-E-Be-Nash-She-Wish Band of Pottawatomi Indians, said the echoes of the grief, pain and loss continue across the generations. 'My muscle and my blood remember things.' She said the day of remembrance could bring emotional, mental, spiritual and physical healing as Native people struggle to regain their language, family, culture and ceremony.'"

(Source: Tribe remembers boarding school era, begins healing in Michigan, www.morningsun.com)

"As in this ancient story, as throughout all of human history, and in my deepest family traditions, the ultimate gift of story is two-fold; that at least one soul remains who can tell the story, and that by recounting of the tale, the greater forces of love, mercy, generosity and strength are continuously called into being in the world... the telling of a story is considered an essential spiritual practice... Tales, legends, myths and folklore are learned, developed, numbered and preserved the way a pharmacopoeia is kept. A collection of cultural stories, and especially family stories, is considered as necessary for long and strong life as decent food, decent relationship and decent work. The life of a keeper of stories is a combination of researcher, healer, linguist in symbolic language, teller of stories, inspiratrice, God talker and time traveler..."

— Clarissa Pinkola Estes, Ph.D., award-winning writer, psychoanalyst, human rights organizer and adoptee, from her book THE GIFT OF STORY

PART II

First Nations Canada

42

Canadian government settles lawsuit over children 'scooped' out of indigenous communities

SIXTIES SCOOP LAWSUITS | October 7, 2017

The Canadian federal government of Justin Trudeau on October 6, 2017 responded to a group of lawsuits by agreeing to pay $750 million to the survivors of the "Sixties Scoop" program, in which 20,000+ First Nations children were removed from their parents' households and placed with non-indigenous foster or adoptive parents. The plaintiffs claimed that this caused them mental and emotional problems, in addition to the loss of their ancestral culture. Carolyn Bennett, Canada's Crown-Indigenous Relations Minister, announced the agreement.

"I have great hope that because we've reached this plateau, this will never, ever happen in Canada again," Marcia Brown Martel, now Chief of the Beaverhouse First Nation, said of the decision. Martel was removed from her home as many as ten times before 1972. She and her sister were among the original plaintiffs. From the 1960s to 1980s, some of the children were sent out of the country to the United States, Europe or New Zealand. Some of the plaintiffs say they were abused by their foster families and others do not. A separate settlement has been offered to the 150,000 children who were instead sent to institutions, such as boarding schools.

"There is also no dispute about the fact that great harm was done," wrote Ontario Supreme Court Justice Edward P. Belobaba in a preliminary decision in February. "The 'scooped' children lost contact with their families. They lost their aboriginal language, culture and identity. Neither the children nor their foster or adoptive parents were given information about the children's aboriginal heritage or about the various educational and other benefits that they were entitled to receive. The removed children vanished 'with scarcely a trace.' " He did concede that the founders of the program meant well, but major sources agree it was subject to major culture clash, with social workers removing children from situations that were later found not to be abusive or neglectful.

According to a lawyer for some of the plaintiffs, Jeffrey Wilson, this is the first time anyone has argued that the loss of a cultural identity in a lawsuit in a Western country: "No First Nations case yet to this day has asked the question as to whether or not the loss of identity is an actionable wrong. Aboriginal title to property has been litigated, aboriginal title to identity has not," he told the *The Guardian.*

The First Nations people make up approximately four percent of Canada's population, at about 1.4 million people, and they suffer disproportionately from poverty, violence, addiction and crime.

Canada is not the only country where native children were taken away from their families. From 1910 to 1970, the Australian government collected Aboriginal children, who came to be called the Stolen Generations, and relocated them to schools and other institutions far from their communities. In 1978, the United States passed the Indian Child Welfare Act to curtail similar actions toward Native American children.

Manitoba was the first of Canada's provinces to apologize for the scoop program, in 2015. The federal government has also announced plans to make a public apology.

MORE

- Reuters. "Canada will pay compensation to thousands of indigenous 'stolen children'" — *The Guardian*, October 6, 2017
- "Canada settles with indigenous 'Sixties Scoop' victims" — *BBC News Online*, October 6, 2017
- Ian Austen. "Canada to Pay Millions in Indigenous Lawsuit Over Forced Adoptions" — *The New York Times*, October 6, 2017
- Jessica Murphy. "Indigenous Canadians taken from homes as children get day in court" — *The Guardian*, August 22, 2016
- Bryce Hoye. "Manitoba Premier Greg Selinger apologizes for Sixties Scoop" — *CBC News*, June 17, 2015

43

Stolen Nation (Canada's 60s Scoop)

For more than 20 years, Canada took Native children from their homes and placed them with white families. Now a lost generation want its history back…

Tom Lyons

Donna Marchand spent 16 years trying to find her birth mother. Now she's suing the government to open up birth records for others

(published in January 2000)

When former Indian Affairs Minister Jane Stewart made her historic apology to the aboriginal peoples of Canada on Jan. 8, 1998, she singled out Native residential schools as the most reprehensible example of Canada's degrading and paternalistic Indian policies. Designed to assimilate Native children into English ways and strip them of their language and culture, the schools also became notorious for sickening physical and sexual abuse.

Though none would disagree with Stewart's condemnation of residential schools, which were phased out in the 1960s, some wondered why she didn't also apologize for the

243

equally assimilationist—if less well-known—strategy that followed immediately in the schools' wake: the widespread adoption of aboriginal children out to non-Native families in the 1960s, 70s and early 80s.

Commonly referred to as the Sixties Scoop, the practice of removing large numbers of aboriginal children from their families and giving them over to white middle-class parents was discontinued in the mid-1980s, after Ontario chiefs passed resolutions against it and a Manitoba judicial inquiry harshly condemned it.

The passage of the Child and Family Services Act of 1984 ensured that Native adoptees in Ontario would be placed within their extended family, with another aboriginal family or with a non-Native family that promised to respect and nurture the child's cultural heritage. Aboriginal peoples also began to play a much greater role in the child welfare agencies that served them, and the numbers of Native adoptees in general began to decline as more stayed with their birth parents.

However, the act also dictated that old birth records remain sealed, unless both the birth parent and the child asked for them. This has helped keep the period in darkness and frustrated attempts by adoptees to learn about their roots. Those who now feel they were victimized by the adoption process have an extremely difficult time finding out who they are.

Donna Marchand, a 44-year-old Toronto lawyer, is launching a court challenge against the Harris government to strike down the sealed birth records provisions of the Child and Family Services Act.

An adopted child herself, she recalls being terrorized into denying her origin: "When I was about three-and-a-half, it started coming to my attention that I was adopted. My cousins told me. I was only three years old, but I was aware that I was different. I just didn't fit in. I was getting called a little bastard. And I asked my adopted mother what adoption meant. She said, 'Don't ever say that again—if your father hears you he'll kill you.' He'd been sitting there in his drunken stupor. He'd go on binges for days."

"I've lived my whole life being Native because I was called a squaw. I don't look white enough. And I was in working-class, real WASP, downtown Toronto. I got called a squaw and Donna Wanna, and I got tied to my share of trees and got my hair hacked off," Marchand said.

Marchand's constitutional challenge involves Section 7 and Section 15 of the Charter of Rights and Freedoms, according to her lawyer, Jennifer Scott. "Section 7 is the right to life, liberty and security of person," says Scott. "And Section 15 is the equality rights. The 15 provisions are that adoptees are sort of a group that is protected. But different communities of adoptees are particularly affected, and it has a tremendous impact on communities like Native people—where they don't know who their mom and dad are, but they're assimilated into families that don't even know their culture, their history, their background. It goes to who they are."

Permanent Scars

Just as the closing of the residential schools did not mean their legacy of suffering instantly vanished, so the end of the Sixties Scoop did not mean that all the Native adoptees who were farmed out to abusive or alienating non-Native families suddenly found themselves with a clear-cut identity or a secure place in society.

Indeed, many still found themselves not only 'torn between **two worlds,**' but literally unsure if they were Native at all, and not French or Italian as their adoptive parents claimed. Their birth records were sealed and often amended to include the names of the adoptive, rather than biological, parents. Moreover, their adoption records were in many cases inaccurate, incomplete, falsified or simply missing. As a result, many Native adoptees who did try to locate their birth parents or confirm their Native status wasted literally decades on failed searches or frustrating battles with Children's Aid authorities or Indian Affairs officials.

Suzanne Bezuk, a spokesperson for the Ontario Ministry of Community and Social Services, says 'non-identifying information' can be made available to adult adoptees without their birth parents' consent. 'And for Aboriginal peoples in particular, in the case of Native clients, the name of the band and reservation can be provided.'

However, Aboriginal status and band names were seldom recorded on the original birth and adoption records in the '60s and '70s. So even this 'non-identifying information' is rarely available.

Marchand cannot even be sure whether her mother was in fact Native. "All I know is, it's very typical for Native women, and my Uncle Frank says we're Native. And my Aunt June looks Native. Me and my two sisters, we look real

Native. But my mother, she internalized the shame of being a Native woman. Look what she put down [on the adoption record]: 'Ethnicity not stated.' It's a shame. A lot of Native women don't say, because they were going to lose their babies, and they wanted them to be adopted by good people, and good people weren't going to adopt 'little bastard squaws."

Even now, researchers trying to determine exactly how many aboriginal children were removed from their families during the Scoop say the task is all but impossible because adoption records from the '60s and '70s rarely indicated aboriginal status (as they are now required to).

Those records which are complete, however, suggest the adoption of Native children by non-Native families was pervasive, at least in Northern Ontario and Manitoba. In her March, 1999 report, 'Our Way Home: A Report to the Aboriginal Healing and Wellness Strategy on the Repatriation of Aboriginal People Removed by the Child Welfare System,' author Janet Budgell notes that in the Kenora region in 1981, 'a staggering 85 percent of the children in care were First Nations children, although First Nations people made up only 25 per cent of the population. The number of First Nations children adopted by non-First Nations parents increased fivefold from the early 1960s to the late 1970s. Non-First Nations families accounted for 78 per cent of the adoptions of First Nations children.'

Similarly, "One Manitoba community of 800 people lost 150 children to adoption between 1966-1980," reports Budgell, who prepared the report in conjunction with Native Child and Family Services of Toronto.

Though it is rarely possible to determine precise numbers, the practice of Native adoption was widespread enough to be denounced as 'cultural genocide' by Edwin C. Kimelman, the presiding judge at the 1985 Manitoba inquiry.

Many Native adoptees suffered from not only geographical displacement and cultural confusion but also emotional emptiness, violence, physical and sexual abuse, and drug or alcohol abuse.

"My brother was adopted at four years old," recalls one of the birth relatives of Native adoptees interviewed for 'Our Way Home.' "His adoptive parents divorced when he was 12 and they gave him back to the agency like returning merchandise. His life after that was a living hell of abuse, violence and alcoholism. My brother hanged himself at 20 years old."

Joanne Dallaire

Joanne Dallaire is a Native adoptee who conducts healing sessions for adoptees at the Anishnawbe Health Centre in Toronto. She too was told by her adoptive family that she wasn't Native. "I myself was raised by a non-Native, and my whole history was denied. Like in school, I was teased. You know how kids can be rather cruel with each other, and I was called a squaw and stuff like that, and when I'd come home, I'd be like crying and stuff, and they'd say, 'You're not Indian, you're French. So you make sure you tell them you're French.' It was years and years of misinformation."

Dallaire's attempts to find her birth mother or at least learn the truth of her Native status began early. "The first time I started searching was when I was 15, so that was 1966. But it wasn't until I was an adult and on my own that I really began to search. I didn't have any proof, either, until 1998. Anishnawbe [Native] people would come up to me and say, 'Oh, so you're Anishnawbe.' And I'd say, 'No, no, I'm French.' And I remember one man said to me—I remember profoundly— he looked at me and he said, 'Someone's lying to you. You're Anishnawbe.'"

"I remember when I got the phone call from the social services department. One of my first questions was: 'Is there Native in my background?' So my mother wanted to know how I'd feel about it if I was, and I said, 'Very pleased,' because my whole spirituality and stuff was drawn to Native culture. So I've come to find out that I am [First Nations]—to what degree, I don't know, because my mother is still very evasive about my father. But at least I know part of my heritage is Cree—James Bay Cree."

Donna Marchand's own search for her birth mother took 16 years through the Ministry of Community and Social Services and the Adoption Disclosure Record. When government officials finally contacted her in the spring of 1999, they said her mother had died 26 years earlier.

"It's a big area that most people never even thought of," says Dallaire, "because it goes so quietly and privately. It's not as out there as the residential schools. And because everything's secret, you can literally throw your hands in the air and go, 'Well?' You quickly run up against one wall and then another, so it takes perseverance, like with Donna having to fight and fight again to get what she wants. Most people get battle-weary and never win."

Was it Genocide?

According to the UN Declaration of Indigenous Rights, Justice Kimelman's description of the Sixties Scoop as cultural genocide is accurate. It reads: 'Indigenous peoples have the collective right to live in freedom, peace and security as distinct people with guarantees against genocide or any other act of violence, including the removal of indigenous children from their families and communities under any pretext.'

So why was the wholesale removal of aboriginal children not considered a crime, or even a wrong, that the Minister of Indian Affairs felt obliged to redress along with the residential school system?

Kenn Richard

The answer isn't that complicated, says Kenn Richard, director of Native Child and Family Services of Toronto and the man who commissioned the 'Our Way Home' report.

"British colonialism has a certain process and formula, and it's been applied around the world with different populations, often indigenous populations, in different countries that they choose to colonize," says Richard. "And that is to make people into good little Englishmen. Because the best ally you have is someone just like you. One of the ones you hear most about is obviously the residential schools, and residential schools have gotten considerable media attention over the past decade or so. And so it should, because it had a dramatic impact that we're still feeling today. But child welfare to a large extent picked up where residential schools left off."

"The lesser-known story is the child welfare story and its assimilationist program. And you have to remember that none of this was written down as policy: 'We'll assimilate aboriginal kids openly through the residential schools. And after we close the residential schools we'll quietly pick it up with child welfare.' It was never written down. But it was an organic process, part of the colonial process in general."

Simon's cousin, 42-year-old Katherine Pelletier, who works at the Assembly of First Nations in Ottawa, applauds the aims of the proposed strategy.

Pelletier was adopted in infancy by a French family and only found her birth family six years ago. Despite having 'a very happy childhood,' and 'wonderful' adoptive parents, she says her identity crisis began at five years of age when she started kindergarten and physical differences between her and her adoptive family began to emerge into consciousness.

"It was very traumatic for me at that age . . . I was made fun of [by peers at school] . . . I grew up thinking I was ugly."

"If I had been within my own community, that never would have happened, because I would have looked like them—I would have fit in," Pelletier explained.

Discovering her roots became 'very consuming—not painful,' she said.

She located her birth mother in 1990 after the Secrecy Act was lifted, she says, and her mother provided her the name of her deceased birth father, who had come from Wickwemikong. Through a series of inquiries, Pelletier then found Donna Simon's mother, who is her closest natural relative on her father's side.

"When I found my father's side, lo and behold, I found I was like them. I act like them, I feel like them, I look like them. I realize my spirituality, my heart, it comes from there," Pelletier said. The search for her identity was confounded to some extent by the Children's Aid Society, who 'either were not astute enough, or did not care enough' to provide her with correct information about her lineage.

"They gave me false information," Pelletier asserts. Not only that, but inaccuracies were recorded in her birth records. Pelletier says as Aboriginal people assume more responsibility for their own affairs, problems such as she had will diminish.

[Source: http://www.eye.net/eye/issue/issue_01.13.00/news/nation.html]

44

The Innocent

Debby Poitras (Metis-Cree)

Debby's photo was used in advertising in local newspapers offering children for adoption. "...Kind of like the Humane Society advertising for puppies and kittens, they were having an adoption conference and my picture used for folks interested in adoption...which is why I guess my A-mother told me I was from a catalogue," she emailed Trace

It was as though it happened yesterday, still vivid in my memories some fifty years later.

"Daddy, where did I come from?" I remember hanging over the back of the front seat as we drove home from my Auntie's funeral. I was about five or six years old.

My mother quickly answered, 'Your dad picked you out from a catalogue of baby girls, HE wanted a girl.'

Although the topic never came up in conversation until I was older, I knew I was different. Due to the tension from my early childhood experience, I never felt brave enough to approach my parents to discuss my true identity until MUCH later in life.

I was placed in my new home at eighteen months. In my new family I had two older brothers. They were ten and twelve years older than me. I was very close to my eldest brother, Allan. When he was home I followed him everywhere.

I grew up on a farm near a very small village in Saskatchewan. My life was somewhat normal. There were all of one hundred and twenty-five people living in the village. Every day I rode the bus nine miles to and from school.

Growing up on the farm, the summers were always fun. I also spent a lot of time in the city with my paternal grandmother. My favorite times with her were the city fairs. Being farmers, our entire family attended the animal exhibits. During the fair the local First Nations would have their pow-wow. When I got tired of looking at the animals, I would sneak off to the pow-wow and hide in the teepees. There to the sound of the beating drums, this little Indian Princess would secretly dance her heart and soul out. This was an Indian Princess' dream-come-true. I felt so alive. But alas, my parents or grandmother would find me and a spanking would follow when we got home. I spent a lot of time hiding under tables to avoid the spankings. Time and time again, I was reminded, 'You're not an Indian, you are French and Ukrainian.'

Growing up there were a lot of drunken parties and a lot of arguing. On a regular basis I was left to sit in the grain truck outside the local bar as my parents sat inside and drank until all hours of the night. It didn't matter what season it was, even winter. Back then; it was a regular occurrence with farm children. I always tried to make it as inconvenient as possible for them by knocking on the bar door. I always asked for my Daddy. I was tired, hot, cold, or hungry and I wanted to go home. Money always kept me quiet for another hour. I would go to the café and order a cheeseburger and strawberry milkshake, or a root beer float. Now, a Children's Aid Society would have a field day in court with those same parental actions.

After high school, I moved to Regina and got a part-time job with the government. I enrolled in an accounting course at the local college. I also became involved with my first real boyfriend. By the end of the summer I discovered I was pregnant. I also discovered that my boyfriend was married!

My parents disowned me and we did not speak until the day I had my baby girl seven and a half months later. It was an early delivery due to gestational diabetes, though it wasn't diagnosed until much later in my life. At the time, they treated me for toxemia, a common ailment in pregnant women. During the pregnancy my parents tried to place me in a home for unwed mothers, but I moved many times and they couldn't find me. On May 27, 1974, I remember calling my parents from the delivery table at the insistence of my nurse. She told me to call before the Social Worker came to speak to me about adoption. Adoption? I never mentioned anything about putting my child up for adoption to anyone. I'm not sure who contacted who first, perhaps my parents had contacted Social Services or vice versa.

The next day my parents showed up for a visit. Their first words were a lecture. They asked how I was going to look after a baby, work, and go to school. I told them, 'I'm keeping my baby; no stranger is going to raise my child.' At the end of the visit, my father went out to the car to bring in a gift consisting of a blanket, sleepers, undershirts and a sweater set. They weren't very happy with my decision and we lost contact for about three months. I managed to find a room for rent with a single mom. I was able to babysit for her, and stay home with my baby for the first few months.

September came and it was time to return to work and school. It was hell. I was faced with a baby that cried all night due to colic. I had to be at work early in the morning and I attended school in the evenings. I broke down and called my parents. Dad was now retired. He asked if they could keep the baby so I could concentrate on school and work.

By 1976 I married and birthed a son. This birth was also premature. I was diagnosed with toxemia during this pregnancy too. Prior to my hospital discharge the doctor announced that I had gestational diabetes. He asked me if I had a history of diabetes in my family? I told him I didn't know. I was adopted. The doctor suggested, 'You may want to find out from the adoption province as you may discover health problems later in life.' He went on to tell me that the adoption office always kept health information on the mother and her family, he said.

I wasn't sure how to approach my parents about my natural mother. That Christmas holiday season, I casually mentioned my conversation with the doctor to my parents on a return to Saskatchewan. 'Do you know anything? Do I have brothers and sisters? What about my last name? What about my adoption papers?' They knew nothing of the sort. Not exactly what I had expected. It was as though I just dropped on their doorstep with nothing. I have no history, no natural family and no last name. I was French and Ukrainian.

At the end of my vacation, my mother came to me with a baby photo of myself on a woman's knee. 'Who is that? A social worker?' End of conversation.

I suppose you could say that I have been searching my entire life for family but where did I truly start? The picture my Mother gave me was the beginning of my current search that has been ongoing since 1978. It is now 2011. That little picture held so much information for me. I truly never paid much attention to the back of the picture until one day while cleaning the frame, I noticed something was scratched out on the back of the photo. It read: Debrah Anne, DOB October 26, 1955, weight 5 lbs.,6 oz. On the far right corner something was scratched out with blue pen. Wondering what it may have been, I took an ink eraser and ever so gently began to lightly erase the ink. Afraid to damage the twenty-three year old photo, I gave up. It wasn't getting me anywhere. I could make out a P and a TR but the other letters were still covered. *Could it have been my last name? Perhaps, but unlikely. Why would they actually print my birth name on my picture and give it to my parents. Who scratched out the word? Was it the agency or my parents?* Curiosity was killing me for weeks. Again, I went at my tattered picture. For days I would gently try to uncover the letters remaining. This was twenty-year-old ink... what were my chances?

Wherever the photo was kept originally, it had been folded in half. Hidden away from everyone I suppose. Personally I had never seen the picture of me at that age. I was sitting on a Social workers lap looking frightened. Kind of a 'deer in the headlights' look. The first time I saw this picture was the day my mother gave it to me. The youngest picture my parents had of me in family albums was around the age of three. The reasons would make sense later on as I progressed through various stages of my search and as more information became available.

At some point, I thought what I had uncovered was a last name. It wasn't looking Ukrainian but indeed it looked French. I could actually read the name

POITRAS. That was me? Maybe this wasn't even my baby picture. Maybe it was the doctor's name. It was worth a shot.

After calling Alberta Social Services earlier in 1978, I was provided some information about adoption in Saskatchewan and a program called 'REACH'. The program would assist adopted adult children and provide them with biological medical information. Yes, this was exactly what I had wanted… or was it? I quickly wrote a letter to REACH and explained that I needed some medical background information as I was having issues with my pregnancies. It took about two months to get a reply but I wasn't expecting what I did receive one spring morning.

The letter from REACH thanked me for contacting them but explained that there were some very sensitive issues surrounding my birth and I must call them. No medical information was in their letter. What could be so serious that I had to call them? After two days of calling, I finally was able to speak with my post adoption worker, Mrs. D.

Mrs. D. explained there were sensitive issues surrounding my case, plus little known facts about my Mother's background, so she would gladly meet with me should I ever be in the Regina area. The only medical information given during our phone call was a disclosure of TB, diabetes and high blood pressure. With Easter right around the corner, we had already made plans to visit my family in Saskatchewan so I made an appointment to meet with Mrs. D then. Our conversation ended there.

I couldn't wait to meet her. Those words 'sensitive issues' haunted me day and night. Again I called her. 'Would it be possible to have contact with my mother?' She would do her best to somehow get in touch with my mother and try to set something up if I were serious. Several weeks and many phone calls later, Mrs. D called. My Mother had agreed to meet with me, however I needed to understand there was no guarantee she would show up for the appointment. My Mother was an alcoholic and somewhat unreliable, Mrs. D. explained.

On the day of my appointment, I arrived early, sitting outside in my van with my husband and children. I left them there and started walking toward the front doors and I could feel my heart pounding in my chest. My meeting would be first with Mrs. D. then my Mother. As I entered the building, an older Aboriginal lady brushed by me. She looked as though she had been crying but I never thought anything of it. I assumed this was the main office for Social Services, so possibly she had a child welfare case with the system. I advised reception I was there and took a seat. Several minutes passed and finally the receptionist called me over to the desk. 'I'm sorry for the delay however it seems that your mother will not attend the meeting. She has had a change of heart. Would you still like to meet with Mrs. D?' Although disappointed, I agreed to meet with Mrs. D. There were still issues to discuss.

In the meeting, Mrs. D asked, 'How much do you know about your background?'

'Not much,' I said. 'My parents told me I was French and Ukrainian but said they didn't know anything else.'

Mrs. D smiled. 'French and Ukrainian? That is incorrect. Let me provide you with some background information. First of all, your Mother was just here and left crying. She had a change of heart and could not meet with you today. Debby, you were born to a single mom who was unable to care for you. Although I cannot give you any identifying information, I can tell you that you do have a few male siblings. You were the fifth child born to your Mother. She was 28 when you were born. If any of your siblings wish to have contact at any point, we will contact you. Your Mother had very little education, Grade four and was unable to obtain a decent job so she turned to prostitution at an early age. The entire family was alcoholics and none of them had stability in their lives. You have several aunts and uncles and only two of them lead normal lives with their family today. With regards to health, I have already disclosed to you that there are some tuberculosis, diabetes and high blood pressure issues. Your ancestral background is not French and Ukrainian. Your Mother was Metis. Your grandparents are Metis and Chippewa Cree. Your grandfather was a stonemason and built a very beautiful church locally. Your father's name is not listed on your adoption file or birth certificate but we do note that he is possibly of Aboriginal descent. It seems that your mother was in a long-standing relationship with him. At that time, not listing a paternal name is no surprise as she was a *prostitute* and DNA tests were not available.' (*Damn, I wish she would stop throwing that word at me*)

Metis and Cree? My heart sank. I wondered if the lady I just passed in the doorway was my Mother?

'Is there anything else you would like to know?'

I thought, Jesus woman, you pretty much blew apart my entire world. What else could you possibly tell me that would make a bit of difference right now?

As I sat there with tears running down my cheeks, my body felt numb. I'm not sure why I was crying. Was it the fact that I wouldn't meet my mother or that I felt someone had lied to me about my heritage. My head was spinning. I have siblings and I'm Metis. My Mother was a prostitute and her family are unstable and alcoholics.

'Mrs. D, I have a name that is on the back of my baby picture. Does the name Poitras mean anything?' I asked.

'I'm sorry, I cannot disclose any identifying information even if it were your birth name.' *My gut instinct immediately told me I am a Poitras.*

'Everything we have discussed today will follow in a letter. I'm sorry I don't have better news for you but it did answer your questions surrounding health issues. I'm sure you can understand why I didn't want to tell you these things over the phone.'

I thanked Mrs. D. and closed the door behind me.

The next few days were tear-filled but at some point I decided that my search would continue. I had one more week of vacation and I was going to make use of it.

Hours upon hours were spent looking through the local phonebook. I called every Poitras in Saskatchewan explaining I was adopted and searching for my family. Many times I was told no, but often they would suggest another Poitras to call. At some point, the information about my grandfather's trade as a stone-mason came to mind. My next fifty calls were unsuccessful but then it happened. Yes, they knew a Poitras who was a stone mason and he did work on the church in Lebret, just outside of Regina. 'Old Zachary had a few daughters but only two of them were not married. They'd heard that the two girls had their children taken away from them and adopted. Try Olive, she was a Poitras. If you are a daughter of either, Olive will be able to confirm.'

I called Olive immediately.

'Is this Olive?'

'Yes it is, who is calling?'

'My name is Debby and I was adopted. I'm trying to locate my birthfamily and I think my last name is Poitras. That name is on the back of my baby picture.'

'So which one of the girls do you belong to? I don't think it is Doris as she has one daughter in foster care and the rest were boys. Was your Mom Nora?'

'I'm not sure; I was hoping you could help me with that.'

'Why don't you pop by for a coffee and we can talk. I'd love to meet you.'

Within minutes I was knocking on Olive's door. A tiny dark skinned lady answered the door; she almost looked Polynesian.

'Olive?'

'Yes, Debby? Oh my God, dear, you look just like your mother!!! Look at you, you're beautiful! If I didn't know any better I would have sworn you were your mother twenty years ago. You are definitely Nora's daughter. You have the same build, the same eyes, the same smile.' She held me so tight, I swore I was going to pass out if I didn't crush her first. 'Let's go inside dear.'

Inside Olive introduced me to Uncle Albert. Uncle Albert was a very old man who seemed to be very ill and perhaps a bit senile. I thought perhaps this was her Uncle but discovered later that he was her father and my uncle.

After a few phone calls, Olive quickly determined that I was in fact Nora's daughter. I described the woman who brushed past me at my appointment and Olive agreed it was probably my mother. No one had heard from her or seen her in months until that week. They'd heard that she was in Regina visiting friends. The description fit her perfectly and why else would she be in Regina unannounced in the middle of the week after so many months. I will never know. *Why did you leave?*

Thirty years later, my visit with Olive is pretty much a blur but I remember hearing name after name, story after story for the next two hours. All of the personal information provided by Mrs. D. matched information that Olive could confirm. Olive said Nora had a baby girl that was given up for adoption around the time of my birth.

None of the family names or stories made sense to me then. It was all so brand new to me. I had a family of names but no faces. I ended my visit with Olive and we promised to keep in touch often. I left with a smile on my face.

I am now the daughter of Nora Poitras.

1988 and relationship changes

Once registered with Post Adoption, nothing happened for about ten years. Greatly disappointed with everything in life at that point, I had given up. In those ten years I had gone from being in a stable relationship to being a single mom with three children. My husband was a drug-induced psychotic who suffered from manic depression. Life was mostly down those days and I married on the rebound to an older gentleman who was a total control freak.

After seven years of marriage, I left him. Five years after we separated, my husband drank himself to death: nail polish remover mixed with soda water.

Just prior to leaving my second husband, I received a call from one of my siblings born in 1952. We agreed to write regularly but one day he showed up at my door. A heavy drinker, he had left his spouse in the next province and asked if he could move in with my family. The man scared me during our visit. He asked me to meet with him later in the evening and we could party. I hadn't even touched a drop since I found out our Mom was an alcoholic. *We exchanged two letters and you are already on my doorstep?*

The conversation that day was a little abnormal for a sibling meeting. I was not looking for a boyfriend. Needless to say, when he came to pick me up later that evening I never answered the door. *Was I afraid of him and his lifestyle or his intentions?* This brother never re-entered my life for another twenty years.

Within two months, I met another brother, three years younger than me. This brother was raised like an only child but had no interest in his Aboriginal heritage. He was white as far as he was concerned. The people that raised him were his family. We lost contact and he lost interest for another twenty years.

With two reunions being somewhat unsuccessful, I had given up hope. Then it happened again. While doing some family research in 2008, I came across someone that was a Poitras living in Germany. After a few emails, we discovered it was the first brother that I had met. He apologized for his bad behavior during our initial meeting but explained he was going through some bad times and ended up in rehab. While recovering, he had been focusing on his love of painting. Today, this brother is well known and is living in Germany teaching our culture and painting. We both apologized, as we were both experiencing marital problems back then.

In January 2009, I hit the jackpot again! My Post Adoption worker contacted with news of another brother born in 1951.

Although this brother had been searching awhile, he was having medical issues with Type II diabetes: first, a toe amputation in January, a foot amputation in July, followed by a knee amputation on my birthday, October 26th. We spoke often on the phone and got along famously. We were so much alike in so many ways, yet so different physically. I am just over 5 ft. tall, 130 lbs. while he is well over 6 ft. tall and 300 lbs. We decided to meet. I booked a flight in May 2010 and off I went. At the airport we were met by CBC radio reporters wanting to cover our reunion. 'What do you think? What do you want to say to him/her?' Not a word, just hugs and tears followed. The entire week staying with him at his house was spent laughing, crying, and learning about our lives apart. We met several cousins I had located. We visited our Mother's grave for the first time together and placed flowers there for her. (Nora had died in 1982 but I found out four years later.) We took a tour of the church my grandfather built and took hundreds of pictures of gravestones, houses and places where family once lived.

I received my name from a second cousin, 'Mahkeechap' which means 'One with big eyes.' My favorite reunion picture is of me sitting on my big brother's knee for the first time. This particular reunion was a success. Rick and I speak several times a week and I can truly say I love my big brother with all my heart. Nothing would make me happier than to move back home to be closer to him. He has even offered me his spare room until I can get on my feet.

But wait, we're not done yet. November 2010 brings forth the baby of all siblings, born in 1965. This child was never listed on our adoption files as he was a foster child. Post Adoption has informed me that foster children are not tracked in the same manner as adopted siblings. Now we keep in contact over the internet and have talked a few times via telephone. We are close but have not yet met.

December 2010 brings forth another two brothers, one born in 1947, the eldest of us siblings and another born in 1957. I have not yet met them or received details on them. I look forward to our reunion via letters (in 2011 and later). My request to the social worker is to reunite me with the eldest soon as our lives are quickly passing.

We do not know how many other siblings there are between 1959 and 1965 as nothing was listed after 1959. For that matter, we do not know if perhaps there are siblings between 1947 and 1965 that remained in foster care. We can only pray more details come to light with each reunion.

In June 2011, five of the six siblings reunited together at our brother Brian's wedding in Saskatoon, Saskatchewan.

After fifty or more years, we will know the meaning of being a family.

Debby lives near Toronto, Ontario, Canada and is employed by a generic pharmaceutical company. A mother of three and grandmother of six, she has been searching since 1978 for her biological family. With culture and heritage denied from birth, Debby enjoys sharing her discoveries with her family to ensure both are never lost again. She is writing a memoir.

45

Nice-shaped head

Alice Diver (Mi'kmaq Newfoundland)

Alice Diver

I am an adoptee, born January 9, 1967 in Montreal (as far as I know since I cannot access an OBC, my original birth certificate). I sought information and reunion in the late 1980s, eventually receiving two anonymous letters from my birth/first mother via a confidential intermediary. She was adamant that she would not be revealing any identifying information and that she had been very upset by my contacting her. (I had responded to her letters, enclosing photos of myself and my eldest daughter). Although she then vetoed any further contact, she did leave me with some amazing information: she was herself of

Native descent, from Newfoundland, and had eight siblings. She had subsequently married and had four children.

When my youngest child was born (I have three daughters and a son) I sent a card and several photos to the social services agency that had made the initial contact, just to let her know that she had grandchildren and that I would remain open to contact/ correspondence if she ever changed her mind. As I have been living in Northern Ireland since 1979, I wanted to reassure her that I had no intention of turning up out of the blue. The agency returned this unopened, citing federal law on contact, and stressing that they were unable to ever contact her again.

Several years later I contacted the agency to enquire about whether there was any information about my birth father. There was apparently a name on the file but it was a 'very common' surname. After three years of searching 'all of Canada' for him, the agency informed me last year that the search was futile, that they were not at liberty to release any identifying information and that my file would be closed. (I asked about the possibility of appealing this decision but I have not heard back from them on this. I assume no appeal process exists.) I have registered with many reunion registries in the hope that someone related to me might recognize the details and get in touch. I hope to visit Newfoundland someday even if only to learn more about the Indigenous people and culture. I will bring my children—now aged 16 to 23—with me. Two of them are quite fair, taking after my genetic father's side, while two are very dark—I like to think they look like our Native ancestors. I have met some First Nations people when they visited Ireland and they very kindly took much time to talk to me—they told me that I resemble some Maliseet people they know but that I could perhaps be descended from the Mi'kmaq people. I would give anything to find out. Hopefully the law will change one day to end discrimination such as this. Heritage should be protected by law and policy not hidden or removed by it.

Being adopted has not in itself been a major issue for me. I started going deaf in my twenties (otosclerosis, probably hereditary) but otherwise have been very lucky to marry, have children and gain an education. I never told my late parents that I was searching for my birth relatives as they had always made it clear that they would be very hurt by this.

Several instances do stand out however when 'being adopted' was an unexpected source of mortification. A couple of years ago I was involved in a seminar on post-adoption contact, giving a talk to a group of Adoption Social Workers on how the law on this area might be reformed, based on recent case law from Strasbourg on kin contact and identity rights. My observations and suggestions were not well-received, to say the least, and I was lucky to escape with only a few disparaging comments.

This was not the traumatizing thing about the day however. A senior social worker, whose talk was just before mine, produced a doll which the audience had to pass around and 'cuddle.' The purpose of this, she advised, was to show us how she dealt with traumatized adopted children. She would encourage them to hold the doll in their arms and would apparently tell them, '*You should feel no guilt about being adopted, as this is all the size you were when you were given up for adoption.*'

I have never liked dolls anyway but somehow managed to resist the urge to launch this one at high speed through the nearest window or at the top of her head when it was passed to me. I didn't pause to cuddle it either. (I did ask her later if she'd ever read any of Nancy Verrier's work and was met with what can only be described as a death glare).

One of the audience members also bellowed at me with great authority that he was an adopter, that his children would never have any interest in searching, nor could he even remember which of his children had been adopted or 'natural.' I was sorely tempted to suggest to him that the adoptees are probably the ones who don't resemble him or his wife and that they probably have their original birth certificates well hidden under their beds. I managed to bite my tongue.

The other occasion was during my PhD viva. The opening question by the external examiner, which is meant to put the student at ease was, '*Clearly you are adopted. Explain how you were able to write fairly.*' I have little recollection of whatever answer I managed to garble back at him but I did argue that not only did I possess a certificate of mental hygiene from the Quebec authorities (a pre-requisite then to being 'adoptable') but that my non-identifying information confirmed that I'd apparently had 'a nice-shaped head' in infancy. (The thesis re-write is going well.)

Alice lives in Ireland and teaches family law.

46

Adoption and Repatriation Services to First Nations People of Canada

Resolution by Assembly of First Nations 1999

Moved by: Chief Gerald Esquash, Swan Lake First Nation; Seconded by: Chief Ted Quewezance, Keeseekoose First Nation; Carried. Certified copy of a Resolution made the 22nd day of July, 1999 in Vancouver, B.C.; Phil Fontaine, National Chief **Resolution No. 10/99**

SUBJECT: Adoption and repatriation services to First Nations people of Canada

WHEREAS First Nation's people across Canada have been tragically affected by the adoption of their children, (16,810 treaty status children, DIAND Statistics, 1996) in the last thirty years; and,

WHEREAS adoption of First Nations children by the governments in Canada is a continuation from the boarding school policies of the assimilation of First Nations through First Nations Children; and,

WHEREAS the affects of these government policies of assimilation has devastated and tragically affected First Nation's children, families and communities, culture; and,

WHEREAS the 'sixties scoop' was a massive failure on First Nations families and was effectively a form of genocide; and

WHEREAS the long term effects of the 'sixties scoop' continue to be felt

in every First Nations community in Canada as parents and children deal with the children problems of lost relatives and ensuing social problems; and

WHEREAS these children, now adults, are searching for family, culture and identity and,

WHEREAS birth families, grandparents, mothers, fathers, siblings and extended family are searching for their children lost to adoption; and,

WHEREAS the demand for service to assist and facilitate searches and reunions is enormous; and,

WHEREAS the funding for repatriation services are inadequately funded or non-existent in most provinces; and,

WHEREAS the Federal and Provincial Governments are responsible for this destruction of First Nations families and their communities; and,

THEREFORE BE IT RESOLVED that National Chief Phil Fontaine support and assist the First Nations communities of Canada in their efforts to secure adequate funding for repatriation programs from the Federal and Provincial Governments of Canada.

47

I am a tiguak panik (adopted daughter)

Birds of a Feather

Bridget Sweet (Inuit Newfoundland)

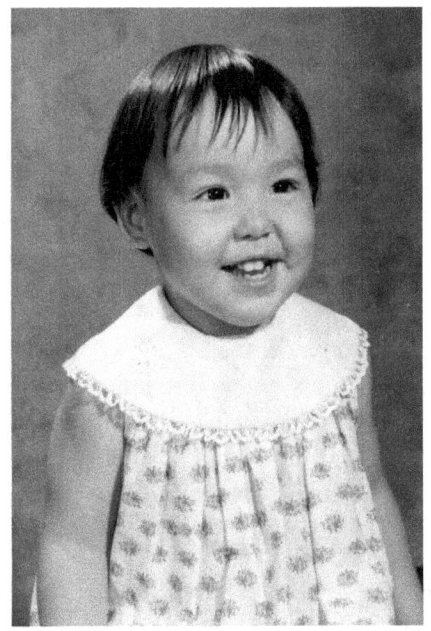

Bridget Sweet (Family Photo)

Governmental decisions to relocate, introduce alcohol, and give education to Natives while smiling to cause erasure was depicted in the 1986 movie, 'Babakiueria.' The similarities between my families' history and the movie caused me to shake. All my life I've tried to deny and/or disguise my family's deep ugly scars.

One character in the movie, 'Wagwan,' the Minister of White Affairs, illustrated the sentiments of the government official my Inuit mother, Millicent encountered. He spoke with the same patronizing tone as he expressed how wonderful boarding schools were. He said taking people away from their homes was fine.

My grandmother, Maria Deborah, oldest of eight, went to a boarding school. She was made to forget her language and forced to study the Bible. When she returned home and had children of her own, her zest for Inuit life and culture had dwindled.

Fortunately, Maria's younger siblings (at the time of writing this were alive and holding Nunatsiavut Government positions) reminded her of her culture before she passed on.

By 1950, my grandfather, Julius, was moved out of Hebron. I read online that the government closed it down because it was too small. He too lost his home.

I will never forget my own relocation, loss of culture, language, and family because of my adoption in Massachusetts.

'Bunji Gunji,' the policeman in the movie, spoke of how the people committed crimes due to alcohol. It was the alcohol the Europeans introduced to my family that decided my fate.

My mother Millicent did not know the 'spirits' would cause her to be in unsafe bars, make her lose her memory and bodily functions. She did not know the military man would take advantage of her when she was nineteen. She thought because she worked hard for her ailing, alcohol dependent parents, that she could play after work. She did not know alcohol would eventually kill her sister on the street.

When my dear friend Trace asked me to write about my adoption I was hesitant. I contemplated it for weeks. I worried it would embarrass my family or myself. Then I realized that my silence would only perpetuate the cycle of relocation and erasure of my people, the Canadian Inuit. It has not been easy for my Inuit family.

I am a *tiguak panik* — adopted daughter. I am an enrolled member of Nunatsiavut Government in Labrador, Canada. It is a crime what the government allowed, peddled, encouraged and did in the 1970s. Their apology does not help me.

My adoption papers state that Dr. Dominic approved of my adoption in March 1971. An eye problem delayed the process by two months.

The name my mother gave me is private and only known by a few. In 2005, I decided on a new public name. A fellow adoptee and I chose it.

I have mixed feelings regarding my adoption. I go back and forth.

Some days, I tell myself:

It wasn't Her fault. I forgive her. She had me at least.

My dear mother wasn't given the option to keep me.

It wasn't Her fault. I forgive her. She had me at least.

My dear mother, then 20, didn't know what my removal would do to her. It wasn't Her fault. I forgive her. She had me at least.

She had to. It wasn't Her fault. I forgive her. She had me at least.

I look like her. I have her height, her shoe size, and her petite stature. We even have the same placement of where our gray hairs grow. It wasn't Her fault. I forgive her. She had me at least.

Other days, I tell myself a different story:

I'm lost. I want to know who my dad was. I want 'the hole in my soul' filled. I'm envious of families with different generations that are connected. I'm a statistic, a victim of betrayal. I'm alone to fend for myself. I don't want to cry again tonight. There is no good news. There is no easy fix.

And then, I realize I must make my good news. I do have good news:

I have a baby girl. She is mine – forever and ever. She's amazing. She's with me. She has my eyes. My idiosyncrasies. My brains. My name. My cooking ability. My love of books. My sense of humor. My love for baseball, water, and driving. I can check on her fifteen times a night if I want. She's in my house. She calls me Mum or Momma. We are a close-knit family. We laugh and cry together. I know the beauty of raising a daughter.

I am loved in my adopted family and I was taught lots of things. I was gifted with education. I was told I was wanted. I wasn't the only adoptee in my chosen family. Yes, I can recall some childhood memories that were not okay, but I can also recall some beautiful memories that I still laugh and reminisce about.

I now know I have a purpose. It took me a long time to discover that my life was not a waste. After trials and tribulations, and years of therapy, I know this. Though my life has mirrored the movie 'Babakiueria,' it no longer defines me. My life is good. My life is blessed with a loving family.

I recall the words of my high school vice principal. It was the early 1980s. 'Birds of a feather flock together.' Growing up with Caucasian parents, I had never heard the term 'Lost Bird.' He must have known I was a Lost Bird.

Fly with me! Honk, if you pass me! Or Honk if you need a wing up. I'll be there. I am a *tiguak panik*.

Bridget Sweet, 40, graduated from University of Massachusetts–Amherst with a second degree in Journalism and a Certificate Program in Native American Indian Studies. She is raising her teenage daughter in the Native community. She has yet to return home to Labrador and personally meet her family, though she has contact with them via internet.

48

Our Future

"The family is the foundation of Inuit culture, society and economy. All our social and economic structures, customary laws, traditions and actions have tried to recognize and affirm the strength of the family unit....Only positive constructive action by community governments and families and individuals can help recover our vision and zest for life."

—Henoch Obed, Labrador Inuit Alcohol and Drug Abuse Program, Nain, Newfoundland and Labrador

"We believe that the Creator has entrusted us with the sacred responsibility to raise our families...for we realize healthy families are the foundation of strong and healthy communities. The future of our communities lies with our children, who need to be nurtured within their families and communities."

—Charles Morris, Executive Director, Tikinagan Child and Family Services, Sioux Lookout, Ontario

"There is a part of the Canadian discussion I've wanted to comment on. Most of this discussion is the result of the Tom Flanagan book, *First Nations: Second Thoughts*. Despite his never having any relationship with the First Nations, Flanagan was able to start a new Canadian thought: Get Indians off the reserves. The new thinking (and Flanagan's horse to flog) is that the Canadian government is keeping us on reserves and, thus, keeping us from being Canadians and enjoying the good life. Many who adhere to this line of thought really want only to do away with the First Nations, period. And some mean well, but are misguided. Has Canada been given the job of the Creator; to decide who should be a certain race? .... I have asked as many Aboriginals as I could, 'Would you like to be made

273

Canadian against your will?' To an individual, they said "no." In the days of the residential schools, many Indians did not know who they were. Today, most Aboriginals know who they are and why they are — Cree, Ojibwe, Lenni, Lenape or Lakota. The Creator made me who I am. No man can make me something I'm not. Even if they make me Canadian I will still be brown and Indian. We are communities, not ghettos of the Canadian mosaic. We haven't adjusted as rapidly as the Flanagan thinkers want—to the European way, to European thinking. Even if, in large part (and I have no data to say one way or another) we wanted to be European, how fast can a people recover from 150 years of imprisonment?

—Bud Whiteye, Osprey Writers Group (online)

49

Our Way Home: Strategy will ease pain of family reunification

Joan Black, Windspeaker Staff Writer

Windspeaker Magazine, Toronto, Volume: 17 Issue: 5 Year: 1999

The joint management committee of the Aboriginal Healing and Wellness Strategy has released a report of a six-month study into the issues of Ontario-born Aboriginal children put in the custody of non-Native care providers outside their communities of origin.

The report, titled **Our Way Home,** was prepared by Native Child and Family Services in conjunction with the consultants Stevenato and Associates and Janet Budgell. It focuses on the problems of families that had children removed by provincial child welfare authorities during the late 1960s to early 1980s—the phenomenon known to Aboriginal people as the infamous "60s Scoop."

The study details the effects of adoption and foster care on children disconnected from their tribe and culture. It also identifies a variety of obstacles that Aboriginal people face in trying to re-establish family ties, and it sets out a four-phase strategy aimed at easing repatriation for those who desire it.

The study was undertaken by the Repatriation Research Working Group of the Aboriginal Healing and Wellness Strategy in Toronto. Participants included the Association of Iroquois and Allied Indians; Grand Council Treaty No. 3; Nishnawbe Aski Nation; Union of Ontario Indians; independent First Nations' representatives; Federation of Indian Friendship Centres; Ontario Native Women's Association; Ontario Métis Aboriginal Association; Ontario Ministry of Health; Ontario Native Affairs Secretariat, Ontario Women's Directorate and the Ministry of Community and Social Services. The Ministry of the Attorney

General was supposed to be on the committee, but was not an active participant, a spokesperson said.

"Through this report we are consulting with our communities and organizations as to how we can effectively assist these people and communities in this emotional healing process," said Garnet Angeconeb, Aboriginal co-chair of the Aboriginal Healing and Wellness Strategy's joint management committee.

The Ontario's Children's Aid Society was empowered by the 1965 federal-provincial Indian Welfare Agreement to reach into reserve communities and administer provisions of the Child Welfare Act. Large numbers of Indian children were removed from their homes, often as a result of distorted suppositions of Children's Aid Society workers about what constitutes adequate parental care and supervision in a culture unlike their own. Loss of the children's identities was the result.

"[The children] were not given any exposure to their culture; they have to know it's OK to be who they are," said Donna Simon, health policy analyst at the Ontario Native Women's Association, which was a partner in the study. "Denial of who a child is is a real travesty," she added.

It is not known how many Aboriginal children were claimed by the Sixties Scoop in Ontario or how many of them desire to repatriate. Those seeking repatriation typically want to meet or re-establish relationships with birth families. Some seek repatriation to regain Indian status, to live in their community of origin, or to uncover their families' medical histories, the report says.

The project came about because many Aboriginal people are seeking information from agencies that mostly don't have the will or the resources to offer repatriation services, according to Simon.

Mainly, the investigators wanted to find jurisdictions having a repatriation model that might be transportable to Ontario. Extensive consultation with Aboriginal and non-Aboriginal repatriation organizations and child welfare authorities, Elders, "experts" in Canada, the US, Australia and New Zealand, and with adoptees, adult foster children or Crown wards, birth families and adoptive parents took place.

They found three Aboriginal organizations focusing on repatriation based in British Columbia, and one in Manitoba. These are the United Native Nations, the Gitxsan Reconnection Program, the Wet'su wet'en Repatriation Program, and the Manitoba First Nations Repatriation Program. According to the Aboriginal Healing and Wellness Strategy report, there are no others working full-time on repatriation issues in Canada. It also discloses there is a seven-year wait for a search by the Ontario government's Adoption Disclosure Register.

The report recommends establishing a **central Aboriginal repatriation office** under the umbrella of an existing Aboriginal organization. The office would employ at least two staff: one to address policy, education and awareness issues, the other to fulfill the role of counsellor. The report further proposes access to Canadian adoption databases to conduct searches, access to internet databases, better co-ordination with other agencies and referrals to culturally sensitive professionals when required.

Repatriation services would include training and educating family support workers, and undertaking education and awareness campaigns. Counselling would be available to adult adoptees, foster children, birth families and adoptive families, the report says.

SOURCE: http://www.ammsa.com/node/12907

50

Adopted Mohawk finds Birth Parent: Indian Roots Grow Deep

David Kanowakeron Hill Morrison UE

(This first chapter was written and posted on my website in 1994)

Sekoh! And hello from Rochester, New York. I'm a Six Nations Mohawk who was born and raised in the Rochester area and while it may not be readily apparent, I consider myself to be a Native Canadian.

I was born in 1954 to a single Mohawk woman who had travelled to Rochester from the Six Nations reserve in search of a job. She was from a large family and when she found that she was pregnant, she didn't wish to be a burden to her mother. As difficult as it was, she decided to place her first-born child up for adoption with a sincere desire for a better life for the child. It would be a decision proven correct many years later.

A white, hard-working, middle-class couple adopted me, and another boy. We lived in the city of Rochester for a few weeks and then joined the legion of those seeking the sanctity of the suburbs. The surroundings were typically suburban; three-bedroom ranch, dog, station wagon, large yard and a yearly vacation to a cottage on the Rideau River. It was a very secure family and although discipline was never withheld when needed, there was a lot of love. Both of us boys knew we were adopted, and I was told that MY birth mother was a Canadian Indian and that her last name was Hill. That was the only information my parents were given by the adoption agency. My life-long affinity with Canada started early. Later I would find that I was more 'Canadian' than anybody knew.

Looking back, my suburban childhood was cushy and insular—not exactly coddled, but definitely naive in the ways of ethnic and cultural differences.

Out of 580 members of my graduating high school class, there were three African-Americans, a few Asians and one North American Indian who couldn't (wouldn't?) decide if he was or wasn't an Indian. How could I? Minorities weren't 'in' then and how would I 'prove' I was an Indian? Despite feelings of definitely being different, the embarrassment was kept to myself.

All adoptees think about the circumstances surrounding their adoption at some time… how could you NOT think about it when the creepy kid comes out with, 'Your REAL mother didn't even want you.' The worst scars are often caused by words. My mother would explain that I was wanted and loved more than I'd ever know, but someday, somehow and somewhere.

The U.S. in the late Sixties was in social turmoil and it probably was a tough time to be teaching a fourteen-year-old that the police are our friends while he watched live TV showing 'our friends' pummeling and gassing demonstrators at the 1968 Democratic Convention. It was the time of 'self-actualization' when we were repeatedly told, above all else, 'Be Yourself'. Today, I may owe some gratitude to the people asking the 'idiotic' question, 'Who am I?'

My dirty little adoption secret was a source of embarrassment, and with my darker skin, it was a quite a stretch to pretend to be the Scotsman or Dutch-English that my adoptive parents were. The whole issue was deftly sidestepped.

Repression and denial aren't the healthiest of reactions for a kid to carry around during his formative years. Neither are inferiority, insecurity and doubt. My parents tried their best… really… but as any parent will tell you, 'they don't come with instructions'.

At thirteen, I found there WAS something I could do better than almost anyone else—consume alcohol. Finally, a vocation I excelled at! This was to be a source of pointless pride throughout high school and college. My drinking progressed until 1980. Out of work, out of hope, and rapidly running out of life, I finally got help. Thirteen years later, I am still sober.

After mending the body, I decided I needed to find out more about my Indian heritage. What WAS my identity? With a renewed determination, I began to deal with a legal system that treated me as if I was legally swapped chattel. The sealed adoption records contained information about me, and my birth mother. Regardless of what the State law dictated, I should be entitled to the same knowledge that the rest of the non-adopted world took for granted. It would only be possible to find my birthmother (and my heritage) by this means.

What followed was ten years of legal bantering and red tape. I dealt with two federal governments, a state and provincial government, local courts, and smug office workers. I encountered more 'you can't's' than 'you can's', and enough 'I-don't-know's' to fill a file cabinet. My determination reached its maximum and I threw caution to the wind. I spoke with an attorney who quietly stated he WOULD get the name of my birthmother from the adoption records to DIAND in Ottawa for a determination of status. Lawyers seem to be able to work miracles for the right price and a steady stream of inquiring phone calls.

The Family Court judge agreed to release the name of my birthmother to DIAND for C-31 purposes on the provision that I was not informed of her name. DIAND agreed and within weeks, I called and was told, 'You ARE banded as an Upper Mohawk of the Six Nations Reserve.' My disbelief was beyond description... I had BEEN to the Six Nations reserve with my ex-wife on several occasions on our bi-monthly exploration of the province of Ontario which lasted five years. (Yes, I'm FAIRLY familiar with the southern part of the province.)

Within two days I made a beeline to Ohsweken and spoke with ANYBODY in the Administration Building who could suggest how my birthmother could be found. Was she still alive? Did she live on the reserve? How should this be handled? Would I be a disruptive secret from the past? Would this be an embarrassment? What if she married and her husband didn't know about me? How do I go about finding an Indian woman with MAYBE a last name of Hill and fifty-six to fifty-eight years old? The odds were not encouraging, but after ten years of what I'd just been through, it was WAY too close to be giving up.

After meeting with a social worker from the reserve, it was suggested that a personals classified be submitted in the reserve paper, The Tekawennake. This was done reluctantly because even above MY desires, I wanted to make sure anonymity of my birthmother was respected and protected. The social worker pointed out that if she didn't want to respond, she wouldn't, and I should at least give her the opportunity to meet me if indeed she was alive AND living on Six Nations. The classified had a brief, non-identifying description of my birthday, place of birth, adoption agency, my surname at birth (as far as I knew) and stated that I wanted to express thanks and appreciation for what must have been a difficult decision for a 20-year-old. Then I waited.

At the end of the first week, there had been no response sent back to the Teka and I started to believe this REALLY may be the end of the line. The ad ran another week with the understanding that if there were no responses, I'd have to be content knowing I'd at least found my reserve and was a Status Mohawk. That by itself was no small accomplishment considering the odds to get to THAT point.

Ten days after the ad first appeared, a call came from the social worker telling me there had been a response. Her voice was shrill from excitement and she said she knew the family and the woman who was reportedly my birthmother. Excited? Yes, but my expectations had been raised and dashed so many times that I thought, 'Well, maybe it IS and maybe it ISN'T. This may be a person who's clutching at straws and I just happen to be a close enough description.' I was somewhat dubious and who wouldn't be after thirty-seven years? I was told I had three brothers and four sisters; one of my brothers had died. I hadn't even met the family and already a sense of loss. Coming from a very small family and being the youngest, to being the oldest of seven siblings was more than a shock… it was something I hadn't even thought about. Nothing she said to me on the phone for three of four sentences was heard.

I was to call this particular number at 6:30pm that night. I waited. 6:25, 6:26, 6:27. Finally, after grabbing the phone and dialing, a voice answered and I asked to speak with her. Then a 'Hello?' and a, 'Hi, I think I may be your son.' 'I think you're my son, too.'

We spoke for a short while and thought it would be a good idea if we could meet. Driving to Six Nations by that point was almost a weekly thing (some 230 miles), so I said it'd be no problem for me to meet her at her house. We agreed upon the following weekend.

I can't remember a lot of the following week. What went through my mind was a variety of doubt, anxiety, relief, fear, contentment, anticipation and awe. You need to remember I'd never had any contact with Indians before and here I am going to a house on a reserve in Canada to meet my birthmother for the first time in thirty-seven years. Nervous? Well, maybe just a LITTLE.

Driving to Six Nations that Saturday I was strangely NOT nervous. Finding the house, I drove in the driveway and immediately saw a guy with a pony-tail to his butt. 'Ah, that must be one of my brothers', and sure enough it was. 'G'won in the house, they're waiting for you'. I went in and saw a lady in her thirties with eyes wet with tears who said, 'Hi, I'm your sister.' I looked up and saw a woman in her fifties (also with tears) come toward me. When my eyes met hers, my search officially came to an end. There was no doubt; this WAS my mother.

We hugged and said, 'It's been a long time' then proceeded to cry almost as if it were a movie script. I could have been in Oz; the whole thing didn't seem real. Meeting my other brother and my four sisters and their families (TEN nieces and nephews), we sat around the kitchen table with people looking at me to see who I looked like from the family. I was introduced to my Indian Dad (my Mom's husband) who said, 'My home is your home. You don't ever need an invitation to come home.' More tears.

What followed must have been orchestrated prior to my arrival. I noticed people on the phone and within thirty minutes, the driveway was packed with cars and the house was crammed with, 'I'm your aunt, I'm your cousin, he's your uncle, you look like one of your uncles, you look like one of your cousins, I'm your sister; what's my name?' Stunned and overwhelmed.

There were many, many trips back 'home' in the following weeks. It was a rebirth of sorts but fate was to intervene again.

My adoptive parents had been supportive of my search and encouraged me even when the legal systems had been stacked against me. My 'mother-over-here' was in failing health due to the debilitating effects of diabetes. Six weeks after finding my family, my adopted mother died. I'll always remember the contented smile she had when seeing pictures of my Indian family the day I met all of them. My father asked that my birthmother and my Indian dad be invited to the memorial service, which they attended along with my Indian aunt. My two families met for the first time at the service. I had found a mother and I had lost a mother.

My pony-tailed brother was in a great deal of pain from accidents that had severely damaged his leg and he was permanently disabled. He had a gentleness, which belied his gruff exterior (my little brother is the same) and I was anxious to get to know both of my 'little' brothers. Actually, both of them could toss their big brother around like a snowflake, but I knew they wouldn't. Three weeks after my mother had died, I got a call from the rez; my oldest little brother was hemorrhaging and in a coma.

I went to the hospital and saw him connected to the machines. My family was there and I was told it was just a matter of time. As he faded, we gathered around the bed... touching and holding his hands as if to help him get ready for the trip he was about to take. Finally, he left and a mother and father said good-bye to a second son. My mother had found a son and had lost a son.

My only little brother left is special to me; not because he's had to endure the loss of two of his brothers, or because he's my only Indian brother remaining. He's special because he and I grew up in different worlds, and I need him to teach me the things HIS older brothers taught him. In return, we'll find the things that I can share with him from what I've learned from my world.

My four sisters are amazing. They've captured the strength and determination that Indian women are known for, from my mother. It's been a great experience witnessing a matriarchal culture in action and as in many other things, there's a lot the non-Indian world can learn from our families. Tough, yet gentle.

My Indian Dad is a survivor. A survivor of raising seven children while moving from one coast of the United States to the other in search of work. He insisted that his family be with him; not an easy undertaking. He survived the 'Mush House' (Indian residential school); he survived the U.S. Army and he's a survivor of cancer. He has a youth to his spirit, which always brings a smile to me. We both love to laugh because there's already enough to be down about without dwelling on it. Take care of business, but above all, enjoy life and living.

There was another little brother who died in 1977 in a car accident. He'll never be forgotten because I 'feel' he and I were somewhat alike. There's a sense of being cheated from not knowing him, but in a way, his spirit remains alive through the rest of my family.

I feel like the eldest brother who left for a number of years and then returned home. My relationship with my Indian family is one of great joy and love. I know I'm one of the most fortunate of our Creator's children in that I was accepted and welcomed to a beautiful family. There are other similar situations where the 'return' of the long lost child has NOT been a glad time.

In 1994, at 39 I'm an Indian child, having never been exposed to Indian culture. Until 1993, I'd never even been to a pow wow. I'm a Database Administrator at a large company in Rochester which employs some 38,000 people. There's a Native American Council (an employee network) with some fifteen Indians; you might say there's a VERY small minority of Native Americans working here. Every time I go back to the rez, I learn something more about the Indian ways from my nieces, nephews and my family. I study my heritage and attend socials, meetings and pow wows. I'm learning and will probably never stop learning.

There is much I could teach about computers and the ways of the corporate world, but all that can be learned in a university. Learning how to live as an Indian cannot be gleaned from a book. The mysterious feelings and unique view of the world makes sense to me now after all these years. There appear to be certain behavioral traits in me, which make me wonder if it's the Indian in me (even though I was never raised among Indians). Is it possible there's REALLY a special spiritual core in all our people? I'm finding out there IS.

The first half of my life was as a white man by chance; the second half will be an Indian by choice.

The Sequel

Fast forward twenty years to 2011. In the two decades since my reunification, what's been going on?

Life, that's what. The drama of life and never-ending experience of education has shown me that not all journeys follow a prescribed path and that life 'as it should be' rarely turns out that way.

I've become a better observer and more philosophical, possibly due to the unique perspective that's been granted to me, but probably more as a matter of simply growing older and assessing my faults, errors and successes.

I now see that my reunification with my birth-identity and birth-family has been a gift of immeasurable value, one that was largely pre-ordained from an existential vantage but also a generous blessing from a spiritual perspective. The lessons I've been taught could never have been possible had I still been wandering through life without knowledge of who I am or where I came from.

I live in many worlds; on the one hand, a part of each and on the other, not fully integrated with any of these disparate societies. Three nationalities (Mohawk, Canadian, and American), three cultures, three sets of values and priorities, three distinct ways of coping and dealing with life and its challenges…. one person.

'Cross-culturally adopted Native' is the description I use to identify my background. It's a distinct demographic, yet in the years since my search ended, one that I've learned isn't as uncommon as I was once led to believe. Circumstances may vary but the very feelings and experiences I experienced during my younger years are nearly identical to those that all cross-culturally adopted Natives face in their lives.

Some find the resolution and answers that I found, while others are forced to find a workable compromise that allows them to move forward in their lives. For reasons that are yet to be known (if ever), I was one of the fortunate ones while others are left to wander in the darkness, with questions that may never be answered.

Wakatera'swiyohne'. ('I was lucky.')

There have been times when these three personal 'memberships' have clashed, creating frustration and anger. Yet through the tasks of living, the very Aboriginal notion of balance has played a crucial component of developing coping skills in the need to be able to function successfully and find happiness in each society. It's not been easy but there's never been any promise that life itself is guaranteed to be easy.

From 1991 to her passing in 1999, both my birthmother and I experienced the joy of a close and loving mother-son relationship. In terms of a lifetime, it was a brief amount of time but during those years, my birthmother shared her values and wisdom with me, which I'll take to my grave. We had our moments of disagreements and misunderstandings as is the case in any parent-child relationship, but there was never any question of the deep respect and admiration that we each had for the other. As I struggled with resolving my 'nurture versus nature' sensibilities, it's been the memories of my mother's wisdom that have echoed in my mind when I've needed guiding advice.

BOTH my mothers, for I am a product of each.

Living in the States while professing a special affinity for Canada and my natural identity as a Mohawk, hasn't been without its controversy and turmoil. There's a subtle, but very real demand placed upon me to 'choose one' society at the exclusion of the others.

A 'cross cultural' AND a 'cross border' lifestyle has meant receiving the benefits of multiple societies, even though the pitfalls of not being fully integrated in any has been a source of frustration. Throughout the years, I've come to the acceptance and understanding that a higher power has placed me exactly where I belong, if not fully desire.

Balance. That's been the saving lesson I've learned from my Native 'upbringing'. For me, a life in balance—emotionally, spiritually, mentally and physically—has shown that an Aboriginal circular model of living is healthier than a non-Native linear model but granted, that may be simply a matter of appropriateness to my own life.

It's not an ethic for everyone else's life, but as unique individuals we each need to approach life on our own terms and discover what works and what doesn't.

On one level, the older I get the more questions I have. Why was I allowed to live with alcoholism and addiction when my own birth-brother and ex-wife weren't? Why did fate allow me to (1) find my birthmother and (2) develop a close relationship with her when so many others were outright rejected? Who do I turn to in order to find knowledgeable advice when absolutes in life are rarely available anyway?

There are dilemmas that non-Native adoptees face when trying to resolve issues that face them on their life's journey which are unique from the Native adoptee. Trying to define the Native experience to non-Natives is an exercise in futility as the adage, 'you need to be one to understand one' is all important.

This makes the Native adoptee experience require special considerations that aren't as critical as what non-Native adoptees face. It may be safer to say the Native adoptee WILL see the world differently (without necessarily understanding why) rather than assume there's no fundamental difference between them and non-Native adoptees.

For parents and caregivers of Native adoptees, the benefit of doubt is less damaging then the presumption of knowledge. Not understanding the Native psyche is no reason to ignore it and children who are deprived of expressing their natural talents and interests are often left filled with resentment, confusion and frustration.

In the years since my search ended, I've experienced a number of serious health issues which has left me disabled but fortunately, not incapable of taking care of myself. I've learned that a disability doesn't necessarily imply incapacitation and patience is not only a virtue, but a powerful tool for coping.

The occasional financial challenge has taught me to appreciate what I have and not lament what I don't. While I'm faced with the temptation to live up to the standards of the society I was raised in, I'm more comfortable with living my life according to a set of standards that I've defined and set for myself.

This seeming rejection of my learned values has not been well received by many of those who have only seen my non-Native past. Apparently, not playing the game according to the prescribed rules has consequences including condemnation, skepticism and outright scorn.

As a result, I've lost many friends and acquaintances from my past who have not seen or embraced the remarkable joy that comes from achieving a personal success not based on material gain.

My twenties were turbulent and filled with doubt, anxiety and a lack of direction. While the physical and personal damage I did to myself was profound and would affect me for decades to come, the resiliency of being a young adult was on my side.

My thirties were about rebuilding a life that had all the makings of a middle-class American dream: a wife, good job and on track with following the course that made others happy but was somehow missing the personal satisfaction I was seeking.

My forties were a time of self-examination, introspection and discovery... free to be me and chart my own course according to my own terms. It was a time of learning to be assertive without being offensive and showed me the delicate art of diplomacy when relating to others.

My fifties have been quietly remarkable. Finally achieving contentment and not falling apart over small setbacks has allowed me to focus on greater goals. To most, I live a life of an enigmatic recluse with brief bursts of intense sociability followed by a retreat into a world of serenity and spiritual reflection. It's not hyperbole to describe myself as a 'student of life' when in fact, we're all students from the day we're born until we take our last breath. Even the act of dying is a new learning experience.

From a source of embarrassment to a celebration of great pride, my life as a Native adoptee has been a journey of discovery filled with one unforeseen twist and turn after the other. At times, I've lost my way... which is to be expected when there have been no maps into uncharted territories.

But through it all, the rewards of finding one's own way have provided me with the skills to see when something isn't working, then correct and rebalance to be on my journey.

Life is truly about the journey and not a destination. Goals are needed but merely as an impetus to move forward; those who maintain they're in absolute control of all aspects of their lives are arrogantly dismissive of the power of fate and luck.

And it was both fate and luck that returned me to my natural heritage and birth-family as well as delivered me to a close, loving and nurturing adopted family.

Wakatera'swiyohne'.

David currently spends his time living in Two Worlds and two countries.

Bibliography

Indian Adoption Project

DeMeyer, Trace A., *One Small Sacrifice: A Memoir*. Lost Children of the Indian Adoption Projects, 2010 (1st Ed.) 2012 (2nd Ed.)

Busbee, Patricia, DeMeyer, Trace., *Two Worlds: Lost Children of the Indian Adoption Projects*, (Book One) Blue Hand Books, 2012, First Edition

Busbee, Patricia, DeMeyer, Trace., *Called Home: The Road Map, Lost Children of the Indian Adoption Projects*, (Vol. 2) Blue Hand Books, 2014 and 2016 (second edition)

Bilchik, S. (2001, April 24). [Keynote address]. Speech presented at the 19th Annual Protecting our Children Conference, Anchorage, AK.

Child Welfare League of America. (1960, April). Indian Adoption Project. New York: Author.

Demer, L. (2001, May). Native receive apology for 1950s racial adoptions. Pathways Practice Digest, 1-2.

Harness, Susan Devan, *Mixing Cultural Identities Through Transracial Adoption: Outcomes of the Indian Adoption Project* (1958-1967) Edwin Mellen Press, NY. 2009

Hentz, Trace, *Two Worlds: Lost Children of the Indian Adoption Projects*, (Vol. 1) Blue Hand Books, 2017, Second Edition, revised and updated

Hentz, Trace L, *Stolen Generations: Survivors of the Indian Adoption Projects and 60s Scoop*, (Vol. 3) Lost Children of the Indian Adoption Projects book series, Blue Hand Books, 2016.

Jacobs, Margaret D., *White Mother to a Dark Race: Settler Colonialism, Maternalism, and the Removal of Indigenous Children in the American West and Australia, 1880-1940* (2009)

Jacobs, Margaret D., *A Generation Removed: The Fostering and Adoption of Indigenous Children in the Postwar World* (Sept 1, 2014) University of Nebraska Press

Lyslo, A. (1962, December). Suggested criteria to evaluate families to adopt American Indian children through Indian Adoption Project. New York: Child Welfare League of America.

Lyslo, A. (1964). The Indian Adoption Project: An appeal to catholic agencies to participate. Catholic Charities Review, 48(5), 12-16.

Lyslo, A. (1967, March). 1966 year end summary of the Indian Adoption Project. New
York: Child Welfare League of America.

Lyslo, A. (1967). Adoptive placement of Indian children. Catholic Charities Review,
51(2), 23-25.

Lyslo, A. (1968, April). The Indian Adoption Project – 1958 through 1967: Report of its
accomplishments, evaluation and recommendations for adoption services to Indian
children. New York: Child Welfare League of America.

Outcomes for Transracially Adoption Native American Children

Briggs, Laura (2012), Somebody's Children, The Politics of Transracial and Transna-
tional Adoption, Duke University Press. ICWA 121-123.

Brooks, D.; Barth, R. P. (1999). Adult transracial and inracial adoptees: Effect of race,
gender, adoptive family structure, and placement history on adjustment outcomes.
American Journal of Orthopsychiatry, 69(1), 87-99.

Fanshel, D. (1972). Far from the reservation: The transracial adoption of American
Indian children. Metuchen, NJ: The Scarecrow Press, Inc.

Green, B. E., Sack, W. H., Pambrum, A. (1981). A review of child psychiatric epidemi-
ology with special reference to American Indian and Alaska Native children. White
Cloud Journal, 2(2), 22-36).

Green, H. J. (1983). Risks and attitudes associated with extra-cultural placement of
American Indian children: A critical review. Journal of the American Academy of
Child Psychiatry, 22(1), 63-67.

Knapp, J. (2002, March). My adoption meant personal loss, but I don't look for blame.
Pathways Practice Digest, 1-2.

Kowal, L. A., Schilling, K. M. (1985). Adoption through the eyes of adult adoptees.
American Journal of Orthopsychiatry, 55(3), 354-362.

Locust, Carol (2000, October). Split Feathers: Adult American Indians who were placed in non-Indian families as children. Ontario Association of Children's Aid Societies Journal, 44(3), 11-16.

Magagnini, S. (1997, June 5). Indian adoptees go in search of roots. The Sacramento Bee, p. A20.

Massatti, R. R., Vonk, E. M., Gregorie, T. K. (2004). Reliability and validity of the transracial adoption parenting scale. Research on Social Work Practice, 14(1), 43-50.

McDonald, T. P., Propp, J. R, Murphy, K. C. (2001). The post-adoption experience: Child, parent, and family predictors of family adjustment to adoption. Child Welfare, 80(1), 71-94.

Melmer, D. (2004, February 18). 'Split Feather' syndrome addressed at S.D. committee hearing. Indian Country Today. Retrieved May 8, 2006, from http://www.indian-country.com/content

Morse, B. (1984). Native Indian and Metis children in Canada: Victims of the child welfare system.

Rathbun, C., McLaughlin, H., Bennett, C., and Garland, J. A. (1965). Later adjustment of children following radical separation from family and culture. American Journal of Orthopsychiatry, 35, 604-609.

Robin, R. W., Rasmussen, J. K., Gonzalez-Santin, E. (1999). Impact of childhood out-of-home placement on a southwestern American Indian tribe. Journal of Human Behavior in the Social Environment, 2(1/2), 69-89.

Rosene, L. R. (1985). A follow-up study of Indian children adopted by white families. Dissertation Abstracts International.

Rosenthal, R. A. (1981). Triple jeopardy: Family stresses and subsequent divorce following the adoption of racially and ethnically mixed children. Journal of Divorce, 4(4), 43-54.

Ryant, J. C. (1984). Some issues in the adoption of Native children. In P. Sachdev (Ed.), Adoption: Current issues and trends (pp. 169-180). Toronto: Butterworth & Co. Ltd.

Schmidt, B. W. (2001, March). Adopted Indians seek roots. Pathways Practice Digest, 1,10 -11.

Sharma, A. R., McGue, M. K., Benson, P. L. (1996). The emotional and behavioral adjustment of United States adopted adolescents: Part I. An overview. Children and Youth Services Review, 18, 83-100.

Silverman, A. R., Feigleman, W. (1990). Adjustment in interracial adoptees: An overview. In D. K. Brodzinsky and m. D. Schechter, (Eds.), The psychology of adoption (pp. 187-200). New York: Oxford University Press.

Topper, M. D. (1979). Mormon placement: The effects of missionary foster families on Navajo adolescents. Ethos: The Journal of the Society for Psychological Anthropology, 7(2), 162-160.

Verrier, N. M. (1993). The primal wound: Understanding the adopted child. Baltimore, MD: Gateway Press, Inc.

Westermeyer, J. (1979). The Apple Syndrome in Minnesota: A complication of racial-ethnic discontinuity. Journal of Operational Psychiatry, 10(2), 134-140.
WhiteHawk, S. (2001, May). An honor song and pow wow for returning lost birds. Pathways Practice Digest, 4-5.

First Nations Adoption (Canada)

Bagley, C. (1991). Adoption of Native children in Canada: A policy analysis and a research report. In H. Alstein and R. J. Simon (Eds.), Intercountry adoption: A multinational perspective (pp. 56-79). New York: Praeger Publishers.

Fournier, S. Crey, E. (1997). Stolen from our embrace: The abduction of First Nations children and the restoration of Aboriginal communities. Vancouver, BC: Douglas & McIntyre, Ltd.

Johnston, P. (1983). Native children and the child welfare system. Toronto: James Lorimer and Company.

Lipman, M. (1984). Adoption in Canada: Two decades in review. In P. Sachdev (Ed.), Adoption: Current issues and trends, (pp. 30-42). Toronto: Butterworth & Co. Ltd.

K. Verma and C. Bagley (Eds.), Race relations and cultural differences (pp. 259-277). New York: St. Martin's Press.

Swift, S. (1999). One of those kids: AFN and other try to restore faded tribal ties for Canada's Native adoptees. American Indian Report, 15(10), 22-24.

Ward, M. (1984). The adoption of Native Canadian children. Cobalt, Ontario: Highway Book Shop.

Image Credits

Cover and story photos were provided by the adoptees. Some are posted on Facebook.

Adoptees on the book cover include: Andy Hill, Ben Chosa, Bridget Sweet, Suzie Fedorko, Debby Poitras, Diane Tells His Name, Evelyn Red Lodge, Gail Huggard, Jessup Neubert, Joan Kauppi, Leland Morrill, Meschelle Linjean, Anecia Tretikoff, Rhonda Serges, Thomas Pierce, Trace L Hentz, Martina Bodonie, Johnathan Brooks, Drew Rutledge, and the Lost Bird of Wounded Knee.

Zintka Lanuni "Lost Bird" was orphaned in the Battle of Wounded Knee (29-12-1890) and taken away from her tribal family by General Leonard Wright Colby. (No date – Photographer unknown)

Lost Sparrow photos were supplied by filmmaker Chris Billing.

Mary Annette Pember supplied photos for her stories.

Stephanie Woodard supplied a photo for her story.

The Navajo Times granted us permission to run their story and photo.

Cover Design: Kim Pitman (second edition)

About the Author/Editor

Trace L. Hentz

Trace's memoir *ONE SMALL SACRIFICE* was the ground-breaking exposé on the systematic removal of American Indian children from their mothers, families and tribes for adoption to non-Indian families while she weaves in her own personal story. Known for her exceptional print interviews with influential Native Americans such as Leonard Peltier, John Trudell and Floyd Red Crow Westerman, Trace Lara Hentz (who legally dropped the name DeMeyer in 2014) started intensive research on adoptees in 2004. Her discoveries culminated in a fact-filled memoir first published in 2010, then a second revised edition in 2012. Her adoptee journey takes her around the country, finally meeting her birthfather in 1994 and learning about her mixed ancestry (Cherokee-Shawnee-Delaware-French Canadian.) Trace is former editor of tribal newspapers the Pequot Times in Mashantucket, Conn. (1999-2004) and Ojibwe Akiing in Wisconsin (1996-1999). She's also worked and freelanced for News from Indian Country, a national independent Native newspaper. Her chapter HONOR RESTORED on Sac and Fox Olympian Jim Thorpe won critical praise in the 2001 book *Olympics at the Millennium* (published by Rutgers Press). She read from her highly-anticipated memoir manuscript at the Wisconsin Book Festival in October 2008. In 2009, she started her blog about American Indian Adoptees. Her memoir was chosen as Native America Calling's Book of the Month is March 2010.

She was a frequent guest and served as executive producer for Jay Winter Nightwolf's radio program in Washington DC.

Trace has contributed to adoption anthologies: Lost Daughters, Adoption Reunion in the Age of Social Media, and *Adoptionland*: From Orphans to Activists. In 2013, she was co-editor of the anthology *Unraveling the Spreading Cloth of Time: Indigenous Thoughts Concerning the Universe* with MariJoMoore. (She uses the pen-name Laramie Harlow for poetry and short stories, with two chapbooks so far.)

The blog American Indian Adoptees [www.splitfeathers.blogspot.com] ranks in the top 100 adoption blogs and has reached over three-quarters of a million views in 2017.

In 2017, Trace contributed poetry to *Tending the Fire: Native Voices and Portraits* and was a finalist in *The Poet's Seat* competition.

Her writing blog: www.laratracehentz.wordpress.com. She lives at the foot of the Berkshire Mountains in Greenfield, Massachusetts with her husband Herb.

Acknowledgements

From Trace:

Research for this book would never been available to me, if not for the Internet and email. I am very grateful to its inventors. I am profoundly grateful to Facebook and all the people who have educated me and become friends and grew this circle to hundreds of individuals, Indian and non-Indian, adoptee, adopter, supporters and first families from across the globe. I thank the publisher Blue Hand Books. I thank Kim Pitman for the second edition book cover and Barb Burke for the first cover art. I thank Hugh and staff at PressBooks for all their expertise and innovative software. I thank the Mt. Kearsarge Indian Museum, the Pequot Museum and all the locations for readings of my book *One Small Sacrifice* from 2011 and beyond. I thank the many adopteees/Split Feathers for their good words, ideas and prayers who I lovingly call my Think Tank: Anecia, Levi, Adrian, Rhonda, Jessup, Paul, Von, Sue, Lila, Nate, Sally, Susan, Andy, Colleen, Launita, Karen K., Carla, Molly, Christine, Gail, Von, Triona, Marley, Lauren, Karen, Alice, Amanda, Diane, Debby P., Suzie, Leland, Karl M, Janey, Joan, Jazrea, Tom, David, Mary Ann, Mike and Irene in Toronto, Melvin, Tina, Bill, Ben (Ani), Nolan, Eleanor, Wendy, Drew, Aaron, Julie, Sally, Tara, Jeff, Murray/Muggz, Neil, Rhett, Thomas, Ann, Kevin, Evelyn, Meschelle, Patricia B, Jagade and Dan (and many more not listed and more that I have not met but hope to meet). I thank all the adoptees who contacted me on the blog American Indian Adoptees and to all who contributed to the book series. I thank Karen Vigneault who helped make many reunions for us and Tom Lidot and the Pala Band in California for inviting me to speak. I thank all the adoptees who are activists and part of Adoptees Rights demonstrations.

I send constant prayers to all the Lost Children/Split Feathers who are still lost but hoping to open their adoption files and reconnect with their tribal relatives. I thank the amazing and generous Patricia Busbee who contributed to the entire book series. I thank my incredible soul mate, my husband Herb for his strength, humor, love and support while I worked on this manuscript and research. I thank Great Spirit most of all.

Si Otsedoha (We are Still Here)

The Farmer and The Eagle

The old story goes there was a farmer who found a wounded eagle and placed him in a chicken coop to recover. The eagle started to act like a chicken, he bobbed his head like a chicken, he ate like a chicken, and otherwise thought he was a chicken. Until one day an Indian came along and asked what the eagle was doing with the chickens. The farmer told him the story, and the Indian asked if he could remove the eagle. The Farmer gave his permission to do so. So the Indian took the eagle to the mountain and said, 'You have to know who you are and what you stand for...' The eagle started to flex his wings. His keen eyesight started to return, and the strength in him started to come back. The eagle flew and soared and everything came back to him, who he was and that he wasn't a chicken. He gained everything back he lost because of where he was placed.

(Old Indian legend)

Lost Children Book Series

CALLED HOME:
THE ROADMAP

Lost Children of the Indian Adoption Projects
Book Series

Editors Patricia Busbee, Trace L.
Hentz

Book One: Two Worlds: Lost Children of the Indian Adoption Projects
Book Two: Called Home: The Roadmap
Book Three: Stolen Generations: Survivors of the Indian Adoption Projects
and 60s Scoop
Book Four: In The Veins: Poetry 2017

Lost Children of the Indian Adoption Projects Book Series (FOUR VOL-
UMES): now available at www.splifeathers.blogspot.com, at Blue Hand
Books, in fine book stores, on Amazon.com and Kindle.
******

IN THE VEINS (Vol. 4) Lost Children of the Indian Adoption Projects
book series, released in February 2017, was edited by Patricia Busbee and
published by the Blue Hand Books Collective in western Massachusetts.
Over 25 poets from across Turtle Island contributed to this lovely collection.

Please support your local bookseller.
We also recommend buying our books from www.indiebound.org.

BLUE HAND BOOKS Publisher: www.bluehandcollective.com

Afterword

In the earlier edition I had the chapter "Where do we stand as Indians today."

I replace it with **this**:

What do you call it when a woman has a baby and a social worker/ judge/ government has pre-judged her, then decides to take that baby, then it happens again and again... each and every time she gets pregnant. What if this happened 5 times, or 9 times? What do you call that?

Debby, Mitzi, Elizabeth (and countless other Native adoptees) your mothers lost you and other children. What do you call this? How do you tell people or explain to people a history like this?

What did they call your mother? Did they demean her, label her crazy, to justify **this**?
How does anyone define genocide? What is Human Trafficking? Choosing one segment of the population for this treatment? Placing American Indian First Nations Indigenous babies with a non-Indian family? This had a purpose. The government paid for this. And until the Indian Child Welfare Act, **this** decimated tribes to near extinction.
We know with slaves, children were sold. Families separated. Rebellions quashed. Resistors hung from trees. Millions of dollars were made selling human life, with fortunes created, mansions built, and enough wealth for generations.
Who in their right mind would find **this** acceptable?

What do you call taking babies from their own mothers? Do you give this a name, like adoption. Do you market it as something else? How do you sell people on this? Why did people accept this?

How did mothers survive losing their children? How do children survive without them?

If this feels like slavery and heinous and insanity and genocide and cruelty, that's because it is. It is all **this**.

READING GROUP QUESTIONS

We are aware that Two Worlds and this book series is used in classrooms when teaching about the Indian Child Welfare Act and the topic of adoption.

Here are some general questions to consider and discuss after reading this anthology:

The magnitude hits first. It's important first to remember WHY so many were taken.

When we consider these adoptee narratives and the impact on each individual adoptee, what questions are raised?

With the governments of Canada and the US and numerous churches, what was their final goal or end game?

Have we (in North America) made any progress? How?

Has the US offered an apology for the Indian Adoption Projects or ARENA? What is taking place in Canada?

Does reading adoptee stories help? Why?

Does writing help the adoptees?

What are tribes doing to assist with this situation and repatriation?

What are adoptees doing?

Do adoption laws need to be changed? How do we go about this?

What happens to families that are fractured in this way?

Are there resources for healing? Should there be?

What can be improved upon?

How do First Nations and American Indian people without resources and money protect themselves and their families?

How does this impact the adoptee's current families—including their own children? or if they adopted children?

What is it like to <u>not</u> know where you came from? What does that do to the psyche? How do adoptees integrate?

What education/information should be given to adoptive families? Is it important to preserve adoptee's heritage? How would this be done? How can we shed more light on this situation?

What is going on today with adoption?

(Thanks to Patricia Busbee for her assistance on this guide.)

www.ingramcontent.com/pod-product-compliance
Lightning Source LLC
Chambersburg PA
CBHW051235260626
47162CB00002B/438